THE MASTERPIECE IS THE GREATEST COLLECTION OF KNOWLEDGE EVER
ASSEMBLED. YOU BE THE JUDGE, AND KNOW THERE IS MUCH MORE COMING.
PART 1, PART 2, PART 3, AND PART 4, ARE ONLY THE START. THE INFORMATION
THAT THE SECRET SOCIETY'S HAVE, WILL BE SECRET NO MORE. IT HAS TAKEN ME 50
YEARS, BUT THE TRUTH WILL LIGHT YOUR MIND, LIKE AN ATOMIC EXPLOSION.

THE COPYRIGHT OF THE MASTERPIECE PAGE
INDEPENDENT WORK 100% MY LABOR,AND MY PLEASURE.

THE MASTERPIECE BY GERALD JOHNSON, THE VIKING. 50 YEARS OF RESEARCH .
THIS IS MY WORK AND NO ONE HAS HELPED<NOT EVEN ONE STROKE OF A PEN. THIS
IS MY COPYRIGHT>,ALL IS THE TRUTH>.

Table of Contents

IN THE BEGINNING THERE WAS ATLANTIS, AND SHE RULED THE WORLD.SOME WISE MEN SAY FOR 100,000 YEARS, SOME SAY A MILLION. HISTORY IS STILL BEING WROTE.

CHAPTER 1,   BY   GERALD JOHNSON

Back to a time in the northern lands,in what is today the arctic Circle, were people called the Vikings. They would roam many of the northern lands, as they should, because they owned them. Back to a Time, when Greenland had no ice, And thule had a thriving civilization, is where we begin our story. Most Europeans dream about the ancient land of Thule.It was here, the most powerful tribes, would gain their strength. Not much has been passed down to us, about these magical places. This is Thousands of years, before any recorded history. This is thousands of years before the Bible, thousands of years before Rome. In fact these were the days, before the great flood, that every civilization, talk about. These were the days, before the Ice Age, before the shifting of the North Pole. The Egyptians, ancient India, and the wise men of today, know all too well, about the shifting of the poles, North and South. The secret societies, of Germany,Britain, France, keep all information locked away, for reasons of Their Own. The wise men, of the world, say in a matter of seconds, the North Pole, shifted 2,000 miles. Check your internet for all matters concerning the pole shifts, it is most interesting. We're talking at least, 20 thousand to 50 thousand years ago. When the ice age came, yes it was time to leave. The magical lands, of the midnight Sun, were Frozen, and it was time to go. I pass this information on to The Seekers of the truth, So that they may know It all. The packs of wolves would follow the Vikings wherever they went, for the wolves were to be their dogs.The Vikings and the Ferocious wolves, were forming a bond, that no man, or no God, would ever break. The Viking Legends say it happened over many generations, but the Ferocious wolves, and the Ferocious Vikings, would fall In love with each other. One Legend says It Happened One Night, it was snowing and the Vikings were getting drunk around a big bonfire. The Vikings always barbecued, whole animals sometimes, and they loved their booze. The legends say, the Vikings saw the wolves coming by the hundreds to watch the Viking parties, it must have been a sight. The legend say, the wolves would howl for hours, wow the Vikings partying. Then one night, the Viking Legend say, some Vikings were passing out drunk. The wolves could smell the meat cooking, and they took their chance. They rushed in to cover the Fallen Vikings from the snow. The Vikings that passed out drunk would have surely died in the snow storm. They covered the Viking warriors completely. The oldest Legends say the packs of wolves, covered many Vikings that night, it must have been a hell of a party, but then, that's how the Vikings do it . The drunken, but not Fallen Vikings, said this could be a good thing. The Vikings cut meat from the barbecue and gave it to the wolves. This night started A Love Affair between Vikings and their wolves, and the Vikings saw they needed them. This is how wolves became the first dogs, and don't forget, they ate well.The Vikings celebrated while thousands of wolves watched, and waited for their turn, for a better life. By the way, just to put some knowledge in the brain, the Vikings invented whiskey, and ale. They didn't invent barbecuing, but you would sure think so. As long as the Vikings fed the wolves well, the wolves they would never leave, the rest is history. As the Viking tribes gathered together to leave the northern lands, that were covered in ice, huge packs of wolves went with them. The oldest of the Viking Legends say the wolves covered the Vikings every night, with a full belly of meat. From that day on, wherever the Viking went, the wolves would follow. Soon they Carried many things, and became sled animals, to pull the loads. The future German Shepherds were very loyal, and certainly man's best friend. The Viking leaders laughed and said, from now on, we will barbecue several animals. In battle the wolves fought with them, and many times saved their lives.

When the ice age started, it would not end, until it wanted to. Most of the populations in The northern lands would not survive. They had never seen anything like the Ice Age, and never would again. All the Viking tribes from all the old countries, would have to leave to survive.The Ice Age would leave no food behind, the cold would kill everyone who stayed. Sweden, and Norway, Denmark, Great Britain, and most of Europe, were hit hard. There were pockets of decent weather in certain spots, that allowed some to live on. There were cave Communities in France, and Spain and Germany. Science says these were Cavemen, and this is a lie. Man was learning how to adjust, to a situation, he had never seen before. Thousands were saved by the caves, that offered them shelter, from the coldest weather, they would ever know. So many of today's theories and ideas, are wrong. Science has had only a few hundred years to progress. As the modern scientist go back to these cave communities, he see things Like worked metal jewelry on the skeletons, in the caves. These were not cave people, they were Viking tribes seeking shelter. The wise men of the Vikings had to learn as they went.They were huge migrating tribes, running for their lives. These migrations went on for years, but eventually the ice stopped. The northern world of Canada ,and parts of the US where held in the grip of the Frozen ice age. Many of the northern tribes, the Great Danes, the Goths, the Saxons, the Franks, and hundreds more, out ran the ice.A few of the tribes, settled in parts of Russia. The Caucasian mountains would be their new home. They would be called the Caucasians. Many tribes would settle in Asia, Turkey, Iran, and those areas. Being Vikings they settled wherever they wanted to. As a rule of thumb, they say, if you cannot hold it militarily, it's not yours. As Viking tribes traveled through their new world, they fell in love with the adventure of it all. They heard stories of the great Himalaya Mountains and Tibet, and many tribes pushed on. As the Vikings traveled all the new lands, they heard about interesting Underground civilizations. To escape the Ice Age, many of the Earth's people went underground. There are millions of caves and caverns Underground. The legends of Tibet speak of underground cities.
Ancient India speaks of an inner earth world. Thousands of underground communities some holding thousands have been found. Shamballa and Agartha are only two of the Great Underground civilizations, that are still there. The Germans with their huge submarine fleets made contact with them under Antarctica before World War II . Before they would stop, the Viking tribes would bust through to Northern India. India's long ancient history would call

Northern India the land of the Aryans. As you can see the masterpiece it's going to be about a lot more than just the Vikings. The Viking legends we're passed down one Viking to another. The stories of the sea monsters let's put to rest right now. As the Vikings traveled the oceans, they encountered many sea creatures, that were just as ferocious as they were. The great whales crushed many Viking ships. Especially the great predators of the ocean, the killer whales. The Viking ships, were not that big, and if a great white, or killer whales were starving, the Vikings and their small ships were easy prey. The Viking ships were made of wood, and the killer whales would Ram them. Enough hits on a wooden ship and they would sink slowly. I bet there were some heavy battles between the killer whales and the Vikings. I would wager the Vikings lost thousands of warriors to the monsters of the deep. There are many so-called Monsters of the deep of the sea, that would crush the Viking ships, these were no stories. The Vikings lust for adventure , is both a curse and a blessing, and this I know, for it is in my blood too. There were many waves of Destruction on planet Earth, when the ice from the Ice Age began to melt, a huge flood followed. Most of the Cities along the coastlines of the Earth were sunk. Man is still finding them. Not just Atlantis, but cities all over the world . In the shallow Waters off India, great cities are still being found. There are huge structures off the coast of Japan. Small cities with pyramids are found off the Bahama Islands. Beautiful paved roads 10,000 years old, are in the same places. There are miles of ruins and structures all over the bottom of the ocean. Many of these have been robbed of their Treasures. The treasure Seekers have their own submarines, and huge ships to store everything. The coast of Portugal has a huge pyramid underwater, and paved roads, that date back thousands of yours. The dragons of today, or scientists, tell us at the same time as the great flood hit, Part of a comet hit the Earth . A shower of meteors came off the comet, and this helped with the worldwide destruction. Once again when the great flood did come, the Viking tribes had no choice, but to go to the highest elevations. The dragons, or wise men, say the tribes, assembled at the top of Tibet. Tibet Is the Rooftop of the world. As the waters came up the Himalaya Mountains, the wise men had to make a decision, to stay on top of Tibet, or go over the mountains into India. Many of the tribes Went Over the Mountain into India, which became known as, the land of the Aryans. As the waters receded, the Aryan tribes came down over many years. As the fresh land came up, the Aryans took it as their own. This is why it is always referred to, as Indo European. The lands between India and Europe, became theirs. Some of the tribes went into, what is now modern Iran. Later in history Genghis Khan's Army would change the bloodline of Iran, and they would be different from then on. The Indo-European language has held, for many thousands of years. The mother of all these languages was Sanskrit, the language doctors use writing prescriptions. It wasn't until modern day, the wise men realized that Greek and Latin came from Sanskrit. These were the centuries of raw Adventure. Actually much of this took place over thousands of years.

The World War II Germans sent scientists digging all over the world, to answer questions for the High Command. They sent diggers to Ancient India, and to Tibet. In Tibet the diggers dug up Many ancient whale bones to prove, the waters did come that far. While the Germans were in Tibet, they made contact, with the cave communities. The llamas and the Buddhist monks showed the Germans many passageways into the Earth. It is written the monks had been tunneling thousands of years. Their were records written in Gold pages waiting for the modern

Aryans to take with them. At this time the High Command was shown the tunnels, that lead to the big tunnel, that allows you to go into the inner earth. This is what the wise men call Shambala, and it has been there, a long, long time. Teams of scientists were sent into the tunnel system underneath the Himalayas. What they found we will never know. All the ancient records from thousands of years ago, were taken back to Germany. The most ancient civilizations in the world, Tibet, and ancient India provided the high command, illustrations of everything they came for. Before World War II actually started, the German submarine Fleet was sent to Antarctica. Under the ice of Antarctica the German submarines came out. Many Structures and Cities were found, some flash Frozen by Ice, some still there. We may never know what the Germans found, but when the submarines left, they came back with even more scientists, to try to power up the cities. Antarctica is the lost continent of Atlantis, and of this, there is no doubt. Atlantis was sunk, and the reason it was never found, is because it's been covered with ice, 3 miles thick. The high command of Germany sent scientists, all over the world to find what they needed. Ever since those days, technology has improved, 5000 %. Ever since the days of the mass migrations of the Ice Age, and the great flood, the Viking tribes have wanted to return to their ancient home lands. It took the science and great minds of Germany, to make this happen. It was their past, and they had to know. This is the greatest story never told, but now it will be. All the European nations have been looking for Atlantis for two thousand years. But how could they find it, if it was under 3 miles of ice. It is written in the secret Library's that Atlantis, was the true Homeland of the Aryans. This is what all Europeans believe, and it is certainly true. The lamas of Tibet had shown the map Made of gold to the Germans, showing exactly where the entrance to the inner world begins.. The entrance of course was in Tibet, But also in Antarctica. Much was learned by the scientists, And much technology was taken from the city, under the ice. It is ironic, and after all these centuries, everything would come full circle. Some dragons, or wise men, said that the information taken from Antarctica, Tibet, and ancient India, helped the German scientists To Perfect the rocket engines, and begin their space program.

Nothing is new Under the Sun. The ancient civilizations had many of the luxuries we enjoy today. Ancient India and Tibet are very old civilizations dating back, 30,000 years. There is no way to really know, at my level, but the secret societies say the underground civilizations, under the Himalayas, date back 60,000 years. The ancient legends, written down on paper and Stone, tell us everything. Flying machines are mentioned thousands of times. They are so precise, explaining in illustrated pictures these flying machines. I've seen a few, and millions of men and women have. The manuscripts go on explaining things like the proportion systems, and even fuel. They talk about the construction of their flying machines, and how they were put together. Don't take my word for it, consult the internet, and open your eyes. Research the thousands, if not Millions of tunnels Underground, that link the world together. Remember, the world has suffered many disasters, and ice ages. Man had no choice but to go underground, where he was safe.In Turkey there's a great example, of a small Underground city. It is at least 10 floors, maybe more.Its gigantic down there, even room for thousands of People, and special underground rooms for the livestock. Yes, the world has seen many tragedies, this is life. Only the Strong Survive well, the others, just get along. The ancient manuscripts from India and Tibet, number in the thousands. These were educated people beyond belief, in the land of the Aryans.It is in their blood, intelligence. That's the main reason they were taught, do not mix the blood.Ancient India had very strict laws dealing with mixing of the blood.I'm covering so much ground, I must toss in a few things I left out. When the ice was melting from the great Ice Age, making floods like the world had never seen, still more was coming. To add insult to injury, the great comet Typhon had a close encounter with the Earth. The comet was nicknamed, the Dragon and crashed into the sea, hitting the Earth, with the force of Millions of atomic bombs. This caused total darkness for a while, massive rain storms, and tidal waves 600 feet tall. This happened all over the world, at the same time. This was perhaps the greatest Mega disaster, the world would ever see. The great flood, and meteor strike would send the survivors back to the Stone Age.All would be lost, even things like writing, math, and astronomy would have to wait to be rediscovered. It would take a long,long time to recover.

CHAPTER 2

The Aryans are not the name of a tribe, but the name of a civilization. The Aryan Homeland, was Atlantis , and stretched all the way, to ancient India. They touched every civilization, and built the pyramids in ancient Egypt. Ancient Egypt goes back at least 15,000 years, and has truly seen it all. The wise men on planet Earth, say the pyramids in Egypt, are but a huge marker for what is underneath. Modern Scholars argue over the age of the pyramids, and the Sphinx. If they ever find out, their brains will explode, like a grape. Underneath the pyramid complex at Giza, there is a metropolis. Some wise men say the Metropolis is a million years old. The pyramids in Egypt, are an ancient marker, for another entrance to the inner world. Sometimes I Often wonder, if ancient Egypt was Atlantis. Plato and the rest of the Greek historians always talked of all the pyramids in Atlantis. However history is a maze, that cannot be worked through. Lies and deceit, are the orders of the day. To the Greeks and the Egyptians to give up knowledge was punishable by Death. To even mention what direction these fabled cities were, would get you killed. It was a law to lie, to preserve what you had, and All Nations played the same game. If other ships were Seen near your trading partners, they had to be sunk. These are the rules of greed, and Power, and all played. The future of a Nation, depends on secrecy. The Greeks and Egyptians exchanged knowledge a little, but they were not family, and told many, many lies. Would any Nation point the way, to The Riches of the world, I don't think so. Greed and jealousy will always be the strongest powers on Earth. The Serpent's and Dragons, and the wisest, know.

 Atlantis was a global civilization . For a million years the high priests were the wisest of men. On some levels ancient Egypt, was considered, a colony of Atlantis, but if Atlantis was gone, and the survivors, went to Egypt, wouldn't that make Egypt, the new Atlantis. We've all heard many stories of the great wealth of ancient Egypt.They say the tops of the pyramids, long, long ago, were covered with sheets of gold. Plato the great Greek historians said to find Atlantis, one had to sail West through the Mediterranean. They said one must sail past Spain to the right and North Africa to the left, the pillars of Hercules, this area is called. Once out into the big ocean, one had to sail West, and he would run right into it. Sounds good, a likely story, but I know a little too much. The Greeks always Drew their Maps backwards just in case, they fell into enemy hands. So what does that mean, it means instead of sailing West to the Atlantic Ocean, one must sail east which would bring us to Egypt. The Greek storytellers always talk, about the wealth of Atlantis, even though they never saw it, interesting. They claimed the caskets we're covered with gold, and sprinkled with diamonds. They said the plumbing of Atlantis was made of silver, and gold was used for everything. The Nile River in Egypt, has fed Millions, for thousands of years. She truly is the mother of Egypt. Thousands of pounds of gold, have been taken from her. The wealth of an Empire, was on the line. You know, as the mystery unfolds to me, the more I learn. Ancient Egypt had a dozen pyramids, and most are still beneath the sands. Hundreds of temples, and other structures, are under the sand for many miles. It almost seems like they don't want all of this exposed. That can be the only reason, why it's not being dug up right now. I understand the US has an underground base right there. The reason I believe, it's because Atlantis was famous For their high tech technology. It's probably hundreds of years ahead of us, right now. Today with modern scanning computers and satellites, we can locate everything under the Sands of Egypt. Atlantis was known for their lasers,and technologies, this is kind of a hot potato situation, and you hope you don't get burned. And if this was not the truth, all the pyramids and temples would be dug up this year. Millions of people come to see the three pyramids at Giza, think how many would come to see much more. Tourism brings billions of dollars to Egypt . The hundred pyramids and temples are all located in the Giza area. They are hiding a lot here,and the U.S. has an underground base there to protect everything.

For the last 30 years underneath the pyramids of Giza, there has been a project top secret. The underground Metropolis called the city of the Gods has been searched. It has been classified for 30 years. I guess we got to give them all plenty of time, to move out all the good stuff. Modern ground-penetrating radar has been used, as well as all top technologies available to us. It's amazing how even our own government, hides so much from us. The only reason we know anything, just recently, it was Declassified. But still let's not forget, beyond that is an entrance to the inner world. The inner world is very mysterious, and totally unknown to most. I would suppose that during the last ice age, most survivors had no choice, but to go underground. We're not talking about to the Center of the Earth, we're talking maybe a mile or two down, where cracks and crevices open up, into underground valleys. In the books of the secret societies, it is written, hundreds of small cities are inside the Earth. Just think of it , no more great floods. no more meteors, no more comets hitting the outside of earth. And best of all, no more rain, no more wind, and no more bad weather. The air would be cleaner, and the water would be pure. Consult your internet, and read about the tens of thousands of tunnels throughout the Earth. In the secret Doctrine of the East, it says there is a large population, that live underneath the great Himalaya Mountains. It is written in the books of Truth, that the Garden of Eden, was inside the Earth. All civilizations throughout the Earth, speak of the great tunnel systems, that link all continents together. In South America, when the Conquistadors invaded looking for gold, many of the Great Treasures, we're taking into the tunnels. It is also written,that many of the Indian populations went deep into the tunnel systems, to escape the gold hungry blue-eyed devils. Some of the South American Indian tribes brag about having as many as 40 cities, 1 or 2 miles down. Like I said, check your internet, and enlarge your brain. Some say the tunnel systems have been there a million years. But know this, if you find the inner world, it will be beautiful. Know this too, you cannot come back out. The Indians or whoever guard the entrances, and the exits, don't want anyone leaving, and telling the rest of the world. Not many citizens of the world, know anything about the inner world. That's the way they want to keep it.

In South America, the so-called new world has plenty of activity Underground. At the end of the Amazon River, there is a pyramid complex. The Atlanteans built that complex too. Underneath the Great Andes mountain chain, there are cities. Once again the Conquistadors chased thousands of Indians into the tunnel systems, and this was noted in the logs of Spain. The Andes Mountains of course had many tunnels dug for the gold. It is written that the Andes Mountains produced more gold than any other spot on earth.The tunnel systems were designed and developed by those with the Elongated skulls.It is interesting to note hundreds of the long skulls found, had red hair still growing on them,some had streaks of white also.

Seek and you will find, and don't expect anyone to show you the way.

The most interesting thing about South America, it's the amount of elongated skulls found. The elongated skulls we're from the shot callers of the gold mines. Some like to call them aliens, which I think is rather childish. I think this race of beings has been with us for a long, long time. I think they've lived inside the Earth for millions of years. Someone's got to have the brains. These elongated skulls, have also been found in Egypt, and Tibet, and ancient India. Man likes to think he's the top of the food chain, and that the world was created for him. But this is a lie and there are other species we will encounter. To think that all this has been going on, beneath our feet for thousands of years, is mind-boggling. The elongated skulls have been found in Europe too, even on the island of Malta. On the island of Malta , there were huge graveyards Underground, with hundreds of thousands of Bones and skulls. The elongated skulls were moved out of the great piles. Of course there is a cover-up going on, they're always is. Even ancient Egypt had rulers with elongated skulls, and they did sit on the throne. These were the ancient architects of civilization all over the world.It makes one Wonder, who was really sitting in the oracles of ancient Greece, and ancient Rome.

In Antarctica, under the miles of ice, The same creatures are being thawed out. Antarctica is definitely hiding secrets that will shake the world. For thousands of years, man has looked for Atlantis, knowing Atlantis was the mother of all civilizations. Rumors are already flying, saying the world is not ready for what has been found. The rumors say Society could not handle the truth. The rumors also say, only over the next hundred years, will man learn bit by bit. Knowledge is power, and they will keep most of it from us. We can only hope for whistleblowers and paid informants. The complete truth of ancient history, is before us. Time will tell how much they let us know.We must protest loudly,with any means to find out about our real family tree.The story of creation and adam and eve,stopped all research into history.To even attempt to know anything outside the bible,would get you burned to the stake.John F. Kennedy demanded a separate power of church and state.10 years later we were on the moon.

OF COURSE THE WHEELS<HAD ALREADY BEEN SET IN MOTION YEARS BEFORE>

The modern scientists will not agree, that ancient civilizations knew more than us, but the more we dig, the more we find traces of superior intelligence. Thousands of years ago, and maybe as many as 75,000 years ago, the Ancients knew about the Earth tilts, and the shifting of the North and South Poles. It is only because of the ancient knowledge left behind, that Modern Man has progressed to the point, where he is today. It is because of our knowledge today, that we can unlock all the ancient Mysteries. It was a Frenchman M De Sacy that found some hidden messages in the Bible. The Book of Enoch, it says when the angel tells Enoch, behold I have showed the all things, and all things have I revealed to you.Thou seeith the Sun, the Moon, and those which conduct the Stars of Heaven, and which caused all their operations, seasons, and arrivals in return. In those days with sinners, the years shall be shortened, and the moon shall change its laws. The hidden message is once the Earth has inclined, the order and positions of the planets and stars would have changed. Enoch was taking up to the heavens, to see all things, and brought back to tell everyone, according to the Bible. Enoch was also the grandfather of Noah from the great flood. In The Book of Enoch it says, and lo, I cried with a bitter voice, hear me, hear me, hear me 3 times. And then he said , the Earth labors and is violently shaking, surely I will perish with it. Open your mind, to the ancient scriptures, an angel had two meanings.One was that the serpent, or Wiseman, was the angel, the initiate's which most people call them. The initiate or wise man that had schooled Noah, in the laws of nature, and the Motions of the world, knew very well the axis had already inclined. He also knew it was only a matter of time before the world, would go into convulsions. We're talking major earthquakes, and major flooding, it happens every time. The Ancients kept perfect records, and they knew. It was like charging into battle, knowing it was only a matter of time, before death comes, for The Unlucky ones. The power of nature, are stronger than the biggest battles, and The destruction that comes with them. This was no mirror prediction, it was the law of nature.At the appointed time, the deluge of waters, would be the instrument, of man's evolution.

The great initiate Frederick Klees did work on the deluge. He says the position of the globe with reference to the Sun, had evidently been in primitive times, much different Then it is today. And the difference must have been caused by a displacement of the axis, and the rotation of the Earth.

When the wisest of the ancient Greeks Traveled to ancient Egypt, the Egyptians were the keepers of all sacred knowledge. The high priests, were actually scientists of their day. The keepers of the knowledge, had to be trusted, and kept away, from everyone else. The high priest of Egypt, told the Greeks, the Sun has not always risen in the east.

In Ancient Egypt the priests told Herodotus that tens of thousands of years ago, the ecliptic had crossed the Equator, at right angles. The masterminds of the ancient civilizations, cleverly disguised all their messages, because they had to. The ancient god Phaeton was created for this Mystic tale. It is written that Phaeton in his desire to learn the hidden truth, made the sun take a different route through the ancient Skies. The legend goes on to say, the Phaeton ordered the Sun towards another country. I guess that's the easiest way, to explain the great changes, that do happen. The ancient knowledge was kept in such small circles anyway, because knowledge is power.

THE SUN DID NOT ALWAYS RISE IN THE EAST

In the Legends of the northern mythology, it tells that In even more ancient times, the sun rose in the south, , and the ice cap was in the east. It is interesting to Note, The Book of Enoch was not allowed into the Bible. because it did not go along with the Christian churches timetable. The Christian church, gave the year 4004 BC, as the date the Earth was created. The Christian church were the Masters of total mind enslavement. They're 4004 BC date for creation of the world, is utterly ridiculous. It was perfect then, because no one was educated, and to speak out against them was blasphemy, and you were killed. That's one great form of Mind Control. A wise man once said, one must look outside His own religion, to find the truth. The Christian books put together as one , we're called, the cannon. There are even books in today's Library's that collect, the books that were not allowed into the Christian Bible. I've read them, and it's easy to see, why they weren't let in. The Jewish scriptures have their own Cannon, or order. The Jews of the Middle Ages disliked the Christians, and the Christians hated the Jews. After all it was the Jewish High Priests they gave the order to execute Jesus. Jesus blood was on their hands only. Pontius Pilate the Roman governor took out a bowl of water, and washed his hands symbolically, at the same time he said to his court, I wash my hands of this whole affair, the Jews shall decide. And for this reason the Christian Knights, and later the Christian Soldiers would Massacre the Jews. This was all done in Revenge, and it was done many times throughout history. When the Roman Emperor in Rome Heard the news of the execution of Jesus Christ he hit the roof . He gathered together, the greatest commanders of all the world, and explained just what had happened. The decision came down from the Throne of Rome, that immediately the greatest battle-hardened divisions the Romans had, would begin a March to Jerusalem . The veterans of many Foreign Wars would soon travel to Jerusalem, to set the record straight. The hand of karma was about to be lowered on the Jews. It is written in many languages , that rivers of blood and intestines flowed through the streets of Jerusalem. Yes I said rivers of blood, for this was Justice. 100,000 Jews were killed, for what they did to Jesus that day, when they ordered him to the cross. As Jesus lay bleeding on the cross, the blood poured down his legs. Mary Matalin collected it in a cup. This cup would forever be called the Holy Grail. Later armies would fight for possession of the Grail, and the contents inside. It was said in many circles the blood of Jesus was magical. Of this we cannot be sure, about the Holy part, but we can be certain he died that day. His body was taken by the secret societies, and no one is sure where.

The Jews paid for their treachery against Jesus. Even though he was a Jew too, he was also a threat to their power. Just for the readers of the masterpiece, the name of the Roman Centurion on the White Horse was Longinus the spear man. The name Longinus is known in every home in Europe, but not in America, strange. But it will be known now. The story of Longinus the Spearman must be told to the rest of the world. Longinus had been a Roman Commander of many armies, and had won many Wars for Rome. Over the long course of his life he developed cataracts on both eyes, and was no longer fit to command. He could not see as good as when he was young, and now it was time to serve Rome in another way. Rome had a huge spy Network and intelligence Division. There were spies everywhere in the Empire. There had to be, and so it was done. The Roman high command put Longinus in charge of spying in Jerusalem. It seems, the Jews were always a rebellious bunch, and they would be dealt with. As a matter of fact, Longinus followed Jesus for two years before the crucifixion. He personally loved Jesus and thought he was a great man. On that day on Calvary Hill when Jesus final heart beats were happening, longinus saw his chance for immortal Fame. The Jews had went to Pontius Pilate the Roman governor , and said in Jewish law, no man can be crucified on their Sabbath day.They said to Pontius Pilate, the Sabbath day was approaching quickly in a matter of hours, and they waited for his response. It was then the Jews got their answer. It was then that Pontius Pilate said, I wash my hands of this whole affair, and Jesus blood will not be on my hands. He said if you want Jesus dead do it yourself. It was then, that the Jewish so-called High priests marched up Calvary Hill. There were three men crucified on Calvary Hill that day, and the Jews smashed the bodies of the other two men with clubs. It certainly was a high pressure situation, but Longinus loved it. Everyone knew the prophecies, and it said, not a single bone shall be broken. The pressure increased as the thieves on Jesus's left and right were smashed, and even their mothers could not have recognized them. As the Jewish priests or killers started walking towards Jesus on the cross, it was then that Longinus made his mark on history. He plunged his spear very carefully under the rib bones of Jesus, so as not to break a single bone. The final prophecy, not a single bone shall be broken, was filled. Immediately the sky went purple and black, an earthquake hit Jerusalem that day, that moment. That spear point would become the most famous religious Relic of all time, even though the Americans know nothing about it, until now. The Knights Templars would come in the future to take this spear back to Europe, and also to take the Holy Grail, and the cross, and the robe.
To the students of History, The Jews were massacred in Jerusalem, and everywhere else the Roman Legions could find them. For their treachery against Jesus, the Jews would lose their Homeland. From that day forward, the Jews would be dispersed, and would never know their own Nation until after World War II. The Jewish state was reinstated by Great Britain and

America. The pages of History, would call this, the great dispersion. The Jews would be dispersed from Jerusalem and all surrounding areas. Make no mistake, this was the dispersion, and they were gone forever. So you see the death of Jesus, set in motion great things. That spear of Longinus,and the spear man, would become immortal too. Kings and Queens in Europe, would fight for this spear, And one of the mightiest Kings would have it. The spear was brought out on many occasions, to Rally the Christian Warriors, and increase their power in combat. We will get to that later in the Masterpiece.

The Aryans had the greatest civilizations in the world. The new religion Christianity, replaced the old religion,pagan. It caused great turmoil and many wars, before it was settled. What was once the greatest Empire in the world, Rome, and then the Holy Roman Empire, was Torn to Pieces by the new religion. The countries ended up fighting for over a thousand years, for they were deeply divided into Catholic and Protestant armies. Many refused to turn their backs on their gods, to worship a man of peace. Christianity was the Jewish consequence. The Jews had the last laugh, and laughed all the way to the bank , as they took over the business transactions of the empire, or at least as many as they could get their hands on. They laughed at their ignorant Christian Soldiers, and helped send them into battle, for 2000 years. The Jews it is true are 8,000 years old, old by anyone's standards. But the Aryan Empire went back 75,000 years. When Atlantis was sinking slowly, the Aryans left and built the super ancient Egypt. The Aryan Warriors settled in Egypt long before France and Britain were above the water. In the secret Doctrine it says that man has lived on the Delta of Egypt over 100 thousand years, and the proof is marked in the Great Pyramid, and also in the temples. The secret Doctrine is preserved also at the foothills of the Himalayas. The secret doctrine of India is the mother of all religions, and occult knowledge. It also says the world has been destroyed 3 times.

Herodotus the great Greek Historian, traveled to the wise men of Egypt, searching for the true knowledge of the ancients. Believe me, he was shocked at what he found. The Egyptian High priests were only two happy to brag and boast of their great ancient civilization. At the time of Herodotus, Egyptians had all their records in order and thoroughly complete. Their 341 statues of their Egyptian kings, were each made in the exact likeness of that King. Egyptians we're only hinting at their ancient past, for each statue Herodotus was told, was a generation. The Egyptians said to Herodotus, that these 341 Generations had ruled for a period of 11,340 years.

The high priest went on to tell Herodotus, that for these 341 Generations, the gods had lived amongst men. Herodotus was not known to lie, for he was a historian, and a scholar. In the library at Oxford University there was a manuscript that says, an Egyptian king named Surid , had the Great Pyramid built. It is interesting to note that King Surid lived before the great flood. The wise King ordered his high priests to write down everything known to them, and to place this knowledge, inside the Great Pyramid.

The only reason anyone says that Pharaoh Khufu was the Builder, is because his name is found inscribed in it. Of course I'm sure he just wanted to be remembered, so he told the big lie. If one would think about this man-made Mountain, it's almost 500 feet high, and weighs over 6 million tons, one would surely realize it was not built in one lifetime. History also teaches us, that if 1 ruler wanted the fame of many, all he had to do was Wipeout all knowledge of the others. Throughout history this has been done many times. Not only the Egyptians, but every civilization on Earth mention the famous Atlantis.Egypt it is written was a colony of Atlantis,and Atlantis had many.

Science today tells us, Cro-Magnon men migrated to Europe over 30 thousand years ago. This is not a wild guess, many skeletons have been dug up. Modern science also tells us that the Cro-Magnon man, did not actually walk hunched over, but instead, straight as today. The Cro-Magnon spines were bent when they were dug up, but upon further investigation, it was found this Bunch all had arthritis, or curvature of the spine. Modern science also tells us, at one time Europe and Africa were hooked together, before ripping apart. Brilliant modern geologists tell us this is true, and they had taken many samples, on both sides of the Atlantic. If one examines the west coast of Africa and the east coast of South America, it fits together perfectly like a child's puzzle. To go one step further, science tells us that Millions of years ago, all 7 continents we're hooked together, into 1 land called Pangea. Is this the simple explanation, for all civilizations having the same Legends , and all having pyramids, and all telling of the great flood.

Plato is probably the best known philosopher and historian, that the Greeks ever produced. Plato- had a teacher too, his name was Salon.He was a Master Adept, and this is what he learned from the master players of Egypt. You are unacquainted with the most noble and excellent race of men, who once lived in your country. From whom you, and your whole present state are descended. Only a small remnant of this admirable people is now remaining. There are Egyptian writings telling me about a huge Force attacking your cities. These forces came from the sea, and spread themselves with hostile Fury, over Europe and Asia.

The high priest's said the Greeks were but dwarfed and weak remnants, of that once glorious Nation. The secret doctrine of the East tells us, it was at this time, that the blood mixed with the Aryan stock of Europe.The man gods were born.The Bible likes to mention the Man Gods, that were created, when those from Atlantis had sex with the European women.The Man Gods were born. That made the northern Nations invincible. The secret Doctrine tells us the Atlanteans then divided into many family races, and then in turn into many nations. The secret Doctrine tells us, thousands of years after the Aryans colonized Europe and much of Asia, the race Wars began. Brown, black, and yellow tribes, assaulted the Aryans, but they were beaten and driven to the other areas of the planet. The Secret Doctrine tells us that many of these lands became Islands, as the Land Tore Off from the mainland. The high priest of Egypt insisted, it was at this time, the great lands of Egypt and Greece became the strongest powers on Earth. The Secret Doctrine says many of the dark tribes became isolated, as the continents moved apart, and the result was, that many tribes fell into a Savage state.

In the age of discovery, when science was finally free to examine everything, much was learned. The Jewish Bible, with the Jewish writers, saw things only from their point of view, and from their propaganda. Science, would set the world stage. On the banks of many small rivers of Europe, were found many skeletons, of the men from that era. History does leave a trail, but it needs someone to follow it. After the Christian Church came to power, and became the government, men of science were executed. No one or no thing, Had the right, to challenge the almighty Church.They wanted all the power,and also wanted a herd of timid sheep.

But let's go back to the cave Communities along the Lesse River. It was said by many, that this prehistoric man, was the lowest man of all, he had what the men and women of

science calls the naulette jaw. These jaws did look Savage and very animalistic, but as I said before in the masterpiece, they had much jewelry of precious stones, on the ancient skeletons. Some scientists believe it was a negro skeleton, and some say it was a Mongolian, but neither one was right, for many more skeletons would be found by the serpents and Dragons. The Serpent's and Dragons for the new Scientists said, nothing would hold them back ever again. The most famous of these cave communities, was called the Bear Cave. There were hundreds of small cave Communities found, with much jewelry, on many skeletons. In France were found the remains of many Aryans, mostly in the caves of Aquitaine The Egyptians of ancient Egypt,kept records of everything, and there are thousands of ruins from days gone by. Napoleon brought with his army, some of the wisest men of that time. They were called savants, and they were the best. Among the thousands of Records the savants devoured, they came across extremely interesting things. They learned in ancient times, the wise men of Egypt, met often with the wise men of France, Britain and Belgium. In the records it says the Egyptian High priests traveled in a Northwest Direction. Their travels took them all the way to what is now Normandy, the beaches of France. They walked the entire distance. The prehistory records, let us know the high priestess of Egypt, met with the Druids. These records are so old, there are pictures of the wise men walking across the land bridge that connected Europe to Africa. That land bridge was destroyed long, long ago. Modern Science claims that Africa and Europe, ripped apart from each other, at least 10 to 20 thousand years ago. Now of course, The Straits of Gibraltars water, separate the two. It will forever be called, the pillars of Hercules, with two Stone mountains separating each other. It is written that the Egyptian Master Adepts met on these beaches every year, with The Druids from Britain. Every year fellow magicians and sorcerers, came also from Gaul, and modern Belgium.Some wise men say the melting of the ice age is what divided Africa and Europe.

On many occasions these meetings took place in Britain, at the Sacred Circle, called Stonehenge. This ancient Brotherhood, supervised the building of all the ancient stone monuments that covered the Aryan lands.

It is true at this ancient time in history, Britain was hooked to the continent by a land bridge that is now beneath the water. It is a fact that these meetings of the Ancient Brotherhood, took place and every nation loved them. This was where the Aryan Brotherhood ruled the world, and it was strong, and would remain that way. The famous Merlin, was one of the worlds famous Druids, and history tells us, they were great. These ancient meetings did take place, and I'm sure they all looked forward to them. The secret knowledge of the world was discussed, and so was the future. Science has a hard time putting an actual date on all these meetings, and land bridges that no longer are there. But they still do, the modern serpents and Dragons, the scientists, love this sort of challenge. This ancient time science tells us, was 50,000 years ago, and the Christian church says the world was created a little over 4000 years ago. So we see exactly where the real knowledge lies. It was at this same time in history, that Sicily was hooked to Africa and Spain to the Barbary coast of Africa. This period of time, coincides with Atlantis Sinking and the mountain chain of the Alps Rising. These were the days of Adventure, Read on modern serpents and Dragons. Let's take this time to note, that for hundreds of thousands of years the dragons and the serpents, stood for knowledge, for men and women. It was this way for thousands of years, maybe Millions, and the Catholic Church turned the serpent into an evil thing. When the Christian armies invaded the whole world, wherever the symbols of the snakes and the Dragons Were, the Christians soldiers destroyed. By doing this, the church had all other knowledge ruined and destroyed. At this time there was a war going on for the minds of men, and the Christian church would dominate for years. And as their greatest Ally, there was no education to prove them wrong.Total mind control was the order of the day,and the masses were brainwashed completely.

The giant monuments of stone are not just found at Stonehenge, but they are found in America, Asia, Africa, and Europe. All over Europe are massive blocks of stone, and many are found in Long rows But believe me they are there, as monuments to the Pagan religions. The Christian church called them the devil's altars, and some said they were the tombs of giants. The message stones of Carnac and Brittany are lined up for a mile, and there are 11,000 of the message stones, arranged in 11 rows. The giant Stone monuments, or Devil's alters are found in Denmark, Sweden, Germany,and Spain. The tombs of the Giants, are found in Denmark, and Sweden too. The tombs are also found in Germany. The tombs of the Giants go all the way to Palestine, to Algeria, and of course all the way to India. The tombs of the Giants, are also found in Siberia and throughout Russia, Peru, and Bolivia. All these locations, are known as the burial places, of the Giants that once walked the Earth. In the Mississippi Valley of America, and in Ohio, there are two gigantic mounds of Earth, that resemble the mounds of Aryan Europe. One of these giant Mounds is called the alligator Mound, and the other is the mound of the Great Serpent. The giant alligator Mound is designed in great detail, and is at least 250 feet long. The original Mound was constructed with mounds of stones. The Great Serpent in shown with his mouth open and in his mouth is an egg, the egg is 100 foot in diameter. The serpent is drawn with considerable detail, and the complete length is 1100 feet. Some of the excavations have Unearthed men with bone necklaces, and of course weapons of stone. That's how old American Mounds are, bone necklaces, and still in the Stone Age. In all the tombs of the Giants, there are no bones. Cremation was the universal way of dealing with the Dead, and it was also the healthiest way. The wise men in the world believe that most of the Giants were killed in the great submersion of Atlantis, and they also believe that there size during the Ice Age , was dwarfed from 15 feet to 10 . The ancient Greeks had their Titans, India had her daityas, and the Egyptians and Phoenicians had there Kabiri. The religion of the ancients worshiped the sun, and the powers of nature, the sons of God, and also the sons of Light. In the extreme North The Sun Shines for 6 months of the year straight. It is the man gods that taught the Egyptians the Greeks, the Babylonians, everything they knew about astronomy, architecture, and Mathematics. The pyramids scattered around the world, are proof of ancient man's intelligence. The ancient land of Australia, and all the Pacific Islands, once belonged to Lemuria. All that's left of Lemuria are these hundreds of mountain tops called Islands in the South Pacific. They are the tops of the continent that sits below.Lemuria was a huge landmass, south of the Equator, most often found in the South Pacific. Many maps show many places, of this powerful ancient continent. Just exactly how it broke up, into how many pieces, we may never really know. All of these so-called Sciences, are actually still in their infant age. Man is being shielded from as much information, as he has ever learned, for this is the way of greed and power, thus the way of man. The Lemurians built monuments to their gods, and many are still scattered everywhere, throughout the southern hemisphere. In the secret doctrine of India, it shows us that 30 miles west of Easter Island, under the ocean, there are huge ruins of the once great civilization. The cities on the ocean floor, of all the Earth all show heavy traces of lava, from ancient times, enormous eruptions. What remains of the Pacific continent is shown on Easter Island, thousands of miles, from South America. When the famous Captain Cook arrived at Easter Island, his men were shocked to find these colossal statues that are all over the island. It is written in the book of knowledge, Easter Island, with its beautiful colossal statues,that look out to the ocean, is magnificent. It is a fact that Easter Island, with all its beautiful magnetism, was the sacred island of the Lemurians.It is amazing when we match the stone idols of Easter Island, with the stone idols and all the ancient ruins of Tiahuanaco in the high mountains of Peru, they are the same. In South America, there are many Legends of giants too, and where there is smoke there is fire. It is interesting to note, the Indians of South America, had their own sun cult, and the Indians of South America, had the science of astronomy exact. It is written in the book of knowledge, that the Lemurians crossbred with the lower races, and this is how they lost they're flame of intelligence. What the crossbreeding did, was bring about a group of savages. While some groups of men, are walking on the moon and Mars.

Some groups are still living in the jungles of South America and Africa. While some groups are developing lasers, some are still using blowguns. Intelligence must be kept in certain circles or else they will lose it, and this has happened many times on planet Earth.This is not a racist Doctrine, but the truth with no sugar coating. This is the main reason the Aryan Doctrine

places so much emphasis on keeping the blood pure.It is done so, so they will remain the sons of wisdom.When the Aryans busted through the Himalayas to India,The Aryan rulers separated the races. India became one of the greatest civilizations in the history of the world. When India lost its power, and also their high standard of living, was when the cast laws were relaxed. All were free to mix. At the height of India's great civilization, to mix the blood was punishable by Death. Once the blood of India flowed freely, the civilization was doomed, and became caught in a downward spiral. In ancient Rome when only a handful of families ruled, Rome created one of the greatest civilizations in the history of the world. But once the blood from the world was mixed with it, it no longer held its strength. Their were great operas in Europe written about all this, but only the upper class was treated to it. The lessons of History are tough, but we must not ignore them. Even in the armies of ancient Rome, the commands were given to foreigners. What this did was cause Civil Wars and outright Rebellion. It was not the powers of the outside world that defeated Rome, it was the decay from Within. It seems then, Modern Man, makes the same mistakes as Ancient Man, sometimes I guess we just do not learn. Geologists have told us that Lemuria at one time, went all the way to the foothills of the himalayas. Geologists say this was hn800,000 years ago. They say Tibet and Mongolia were on the ocean floor. The ancient teachings of the secret Doctrine tell us the northern polar region, and the southern polar region, are the cradle of civilization. This is where it happened, and now they're covered with miles of ice. Change is the order of the universe, and things change. The older civilizations in the history of the world, are under the ice of the areas around the North Pole and the South Pole. The gigantic continent of Lemuria stretched from Southern India to the South Pole. The Ancients tell us that Lemuria some 800,000 years ago, began breaking into pieces, much like Atlantis. The ancient wise men say this happens due to a decrease in the velocity of the Earth's rotation. When the Great Wheel runs slower, the poles tilt and the Earth is caught in a violent struggle. In the case of both Lemuria and Atlantis, the under sea floor was broken to bits by enormous volcanic action and earthquakes. The ocean floor at both spots has been thoroughly checked by today's scientists, and both places are covered with huge lava formations. When the poles of the Earth are Tilted soon after, all the water rushes to the ends of the Earth and soon sink everything. As the poles shift again at some later time, the oceans swell in the middle of the planet, and drown that area. It is at this time, that the polar lands North and South, rise up, this cycle happens every 26,000 years. To the man or woman with wisdom,the 26,000 year cycle is called the great year. It takes 26 thousand years for all the zodiac star signs to pass through the skies of the Earth. This is why the ancient astronomers watched the stars and planets. Every cluster of stars, that are represented as the signs of the zodiac, take their turn as the main star constellation, that brightens the skies on Earth. The universe is so large, that each zodiac sign dominates for over two thousand years. This is why in ancient history, one finds the cult of the ram, or the cult of a lion.These 2,000 year Cults last until the next zodiac animal, takes its place as Master of the heavens. In fact the star signs are like an enormous Cosmic clock. When the poles of the heavens match up with the North Pole on Earth, Titanic forces are

Unleashed. The Earth as it goes around the Sun, in 365 days, it is a year. The Earth is also moving around the galaxy and this cycle is the great year or 26,000 years. In this way by reading the zodiacs of Egypt and India, we know exactly the year, It was. One might ask themselves, how did the civilizations know this. This is concrete proof just how old these civilizations were. It would take 26,000 years to chart 1 year, and another 26,000 years to recognize it's repeating itself, so you see my friends, were talking about huge periods of time. Modern civilizations, even in the Bible, Babylon, and Iraq, go back 6000 years, maybe 8. To see the great cycle display itself in the skies, would take at least 52,000 years. That's sort of time is unheard of, so now the plot thickens. All ancient knowledge, is on a need-to-know basis, and the majority of the truth is kept from us. We have reached the time in history, where it is time to take off the blinders from our eyes and ears. The ancient Babylonians knew the exact time of the great year. The Babylonians received their knowledge from the much more ancient Sumerians. It was the ancient Sumerians who gave the name to the zodiac. It was the Sumerians, who designed the animal figures around the clusters of stars. Zodiac means, the animal Circle, and that is exactly what they are. The Sumerians also called these star signs the shiny herd. The Sumerians and the Babylonians Left Behind great records and their knowledge was unbelievable.

Our story will move on to the Hopi Indians of the Americas. The Hopi Indians with their own Legends of the shifting of the poles, blew everybody's mind. The Hopi Legend says the second world ended when the Guardians of the North and South poles deserted their posts. The legend is amazing, for It lines up perfectly with the secret Doctrine, of all the ancient civilizations. The legend goes on to say that once the twins abandon the axis, the Earth shot off into space. The legend says that the Earth changed its shape, but finally a new axis, and a new world, was created.

Even more amazing is the fact,that ancient civilizations in Europe and America gave the same names to the Stars. It must be noted, or at least that's what science tells us, the Babylonians and the Mayas Of Central America"s bold name, figure of the Scorpion. How did they know that what star sign had in it a stinger. The Stinger in reality was a comet. The ancient Greeks and the ancient Babylonians both realized,that the planet Uranus, regularly covered its Moons. This could not be seen by the naked eye, and a legend was born. The legend states that the god Uranus had the habit of eating his children, and then throwing them up. How cleverly the ancients, concealed their knowledge. As soon as the moons we're no longer covered from view they popped up again, and this went on and on and on, and a legend was born. Uranus would eat her children, and then spit them up, and then eat them again. in reality the moons were just circling the planet. The Ancients went to any lengths to cover any information.

In the ancient mythology of Mars, the God of War, it says Mars had two horses. His two Mighty horses pulled the chariot of Mars into the battle. Once again the ancients disguised their Wisdom. For they knew all too well, that Mars has two moons. In 1877, a Wise man saw the moons of Mar, and announced it to the world. Yeah of course he had a telescope, and when he spotted them, he named them phobos, and Deimos, Mars two great horses.Science has taken pictures of a square monument on one of the moons.

It seems to the wise man of today,that all the legends of the Gods, we're actually astronomical knowledge disguised as Legends. Science tells us the first telescope was invented in 1604 but history tells us a completely different story.

In ancient Egypt, at the sight of Nirvana, telescopes were used everyday. Great lenses have been found all over Egypt, Babylon, and Sumeria. The Serpent's and Dragons, the wise men, must sit through mountains of theories and lies. The Museum's of Great Britain, display these ancient lenses. The blindfold of the church has been lifted, and education will prevail. Man is beginning to Rediscover his real ancient past. The submarines of the Aryan Nations have searched the ocean floor, and have found thousands of ruins and artifacts. Many have been brought back up. The lenses for telescopes have been found on the ocean floor.In Ecuador,and in Mexico, at La Venta, the lenses have been Unearthed. Jewel like lenses have been found in the ancient tombs of Libya. In the caves of Italy, drawings of a wolf have been found on carved bones, many dots to make a figure Of the Skies. Scientists date this find, Millions of years ago, before the Ice Age. The best Minds on Earth have tried to decipher The Mystery of the carved figure. The scientists know all too well, these dots Form a star chart, of a constellation looking like a wolf. Other dots on the bones are explained as Libra and Scorpio, and other star groups. It is ironic that Rome was built on the cult of the Wolf, but knowledge has been so cleverly disguised.

The history of man is written in the stars. The high priests or initiates wrote down the sacred knowledge, and much is still hidden from those that would destroy it. The secret societies, the adepts, have let much of it come in the form of Legends, but without the keys, it's speaks only in Mysteries. The secret doctrine of the East, does not try to conceal the Mysteries , but one needs to speak the master tongue, to decode them. The oldest astronomical work in the world, can be found in the Sanskrit Legends. In these Legends they speak of Atlantis and Lemuria. The seven sacred Islands, or land masses, appear in the works of the Sanskrit Surja, and Siddhanta. It is written in these Sanskrit Legends that the continents Lemuria and Atlantis, overlapped each other. This brought the wars,that the ancient writings are about. The sons of Light, against the sons of Darkness, are what these extremely ancient wars.

At this point of the history of the world, the heavy volcanic eruptions, and the enormous earthquakes, kept these two races moving. The high Priests of the Himalayas, and the modern geologists, tell us in these prehistoric days, when Lemuria and Atlantis, stood above the waves, Europe and America we're beneath the waves. The wise men of today would find it interesting to know, the coast of California was part of Lemuria.It seems all the talk of the land masses breaking up,is possibly the real story of Pangea breaking up.Atlantis was a world civilization,that broke up into many colonies.The writing is on the wall.

The world has changed its face many times. A great example would be, under the ice of the North Pole region, man has found tropical plants. When the last tilting of the poles happened, the Ice Age was on, and quickly. The once giant men and animals and plants were covered with ice. Because of the extreme cold, Plants and animals were dwarfed to a smaller scale. Due to the extreme cold, things shrink. Wise men call this the Great adjuster. The eternal law of nature is cold contracts, and Heat expands. There is no way governments wants to admit to the ancient knowledge, but they would also have to admit, they have been lying to the masses forever. The government's will say the good civilized world needs it's religious dogmas, and set order of things and events. Governments say knowledge causes Revolution, not the other way around. However science will admit the Ice Age ended from 30,000 years ago, to 18,000 years ago.At about 13,000 years ago to 9,000 years ago,the world wide melting was at its peak period,and the biggest flood the earth would ever see,was sinking much of the earth.

The extreme cold of the Ice Age, took its toll on man, animals, and plants. Not only did everything grow smaller, it also shortened man's life.Man used to live twice as long, the wise men say.Change is the order of the universe.

The ancient Egyptians left Behind complete records, and most were destroyed by the Romans at the library of Alexandria. I know the Romans set fire to them, but I don't believe for a single second, they destroyed the ancient knowledge. They would most certainly keep it, to add to their knowledge, of which was very limited. Rome was in its infant stage, compared to the ancient Egyptians. Only modern man can interpret the drawings of the zodiac in the Egyptian secret temples. The Egyptians Left Behind zodiacs that proved, they had seen three and a half SideReel years Or 87,000 years. All the civilizations, we're basically infants to the Egyptians, by a long, long, way. But don't forget the survivors of Atlantis built the most ancient of Egypts civilization. Not to be outdone, the Hindus of the Himalayas have protected with their lives, calculations that cover 33 sidereal years, or basically 850,000 years. Man is much older, than anyone will ever tell you. Knowledge is power, and they do not want to share. The Egyptian High priests told Herodotus, the poles of the heavens, and the poles of Earth, have lined up 3 times, and they would be the only ones to know.

Herodotus, one of The Grandfather's of History, traveled to Egypt to learn the mysteries of life and death. You might as well go to the source, if you expect the truth. Herodotus tells Us the ancient Egyptians showed him a complete written history of 12,000 years, before the time of Christ. This is twice as old as any civilization . The secret writings of the Egyptians, are just beginning to see the light of day.

Like a modern doctor writes in Latin to confuse the average man, the ancients wrote in even stranger languages. This writing is called occult science, and only the initiated can read it. Often this secret writing is done in their forgotten language of Sanskrit, and some is written in picture writing. To make it even more difficult, words are written only symbolically, and they are written in disguises. Every letter of every word means a separate Word. Every proper name in The Aryan Vedas, or the Egyptian Book of the Dead, are written in the Serpent's language. Even the Christian Bible is written symbolically, so only the trained eye can understand.This is called a code,for those that do not quite understand.

For anyone to truly know what is really meant in the ancient books of Mysteries, one must first master the secret meaning, of every letter that make up the symbolic words. Rod Stewart said

Every Picture Tells a different story, but to the ancients, it was every letter. To the adepts these are called Logo Grams, and they are only Read by those who can see behind the veil of the ancient Mysteries.

The Giants of the ancient legends have been communicated to us through oral history, and also to the written records. Egypt had her giant Kings and heroes, and the Greeks had their giant Titans. The Jews in the land of moab had their Giants, and also their Giant Akim. The ancient Chaldeans had their Giant Nimrod, and the Chinese and the South Americans all had Giants in their Legends. And of course the legends, we're filled with stories of war between Giants and regular men.

Moses wrote of one giant, whose bed was 15 ft long. And it is written Goliath was 10 foot 7 or 6 cubits. All the ancient writers, tell of Actually seeing the skeletons of the Giants. The Bible tells us, in the days of Moses, giants still lived in several countries, but you know man would hunt them down. On the inside walls of the pyramids, there are painted pictures of giants, and pictures of men standing next to them. Yes I would imagine the smaller men were the servants, of the Giants. But that is the way of the world, for might does make right.

The beautiful pyramids of South America all had pictures of giants in them. There are many temples, that go for many miles, on top of the Himalaya Mountains. These temples on the Himalayas show pictures of The Giants there once ruled the world. The Giants from the Atlantean age, are said to have built all the giant temples that cover the face of the Earth.From the pyramids of Egypt, to the pyramids of the Americas, the Giants from Atlantis built huge stone temples. Their work can be found scattered, all over the world, in Asia there is a place that man calls Bamiyan. It is here that the largest statues on the face of the Earth rest. They are the gigantic statues of Bamiyan, and its statues are huge. The Statue of Liberty in New York City, looks small to these wonders. The statues stand at a mountain that has secret passageways all through it. The mountain is honeycombed with many secret passageways. Inside the mountain there are more passageways then man can count, and no one will tell you where they lead. At this Giant mountain, the giant statues are cut into Solid Rock. The legends of Central Asia say the giant cyclops had ran mad there, Built them himself. Bamiyan is a very deserted place today, and much of it, are ruins. It stands at the foot of Kohibaba, which is an enormous Mountain in the Hindu Kush mountain chain. The mountain stands 8500 ft above sea level. This ancient city was destroyed down to the last Stone by Genghis Khan and the Mongols, in the 13th century. The whole valley, is now hemmed in by gigantic rocks. The valley is full of caves and most of the caves, are carved out of solid rock, by Ancient Man. It was in these man-made caves, that Buddhist monks, made their temples. These temples remain to this day. The modern Buddhist still live in these Rock temples. In front of the rock Temples stand the giant statues, and some say they can see the face of Buddha in them.The biggest statues in the world were covered with thin sheets of gold to add to their beauty,and could be seen for many miles.

The statues were discovered in the 18 hundreds, as the Europeans lived in their age of discovery. Ancient historical records tell us that a Chinese Traveler, Row gave them their name when he saw them in the 7th century, or about the time that the Roman Empire fell to the Germanic tribes. It is a fact that no statues on Earth are taller, And their measurements will blow your mind. The largest of the five statues is 173 ft High, the Statue of Liberty in New York City, is 105 feet high. The second largest of the statues stands at 120 ft, and it to is taller than the statue of Liberty by 15 feet. The legends say these gigantic statues were made by the Giants. The giant statues all have long ears, which is symbolic for the ones that know it all. This was the great Buddha's part of the world, and man must find out, that Buddha was actually a Aryan Hindu. The Buddhist monks that live inside the mountain, were there long before the Chinese Traveler Saw them. The Buddhist say it is written, they were there at least 500 years before. Even 500 years is a long time, it's longer than the United States has been around. When the Chinese traveler saw the giant statues, he wrote that to look at them Dazzled the eyes. For the outside of these magnificent statues, were overlaid with gold. When the British Came Upon the largest statues in the world, there was no gold. Historians say that Genghis Khan, and his Mongols took it. But then the Mongols always took it all, rape, pillage and plunder, was the name of that tune. Complete records of course were Left Behind explaining the mystery of these giant statues. In the records it explains, as the Buddhist monks moved into the Rock Cut temples, they even changed the appearance of the statues. With the new coat of plaster, they put on a new face on the largest statue, to represent of course they're favorite. As one travels through the network of secret passageways, you will come to many rooms inside the mountain. Even today, one can still see, many brightly colored pictures of the Sacred image of Buddha. The great statues belong to the ancient descendants of Lemuria. Some historians believe, they are 1 million years old. Science now in the modern world, is only beginning to release the ancient information. Some are getting famous for their so-called discoveries. Because many nations are freely discussing the Mysteries, we will someday know for sure. With money as the biggest reward modern man will do most everything. The face was changed to buddha, on the biggest statue. The extra long ears were the wise ones from Lemuria.

Whenever the Earth experienced great floods, title waves, and great earthquakes, the survivors always went to the highest ground. This is why they Himalayas are the sacred ground, or the cradle of civilization. Every time there was a major catastrophe, the survivors headed for The High Ground, which makes Tibet and the Himalayas The new world. This is probably why the biggest statues in the history of the world, stand on the highest ground, where the forces of nature leave them alone. It is because of these monuments, like the pyramids, and all the statues in the world, that mankind will be able to see the truth, and not just listen to some so-called Authority, with his theories.

The ancient civilizations always worked in stone, so the memory would last for millions of years. Besides the great statues of Bamiyan, the pyramids are scattered all over the world.
There were many other Cults of stone. In ancient times when Miracles were plenty, Legends were born, and stones that talked, gave counsel to those that knew their powers. There are legends of pagan and biblical stones, that had the power of the Gods inside them. The Giants of ancient times had super strength, but they were also known to be Master Adepts, or magicians. Legends tell us the Giants of ancient times moved the enormous stones of Stonehenge into the circle, that they form. The men of wisdom, say it was either the Giants, or The Magicians, like

Merlin and The Druids. There are many ancient legends, that tell of the talking stones that thousands listened to at the sacred oracles.

The greatest civilizations the world will ever see, had Stone idols and they worshiped them, and that was okay. And then Christianity came along , and made worshipping Stone idols taboo, and executed everyone that did. And of course, they put up their Stone and plaster idols. Yeah the Catholic churches still have many idols and statues, but like Ancient Man did, this is the way of man. The Seeker of occult knowledge , will be pointed to a most interesting piece of work called Academic Des Inscriptions. In this book that many call satanic, is the study of psychic and magical powers of certain stones, and Flint's. It is written that the Atlanteans, taught the Aryans, all the properties of magic and sorcery, and Stonehenge is where the rituals were performed.

Is a fact that the enormous stones at Stonehenge were called Choir Gaur, which meant Dance of the Giants. It seems the Giants Stones danced and rocked just like the ancient magical stones of Sweden. The Swedish had their dancing and talking stones, for a million years. The Celts called their talking stones Clac Ha Brat.This was translated to Destiny or judgment Stones. The ancient Phoenicians also had their talking Stone Idol, and everyone who knows anything, knows that stone is alive. In fact the stone idols that the spirits talked through, are found all the British Islands, France, Russia, Spain, North America, and even Germany. The ancient writer, historian, Pliny saw talking Stone idols in Asia.

It is written that the ancient High Priestess, and Priests, were said to have the mental power to move huge stones. It is said, they could move these stones from even a great distance. Many books have been written on the enormous stones of Stonehenge, and many of the writers are misguided fools. Around the region of Stonehenge, there are rock pillars. Some of the biggest of these stones weigh over a million pounds, and no one of course can explain what force moved them into place. These monster stones are of course, said to be the remains of the great Druid temples. These gigantic stones, are not limited to Stonehenge, and are scattered all over Southern Russia and Siberia. What is amazing, is where these gigantic Stone Temples stand, there are no other rocks or stones, and there are no mountains, from which to cut them. The modern scientists all agree, because they have to, that these enormous stones, come from far away lands. And of course they also have to agree, that a fantastic amount of energy was used to move them into place. Long Live Merlin and the Brotherhood, you did a hell of a job.

A great writer named Charton speaks about a great block of stone, that was brought to Ireland. all English geologists agree, it definitely is from a foreign land. In Irish Legends the stone is said to come from Africa, and the Legends say, the stone was brought over by a Warlock. It is most interesting to note, that all secret societies of the world Agree that Great Britain and Ireland were part of the fabled Atlantis. Of course they were, and so was Sweden, Norway, Germany and Northern Russia. The giant continent, covered many countries, and the continents were always ripping apart, and forming new continents. I think the story of Atlantis breaking into three different pieces, belongs to an even older story about Pangea. It might have been Pangea breaking into pieces,for Atlantis was supposed to be millions of years ago. But let me tell you right now, just in case I have forgotten, that Atlantis was a world Empire. Make no mistake, to their long, long, history, they ruled it. Atlanteans built The pyramid complexes all over the world.

Greek writer Plato loved to speak about the fog in The Mists of Atlantis, and how they surrounded the island of Atlantis. Are not the British Isles the home of the London Fog and the home of the leprechauns and fairies. Let's don't forget about Merlin the magician the famous sorcerer, And of course his brothers The Druids. The British have always been a mystical and magical race. In King Arthur's Court The Serpent of course was Merlin the magician, and the gods only know how many more serpents there were. The magical stones of Stonehenge rocked and moved, and The Druids were able to read their movements. It is written that once a year all The Druids would Assemble at the stone circle of Stonehenge. It was on these occasions, that human sacrifices were given to the Gods, and the gods answered back, through the stones themselves. These were miracles, and miracles of the Aryan kind. The Serpent's of The Druids were in the Brotherhood with the Serpent's of Egypt, and Babylonia. Both countries made the walk to Great Britain for probably 10 to 30 thousand years. The Egyptians leave behind records and maps that show how they walked from North Africa across the Mediterranean to Spain and then on to Great Britain. There was no Mediterranean Ocean then, the continents had not ripped apart yet. This is how old the Brotherhood was. The Serpent's from India came to the Gatherings also, for the Aryan Empire went from India to Great Britain. History is so damn exciting, but you must have the truth, and it becomes much better than all the lies. The very least known island of the British Islands is Mona, And Mona has her Legends too. The Vikings and the Romans on many occasions traveled to Mona, to learn the wisdom of the Sacred Island. On the island of Mona there is another magical stone with its own Legend.

No matter what efforts are made to remove this Stone from its sacred place, it returns. When King Henry was conquering Ireland, count Hugo heard of The Legend of the mystical Stone, set out to disprove it. The count and his men tied the stone of Mona to an even bigger Stone, and push them into the sea. The following morning the count and his men, could not believe their eyes.The Mona Stone was right back in the exact same spot, and the Gods were pleased. The legend does not end there, for the Christians knew the power of the sacred stone. They built a church around the Mona Stone. The sacred stone is in the wall of the church. Some things, man cannot change, he is not the supreme power any place. In the year 1554 William of Salisbury, testified to the stone in the wall, and it is still there, and quite a tourist attraction. The pagans have their strength too, and much of it, is still in practice. You cannot change the hearts and Minds of men.

Another great story, is the sacred stone that Jason and the Argonauts left at Kyzylkum. It was there, that it was placed in the temple. Legend has it that the stone, ran away and was found by the Cyzicans,On several occasions, the legend says this happened too often, and the holders of the Stone, we're forced to weigh it down with lead. Stone Idols that moved, were given the nickname routers, which means to put to flight. The ancient stones idols were also prophetic and sometimes were called, mad stones.To millions of Pagans these stones were the most powerful forces in their lives.

In Sweden, Denmark, and Norway, the land of the great ones, the magical stones, have the legends of their Heroes written on them. The Legends say many of the Sacred Stones of

Sweden were transported to Ireland, by the Giants. They were legendary warlocks,and the Irish knew their names.

The Druids were mysterious and spoke only of the power and Magic of nature. Mother Nature always ruled the world. It must be noted here, that all the enormous temples and pyramids, were built by the Giants. The secret societies say, there were never more than 100 alive at any given time. This is how it is written, and this is how you will receive it, this is not my opinion. Remember Sweden and Norway,were once part of the Great continent Atlantis, and also remember, that Odin was a giant himself. One must look to the legends of the Aryans from Scandinavia, if one desires the complete truth. The Scandinavians believe they are the chosen people, and that the Gods have created them to build the Great civilizations that lead mankind to the Arts and the Science's.The Scandinavian Vikings have conquered most of the world with weapons of steel, good Swedish Steel. Talk is cheap and words are for preachers. The field of combat belongs to those that win it. When the magical and unbeatable Aryan Warriors conquered the lands of the Earth, they had their gods, and a very close association with them. These Viking warriors were men of action, and travelers of the globe, plus The Seekers of the ultimate wisdom, and of course gold. Let's get real for a moment, what did this have to do with a carpenter from Israel a pacifist, who would not even fight for his own life, nothing, absolutely nothing at all. The Aryan Vikings we're all about the adventure of life, and they did live it. Many scholars have said, the Christian religion was the religion of no, you can't do this you can't do that, mere children in the grand scheme of things.

But what the Jewish writers of the Bible could not take by War, they took with a book.Every race has their masters, and the Jews were no exception. But the Bible was the Jewish blueprint to power, and it worked perfectly. That's another subject, and we'll definitely get to it in the masterpiece, but right now let's get back to our history.

But like Britain found herself in World War II, when she was being terrorized by the superior German air force, the Luftwaffe, major cities laid in Ruins. With no thought of giving up, this made the Vikings of Great Britain even more determined to win back, all they had lost. Listen to the gothic gods as they speak to the Vikings today through the heavy metal music. Stay true to your people and stay true to your hearts. Let no race or no people take what your great-grandfather's won for you.

Search for the truth and the power in your Noble history's, and do not go down, the road that others try to prepare for you. In Sweden, Norway, and Denmark, and Great Britain, the Viking history awaits them.It is most difficult to write about the ancient knowledge of thousands of years ago, and sometimes tens of thousands of years ago, but for the seekers of the truth it will be written.

If you believe in Magic, nothing can stand in your way. There is a name to those who know of the magic of the stone sacred idols, and they are the Dracontia. The moon and the serpent are there symbols, look for them. The Serpent's of the Aryan Nations knew the sacred rocks were the destiny of All Nations. The Serpent's or wise men of the ancients,knew just by reading the rock motions of the rocks, they could do this. This code was known of course, to the Inner Circle of the Serpent's. It is most interesting to know that in the Viking lands, the great stones were the Unseen powers behind the Viking Thrones. The wise men of the Teutonic tribes, the Vikings, watched these rocking stones, every time a new king needed to be elected. This is how it was done, and now you know. The greatest warriors were in step with the greatest gods in the world, and it soon belonged to them.The great ones were in touch with the real forces that rule them all.

For those with wisdom, for those that seek it, not only were the Aryans of Sweden and Norway and Denmark and Great Britain, the keys to the destiny of our world. They were a major power in it. All of our destiny is mixed and Blended with their destiny, as far away as ancient India, and in ancient Iran. You know it is amazing, right up to today, the Persians worship their black stones, as their most sacred objects. Yes, those sacred black stones of the Muslims, are the most sacred relics in the world to them. It was from these black stones, that Muhammad ascended into heaven. The Muslims have built their Finest temples around them, and all the holy lands. The Muslims to this day have a sacred Church in Jerusalem, and the black stones are kept there. All the Sacred Stones on planet Earth are the relics of the Atlanteans, And they definitely are a precious gift to man. Much of ancient information about the power of these stones was destroyed by the Catholic Church, so she could have no rivals. It was just another brick in the wall, of the ancient knowledge, so that soon the wall could be destroyed, and the new wall put up.

The Catholic Bishops destroyed so much of the ancient records, and then did their best to keep their flock in a blind sleep, from ever seeing the rest of it. But what the Catholic Church could not destroy was the supreme power of the Pagan Church. The Pagan religion, or mother earth religion, was half a million years old. Of course they worshiped the Earth, what else did they have better. Once Christianity did take over, it was only a matter of time, before pollution of the planet began. Many of the pagans, hundreds of thousands, fought to the death, to die with their own beliefs. The Holy Roman Empire of the German Empire , set forth the first protest against the Latin slavery. Martin Luther was the first official protester and declared he protested. Martin Luther and his followers became known as the Protestants, or people that protest. Up until the time, that Martin Luther protested, a Christian could not even lay his hands on a Bible. He was let around like a dog with a ring in his nose, and blindfolded too. From those moments on, the power of the Roman Catholics weakened, and Protestant nations would fight Catholic Nations, in bloody wars. All the kingdoms or nations of Northern Europe went this route, and freedom to think and worship was born again.

It was at this time that the knights began seeking once again, their paths to the Gods. Make no mistake the bitter Catholic pill was never swallowed by the masses,and Many religious wars were fought, just for the freedom of thought. They were sick and tired of being told what to do. The religious wars which history calls them, Were really wars of the Pagans fighting back. The power of the Pagans would never really leave, and it was underground mostly. The Pagans fought on generation after generation, until they got their part. Even in the most Catholic Nations, the power of the Pagans never died. But make no mistake it did go underground. In all the European nations, the Pagans took the images of their gods, to safe places. Here's a real reality check, the Great knowledgeable priests of the Catholic Church told us the world was flat, so you tell me, just what the hell did they know. They said the world was created in 4004, and I think they were just a little bit off. The masterminds of the church government of Europe we're not that bright, but they were very ruthless. The pope went on at many occasions, to say the world it's not that old, 4004 BC is Right. When men started dragging the bones of dinosaurs in front of the bishops and Popes, they said these are just a work of the devil. Believe it or not, in the greatest con game in the history of the world, the Catholic church and the pope would tell you, he had the exact minute the world was created. With no schools and books, all of Europe believed them. Just remember serpents and Dragons, there is no religion higher than the truth. Remember too it was the Catholic Church that held back all science for 1500 years in Europe. The scientists were jailed or executed. All the knowledge and wisdom from the Roman and the Greek Empires was erased, and all the Europeans were meant to be just sheep, easily herded.The church needed soldiers and peasants,nothing else.

Please remember so much knowledge was covered up, the new knowledge never made it to the people. A man,E. Biot Who belonged to the Institute of France, published his own beliefs in his book The Antiquities de France. In it was some stunning information. In his book Biot writes of his knowledge of the place called the field of death. It was an ancient burial round, in Malabar. The burial ground was identical to the ancient tombs at Carnac. Biot writes that in the tombs were enormous bones, that were definitely human. The natives of Malabar, told him this was the tomb of giants. They were several circles of enormous stone blocks, And the legends say they were the work of the 5 Giants, called the five Pandus. In Aryan India, the five giants created all the enormous monuments that are scattered all over the country. The Indian king Rajah had the tombs opened. He was amazed when he saw, enormous human bones. It was while staring at the giant bones, the king knew the Legends were true.India has some of the greatest and wisest men, that ever lived.

In ancient times, in every major flood of the Earth, with the huge tidal Waves, and enormous earthquakes, the huge giants went for The High Ground of the Himalayas. It was only fitting, that this is where they would rest in peace.

CHAPTER 3

 To the seekers of the true knowledge, that has not been destroyed, like the ancient library of Alexandria, read on. The Romans and the Greeks, and yes even the Catholic Church destroyed as many of the ancient library as they could. We're talking literally millions of books of History and Science and medicine too. This was done of course, so there would be no resistance to their thorough brainwashing. However we are most fortunate, they could never get all the knowledge. Much of it was hidden from them, the Secret Societies you did well. Since the beginning of time there have been secret societies, and of course secret library's. This has been done to safeguard the truth.In 1799 Napoleon and his troops broke into the Great Pyramid in Egypt. Napoleon said he knew exactly where the high priests kept their records. Napoleon was a great General, and he defeated most of the troops of Europe, and even forced his way into the secret libraries of the Vatican. The Vatican had a lot of answers, that nobody else ever will. Napoleon took his armies to Egypt, and they fought there massive battle, in the shadow of the pyramids. Napoleon had many questions, like the rest of us, and he decided he would have all the answers too. Napoleon instructed his savants, to conquer the mysteries of the pyramids. You see Napoleon brought his wise men with him, and his savants were among the wisest of the men in Europe. It is said that Napoleon had over 100 savants with him, and that he would have his answers to it all. Some of the most brilliant men in the world Napoleon had. His engineers, knew that Plato, Herodotus, called Egypt as the birthplace of geometry and advanced mathematics. In fact the most ancient Egypt, Was the first place, of everything good, they truly were the beginning of it all. The french generals turned the entire region upside down, to get to the real truth they wanted and needed. It was General De Saix,that found the most beautiful Temple of them all. The temple was near the town of Thebes. When the French General found the temple, it was like most temples and pyramids in Egypt, it was almost buried in the sands of the ancient empire.

When his savants went inside, their eyes were opened and glued, to the zodiac, painted on the ceiling. The savants immediately recognized the constellations, but their positions were not where they should be. After talking amongst themselves, the savants agreed,that this painting was done in ancient times, and represented the heavens, then. While most savants we're decoding the ancient pictures, Napoleon was figuring out things for himself. Napoleon had a brilliant mind himself, you don't make it to the top, being stupid. Napoleon figure it out,that all the stone blocks in the Great Pyramid, plus the smaller pyramids at Giza, that he could build a wall all around France 9 feet high and 3 foot thick. That's a lot of stone.He was there for a lot more than that,they were the rulers of the world,and had the wealth too.

On August 12th 1799 Napoleon visited the Great Pyramid. He asked to be left alone in the king's chamber. He was not the first conqueror to do this, for Alexander the Great had done it before him. When Napoleon came out of the king's chamber his officers and savants, asked if anything mysterious had happened. Napoleon's reply was no, the rumors have it, he looked very pale and severely shaking. It is a fact, that he snapped at all his staff, and he wanted this never mentioned again.

At this point, everyone hushed for years. In the pages of History we find our answer. Napoleon did have a vision in the king's chamber. We all know he did, for this is one of the main purposes of the king's chamber. That is a finely tuned structure,it was supposed to be.The third eye will open at the right frequency,

As Napoleon many years later, was dying, he's tried to tell his trusted friend About the most interesting night of his life, in that chamber. And all of a sudden Napoleon stopped, and he shook his head, and said no what would be the use, you would never believe me. When Napoleon was finished with his discoveries in ancient Egypt, he returned to his beloved France. Napoleon ordered his savants to bring forth all the information they had collected on their expedition to Egypt. Napoleon wanted to see all the measurements, and all the drawings. As for that zodiac in the temple of Thebes, Napoleon had it dynamited from the ceiling and taken back to the land of the western Franks, which of course was France .

The savants had done their work in Egypt, and over a 25 year span of time, the facts and information, were studied, and then released in France. It took a long time for the Franks To understand, and to piece the puzzle together. This was like another world , they had found, but you knew they would get to the bottom of it eventually. The savants had learned so much for themselves and for the world, and I wonder how much was released to the world. The knowledge of the savants filled up 9 very large books.

The highlight of the French Expedition was a 3 foot slab of stone, filled with hieroglyphics. That one important Stone was called the now-famous, Rosetta Stone. From this one terrific find the French and British, and the other nations, were able to decipher the hieroglyphics of the Egyptian language. Because of the invaluable Rosetta Stone, the code of all the picture writings were broken, and the world immediately was filled with knowledge.

It was Napoleon's Generals that agreed with him, that the only true Conquest, are those gained by knowledge over ignorance. Napoleon changed the world, and filled the world with knowledge, and left behind a greater civilization, then he had been born into. The world is still using the Rosetta Stone, and it's job will never ever be done. There are hundreds of temples, structures, and pyramids, still buried under the Sands of Egypt, or was it Atlantis. Napoleon became so powerful militarily, in his own mind, that he did not listen to his generals. No European armies could match the genius of Napoleon on the battlefield. It would be the Russian winter, that would hand Napoleon his greatest, and crushing defeat. The army of France, and their power, was forever changed after their invasion of Russia.

Napoleon was beaten soundly by the Russian winter, not the Russian generals. To add to Napoleon's crushing defeat at Waterloo, he would never ever get to return to Egypt. He would spend the rest of his days, on the island of St. Helena in permanent exile from France. Oh the winding road of life, can we ever know what's next. However, because of this one great man, the doors of knowledge, were opened wide. This one man changed the levels of knowledge on many things.The top secret wisdom,we may know someday.

 No power of the masterpiece, would be complete, without the story of Italian captain, Caviglia. The captain from Italy left the love of his life, The Maltese ship he owned, to explore the Wonders of the pyramids in Giza. By the time of the captain's arrival, hundreds of the richest Europeans were also Landing, to explore The wonders of the world. These treasure Hunters began searching for The Riches of the world. and of course, each and every one of them thought they might unlock the secrets of the Mysteries, of the Great Pyramid.Although Millions before them have tried, none would be very successful, but they would still try.The Italian captain began leading search parties for the Filthy Rich tourists. The search party of course followed Napoleon and his hundred savants, so of course,they would only get what Napoleon did not want. However there were thousands of ruins for them to play in, and they did.

It seems the Italian captain was a student of the occult, And it was said he almost killed himself.He put his Magic, and animal magnetism inside the pyramid. The captain told many of his friends of his occult experiences inside the pyramid, and this only spurred him on to Greater Heights.Every great and powerful man had visions of the secret rooms in the pyramids. But just who would find them, that's the question the captain like many others, devoted their expedition to. Finding the secret wealth, and power of these cult triangles. The captain made a ton of money from the rich European Travelers, and he began hiring Arabs to dig tunnels into the pyramid. The captain descended into a passageway over 100 ft, and the air was so thin he could hardly breathe. To add insult to injury, the batshit was so thick , it made him gag constantly.

At the time the captain finally stopped, he realized it was cluttered with sand and rocks, and he knew something was beyond it. It took a long time before the well area was cleaned out, but once it was, the airflow was fine. Then, as if out of a dream, the plot thickens, as another unlikely person appeared at the pyramid. Of course this Traveler was also seeking that treasure and occult knowledge that the pyramid did offer. Occult for those with the minds of a child, only means Supernatural, nothing more. It is a way for the wise ones, to scare off the others, and it most certainly works. Eliminate the competition, is not that, the nature of the game. Our new treasure Seeker was named Richard Vyse. He was an officer in the British army, and of course the British talk of the pyramid daily. What is so ironic, is that he had served under Wellington at Waterloo. Perhaps Napoleon had told the high command of Britain about his expedition, it certainly seems so.

Before the British officer was through, he would spend over 10,000 pounds sterling on his quest for greatness. This added much flame to the fire, with money being No Object. And of course, the pace quickened immediately. Soon officer Vyse Hired a professional engineer who was an assistant to Muhammad Ali, Who was the Shot Caller of Egypt. With the new engineer, in the forces of the British officer, he was soon taking measurements, of all the pyramids and tombs in

Egypt. Now that was a major job, but somebody had to do it. The British officer did not mess around and soon him and the captain has over 700 laborers.

It was at this point, the British officer took out on another Expedition, up the Nile to a newly found pyramid complex. The captain was left behind, As the big boss, over the 700 laborers. It was real quick that the captain used them for his own ambitions. It seems the captain had greed in his heart, like most men, and he ordered his 700 men to search for mummies. There were very old fields Nearby with the mummies. It seems that mummy flesh was in high demand in Europe, in the use of medicines. It was also used to heal bad bruises and cuts. It is said that mummy flesh could make fractures Unite in no time. Sometimes the mummy flesh healed fractures in minutes, if not hours. It truly was the rage of Europe, and if you had any cash at all, you wanted some. It was also believed to be a great cure for many problems inside the body. A whole network of traitors and thieves developed, to trade in these occult objects.

It was believed, that through the flesh of mummies, one could speak to the spirits, and cults sprung up. It also is a fact, that the shape of the Great Pyramid, made a magnetic power, that made it so that human, or vegetables, or animals could become mummy's. This all happened within the occult King's chamber. This is not a belief, this is a fact, and experiments were held inside the king's chamber. The first experiment was done with an unclean fish, a trout in fact, it took a total of 13 days and the trout was mummified. The next experiment was with the radish, and it took 15 days to mummify. Finally, the pace quickened, and the Heart of a sheep, was placed in the king's chamber. it was mummified in 40 days.

The Egyptians were the Masters, at making mummies, and it was a bizarre cult. When the ancients mummified a man, there were certain steps to be followed. First the brain, was pulled out through the nose. The rest of the organs were a slightly harder process, for these were pulled out the anal aperture, or more commonly referred to as the hole of the ass.

Making mummies was a form of suspended animation, and this came from much more intelligent sources that mere humans. The DNA left in the Mummy technically could still live on for a couple thousand years. It is in this way, Immortal Life Could Be Lived. Modern science tells us the DNA could definitely be Amplified, and the life force could be brought back. This is the reason, for all the extra effort to make things happen.

Before the process was completed the body had to be soaked in brine for at least 30 days, and then sweet smelling plugs were placed in the nostrils and the other holes. The Pharaohs believed this Final Act, ensured them there would be no reincarnation, for to reach this level, they passed their initiation.

When the British Colonel returned from his trip, and found out that work had come to a halt inside the pyramid, he became very angry, and huge arguments erupted. It was at this point that the sea captain went back to Europe, and with him, he took all the mummy flesh he could haul away.

The British Colonel now began to drive his workers, 7 days a week, they had to get to the treasure. The colonel ordered his men to Chisel their way through the enormous Granite blocks. They made no Headway, the pyramid was built to last a million years. Mountains last longer than that, so why not the pyramid. The chisels did not work at all, so the colonel next decided to use Dynamite, and this Worked really well. It wasn't long before the colonel and his men, found themselves breaking through to the next chamber. The colonel named this the Wellington chamber, and he found himself staring at the ceiling, with 8 monster blocks of granite. The granite blocks were 50 tons a piece. After blasting into the next chamber, instead of finding piles of batshit, he found black powder. It turned out to be Millions of dead skins and shells of insects. I'm sure this really pissed him off. The Colonel ordered more blasting with dynamite. The higher the colonel blasted in the pyramid, the stronger the structure. Of course this made it much more difficult to Dynamite. However the British officer was not a quitter, and he continued blasting for over 4 months. The results of 4 months of blasting was 40 feet only, this was the hardest Stone he had ever encountered. However there was much success in the blasting, for the colonel had blasted into five different chambers or rooms. Although no mummies were found, with all the riches that they were buried with, no wealth was found.

However this should not come as a surprise, for they were certainly not the first in the king's chamber. The only thing they did find, were some red paint marks. They were able to read these marks, because Napoleon had blasted out The Rosetta Stone from the temple. This Stone by the way, broke the code to all the hieroglyphics. The red marks revealed the pharaoh Cheops have made this great pyramid. This is why the pyramid is named after this pharaoh. He could have just put his markings on it, it really means nothing.

It is most interesting to Note that there were two air vents in the king's chamber, and that this chamber was used for many Mystical and mysterious rights. Once these air vents were found, the outer surface of the pyramid was searched, and two holes were found. The holes from the king's chamber to the outside, went for over 200 feet, through solid Stone, and whoever made them we're geniuses. When the air holes were finally cleaned out, fresh air rushed in. Imagine This, that in the middle of the Giant pyramid, the temperature stayed at 68 degrees, no matter what kind of weather was outside. Probably the most amazing thing the Colonel's Expedition found , the pyramids had once had a beautiful casing of Whitestone, and the white stones were beautiful. Of course by the time the colonel or Napoleon had reached the pyramids of Egypt, there were no outer casing stones left. The stones had all been Stripped Away. Of course on one end of the pyramid it is obvious, for fragments of the outer casing we're gathered together in a 50 foot High Mound. The way the secret of the beautiful outer casings was found, was the colonel had his laborers dig down to the very bedrock that the pyramid stands on. It was down here on bedrock that the Beautiful polished stones Were found.

The pyramid was designed to be equal in area, to the square of the pyramids height. If you divide the perimeter of the Pyramid, by twice its height, it comes to 3.144, which is pi, the height of the pyramid. In relation to the perimeter of its base, as the radius of a circle, is to its circumference.

The perimeter was intended to represent the circumference of the Earth at the equator, while the height represented the distance from the earth's center to the North Pole. What the pyramid did was to make a record, of the measurement of the Earth. Whoever built the pyramids knew for sure the world was round, so much for the Flat Earth crap. By observing the motion of the heavenly bodies over the Earth's surface, you could figure its circumference.

There are so many mathematical calculations in the pyramid, that you must consult Google to find out, because I do not want to lose anyone with my work. There is a much larger picture. I will add however, mathematicians say that by adding and multiplying certain things, one can come to the exact mileage of the Earth, around the equator. If one multiplies Everything in the calculations of the pyramid, One comes up with 91 million 840,000 miles, and this is the orbit of the Earth and its Journey around the Sun. The Great Pyramid is so precisely lined up with the cardinal points of the compass, that it surpasses any human construction today.

The Pyramid of Cheops, was a perfect marker for all of the ancient cities of the ancient world. Before the use of laser beams or radio waves, to determine latitude and longitude, it was done by accurate astronomical sightings. Many of the ancient temples, and ancient ruins are located in geographical locations, that use the pyramid as its source. After breaking the code of the hieroglyphics the stunned scientists realized the ancient Egyptians,knew the exact circumference of the Earth. They also knew the length of their country, to within a couple inches.

The Babylonians and the Sumerians left behind their own picture writings on stone tablets. 3,000 years before the time of Rome they were both Masters of astronomy and geography. The Babylonians and the Sumerians of course had their own pyramids , and these were called Ziggerknots.They too were built, with all kinds of hidden meanings, for they had the keys to knowledge and mathematics. You know it's funny on some of the Pharaohs Thrones, there were latitudes and longitudes, inscribed on them, and even data. They had the Tropic of Cancer written in at 23 degrees 51.This measurement is exact. At the Temple of Thebes there were also hieroglyphics they gave the exact measurements of ancient Egypt.

The first Jewish center of worship was not Jerusalem, but another mountain which was 4 degrees east of the main axis of Egypt. It was in 980 BC that it was made the occult Center of the Jews.

The ancient religious centers of Greece were Delphi and Dononna. Delphi was on 7 degrees, and Dononna was on 8 degrees. These were there Geographic markers. The Great Pyramid in Egypt, was so advanced that the rest of the capital cities were set to them. Egypt's meridium of course was always set at zero. Even the Muslim shrine was located at 10 degrees east. Mecca had the Black stones, originally arranged to a pyramidal triangle.

The pyramids or ziggurats were found on the ancient sites of Babylon, Ur, and Uruk. Although they were not true pyramids, like the Great Pyramid in Egypt, They were still magnificent. The ancient stone tablets in Babylon tell us in each of the beautiful ziggurats, had a set area, for the area between the North Pole, and the equator. These were divided into 7 zones. The mathematics and the calculations, are incredible, and I refer the seekers of knowledge to the book, the secrets of the pyramids. The pyramids of the ancient east, were set in a pre-arranged pattern, so that the Earth could be measured exactly. The pyramids of Babylon and Sumeria, had shafts of several hundred feet built into them, so that they could see the heavens perfectly, with no interference. Even in the Great Pyramid of Mexico, and the rest of the pyramids of the Middle East, there were water wells, where the sun could shine, and this would confirm their accuracy.

Any astronomer will agree, from the bottom of these deep pits, a bright star could be easily followed with the naked eye.

One must remember that these were the days when man was supposed to have been totally uneducated, but in fact the reverse is true. One must also remember that many of the ancient pyramids do not stand anymore.They stood thousands of years, many were grinded to dust, and many were covered by the sands of the desert. We will examine later, that many of the pyramids were dismantled, and used to build holy shrines and temples. In the picture writing on the walls of the Great Pyramid, it tells of a small pyramid far to the West, in the desert of modern-day Libya. The hieroglyphics say it could be seen at sunset, but this pyramid no longer stands, as many others no longer do.We are not talking about a couple,more like 20.

With the vast Network of pyramids scattered all over the ancient world, it was easy to fix once location. One must remember that every bright star comes to the meridian, of every place on the planet, once every 24 hours.The time that passes between the same star coming to the meridian, up to different places, is the difference in area, of these two places. This is called longitude, and very easy to set.This is how man learned and charted territory. What the network of pyramids did, was when the star they were charting, was at its highest point, Fires were lit on the tops of the platforms, so that the network could you. When the same star reached its highest point at another location, the distance was now known. This is how men truly learned.

The Egyptians and the Eastern people, we're not the only ones that knew the ancient wisdom. The ancient Druids we're doing the same thing throughout Great Britain, France, Germany. They Say the druids, in their homelands for tens of thousands of years, had been lighting their own fires, at the moment of the mid summer solstice, or the longest day of the year. Later these ancient fires were Incorporated into the MayDay fires. The ancient Druids of Britain, France, and Belgium, all gathered each year for the festival's.The festivals were known for their fantastic shows of magic, and of course there was them you would never forget. Merlin the magician of King Arthur's Court was himself a Druid. The Druids and the Goths, also measured the sun's rays in much the same way the Egyptians did. The longest shadow cast would be recorded, and also the shortest shadow cast would be recorded. It was in this way that ancient Man learned the length of the seasons. The Ancient Man of Britain, erected enormous mounds of dirt. They placed what would be called a May Pole on top. These man-made mountains covered 5 Acres.

and in that 5 Acres was over a million tons of dirt. Ancient archaeology say these Hills in England are over 4000 years old.

The Pyramid in Egypt is 484 ft High, and the giant Hill at Silbury is 225 feet high. But Britain is further north at the summer solstice, when the sun is at its highest point in the sky. The shadow of course would be the shortest in the year, and the winter solstice would be when the sun is the lowest in the sky. The shadow cast would be the longest. In the modern world the measuring of the Shadows, is no longer needed for now we have clocks and calendars. However, in the ancient world sometimes it meant the difference between life and death. If one did not know when to plant his crops, and also went to exactly Harvest them, Whole populations would have starved to death. Remember, in nature sometimes the Snows come early, and frosts Come at strange times. Without a set calendar man would have had to just gamble, but that's no way to run a city or a country. Men and Empires lived and died by the science of the Sun.All ancient religions, for as long as time has been, Egypt and Rome, to the Americas, we're all founded on the science of the Sun, and the sun god of course. The sun was truly God, for there was no life without it. Now we will examine further the sun cult.For a million years,man worshiped the sun,and they still should.

Like so many things that the church took away from us, they took the science of astronomy. It was only after Brave Men like Copernicus and Galileo broke the ice, was astronomy even thought of. The Catholic Church said it was evil, even the practice of it, and they threw Copernicus in jail. Most of the ancient astrology was kept from us, and most of it still is, unless one educates oneself. The days of the week are cleverly disguised , by the wise men of the pagans. Sunday the first day of the week, would be for the Sun. Monday would be the day of the Moon.Tuesday it would be named after all the Teutonic tribes. Wednesday which would be Woodens day. Thursday of course would be Thor's day, and Friday would be named after frigg Wooden' s wife. Saturday after Saturn. The Catholic Church was brilliant and it's ways of brainwashing the masses or the Sheep. For the winter solstice is still celebrated like it had been by the pagans for many thousands of years. Now it is the Christmas holidays, and the spring solstice, it's tied to Easter, how brilliant of them.

Everyone at all levels, realize that the movements of the Sun and Moon control the phenomena on Earth. We called this phenomena the seasons, the tides of the ocean, and also the growth of plants and animals.

Higher Learning tells even a deeper understanding, and a more powerful influence over man, plants, and animals. The Sun and its rays have an almost unbelievable impact on life and death. It is the 11 year cycle of sunspots, that should concern us the most, for they are the creators of the occult Sciences. To the modern astronomer, with the aid of a telescope, he can view the Sun spots. The dark spots that appear on the Sun are as flowers to the Earth. As the sunspots appear on the Sun, like the magic mushrooms do on Earth, they are giving birth, grow, and then disappear. In the meantime the Sun throws up enormous clouds of gas and gigantic magnetic winds appear. The sun is like the Earth, and rotates on its own axis. It takes the sun 27 days to complete its cycle. But sometimes the eruptions of the sunspots are aimed at the Earth, then this phenomena is accelerated. When this happens the Earth receives an unusually large amount of particles and waves too small to even be seen.The sun controls everything,without it there is nothing,no life.The pagans were right.This is not faith,it is reality.

According to where the Earth is in its orbit, and where the other planets are, the effects are different, and sometimes deadly.When the Earth and Venus are on the same side of the Sun, all hell breaks loose.The secret power of the sun spots, with the combined forces of the two planets, can cause enormous earthquakes around the world. At this time, the magnetic fields of the earth become distorted and unmanageable. At the same time as the Earth receives the amazing secret streams of power directed by the Sun, there is also doses of rays called Alvarez's cosmic rays from the Galaxy.

The secret power of the stream of particles, have been known to cause strange phenomena, like huge numbers of icebergs breaking loose from the polar region.Some say that during the heaviest of sunspot activities, that the greatest wines are produced. Sunspots also have a tremendous power over the smaller organisms in life. The smallest cells of nature also fall under the spell of the solar winds. The structure of the tiny cells can be irritated so much, that epidemics break out. It was a great doctor, Faure that devoted his attention to this matter. The doctor found out that the 11 year cycle of sunspots caused diptheria cases, in Central Europe every 11 years. The doctor also noted that Chicago is hit every 11 years with a smallpox epidemic. In Europe the Great Plagues of century's gone by, also occurred in 16 year Cycles. in Europe's cycles of plagues, there was typhus and Colorado. These two plagues killed many of the people of Europe and no one knew what caused them.

The more one studies the mysterious power of the sunspots, the more one's eyes are opened. It is amazing when one turns over the stones to look for the serpent, one enters into real knowledge. It is amazing when one learns that all the phenomena of nature fall under the magical spell of solar activity. Sunspots also affect barometric pressure on Earth, and sunspots also influence, the velocity of the Winds.

In fact the ionized streams of particles are also rumored to be an ally of magicians and high priests. In the future when the cloak of religion is taken away fully, science one day will merge themselves in astronomy and astrology, for this is a true and factual art.

In fact the Ancients knew all about it, but the Catholic Church killed all that practiced. Even the crown of the rulers of many kingdoms, wore the emblem of the Sun and the sunspots on their head, which would be the crown. When the Catholic Church took over, it was a long and bitter battle to change from pagan to the Christian Doctrine. It's ironic that the door of knowledge was opened by the ancient religions, and slammed shut by the Catholic Church. But this was done to control the populations Mind and Spirit, but of course the nobility, the wealthy, practiced the age-old Arts.
Even the great king of France, Louie the 14th preferred to call himself the Sun King. In fact the Pagan religion lived on in the hearts and Minds of most of the populations. It was just driven Underground. All secrets of the true knowledge referred to the secret Doctrine, and also to the

Egyptian Book of the Dead. Here one will find many of the mysteries of this life, and the next answered. On the back of the American $1 bill, the sign of the ancient religion can be found, and this is the pyramid, with the all seeing eye at the point. The pyramid is the symbol of the Freemasons, and they are one of the secret societies that still flourish. Thomas Jefferson, John Adams, Ben Franklin, George Washington and many more of our founding fathers were in fact members of this occult Society. It was Manly P. Hall that brought this point to light, and he is the world's top authority on the Freemasons. It is because of Manly Hall, and the other wise men that we know The American Revolution was backed by the Freemasons of Europe. It is most interesting to note, that the secret societies of Europe, also propelled Adolf Hitler to his Summit of power. It is even more interesting to Note, that the Great Seal on the dollar bill was also part of the powerful Freemasons.

After the American Revolution was over, the French Revolution followed quickly. The power was taken from the royal families, and the common everyday people, soared like eagles.

Napoleon like many of the wise men of France, was a Freemason too,and Napoleon spread his power all the way through Europe. The Revolutions of these two countries were deeply connected, for one hand does wash the other. Napoleon took things one step further by doing away with the 7th Day Jewish biblical week, and Napoleon reinstated the Egyptian 10 day week. The old holidays were replaced by great feast days, celebrating nature and the supreme Being, and even the human race.

Napoleon also held feasts to the martyrs of human Liberty, and especially To the truth. This was not all Napoleon had in mind, for he at once adopted the metric system of counting,and forced it on Europe. Napoleon at once ordered that all things would become new, and he had special orders for his wise men. Napoleon ordered his wise men to measure the distance from Paris to the North Pole, and then from Paris to the equator, and then he got the shock of his life. After studying the measurements, Napoleon learned just what he had suspected. From the Pole to the equator was 10 million meters. He then knew for sure he was on the right track. It was then that Napoleon set out for Egypt to conquer and steal the knowledge of the Egyptians. It was in the king's chamber, inside the Great Pyramid that Napoleon saw his vision of greatness.

The Great Pyramid of Egypt was the greatest ever built. So many of the ancient pyramids no longer exist except in Ruins. But that region of the world has not been fully explored, and many pyramids, are still under the sand . So much of super ancient Egypt is still cloaked and in mystery. Yes the Great Pyramid at Giza, was perfect, and so many of the smaller pyramids could not begin to come close to her perfection. We even have the bent pyramid, and it is bent at the top. Maybe it is even older than anybody will admit to. The oldest Pyramid in Egypt, or so they say is the Pyramid of Saqqara, and this pyramid was built in several stages. It does not look like the Great Pyramid, but instead is a step pyramid like those found in Babylon and Mexico. You have the mysteries of the step pyramids.Especially in Egypt and the surrounding areas, are pretty simple. because the step pyramid is the easiest to build.Steps were built going up, the casing Stones were added from the top down. This occult work of art is said to be heavily influenced by the father of Cheops.

One of the greatest authors on the pyramids was a wise man who was also an initiate . The new calendar that was made for him, was done by a light-skinned European. It is interesting to note this light skin European brought to Egypt a much older and more perfect calendar than Cheops had ever known. Egyptians to this point had operated on a two calendar system,one a civil calendar of 365 days, And also a sothic Calendar of 365 days point 25. The extra 1/4 of a day over a period of many years, through all the calculations off. A more perfect calendar was needed desperately. This is amazing and it must have been The Druids. Right next to the Great Pyramid of Cheops is a much smaller pyramid that is dedicated to his daughter. On the walls of the Tomb is a picture of her mother, who Cheops married. The mother was a white skinned European with blonde hair and blue eyes. The daughter of Cheops and his European Beauty was also a blonde with blue eyes.The Mystery becomes even larger, when it comes to the pyramids. There are so many, that have so many opinions, but I say the pictures don't lie.

The blue-eyed Queen, and the blue-eyed daughter, we're not the first Europeans known to the ancient world. For communications between Egypt and The Druids had been going on for many thousands of years. The Monuments in Britain at Stonehenge we're not built on the British foot, but on the megalithic yard of 2.72. In Britain there was even the ruins of an ancient stepped pyramid, It still has three levels. In the pyramids of Egypt there are pictures of the Egyptians with their own maypole. This further cements these two civilizations together. There are many mountains and different shapes in England, Scotland, and Ireland. They all had Maypoles To measure the distance of the Shadows. Even all through the Middle Ages in England,the maypoles all came out on May Day. It was the deed of Cromwell to put the maypoles flying over England. Cromwell was the person who banned the maypole, but it was really the Puritans who pushed for this to happen. The church eventually wanted to control everything, because power corrupts, and absolute power corrupts absolutely.The Puritans said the maypoles were for heathens only, and only wickedness and Superstition followed them.They were definitely a force to reckon with.They Marched to the beat of their own drummer, for their own Wicked Ways. In 1644 the parliament of England ordered, all the maypoles destroyed, and those that still had one, we're find heavily for cash. However history would have the last laugh. The last maypole erected in London was taking down. And here's The Clincher, the last maypole was taking down to support the telescope of Sir Isaac Newton the scientist in 1717.

It's amazing that all the pyramids of the Middle East, like the ancient British observatories, had a sighting Passage aimed to the north. In ancient Britain the round Stone circles, we're calendars of the Sun. So that the British would have the most accurate figures in the world, the Ancients erected 10,000 megaliths across Britain. The accuracy of these thousands of gigantic markers was 0.1, almost perfect. This must be remembered, that this was at least 4000 years ago, but wasn't this the time, the Catholic Church said The world was just being created. Boy did they have a lock on the minds of the Europeans, and without science, they had Doomed them to mental slavery.

The British and the Egyptians did not have a corner on the market either, because 4000 years ago the Greeks were very wise too. The Greeks were schooled in the Mysteries, and they wrote about the seasons, and the Year's rotation around the Sun. This of course was kept from the population, and even today, 4000 years later, not many have heard this information. They were also fully aware of the different climates in the different zones. The Greeks by this time had even named the planets, and they still go by the same names. In the Greek writings they also note the presence of mountains on the moon.

And Ireland not to be outdone, there are still 120 ancient Towers. They were used to follow the Sun. The wise men watched the Shadows on the wall, and they marked them. This is how the Irish, learned the mystery of the seasons. The towers just like the pyramids had subterranean pits, and then they carved markings into the walls. It was a picture found in the Great Pyramid of Cheops that tells this story exactly. There was a picture of a stepped pyramid, with the maypole on top, to show the British and the Egyptians, were tied together in thought and customs.

Inside the Great Pyramid of Egypt, in the king's chamber there is a stone coffin. The measurements were taken and the cubic capacity, is the same as the biblical Ark of covenant. Now it is time to be initiated, to climb Jacob's Ladder, and to see.

The Arks measurements can be found in the Bible, and when reconstructed was found to be an electric battery capable of producing between 500 to 700 volts. The biblical Ark was made from Acacia Wood, it was lined with gold inside and out. So what we have here, is two conductors separated by an insulator, and if placed on dry ground a magnetic field that was produced reached between 550 to 600 volts Per vertical meter. The magnetic field created the same type of magnetic power that fill the pyramids. It was in this Ark of covenant Inside the King's chamber, men received their knowledge of the world Beyond. Yes it was here that Alexander the Great, Napoleon, and the greatest historian in the world at that time, Herodotus, received their initiation into the spirit world. Or speaking of what men have always referred to as the Mysteries. Of course there were many more, thousands more did see the light right here. The modern Freemasons describe the Temple of initiation, as the highest degree of the order. Before one could attempt to Journey to the world Beyond, you must first be a scholar in geometry, astronomy, and astrology, so that he could appreciate the journey more fully. It was a gradual process, and some say the search for the grail, with Grail meaning gradual. Grail would be another of those words with two meanings. The gradual process sometimes lasted years, before the initiate was ready for the final hurdle. The modern world used astronomy as a science of the mechanism of the heavens. To the ancients, it was the opening door.

Astronomy, or the science of the heavens was closely tied to astrology, and these were tied to great Cycles of man's evolution. Of course only the Super wise adepts , who had already been initiated to view it all, in the proper frame of thought. Some Wise men believe the pyramids were built by adepts, for initiates. On the outside of the pyramid, it stood for the symbol of geometry, and Mathematics, and astrology. But on the inside, it was the Egyptian temple of initiation. One must remember that besides the electrical charge in the pyramid, one also has an electrical charge in his body. When he dies, it leaves him, and this would be the spirit or the soul. With these two electrical forces operating together, we also have the electrical magnetic force from the North Pole. Here is your sacred triangle, and here is your blueprint To initiation. This is where the spirit of man rose to meet the higher spirits.

The man seeking the ultimate wisdom was placed in the Mystic Stone Coffin. It is not known if the initiate was given the mind-expanding Soma as the Aryans in India, or they're peyote and their magic mushrooms. It is said by many civilizations these two drugs speak with the voice of the Gods, and this I can testify to.

But what is known, is the subject was allowed to stay in his dream like State for 3 days, and his Spirit flew through the spheres of time and space. In this state, the initiate realized that life was everywhere, and he could comprehend even the atomic structure of himself and the universe. In this state all will be revealed, and man would see as a god. When man learned that it was possible to slip outside his body, and come back without dying, he achieved immortality. It was only at this point,That Man became a true initiate, for now he knew the secrets of life and death. He also knew the secrets of rebirth.

Even Jesus spoke of this, but cleverly disguised his message, When he said, a man must be reborn to enter the kingdom of heaven. Jesus himself, was an initiate, who held the key to life. So were the Teutonic Knights of the Middle Ages. Adolf Hitler himself was an initiate, his mind was strong enough, but still he used drugs. It spoke with the voice of the Gods, peyote. He also use another plant of the Gods called Mandrake. It is most interesting to note, the high command of Germany were all initiates, and so were the Thule group, that pushed them to power.The plot always thickens,as it should.

I feel I must add that many of the Roman emperors had enjoyed this View, of time and space, and that all of these initiates did great things after they viewed their futures. It is extremely important to also say, the US government and the allies, did everything in their power, to keep this knowledge from their populations. But with Hitler things would be much different. He was one of the strongest personalities on Earth for that generation, and he definitely played his hand. Many of the Europeans, knew all too well about his magical Mystery Tour, for once anybody really grows up, they also learn. Everyone I've ever known, have struggled with the question, should I try it. Most are too scared, afraid they can never come back,scared and weak.

Anyone who knew the high command of Germany, knew that this was the source of their Newfound power. Churchill and Roosevelt agreed this knowledge would be suppressed. In the 1960s that message leaked out, and the world became initiated with mescaline, peyote, and LSD. Some laughed and said, LSD stood for love special delivery. America experienced a spiritual rebirth such as the Western World had never seen.It was then that the American government lost its hold on their minds. The new prophets were John Lennon, Jimi Hendrix, Eric Borton, Led Zeppelin, Mick Jagger, and the Jefferson Airplane. These are only a few of the new Prophets, and believe me there were many more. A generation was awakened by the new prophets with the electric guitars. You knew if Hitler sent his armies against the combined strength of what he called the Jewish controlled democracies, and he did not win, he broke the

Jewish Stranglehold on Western Civilization, and Christian minds. The Egyptians like Hitler, were initiated beyond belief, and the Egyptians at heliopolis, had 13,000 High priests that were all members of the occult Brotherhood. In 1425 BC, Moses himself was instructed at the finest University in the world, heliopolis. Moses received the same education as the high priests of the Brotherhood. He was taught medicine, chemistry, geometry, astronomy, geology and meteorology. I would suspect that after Moses received his initiation, is when he gained the true knowledge of his life.

It's funny, this thing called knowledge, the more knowledge we receive and Digest, the more we learn, but as the years go by , we look back, and realize it really wasn't that way, on many things. I know we hate to admit it, because we like to think we know everything, but this is not true. The more knowledge we put together, when you look back and realize how wrong we were. .

Scholars get together and decide, what the truth really was, even if it was a Theory. Many times so-called wise men and governments, all get together and agree to Agree on many things. As time goes by, a lot of this is looked at as nonsense. We hate to admit it, but the Western world, has only had a few hundred years, to try and put everything together. However, men like me, will shine a bright light on the real path for all to enjoy.

You know it's funny, the men that organized governments, give credit to, for figuring out the circumference of the world, in ancient days was a Greek. But now one more time, we will open the door of Truth. He actually gained his information at the Library of Alexandria, while he was put in charge of it. Beware of Greeks bearing gifts , and also Greeks telling lies. Our leader of the 500,000 books at the biggest library in the world of Times Gone by, was a Greek. It is most interesting to note, that the Greeks are also given credit for all higher mathematics like geometry. where did they get it come, the Library of Alexandria. Before the Romans conquered Alexandria, and the rest of Egypt, Egypt like most of the known world, was in Greek hands. It all started with Alexander the Great and his massive Army, they took it all. This is not to say, the Greeks are always takers and Liars, for they did much to add to all civilization. But let's get real for a minute, by the time the Greeks made mathematics known to the world, the Egyptians had used it, for many thousands of years.

Getting back to the pyramids, for much of this masterpiece talks about it, the brilliant Basil Stewart who wrote The Mystery of the Great Pyramid, states it best. He says, there is no more reason to believe, that because the pyramids stand in Egypt, they were built by the Egyptians. Whoever built these pyramids believe me, built them a long time before anybody arrived. It's almost like saying the modern Egyptians built Aswan Dam. In case you don't know, the Russians build Aswan Dam, and did a heck of a job. As the Russians carved up the Earth, to build the greatest damn in that part of the world, they were stunned at what they found. The Russians dug up ancient lenses, that were used for telescopes thousands of years ago. In fact the lenses were grinded so perfectly, that it is hard to imagine the ancient world having the technology to make them. The ancient world might not have had this technology, but obviously certain people did. Lenses were also dug up in Iraq, and again were thousands of years old. Today the same lenses are produced in Laboratories. The modern man uses an abrasive made of oxide, that is produced with electricity.

What we do know about the construction of the Great Pyramid, is the area of the pyramid is on 13 acres, and the 13 acres are level. The Great Pyramid of Cheops, has over 2 million giant blocks of stone. To be exact, it has 2,300,000. The so-called experts tell us the pyramids of Cheops, his wife, and family, on the desert strip were built to house the pharaoh. If you believe this, you're welcome to it, because none of the pyramids had anybody in them. These lies about who the pyramids house, are but a Smokescreen for what they really were for. The tomb of Cheops was called a tomb by the so-called experts, but none of us really know just what really went on in that room. This is what you call Miss information, and they will keep the truth to themselves. You might say it's top secret, because it most certainly is. The Queen's chamber had no Queen, but our leaders are the best Liars in the world. When the experts were asked why did you name this room, the Queen's chamber. The answer from our high level Liars, thats because of the style of the roof. If you can believe that one, I got some land for sale at the bottom of the ocean. Like I was saying, there is a full scale attack on this information. Our government, like every other government, wants to control everything, especially our minds and the way we think.

According to the Super Wise Men of the church, man was born in the Garden of Eden, and that was approximately 6,000 years ago. Because of archaeology and history we know this is nothing but a lie. This worked a couple thousand years, when there was no education. When the Bishops and popes were confronted with dinosaur bones, cavemen, Etc, they really took to telling some major lies. Their favorite was, This was the work of Satan.The church was evil,and losing power.

After Christianity was taken as the religion of Western Civilization, all other knowledge was either burned or placed below the Vatican. In the subterranean world that exists there, the scientists and the scholars were tortured and executed, so there would be no threat to the power of the church. For a long long time in Europe the church was the ultimate Authority, the final word, the government. The light of learning was turned off, and this is why men call this the Dark Ages, until the nations of Northern Europe, the Protestants, separated church and state. After all you would still need hundreds of thousands of troops to fight off the other countries that would come for you. The many invasions of Europe almost worked for lack of a great Defense Force. Not only did the Pope and his Bishops finally lose their commanding positions, but the royal families, also lost their Stranglehold on the masses. Another huge attempt to add this information, happened when the government's, chose to keep the underground temples Secret. I have already spoken of the many underground temples of Asia, especially those found around India, and the Himalayas.The Egyptians had plenty themselves. Many of the Great historians write about the underground passageways and The Mazes under the ground. Some believe in Egypt, beneath the pyramids is an Underground kingdom. They say the kingdom is just like Agartha of Tibet, at the roof of the world, the very top of the Himalayas. this Kingdom has been there for thousands of yours. There are many code names, for these private underground kingdoms, and only the very wise, even think about them. That is the way it is supposed to be.

In 1839 Perring was searching for the Mysteries of the bent pyramid, and something occult happened to him. The workmen were clearing the secret passageways and many began passing out from tremendous Heat, and lack of oxygen. Suddenly a few hours hours of cold wind blew through the passageways. It is written the wind blew hard for 2 days, so hard the workers could not continue. They could not go on, because their lamps would not stay lit. After several days the cold wind stopped, and never blow again, and fear fell over the expedition. Many of the workers would not continue, saying that the force of the pyramid was after them. The wisest of the ancient historians, assure us that even after the pyramids were sealed on the outside, that the high priest still could enter from a secret passageways below. So much of the pyramid complexes are Underground, they do not like to speak about them.

The ancient Greek historian Herodotus tells us that the extremely occult pyramid found in the lake at Moeris, has over 3,500 secret Chambers, or rooms, and most are beneath the lake. Herodotus received a grand tour of all the pyramids in ancient times, and he is considered the ultimate Authority, of at least what they showed him. These Egyptians always played their cards close to the vest. The Egyptians called this pyramid, the pyramid at the entrance to the lake. Every historian who is worth his salt, knows there is much more to be discovered in ancient Egypt, that is not known. It's been estimated only 25% of ancient Egypt has been revealed.

It is also Herodotus the great Greek historian, that brings us all the information of the Tower of Babel, in Babylon. In ancient history we're always covered with half-truths. the Tower of Babylon of course is the stepped pyramid.

Herodotus tells us, on the top step there is a spacious Temple, and inside the temple is a great bed covered with fine bed clothes, with a golden table by its side. There is no statue of any kind set up in the place, nor is the chamber occupied at night, by any but a single native woman, who say the Chaldean Priests is chosen by deity of the land. The priests also say, God comes down in person into this chamber, and sleeps upon the couch.

Of course some Legends have it, that spacecraft landed on top of the tower to the heavens, and the visiting astronauts could meet with the high priests in the inside of the pyramids. I guess some Legends, are more believable than others, but let's continue. Before we dismiss the part in the Legends of the spacecraft, let us remember in the ancient Aryan Legends they speak quite often about flying vehicles. Even in the Bible they speak often of flying vehicles, wasn't Ezekiel taking up to the heavens.

The scientists from the Atlantean age, knew how to tap the Van Allen belts for their own power. It is told in the Legends, at some point in space, laser beams were aimed at the pyramids, and this was their energy source. I know this is true as the power of an atomic explosion is very dangerous, but it is nothing compared to the power that is generated by the Van Allen belts that go around the Earth. It is written that for some reason, the power was left on too long, or too much power was generated. It is written at the last, that there was an enormous explosion, that knocked the world off its axis.

I have Teutonic blood running through my veins and my blood screams out for the facts. I try to make my work the masterpiece deal with only facts, but it is most difficult since I write about many Ancient centuries ago. It is most interesting to note that the great Greek historian Herodotus, also traveled to the Mystic Temple, Luxor. Europe was not quite sure of the truth, of the statements about everything they heard concerning Luxor. But after Napoleon took the wise men from Europe, the savants, he made them make sketches of everything they encountered. It was Napoleon's savants that had the mission, to educate the world. After much studying and deliberating, Napoleon learned that the Temple of Luxor, was perfectly pointed at the summer solstice. When the summer solstice took place, the fireworks begin, a ray of light at Sunset or sunrise, was shot perfectly deep, into the innermost part of the Temple. As the light from the Rays penetrated the temple, it traveled between two rolls of beautifully carved columns, and I do mean beautifully carved columns. Then the ray would go through a chain of Halls, and when the light finally hit the designated spot, it shown on the wall for a couple of minutes. By measuring the light, the Builders of these temples, had an instrument of extremely precise accuracy. The tiny stream of light traveled 500 yards and was funneled to the temple, with pinpoint precision. Herodotus stunned the Greeks back home, when he told them about the Temple at Tyre. It was here Herodotus told Greece that the Sun shined at night, in the dark innermost
 Section of the Temple. The bright star of the North, was able to throw enough light into the temple,and it was beautiful and quite mystical.

For those that did not understand science, this was a show they would never forget. The high priests or serpents, we're not above fraud. and even placed large jewels in the statues to make them shine with brilliance. Temples that were set to the Sun, would last for thousands of years, for the Earth tilts its axes only one degree in 6000 years. However the temples of Egypt that were set to the Stars did not enjoy the same. These temples would last 200 years to 300 years. The wise man knows that this is the main reason, for so many hundreds of ruins throughout ancient Egypt.

The solar year is the time it takes, for the earth to go around the Sun. The temples that were set on the Stars would only be good for between two and three centuries. The stars in near sidereal cycles lay back behind the Sun, or in other words, later each year after the sunset. The Zodiac Cycles are called sidereal cycles, and they marched to a separate drummer. In fact, at first, the difference was 172nd of a degree each year.

But after 200 years it would be off to 3 degrees. All so many of the temples were rebuilt and had their axis changed. And of course on many occasions new temples went up. When the scientists went to the fabulous Temple of Luxor, then measured and observed the changes in the structure at three different points.

As the scientists and serpents checked the temples of the Assyrians, they found they had been altered. The temples of the Egyptians were set to the Stars of alpha major and Alpha centauri. One of the greatest Minds in ancient history belonged to a professor Lockyer, and he said the earliest race in Egypt, Built temples, and Heliopolis. But he also says the Great Pyramids were built by a new invading race, who was more advanced than any earlier race. Well thank you Professor we had that one figured out, thank you.

The Zodiac that Napoleon had dynamited from the ceiling, Louis The 18th bought for a hundred fifty thousand Frank's. Today that great piece of work, is on display at the Louvre Museum in France, thank you Napoleon.

The Temple of Isis is one of the most famous of all temples ever belt, and the great historians say it was directed at the star Sirius in 700 BC. It was at this time in history, that the star of Sirius rose at the same time as the sun, and this happened on the Egyptian New Year. The historians are sure of this date, for on the throne of the Pharaohs, it is inscribed. and it is inscribed forever.

It is most interesting how the historians are able to date the temples with the zodiac, but it is so very simple for the wise men of today. The ancient Egyptians were Masters at recording the movements of the Sun and stars, and they also knew the procession of the equinox. This means they were well aware that the equinox would bring a new constellation behind the Rising Sun every 2,200 years. To check this in Egyptian history, is simple when one learns that the cult of the bull, was before the cult of the ram. This is exactly the way it was in the heavens above, that's the constellation of the bull, and cult of the ram would follow.

The ancient Egyptians knew there were really two poles, 1 the North Pole, and two the pole of the solar system. The Babylonians we're just as sure as the Egyptians, and they were definitely sure there were two poles, because they named them. The belt of constellations that each had their name, control the heavens, and also control life on Earth. This is why the Egyptians believe so much in fate,and the Stars.

The zodiac of course becomes the oldest calendar in the history of the world, measuring not in days or months, but in light years. For those that do not know, a light year is the distance it takes light to travel in one year, that is a light year. But check this out, light travels at 186,000 miles a second, you need your computer, to figure out how far it would travel in a year. Grasshoppers I hope you have enjoyed thoroughly all the pages I have written about, the pyramids and their secret entrances, and secret exits, the small cities down below. I hope you use this information some of you, to uncover even larger secrets. Do not be afraid, someday we must all go on, if there is an on, but know grasshopper , seek and you will find.

THE MASTERPIECE

CHAPTER 4

In March of 1882 in the prime age of discovery, this is what men called the age of discovery, when science was taking off like a rocket, the world witnessed colossal forces at work in the North Atlantic. A British merchant ship named the Jasmine was sailing to New Orleans from Italy, as she passed through the pillars of Hercules out into the Atlantic, the life of every member of the crew was changed. Their position in the Atlantic was 31 degrees by 25 degrees North, and 28 degrees by 40 degrees west, very close to the Islands. The ocean around the ship became extremely muddy and something was going on below. It was not just the muddy water that captured the crews attention but also the large amounts of dead fish. As if killed by an underwater explosion, millions of fish were floating on the surface dead. Captain Robson noted in his log this event, and he called it The Dead Fish Banks. It was also noted that far off on the horizon were clouds of smoke, and the captain thought it might be just another ship.

As the night fell, the next morning came, and the ship's crew was shocked at what they saw. The amounts of dead fish on the surface had grown, and fresh piles were everywhere. The smoke the captain had seen the previous day, was now seen coming from an island to the West. On the island was a mountain, that was burning. The captain quickly pulled out all his sea charts, and there was no Island listed For thousands of miles. The captain not knowing of this island, or if it had coral reefs that would sink the ship if you hit them, he chose to Anchor his ship, 12 miles from the island. The men loaded the small craft, the captain ordered the anchor thrown overboard, and he was shocked when it stopped it only 7 fathoms. The captain's reliable charts told him the water in this part of the world was several thousand fathoms.

The captain and his men, road to shore, and once on the island they were shocked again. On this strange and Mystic Island, there was no plant or animal life at all. There were no sandy beaches, and there was a strange feeling in the air. The only thing on these rocks was cooled lava, and it was found everywhere. The captain and his men tried to get to the part of the island, that had the Smoky Mountains. On their way, They found deep and wide cracks, and they knew it might be weeks, to get to the mountain. The captain and the crew went back to the landing point, and everyone started walking up and down the seashore.

One of the crew spotted an arrowhead, and the captain at this point, sent back to the ship, a few Men to get picks and shovels. The captain and his men, found ruins and stone walls, and for two days they picked and looked for treasure. The crew of the Jasmine found vases with bones in them, and also found a complete skull. The men of the SS Jasmine found many Priceless bronze swords, and many sculptured works of art. The greatest find on the island was a mummy in a rock sarcophagus, and the crew took a better part of a day digging it up, examining it, and transporting it back to the ship.

When the Jasmine finally reached New Orleans, with Her cargo, many of the local reporters came down to examine the artifacts. It must be noted that the search on the Mystic Island, was called off when the weather, began getting bad, the captain feared for their safety. In the times of New Orleans, the paper was full of Stories, of the land the Jasmine had found, and they talked about the treasure they brought back. It is interesting to note that the Captain's Log of his journey was stored at the offices of Watt and Company, the owners of the ship. in 1940 Hitler's Air Force luftwaffe, destroyed much of London and the offices of Watts and company. Of course the British museum Claims, they never received any of the artifacts. What is even stranger than the treasure, is the amounts of dead fish the Jasmine encountered. The area The Dead Fish covered, was 7500 square miles,and of course many of the other sea captains reported to the New York Times, seeing these mountains of dead fish too. The captains of the ships, estimated that close to a half a million tons of fish were floating dead on the surface. Many of the different ships, that passed through this 7500 square miles of death, reported every type of fish imaginable. Many reported they ate the fish, and reported the fish were Cooked by the hot volcanic water,and they said it tasted great.

Modern oceanographers say that this ocean of dead fish and Muddy Waters happened as the island was pushed up by volcanic action. Crew members of the passing ships told the Times newspaper and New York, that the fish were very tasty. Another passing ship said there were millions of pounds of dead fish. The Westbourne was sailing from Southern France to New York when he saw the island. The New York Post newspaper on April 1st 1882 carried the story.

All over the Atlantic, there have been many sightings of buildings and walls, And even roads. The bottom of the ocean floor is covered, and they go all the way down to the Devil's Triangle. Now what kind of book would this be if I did not answer the riddle to the Devil's Triangle.

To put into the proper perspective, the extremely volcanic action in the North Atlantic, we will examine. The disaster at Lisbon Portugal in 1755, before the American Revolution, Lisbon was struck by an earthquake that will go down in history as a Serious jolt . It is written in the pages of History, that day in 3 minutes 60,000 people were killed. Many of the people of Lisbon ran away from the buildings, when they felt the earthquake, and many of them ended up on the solid Stone pathway by the docks. All the stonework fell into the sea, and plunged to the depths of over 600 feet. It is written in the histories of all the European nations,and It was heard in the capital city of Sweden. European history is full of volcanic action, we live only on the crust, with a ball of fire beneath us. Time and time again in history many of the cities of Europe were totally destroyed by volcanic, an earthquake action., not to mention the lava that cooked them good. Pompeii is an excellent example of thousands buried in lava. Many times the massive Atlantic earthquakes can be felt but not seen. In 1929 there was an underwater earthquake, that because of all the mud and Rock shifting, many of our transatlantic cables, were broke and covered in debris. The wise men of those days went and searched, they found that the ocean floor Has Lifted over 1 mile up . In 1963 the ocean floor of the Atlantic rock and rolled again, and new islands came to the surface.

. The first island to pop up, was off the coast of Ireland, and it was named Surtsey. This was named after the Viking god of fire. The island was created with enormous amounts of fire and smoke, and the people of America watched it on television. But watching it on TV, you lose a lot. The fire god of the Vikings kept kicking out fire for 3 years. In that amount of time, two more Islands were born. All over the North Atlantic around the Canary Islands the natives have watched for thousands of years, Islands appearing and then submerging beneath the ocean. In 1974 the Viking god of fire, Buried 2 towns in Iceland. The towns were covered with lava, but because of the slowness of the lava, most of the people just lost their homes. I might add that on the floor of this extremely violent earthquake and Volcanic area, that the world's tallest mountain range stands. Some say it is a Living testament of the mountains of ancient Atlantis.

Plato Of the Greeks, wrote a lot about the hot springs, and the cold springs that were on Atlantis, and today the hot springs still remain in the Azores Islands.In Iceland the hot springs are loved by all, and the hot water is found in enormous quantities. The subterranean Hot Springs provide enough hot water for entire cities.The Azores Islands are filled with many ancient volcanoes, and legends say at the bottom of their Great Lakes are the ruins of Atlantis. Plato in his work of the tropical plants and trees,said on the bottom of the sea, on the ocean floor are hundreds of volcanoes. The Russians Have sent us plenty of photographs of the ocean floor, taken just a few feet above, by underwater cameras. The Americans and the British spy submarines, have also mapped the entire Atlantic Sea bottom. Learning to show the world, that they too are powerful players in science, have recently released many photos that the Western governments have never shown us. The Russians sent their research vessels to the Atlantic, to search on the ocean floor,for places to park there submarines in case of a nuclear war. The Russian wise men, tell us that the land bridge between America, Africa, and Europe did not sink as much as it was drowned by the waters of the Ice Age melting some 13,000 years ago. Although only islands rise above the Waters of the Atlantic, beneath these Waters, are 10,000 foot Peaks that rise up within 200 feet, of the surface of the ocean. A great Russian writer Dimitri, who was perhaps the most honest of all the European writers, said that most modern scientists agree that one day all of Europe will meet the same violent, fiery grave, that Atlantis once did. In 1974 the Russians proved to the world what knowledge really was, when they released photos from one of their finest research vessels. In these photos The scientific Community was rocked. In exactly the place the ancient Greeks had said Atlantis was, there was something. The Russians photographed many underwater buildings, and many ancient ruins. It was in 1979 that the photos were released, in the Russian press. Right after the Russians released their top secret photos, pictures began showing up in all the world's magazines. America and Britain did not want the knowledge leaked to the masses, but the Russians could have cared less. When the Russians carried out their deep sea mapping and investigation, they left no stone unturned. With their prized research ships, the Russians brought their top geologists, and their top oceanographers. When the ships were in their desired places the Russians lowered their underwater cameras. They also lowered some super bright lights to within 9 feet of their targets. The Russians started photographing very close to the Straits of Gibraltar, also known as the pillars of Hercules. They also went up and down the coast of Europe and Africa. The Russians got more than they bargained for, when the underwater cameras snapped the First pictures, of the ruins of Atlantis. it was exactly where Plato said it would be.

It is most interesting to Note, the Russians filmed day and night at the site where the Jasmine found their Treasures of swords and pottery. This site was 300 feet west of the pillars of Hercules, were talking right on top of the whole ball game, just like Plato said it would be. This is a place where the underwater mountains are shaped into a huge horseshoe. This extremely high mountain chain is called the Atlantic Ridge. This mountain chain divides the Atlantic into two enormous underwater plains. The massive melting of the ice age peaked 18,000 down to 13,000 years ago. This was the great flood,and a lot of the world was drowned. 13,000 years ago the comet struck the earth.These two things happening at once,almost ended all life on earth.The earth was knocked off its axis,and the deluge began,and the rest is world history.Make no mistake this happened just like I wrote,and all has been kept from the public,but no more.

Thousands of photographs were taken and studied. On several of the photographs, the Russians became very excited, on what they had found. The Russian photographers we're very good at what they did. Thousands of photographs were taken and studied by everyone. On several of the photographs the Russians became extremely excited, on what they had found.

Here's a few words from the Russian in charge, When I had to develop the photographs, and made the first prints, I realized that I had never seen anything, like it before. The Institute of oceanography of the USSR, had a huge archive of underwater photographs. Russians also had many thousands of photographs taken by The Americans. Nowhere have I seen anything so close, with traces of the life and activity of man, in places which could only have been dry land.

On the first photograph we can see this wall on the left side. stone blocks on the upper edge of the wall are clearly visible. All the lenses were pointing almost vertically downwards, areas of Masonry can be seen quite clearly. One can count five such areas, and the masonry blocks of the wall are 1.5 Meters High, a little longer in length. On the second photograph, we can see the same wall from directly above. It is difficult to calculate, the masonry blocks are clearly visible on both sides of the wall, the seaweed is visible on all the photographs. An area over which lava has flowed can be clearly seen. The wall is broken down in many places, and overgrown with under sea sponges.

The Russian Expedition would be the first to admit ,that due to man's technical breakthroughs in the last 90 years, the door of the Earth's Mysteries have been opened. Modern governments have at their disposal, deep-diving submarines with fantastic cameras to photograph. The most modern of the undersea craft are equipped with robot arms to take samples of whatever they need, or just snatch the loot and run. When they go down with their equipment, make no mistake, this is a business operation, and it's all about the cash. Not only do they have the robot arms on the submersibles, they are equipped with the most powerful searchlights in the history of the world. If that wasn't enough they even have modern sonar.

The area were speaking about had to be checked thoroughly, it's called the Great horseshoe. Believe me every year, that area is visited by the underwater vessels of many nations. That my friends, or serpents and Dragons, the secrets of the real truth will be known, for this is what we live for, this is our Kick. To put all theories aside for a moment, and check all the brands of ancient history, this is definitely the Cradle of all civilization. This is why the submarines of many nations are there. Anything, and I mean anything, taken up from the legendary Atlantis, would be priceless. What I wonder is did the symbol for good luck,the horseshoe, which was passed down to us by the ancients, does it really symbolize this Sacred underwater place.

Please remember if it was not for the destruction of all the ancient libraries, the world would know quite a bit more, in fact they may know everything. The best example of destroying complete knowledge of ancient civilizations, was the destruction of the library at Alexandria, that was a big one. The library at Alexandria had over 5 hundred thousand books. I'm sure they kept the best ones for themselves, and claimed the fire burned everything. The libraries at Carthage, the home of the Phoenicians was also burned. The Phoenicians rank with the best of them for traveling the oceans, they even rank up there with the Vikings, if not further up the ladder. Before the days of Jesus Christ, before the days of Rome, the Phoenicians we're sailing up the Amazon River in South America. They tell us, Everyone thought the Earth was flat, which ranks high with all the other fantastic lies we have all heard.Men stared at the moon, and sun for thousands of years,they knew they were round.The Greeks and the Egyptians knew the earth was too.

 The Roman Empire is another story, and boy how we love a good story, but only if it's true. The Roman empire was divided into East and West, because it was rather large. The Western Empire was Latin dominated by Rome, and the Eastern Empire of the Romans was actually, what was left of the old Greek Empire. Greek was spoken in the east, Latin in the West. The Western Empire fell to all the Germanic tribes, and the rest of the Viking Nations, but the Eastern Empire fell to the Turks. The Eastern Roman Empire with his capital at Constantinople lasted for another thousand years more than the West. But when they fell, they fell.The Eastern Roman Empire fell about 1450,s, but there unlike the West, the Eastern Empire got to fight a rear guard action. What I mean by that exactly, is while the Army retreated, they did so in order. It wasn't a massive retreat, but instead they took their sweet ass time, Gathering Together most of the wealth that they could cram into all the wagons. They definitely headed west. Now as they brought back all the written knowledge of the world, one has to wonder exactly what they did know. The Eastern Roman Empire had the knowledge of the Phoenicians, and the Phoenicians had the knowledge of North and South America, and all the gold in South America.So much for the Phoenicians,their library was supposed to have been burned down too,sure they lie.

Let's not kid ourselves, thousands of shiploads of gold is what every nation wanted. All the wealth that was hidden in the libraries, and the wealth that was hidden in the maps. Now the only question I have, and it's very legitimate, is did Christopher Columbus get his grimy little hands on this knowledge,of course he did.We know now he had thee old maps showing where Atlantis was,i've seen them.He too was after the gold,of course.Its always the gold.

It was at the same time that all this was taken place, they tell us that he was an explorer, he didn't really know what was out there. It is said in the history books for children, that Columbus had to go back to every king or queen, to give him the ships. That's a likely story and a big fat lie, and the serpents and Dragons can see through that easily.

Getting back to the underwater exploits with modern equipment, 50 years is a long time. All along the coast of Morocco, many ancient walls have been found under the sea. Where there's smoke there's fire, and I'm sure somebody's out there right now. In North Africa divers have gone down to take
Pictures of the largest stones ever cut from Rock, and they're located off the coast of North Africa. It is in Lebanon which was ancient Phoenicia, at the most enormous ruins were found underwater. As we move into the South Atlantic, modern scuba divers and Pilots, and treasure Seekers have also made tremendous discoveries in recent years. It is mainly the pilots flying up above the Devil's Triangle, that first saw the underwater buildings and ruins, and yes even pyramids. What is amazing, is all the ancient roads and ruins in the Devil's Triangle have to have been built before the melting of the Ice Age 18,000 years ago. So much for the Catholic Church preaching everything was created a little over 4,000 years ago . The area that has captured the attention of the archaeologists, the most is that under sea region off the coast of the beautiful Bimini. Science is trying to downplay, and done a good job, of all these magnificent

discoveries off the coast of Bimini, especially the part about the ancient roads and walls.They said, they were just natural undersea formations, to keep away everyone else who wants the big cash too. Off the coast of the Bahamas is the largest collection of underwater ruins in the world. Many of the underwater finds resemble the stone Circles of Stonehenge in Great Britain, sounds like the Brotherhood again to me. The government's would have us believe that these enormous undersea constructions are natural formations, but as the photographs show, the stones were cut and designed perfectly. Sometimes the stones were cut in perfect squares, and perfect rectangles. The stones are visible to the divers of all Nations, and nature does not build in these symbols. The walls and ruins under the sea at Bimini,are called the Bimini Road, and these underwater roads are thought to have once linked the islands together.

Enormous blocks of cut stones are lined up perfectly, and sometimes are formed perfect right angles. The underwater divers can follow the Bimini Road only so far, then there is a sharp drop in the seafloor, and the rest is covered with the Sands of the ocean. Thanks to a doctor Valentine and men just like him, the knowledge of these ancient works have been spread around the world. Dr. Valentine has spent over 25 years searching the ancient ocean floor off the coast of the Bahamas. I'm sure it's not the fish that attract this great man, it's the of the treasure seeking. Indiana Jones is Not the Only treasure Seeker in the world, there are many more.

But thanks to Dr. Valentine word has spread around the world, and this is such a huge underwater site, that many have filled their pockets I'm sure. Whoever finds the treasures of Atlantis or any of its colonies, can write his own ticket for the rest of his life. Dr. Valentine found this under water Road and wall in 1968, and of course since then, he and many others have made many private expeditions to the area. You know it's funny, the stones that make up this ancient wall are the hardest rock known to man. Because of all the sand on the ocean floor Searchers do not know how far the wall really goes yet, but then I'm sure they're also looking for any type of treasure. Many of the archaeologists had said all these Stone workings and Roads,are only the very tops of what is down below. These stones that are cut, are so enormous in size, that modern scientists agree they probably built all the ancient sites that had the massive stones. Were talking about Malta in the European Waters, Tijuanaco in South America, and of course the great Stonehenge in Great Britain. You know it's funny, all of these giant stone structures, the legends say the Giants built them,I say ancient man did.

Pilots, not to be outdone are also treasure Seekers of course. They have been the spotters of many of the undersea ruins and structures. Many Expeditions of scientists and divers have spent months surveying the walls, and the roads. But you know as well as I do, they are looking for the priceless artifacts that would certainly make them rich.
A
Stonehead was brought up by 1 Expedition that weighed 300 lbs. Throughout the whole Devil's Triangle on the floor, are ruins, structures, pyramids. Now here's the part that's a little bit funny, but I know my readers will have a big sense of humor. You have to this is life. It is talked about in many circles, that much of the treasure that has been taking up for the last 75 years, belongs to private collections, and wealthy people.

What is puzzling and amazing at the same time, exists in the ocean, off the coast of Portugal. But they also exist in the Devil's Triangle. Fisherman know exactly where to find them of course, and explorers have known for thousands of years, although most would not admit it. Fresh water Springs are also found in the Azores island chain and fishermen have known about them for as long as man could talk to his son.

In the Devil's Triangle scuba divers have announced interesting blue holes, several of them, and they are a half a mile across. The wise men of today say these giant blue holes were caused by meteorites that slammed into the Earth a long time ago, wiping out surrounding areas with huge tidal waves. Some of these deep blue mystic holes, go down to over 1000 feet. What is ironic, is the ocean in this area is only 20 feet deep. Giant holes can be seen by the pilots easily, and the ships can notice them too. These blue holes are shaped like the sacred Wells of the Mayans and legends say, the Mayans holes are made by meteorites too. In the Maya civilization, the high priest threw Jade, and gold, and virgins, to the Wells of the Mayas. They are still to this day considered sacred sites. Of course they're considered sacred sites, the Muslims still have their famous black stones, and many say they are meteorites too. The blue holes in the Bahama Banks have grabbed the attention of many modern wise men and women,
and many have gone to the spot to search for ancient civilizations that were obviously wiped out. Some say these meteorites did one hell of a job on Atlantis. Depth recorders say the bottom has not been found with them. However the depth recorders have not found the bottom even at 2800 feet, which means the meteorites had to have hit with a force of hundreds of atomic bombs, but this is the way of nature. In Canada there is a scar left on the landscape of what happens when an asteroid hits the world. This enormous asteroid strike was discovered by NASA, and it's orbiting vehicles. The scientists of the world,agreed that this huge asteroid, would have hurt hit the Earth, with the force of 100,000 Atomic bonds. This asteroid crater could be perhaps the reason why so much of the Atlantic is underwater, then on the other hand,the asteroid strike could have been the great flood. Any of these asteroid strikes I've just mentioned, could have finished life off everywhere. It's not the size of the meteorite or the asteroid, that determines the damage. It is the kinetic energy that comes with the visitor. The kinetic energy is determined by many things, like did a planet explode and send this meteor a million miles an hour, or just how far did it come from. Every mile it traveled, added to the kinetic energy, or the force that would be Unleashed. I have seen films by scientists explaining kinetic energy and meteors. It is hard to imagine, but when the meteor hits the Earth, or asteroid, the force it hits with goes around the world several times destroying everything. Like I said the asteroid that hit Canada a long ago time, hit with the force of 100,000 atomic bombs. They could have caused the Ice Age. So much debris is thrown up into the atmosphere, that sunlight cannot even come through, and this goes on for years I am told. Without the heat of the Sun, quickly the temperature goes way down and gets ice cold. It is said by scientists of the western world, when an asteroid hits with this much power, it could literally Shake to death every living thing. These asteroids and meteors,have hit hundreds of times in the 4 billion years the man says the Earth has been here. One has only to look at the Moon, to see how many times a planet or Moon could be hit. One thing is for sure after any of these large strikes, the world would never be the same, and anyone living along any Coastline in the world would drown. Here's your reason for

all the great floods. The only safe place for civilization to exist for millions of years, would be inside the earth. The space rocks have brought total destruction to our planet many times, and they will return.

Inside the Devil's Triangle there are many gigantic storms and hurricanes, that shift the underwater Sands around. After some of the biggest storms, Pilots and scuba divers have reported seeing pyramids Rising from the ocean floor. In 1977 inside the Devil's Triangle, a huge pyramid was spotted by a ship on its depth finder. Since that discovery, many undersea expeditions have been launched, and no results are given. That doesn't mean they didn't find anything, that just means they don't want you to have anything. Do not be the one that needs to be told everything, because most people are just not that nice or stupid. Treasure hunting is a great line of work, and don't expect them to point the way for everybody else. Geologists working for the government, of course told the world this underwater pyramid was a natural formation, however freelance scuba divers tell a different story. The research team tell us there are more than one Pyramid on the ocean floor at the Devil's Triangle. This is probably true, for pyramids above the ocean, are always found in groups or complexes.

The Caribbean Sea, and the waters off the Bahamas, have been discovered and photograph many times, but those multi-million-dollar treasure ships, need to get their money back. They will always go first, and allow others to Trail way behind. In 1979 a freelance treasure hunter, took closed circuit television pictures of a pyramid in the Devil's Triangle in 750 feet of water. The man in charge of this huge freelance Expedition, was a Greek industrialist named Ari Marshall. Let's listen to what he had to say.' The first thing we noticed when we got near the area, was all the compasses were going bezerk. How many times have we heard that one. There seems to be a power source still alive in the pyramids on the bottom, whether it be nuclear, we just do not know, or I should have said, I do not know. The Greek industrialist and millionaire said the top of the pyramid was 150 ft from the surface of the ocean. He said the total depth was 650 ft. He said they lowered the cameras and the high intensity lights, and they suddenly came to an opening in the pyramid. Light flashes or shiny white objects were being slapped into the opening by turbulence. They may have been gas, or some sort of energy crystals. Further down, the same thing happened in reverse. It was surprising that the water in this deep area was Green instead of black, near the pyramid, even at night. The Expedition photographed big holes, in the side of this underwater construction, and it also photographed electrically charged particles coming from them.

This may very well be the reason why radios and Compasses, do not work in the area. The power of the pyramids are well-known, but the power of the undersea pyramid is unknown. The pyramids that were built in Mexico, Egypt, Peru, and Brazil, are linked with the pyramids of the Devil's Triangle. You know it's funny again, the treasure seekers of the pyramids, at all these places, went for the wealth that Plato wrote about. Plato said that the palace of Atlantis had Plumbing made of gold, garden tools were made of silver, and I mean pure. In the ancient world I would imagine the veins of gold and silver were just popping out of the Earth. Plato Tells us that the Atlantean Temple to the Sun, a pyramid of course, was lined with sheets of gold, and that diamonds and precious stones were everywhere. So you see why the treasure Hunters fall in love searching. This is the force that propels the modern explorers and if they found it, do you think they would actually tell the world, no I don't think so. Wouldn't they want to possibly find some more.

Plato also tells us the mummies of Atlantis we're completely covered and gold and jewels, and of course one has to wonder about ancient Egypt. Plato tells us that Atlantis, was so filled with precious metals of gold and silver that all the underground pipes were silver. Plato says the entire landscape was covered with gold and silver statues. When one is trying to figure out exactly where Atlantis was, and that Temple to the Sun with all the gold, the list is short to Egypt or Peru. But don't ever forget, all the land on Earth was hooked together at one time in the distant past, and this was called Pangaea. I would imagine that meteor and asteroid hits, at least helped separate the continents.

You know it's funny, the asteroids or meteors when they hit the Earth, it shook the Earth so hard and ended most life on it. I mean you had to be a bird flying real high to escape the Monumental vibrations, and basically the terror of disaster of this magnitude. Life was ended as the Earth was knocked off its axis, ice ages began and lasted a million years, and then the next set of meteorites, or asteroids broke up the ice, and rivers were created. I would imagine the only survivors of these worldwide disasters, where those that went underground. Consult your internet, for the tunnel systems that have been dug throughout the world, and I don't mean channels for a cat or a dog to run through, I mean big boys. There are literally tens of thousands of miles of tunnels, that lead from the caves that catacomb the Himalaya Mountains and South America. It probably took them 10,000 years to dig a network like I'm talking about. Do not take my word for it please, look for yourself, and it will blow your mind, and it was all right there in front of you all this time. There is an old saying of the wise men, that you can't see the forest, because the trees are in the way. That makes a lot of sense when you think about it, we tend to not see the things right in front of us. The only thing I remember about the huge tunnel systems under the crust of the Earth, was when the gold hungry Europeans, swarmed the countries of South America. Much gold was taken, and the total was in the hundreds of Millions, but some did Escape. It was then that I heard that the Indians of South America took their biggest and prized pieces of gold, down into the tunnel systems.They say a few of these ancient tunnels lead to civilizations inside the Earth, however this I cannot say, because I haven't been down there. However after this book is published, and possibly a movie made, I personally will finance many expeditions with modern equipment, to many of the spots I talk about in my work.

When I say that Spain, came for the gold, I do mean The Mercenaries. The Hired Warriors of Europe came for the gold. At the fall of the Roman Empire many of the Viking tribes went all the way to Spain and took it, live stock and Barrel. It was good Viking blood and brawn, that once again boarded the ships they made it to America. The Vikings had spent 40 Generations collecting gold throughout the world, trading for it, or just taking it in battle. But these Generations saw everything that past Generations had worked hard for. The Spanish Fleet with all her Warriors and mercenaries, found more gold than sits in Fort Knox. The world had never seen such stores of gold, and probably never will again. Among the many ship loads of gold they came back from South America, there were many full size solid gold statues. Many solid gold statues were of their prized possessions the llamas. The llamas if fed properly,were as good as any donkey or horse, for packing the gold out. To give you a general idea of just how much gold these people had in Peru, the ancient peruvians had a garden around their palace, and it was man-made of course, and the soil was made of broken bits of gold. From this golden soil, big rube golden corn of real gold, even the leaves and the ears of the Corn,were solid gold of course. Many of the wise men and women in the world today, believe that the gold of the civilization in Peru, was greater than anything ever found in history. Make no mistake Peru was Atlantis, or at least one part of it. I've said before, and I'll say it again, Atlantis was a worldwide civilization. Thousands of years ago there was no major populations in most of the places, not like today. Atlantis had her colonies, and Peru and Egypt were her best. After Atlantis went down below the waters, it is a known fact the survivors, built the most ancient Egypt. I'm sure they did a lot of building in Peru. Not to insult anyone's intelligence, but who do you think built the Pyramid complex, right by the Andes Mountains close to Peru and Bolivia. The pyramids all over the world, of which there are literally hundreds that have been found, we're all built by the same builders, and quite possibly different laborers.

The gold of the Americas, especially South America, was more plentiful than anywhere on Earth, and who can blame the treasure Seekers who still look for it. The ancient historians know perfectly well, the ancient civilization of Egypt and the Americas are strongly linked together and they also know, all of it originated in the fabled land of Atlantis. Some Atlantis Authorities say that the civilizations of Egypt, Mexico, Babylon, and Asia Minor, were fully developed when they were transplanted to their modern sites. In Peru there is a great wall that the Great gold Seekers followed along the mountain tops the stretch for 45 miles. Every Temple in these 45 miles was looted of course.They were asked later on, who built all the temples, and who built the wall. The Indians say that by Legend, it was Auburn haired, white men, most interesting.

When Columbus arrived in the Gulf of Uraba in Panama, he wrote of a city called Atland. It is no mistake that if we add tiss to it, we have Atlantis. For thousands of years maybe 25 to 50 thousand years, men have kept the secrets of Atlantis quiet. At the same time they pointed the rest of the men, in many different directions. For the Golden Rule is, whoever has the gold makes the rules,and they wanted to make the rules.

To get back to another ancient mystery, I feel I must add background information to the Great Sphinx, that guards the pyramids. The Sphinx is not an Egyptian word, but belongs to the Greeks. To the Egyptians the figure of the Sphinx has no wings, the head of the Sphinx Represented a dual role of male and female reproductive powers, and also represented the duel powers of positive and negative. Of course we are more familiar with the great year or 26,000 years cycle of the zodiac.

The Greek civilization also had their own Sphinx, and their symbol was of a winged woman, combined with the demon. It was closely associated with death. Perhaps the Sphinx outside the Great Pyramid is a better indicator of the death that the great year cycle brings.Most of ancient Egypt is buried in the sands,and the sands have millions of seashells in it.

The Mayans also have their own sphinx, And it was said to be much smaller. The Sphinx of the Mayans, also represented the Dual powers of male and female. The Sphinx of the Mayans was cut as the symbol to the great white God Quetzalcoatl. To bind together the prehistoric civilizations on both sides of the Atlantic, we have only to look at the Cults of nature, and the phallic symbols found from Egypt to Greece, to the temples of India. The symbol of the prehistoric druids was the serpent and the symbol of Hu, The Druids creator of all things.

From the Romans to the eskimos of Alaska, the cult to fertility was worshipped, but imagine that, they say we are sex crazy today. The Cults of natures reproducing power was worshipped worldwide, with the cult of the Sun. According to Plato all the ancient legends, say the world has seen Destruction of the Earth 3 times. Plato tells us Atlantis was sunk or submerged By the Waters on 3 separate times. To the trained historian, this veiled language represents three separate locations. The northern Zone, the middle Zone, and the southern Zone. All three have shared in world disasters, and they will share again, for the only thing constant in the world is change.
Atlantis was a world empire with Tibet,Egypt,Peru,North pole region,and south pole at Antarctica.After the melting from the ice age,everything changed.All land bridges were sunk.The Atlantean culture remained.Elongated skulls were found at all sites,and they were probably the leaders.The Elongated skulls have been at all the right places throughout mans history.They are not human,but are the top of the food chain.They are the top dogs on planet earth.Inner earth is their domain,the Greeks called it Hades.Many of D N A tests have been run on them,on mummys,and red hair has been found on them,all over the world.Some are said to be human, some not,some half and half.
Some call these man gods.

IN PERU THE SKULLS ARE IN MUSEUMS>

CHAPTER 5 Part 1   THE TRIBES

As the once great unbeatable Empire of Rome fell, the Rush of even bolder and greater Germans, and assorted Viking tribes came.Every Viking always brought 3 weapons, of which I would think, the battle axe was the best. At least it was the most terrifying, and if it broke in battle, he quickly went to his huge sword. Of course the Viking also carried a large dagger.

The Bible likes to capture our imagination with the story of Moses leading his people to the promised land. It goes on to tell us that the Israelites wandered for 40 years, and tells us all about their struggles. But I for one do not care, for every race of people have their own struggles. I guess that Jews were looking for a new home, but what group of people didn't. With the ice age coming down on the world and floods, and major invasions of other people, many tribes went wandering just looking for a living space, to survive.

The wandering of the Germanic tribes that history calls The Barbarians covered thousands of miles, and some of the wandering took hundreds of years. The Scandinavians suffered Untold hardships, but some of them we're just looking for fertile ground, to grow their food for themselves, and for their livestock. The Goths, a gorgeous and warlike Scandinavian tribe, were mostly known to have come from Sweden, and the Goths will always be Sweden's greatest export. It would be the Goths who would sack Rome in 489. They say the Goths had been moving for a couple of hundred years already, enjoying themselves wherever they went, I suppose. The men would always do their trade in animal furs, weapons, and yes even drugs. They were World Travelers, and when there is a desire for something, the businessman will get it . Plus the so-called Barbarians, always had their Psychedelics, most often the Magic Mushrooms, that were used at all their occasions. And of course even in those days, there was plenty of Opium and Hashish to be had, and the Bold ones had it. The Vikings invented Whiskey and Beer,they were the ones to know.

The Visigoths definitely were related to the Goths, and started on a long journey themselves. The time that man calls the wanderings of the tribes, took place over hundreds of years. The Visigoths, or the so-called Southern Goths took place over 50 years. The northern Goths of course were from Sweden, and their Kinfolk, the Visigoths,were from the mountains of Russia. They traveled across the Balkans and Italy and finally settled in gorgeous lands, of what is today southern France, and southern Spain. Perfect areas for agriculture, and some of the finest wines are still grown there. After the fall of Rome, the empire was gone, and it was every man for himself. Along with the magnificent migration of the blonde haired Vikings came many tribes. The Vandals, the Burgundians, the Lombards, and the Ferocious Franks. All these great tribes from the north would become Nations in Viking Europe. To the readers of the great knowledge keep reading.

Not to be outdone the great Viking migration, that filled the vacuum of the Roman Empire, was not over yet, not by a long shot. The Viking tribes came in waves, one after the other for years and years and years. These were all of the tribes that assembled every 9 years at the Viking Temple of Uppsala which is located in Sweden. Every 9 years everyone had to come to show and honor the Viking gods Thor and Odin, Frigg and Frey. Much has been said about these great parties that the Vikings threw. Hundreds of thousands came every 9 years, and what an event they must have been. The truth has came down to us, but from only several sources. Now you will learn it all, disregard the other sources. First of all in the old days or ancient days, there were no lines in the ground to divide country from country, so when I say Sweden, or Norway, or Denmark, or Northern Germany, or Belgium, we're talking about the tribes. They intermingled,and intermarried for thousands of years. They had nothing in their head to tell them that one of the Viking lands was any different, than the other Viking lands. Basically it was 1 extremely large country. When it was time for the 9 year Festival to begin, tens of thousands or hundreds of thousands, started on their trek to Sweden. They said that When they got within 50 miles of the Great temple, they could see the shiny pure gold chain stretched out over the mountain top. I don't know how many pounds of gold were in it, but the Vikings had no problem taking gold from everybody, so this was not an issue. They said that massive gold chain that stretched out across the Mountaintop, when hit by the sun rays on a good day, would shine for

50 miles. Anyway it was breathtaking. On that night of celebration, the bloody rituals would take place.At the celebration there was a bloody sacrifice that happens, when 9 of all the living males are sacrificed. They were placed in an open coffin in front of the entire crowd, and their arms were extended out of it. The high priest cut their wrists thoroughly, and they did not try to get away. the Vikings believe in reincarnation, probably because all the psychedelics that they have done, they know there is much more, they have seen The Matrix.

Just to let you know a little bit more, the flowers of the high mountains , Magic mushrooms,has psilocybin as the active ingredient, and is as good as LSD. The blood cult from Stone Age days were all on psychedelics,and always knocking on heavens door.

I believe the blood from the 9 sacrifices was mixed, and many amongst the family drank it.
 The party went on Into the Night, a massive orgy took place, and this happened every night for 9 nights. The party was on, and this is how the Vikings lived, and it is said that they had a love for life.

It was said that after the sacrifices, the gods would favor the Vikings again. And it shows to what extent, the Vikings believed and loved their gods. The dead bodies were strung up in a Sacred Grove close to the Viking shrine. Not only men were sacrificed, the dogs and horses, to show how close they all were. At times in the Sacred Grove it was possible to see over 50 men,and dogs and horses hanging at one time. This was their cult of the blood, from the tribes of the northern lands. The cult of the Swedish tribes secured a blood brothership between the Warriors, and this was always good for battle. The Cult of the Sacred Grove are the words of the pages of Viking history. It was this resistance to the invading foreign religion of the Jews, which was Christianity. Jesus was a Jew and they held out Until the 18 hundreds. One can certainly understand why, too. Their gods made them Supreme, wherever they went. But soon after 1000 AD, and the centuries that followed, Sweden looked South to Germany, instead of to the Eastern lands. It was only after Sweden embraced the German Empire, that Christianity began to flow. Once the German Empire, which was called the Holy Roman Empire, Hamburg Germany became the center of worship for Christianity. The Holy Roman Empire was neither holy, nor was it Roman. Roman's not once sat on the throne of the Holy Roman Empire, although many Saxons did, and many other Viking tribes. It was not until Napoleon Marched through Europe, that the Holy Roman Empire of the German nation was dissolved. Even after the Swedish King Olaf became a Christian, the blood Cult of the Uppsala Temple still flourished. It was Hitler, who was a member of the blood Cult, and he brought the Pagan religion back as evidence that the power was still alive. The Jewish hold from the Bible, was not strong enough to capture everybody, no way, but it sure got a lot of them. Soon all the Pagan Nations became Christian, at least their monarchs did. Missionaries from Norway, Denmark, and even Russia descended on Sweden after the 18 hundreds, and many of the Vikings became Christian. However the famous Uppsala Temple stayed famous. All this really did was unite The Cult of the Temple to the pagan gods. Still the blood sacrifices went on despite the Christian cult, and their objections. There were many Christian missionaries killed by the Swedish tribes.They said they had nothing in common with the Jew from Bethlehem. The tribes in the North of Sweden we're still mountain Tribes, even in the 18 hundreds, because they did not believe in selling their gods down the river. After the 1800s the Vikings from Sweden, then learned to become moderates in all things except for their many wives, but then they were real men, and they needed all the extra flesh.

After the 13th century, the pagans were pretty weak in Sweden,and the Pagan images were torn down, and buried. A Christian Church was built on the exact spot, that the temple had stood. In fact all over Europe and Great Britain, Christian churches were built on top of ancient Pagan temples.Sweden could not stay pagan, and advance into the northern countries. It was politics as usual,and cash and power were the reason.

Sweden was a Powerhouse for tens of thousands of years. Most is still full of ice, and their ice is still retreating every year. Sweden played a major part, in keeping together all the tribes from the very bottom of Sweden, along the ocean and Norway too. The ice would freeze up in that part of the world every year, and you could really walk from Sweden, Norway, or Denmark, and then right back. It was the same with the animals. The herds and the wolves, for this is the way they all lived. Not enough can be said about the Warriors from Sweden because they were invincible, just like the Warriors from all the Nordic countries, they were absolutely the best. The emperor's from the Eastern Roman Empire, chose them as Viking bodyguards, and I mean probably 50 To 100. They were the best and the brightest, and all the world knew,and the world feared one to one combat with them.Combat with a viking ended your life.

Back to the wanderings of all the Viking tribes, and there were many, you go back to between the 4 hundreds and the five hundreds, and these were the times of action. In the year 489 is when the Goths sacked Rome. These were the days of Conquest and raw adventure. The waves of Viking tribes could not be stopped, and it would have done no good to even try. For the mass invasion of Europe, the Viking tribes were over 1 million. The Jutes came in full force, the Angles the same. The fearless and ferocious Saxons invaded , and they all tore out a piece of the empire for themselves. These were the days when Rome was dying, and these were the wolves. Every inch of Rome's Empire would be carved up, into-tribal kingdoms. This chapter in this book is intended to shine a bright light on these dark ages, and they are always confusing, but not this time.

From the Ashes of the once-great Roman Empire, a new and greater civilization would emerge, but this of course would take quite some time. For centuries men called them the Dark Ages, but new light from Modern Times will cast a different shadow. Rome disintegrated in the 5th Century, and the 11 Century would see a rebirth of Europe's New cities and Grand churches. But in the early Dark Ages, tremendous powers were turning the wheels of progress. Rome's Germanic conquerors could not read, this is true, and their civilization was one of raising their herds and warfare. The world would be shocked at the energy they added to the whole picture.

The Germanic Warriors of Scandinavia for sure had a fierce look with their fur garments and long hair, but they were no more barbaric, than the Romans themselves. As historians of the 19th century shed their light of learning on the so-called Dark Ages a new story emerged. As the 19th century historians studied all the records of the great Roman Estates, it was revealed that their fortunes, and even their profits were going downhill never to return. This was long before the barbarians, appeared on the scene. By the 4th century some of the greatest Farms now laid bare, and farming was no longer good. As historians look further into the records, they noted that in the 9th century under Barbarian Kings, the same land was extremely productive.

The so-called Germanic barbarians once again showed, they could use simple but reliable methods. Simple devices like the water mill, and good plows, they turned losses into gain. The Barbarians it would seem, had more imagination in many fields. History is reexamining them. They were to be sure, fierce, giving too unpredictable rages, but they were also were cunning, and very resourceful. The bloody tales of the barbarians, struck fear in the hearts of everyone, but any learned man or woman knows of the so-called bloody exploits of the Romans, and they were so Civilized, or so it was told.

It is admitted by all, that at first, the Germanic Warriors or crude tribesman, were totally in awe of the civilization they called Rome.Many of the ancient writers tell us of all the traits of The Barbarians. They also were kind and generous, and much closer to their wives,than the Romans. It was a difficult battle for the new Barbarian conquerors to form governments, but through it all they made it happen. For the first couple centuries The Barbarians could only hope to merge, with the thoughts, and the ways of Rome. This does take a long time for people to separate levels of attainment. It was the same process of merging together, between the two peoples, that brought Rome to her highest levels. The merging is what made Rome the greatest. The Romans when they conquered the Greeks,were very crude themselves, but after centuries they learned the civilized way. The crude early Romans benefited from this sophisticated people, and the same would happen to the Germanic Warriors.

Even today As I write, the world is trying as hard as it can, to merge with the Western powers and their technology. It was good for the dying Empire of Rome to be injected with the energy and the ingenuity of the Scandinavians. It was a long process for the Germanic peoples to think of themselves as a society, instead of living alone with their tribal identity.

One thing the German tribes would not do ever, was give up their rights as individuals, and it was their right of democracy. The Barbarians could not read when they crossed the Frozen Rhine River in Germany, but reading isn't everything. They had survived for many thousands of years in their tribes, passing down the knowledge from one generation to the next. It's amazing in a few centuries, the ones that could not read became fantastic writers and Painters. The Germanic writers would write about their struggles and create Epics for the world to enjoy. They would write for 100 years about their struggles, for even to find a good Homeland, and let us not forget, Scandinavia was mostly covered with ice, miles thick. The so-called Dark Ages, we're in fact the greatest seeding time for Europe, that they will ever know. It took 500 years, from the death of Rome in the 5th Century, for the seeds to germinate, and then explode, and grow into what will forever be called Europe, because of the Renaissance. The Renaissance Period is often misunderstood. In the Renaissance the Germanic Barbarian world recovered all that was good about the Roman Empire's ways, and also the great ones before them, the ancient Greeks.

In 6 centuries, or 600 years, the Germanic Invaders transformed a dying Europe. What they did with it, is turn it into a collection of independent states, spaced to the North Sea and the Atlantic. For 600 years as a matter of fact, the very nucleus of modern Europe.was transformed. They saw these Raw, belligerent kingdoms, breed into the first modern nation-states. Most important to the whole human race, was the first nation states, paved the road for personal freedom, and scientific progress. The Germanic and Teutonic Warriors would never negotiate their independence, and it is only because of them alone, that anyone on the face of the Earth, enjoys any freedom at all. Make no mistake it was them, that even give us our freedom today, and freedom might not appear to be that much, but wait until you lose it, and then you find out. In the 4th century the bishop of Carthage,said all the world has grown old, and lost its former vigor. Even winter no longer gives rain enough to swell the seed, Nor the Summer Sun is not enough to toast the Harvest. The mountains are gutted, and do not give the marble that they used to. The mines are all exhausted , and give less silver and gold. The fields lack the farmers, the seas lack sailors. There is no longer any justice, there is no confidence in trade, and no discipline in daily life. sounds like today.
It was still two nails that needed to be pounded into the coffin, and they would come in the form of two major decisions. In the year 330 emperor Constantine moved the capital city from Rome, to Constantinople in the east.The Emperor divided the Roman Empire into the eastern and western Empires.

Both of these moves were designed to improve things, but both moves only proved to be Nails in the coffin. The Roman Empire was so big, it defeated the purpose of State. The Western empire was populated by different people, who lived much different lives. They were completely different characters, as time went on the differences steadily grew larger. The Eastern Empire was by far the richest, for the lands of the Byzantine Empire had always been extremely wealthy in riches and in trade. Most of the world had to travel through there to do business. These wealthy provinces extended from Greece to Egypt, and these provinces had always led the world in riches. That's why it's the so-called Holy Land, and that's why there were so many crusades to those areas. The Golden Rule, he who has the gold makes the rules. And make no mistake, the area from Greece to Egypt had always led the world with riches. And that's exactly why it was so important. The trade routes of the world went through the so-called holy lands, but what really made them great and powerful,
 was the amount of cash and jewels and whatever else they needed. This was called the Orient from the men from Europe. The culture of the Eastern half of the empire was breached, and these had been Greek lands of Conquest, long before the Romans. Basically they would stay Greek, even in language and culture. The eastern half of the Roman Empire If one studied a map closely, this would be Southwest Asia. Along with being the richest half of the Roman Empire, the Eastern Empire was also the most populated. This is a fact and it had always been that way. The culture of the eastern half of the empire, was always Greek and would remain

Greek. The eastern half of the empire had always been a mix of people, a mix of cultures, and a mix of ways of doing things.

The East was also very Industrial, and this also led to its riches. Most Affairs of the East or business transactions, we're done in the language of the The Greeks. I suppose it's because they had all the money, for this is the way of the world. In the west part of the empire, it was much larger and went all the way to Modern Great Britain. Although the West Was much poorer than the east, time would take care of that also.

The West was very country, while the East was very Urban, with great cities. In fact the western part of the Roman Empire, was one enormous Colonial territory that fed the east. The Church of the Roman Empire was a strong Force that United the two halves, but of course even this would not last.

The Christian church would split between the two halves of the empire. The two halves had bitter arguments over the doctrine of the Christian Church every day about Jesus. Most of the greatest warriors from the north even fought to the death, before they would turn their backs on their gods, that had brought them Halfway Around the World, over 10,000 thousand years.Most great warriors were hunted down,to make way for the brainwashing.

The empire was just too big, and on every border massive enemy tribes fought to get their countries back from the Romans. This was the way the world was, and basically it's still that way. The Roman army fought constant Wars throughout the world, and on many occasions the Roman Legions we're fighting along every square inch of their 10,000 mile long Frontier. The new frontier went all the way from Hadrian's Wall to the Rhine River. Hadrian's Wall in England, went from coast to coast, and believe me they needed it. Hadrian's Wall was a massive Construction, and did go from coast to coast, east to west. It covered every square inch, to keep out the baddest boys with their long blonde hair, from taking over. Not too much is ever said about the blonde hair Beasts from Scotland. The Roman army once said that the Scots we're so ferocious, that they had to build Hadrian's Wall just to keep them out. That's quite a compliment coming from the Roman army, because they were pretty vicious themselves. But it is what it is, and the wall was built, and even stands today as a tourist attraction. The Roman general said because Scotland was so mountainous and hilly, and full of forests, they could not use their formations of soldiers effectively. Therefore any battles with the Scots would take Heavy casualties on both sides. It was always one for them one for us, and they refused to commit tens of thousands of troops to finish the job. Only because the tens of thousands of troops, would probably have never come back.The vicious Warriors to the north we're allowed to live in peace. The Roman generals had enough to worry about, as far as enemies, and they kept a standing army, fully equipped, of 500,000 men. In the end, this would prove to be not enough soldiers. All along the Rhine River in modern-day Germany was where the largest amount of Roman troops were. Along the Rhine, there was a heavy concentration of forts to hold back the Saxons, Vandals, and the rest of them. This was a very difficult job, to hold back the most ferocious Warriors In the history of the world. Not only did the Romans have a great equipped

Army, they also had many secret weapons that the other side didn't. One of course would be the catapults. The catapults we're actually the first artillery. The Romans would load catapult after catapult with Greek fire, which was basically a low-grade of napalm, and light them up. Many forests were burned, after thousands of shots from the catapults. One could even put large stones or huge boulders in the catapults, and it was said they could still throw the boulders at 60 miles an hour. With enough ammo, the Romans could bombard anything.

No where were the Roman troops stronger then along the Rhine River, and they had been there for 500 years. On the other side where the Germans, who were never beaten by anybody, and God help you if you made it to the Saxons, cuz there was no coming back. The Saxons of course would go on to be the Anglo-Saxons of Great Britain, and in fact every one of the German tribes, would go on to be great Nations. The Roman Legions had to fight constant brutal bloody wars, and if the veterans could last 20 years in combat, they were given land, in their empire to retire on. Much of the land that was given to the battle hardened Roman soldiers would be in the land we call Romania. Romania was to the east of Rome, and that's where Rome needed to settle it's best combat troops. Invaders of Rome usually came from the East, so this turned out to be a great plan. Never before in history Had Any Nation seen a collection of forts waiting for the enemy, as they did along the Rhine River. The frontier also followed the complete course that the Danube River ran all the way to the Black Sea. Many fortresses, and many Roman armies were stationed there. The frontier cut through all of Asia Minor and turned South to the Middle East, to Egypt. The frontier also continued across all of North Africa,for That was part of the Roman Empire too. This line went all the way down to the Atlantic Ocean. Rome was greedy, but when you can have it all, take it all, and that's just what they did. With all this great show of strength, it did not scare the Teutonic Warriors one bit. The painted ones or shall we say the Picts,in Britain assaulted the Frontier constantly. There were brief periods of no Warfare, but they did not last long. The painted ones, the Picts Wanted the Romans out of Britain, and these were men, and these were warriors, and realistically the fight had to go on. In North Africa all along the Roman Frontier or BorderLands, the Berbers harassed the Roman army constantly. The Berbers never ever let up either, for once again this was a huge group of warrior men, and they were not about ready to just walk away. The Arabs of the Middle East were always in combat with the Romans, and if they weren't, they were surely planning a major attack. This is the way of men, and always will be. Persians who already had five major Wars with Rome, were always ready for more, and their armies massed along their borders.

If that wasn't enough to worry the Roman Commanders, it was also the terrifying Huns. The Huns Roamed at will, north of the Danube River, all the way to the Caspian Sea. From time to time the Hun's would disappear, but usually that was just a ploy. The wise men knew they would be back to rape, pillage ,and plunder, for this was a way of life. These Warriors from the mountains of Asia struck fear in the heart of the Germanic Warriors In the fourth century. The Hun's would drive on a number of the Germanic tribes, up against the Roman Empire. An old proverb said, the home of a hun, was the back of his horse, and the pages of History tell us, this Is correct.

To stay on top of all the enemies of the state, the Roman Empire had to keep a standing army of half a million troops, with many in reserve. This was a staggering cost to Rome, and always will be to all free civilizations. That my friends, is the price of freedom, and freedom isn't free. In the year 330 the change would come, when emperor Constantine moved his capital from Rome to Constantinople. For all that should matter, this was a brilliant move forward. It placed the strength of the empire, between the Middle East and Europe. It was here that the crossroads of the world intersected, and it was here that the Empire would hold its military strength. Constantine knew from this vantage point, he could control the trade of the world, and that's just what he wanted to do. It also made it so, the strength of the Roman Empire, would be focused on its richest provinces, those of the East. Constantine gave his name gladly to this Majestic capital of Constantinople. At Constantinople the civilization would top all others in luxury and wealth, and this would stand for 1000 years.

In the seventh century Islam, would rise to topple the great Constantinople, but the armies of Islam would be slain one by one. When I say they were slain, I mean each soldier of Islam was cut into at least 200 pieces and fed to the dogs. If it had not been for Constantinople,Europe would have been torn to pieces by The Warriors of Islam. At Constantinople The Fortress was built better than anything on Earth, and the Fortress would hold back the armies of Islam until it's capture in 1453. For 1000 years Constantinople would dictate its policy to the world.

The Roman Legions of the empire, would definitely keep the armies of Islam in check. It would cost them in blood and Treasure of course. But this is the way of men, and this is the way it was. For over a thousand years Islam was kept in check, and her armies were slaughtered on the battlefields, wherever they reared their heads . It wasn't until 1453, that the armies of Islam broke through the defenses Of Constantinople. This time Europe would have a new Defender, because things do change. It would be the three Germany's of the Holy Roman Empire that would stop the armies of Islam. The skin was still White, and the hair was still blonde, and they were just as deadly. It was on the outskirts of Vienna that the massive invasion was stopped dead in its tracks. It was at this time in history,that Vienna Austria was a Powerhouse of Europe. Austria held down the empire, but not on her own. Thousands of armed-to-the-teeth knights rode down to help defend Austria. They came from all over Germany, and Scandinavia, and Poland sent many. This is where history was made, and this is where tens of thousands were killed and buried. Today in the Museum's of Austria,there is a collection of the knights armor they wore in these battles. It is the biggest collection of battle armor in the world. It was here at Vienna, Austria, that the Nordic blood boiled, and Islam was massacred.

The move to Constantinople only enriched the eastern Empire,it did not do much for the West. Another trick the rulers of the East used many times, was to buy off their attackers, with gold, silk, spices, and whatever else they desired. They also helped to save the capital of the East, but it soon sent the same armies In search of more gold to the West.

In the year 395 Theodotus had to divide the great Roman Empire between his two sons Honorius would rule the West, while Arcadius would rule from Constantinople in the east. This was the only option open, and the only move he could make. Each ruler of the east and west agreed to help each other, if they needed military assistance, but after the year 395, the pages of History tell us, the West was really on its own.

At first the citizens of the West felt secure, for the West had the largest military of the two powers, even if they were Barbarian soldiers. However it could not match the wealth of the East, only in raw military power could it hold its own. The West Had an ace up its sleeve, for they had already dealt with the Germanic Warriors for Generations, and when Rome's military tactics failed, their diplomats outright lied, and promised the world, to the naive Kings of the Scandinavian Warriors. Although Things had changed tremendously, the Roman leaders had the same view of the Germans. The German tribes have been crossing the Rhine Frontier for years, and the gap between the cultures was becoming smaller. Many things has drastically changed since the days of Julius Caesar. These were the days before Christ, when the extremely Furious Roman Legions first met the Germans. In the first century before Christ, the Romans met with the first Germanic tribes to come from the Homeland. With the Great Scandinavian tribes, there was no defense. The Romans fought with them for 500 years and each year things looked worse.

In Julius Caesar's book the gallic wars, he spoke of these tribesmen with no fear. He said they were a primitive race who lived off their herds. They also of course, did a little fishing to meet their needs. He saw them as no threat whatsoever, to the Invinceable power of the cult of Rome.

200 years later the story was quite different, when the Great Roman historian Tacitus,said the Germans were now living in villages, and they were also great farmers. He also wrote the German Society was organized for one reason, and that would be War. The Germanic Warriors, had a king, and also Chieftains, and also a tribal council of warriors. The historian noted several times that these tribal councils, would bang their Spears on their Shields, as a sign of approval. This is the way it was done, for thousands of years, and this was the Scandinavian way.The Roman historians also wrote tribal Chieftains Rose to power one way, by winning victories in war. The Riches of their Warfare was split up amongst the Warriors, for this was the Germanic way. the Roman historians also note that for every man in their society, Valor was the only ingredient. The Roman historians were great writers, and left us with a lot of background information about the Germans. It said the Germans and the Scandinavian Warriors had blue eyes as a rule, and reddish hair, and of course great bodies.

The Romans also pointed out, the great Germanic bodies were especially powerful for attack. As time moved on the German and Scandinavian Nation was growing at an alarming rate. By the 3rd century the Warriors that traveled south to modern-day Germany,were more equal in number to the Roman Legions. Now the swelling of the numbers of The Barbarians, was making all the leaders of Rome Shake in their boots. The writing was on the wall, and the Barbarians we're at the gates. Yes it is true, there were many fortresses built along the Rhine River, but the armies of the Scandinavians were without number. So by the 3rd century the Warriors that traveled South from all the Scandinavian lands outnumbered the Roman soldiers and their Legions. No longer were the Roman fortresses that lined the Rhine River, as menacing as they used to be. The Swarms of the Gothic Warriors were growing by the day, and any Roman Commander could see the end was near.

These huge Armies of the Scandinavian wild beasts we're making ready, for the vicious war that would come. There was Now a balance of Germanic strength all along the frontier on the Rhine, and then all along the frontier of the Danube River. By the 3rd century, the Romans had already giving up their dreams of expanding the Frontiers. Things change, and now the Romans were wondering how long they could even hold back the tribes from the north. The cold harsh conditions of Jute land ,Sweden, and Norway could only produce enough food for a few small tribes. The Overflow of the North eventually headed south to modern Germany, along the Rhine River. Of course with food and beautiful blondes of the North, the population would always grow, for the Vikings worship their women, and of course their bodies.

During the 4th century, along the Rhine, the population of the Nordic Warriors was swelling, and it was broken up into five major groups. Among these were the Ferocious Saxons, the Ferocious Franks, the Ferocious Vandals, and of course the greatest and biggest tribes of all, the Goths. You had the Ostrogoths, and the Visigoths, the northern and southern Goths. The 4th century, saw the bow break, and the floodgates opened, and it would never close.

With all of the tribes together, there was no possible way to hold them back, or deny them anything at all. They would write their own ticket, and everyone would have to cash it. The Furious tribes of Scandinavia we're now massing along the Rhine River, and the Danube River. They waited And waited because they respected the military might of Rome.

They also waited as long as they did because they wanted to be assured of a quick bloody victory. The Teutonic tribes are what the Scandinavian tribes are called, and they were so great, they named Tuesday after them. The Teutons we're totally invincible in the days before the gun.

The Visigoths had the greatest strength of all for the Scandinavian tribes, and Rome would find them uncontrollable. The Visigoths swarmed through the Balkans raping, and pillaging as they just love to do. All the tribes that came in contact with Roman civilization benefited from it, and the two peoples, would merge together slowly.

The 4th century was a great and powerful century, and it would dictate the future to all. In the 4th century A barbarian named Ulfilas would play an important part in The Taming of the heathens from the north. Although he was himself a barbarian, he was born in the great capital city of Constantinople, and was well-versed in the ways of the Romans. Once he gained the culture of the Romans, he soon traveled among the northern tribes, who settled north of the Danube. It was this great man of vision that gave the heathens their own Bible. It was translated into their own language, This translation would be known to history as the Gothic Bible. It is admitted that our Warrior left out certain passages in the Old Testament, but he did this for certain reasons. He felt that certain passages in the Old Testament,that would encourage the barbarians in their warlike ways, and his goal was to pacify them. The Visigoths

Received his message of Christianity, and so did the Vandals, and the Ostrogoths. Our Barbarian translator was also a bishop of Constantinople, and the form of Christianity he preached was unacceptable to the Catholic Church. The religion taught by our Barbarian minimized the Divinity of Christ, and it's that he was a man not a god. This form of religion was called Arianism, and would prove to be a major bone of contention between the two peoples. In fact the Church of Rome, would call that Arians heretic's or non-believers. This also made them enemies of the Roman Catholics. Even the German tribes, that became totally civilized,were still enemies of the church.

The Germans however Were an enormous Market for the Romans to exploit, and religion was placed on the back burner, for the good of all the money that would be made by the merchants. This is the way of men, and this is the way it was. The Romans sent many items North for sale, and among them was there wine, jewelry, and farming tools. The Germans were heavy beer drinkers, but they also learned to love the juice of the Grape. In fact students of History it was the Germans then invented beer.

The most saleable item the Nordic Warrior had, were the slaves they took as they pillaged Eastern Europe. These were mostly the Slavic tribes, the word slave came from them, the slavs. The trade in their human product was there greatest marketable item. Originally the word slav meant glorious, but the Germans changed all this, as they always changed everything they came into contact with. Many of the slaves the Germans brought to the Empire, ended up in the arena as gladiators, and many ended up in the fields and Farms, or as domestic servants.

All through the history of the Roman Empire, the top export of the Germans was in truth their Warriors or their Mercenaries, and they would rent them to the highest bidders. After all Longinus the spear man, who stuck the spear into Jesus Christ when he was on the cross, he was a German. From the death of Jesus, the percentage of Germans in the army, kept Mounting, until by the 4th century the legions were mostly Germanic Warriors fighting for the gold. No longer would the Roman army be Roman, even the Commanders were barbarians. For hundreds of years it had been built into this,the Celtics and other tribes had been the backbone of Rome since day one. In the 4th century the whole character of the Roman Army was German, down to the very clothes they wore. When the legions went into battle they wore the hide breeches and the cloaks, The Barbarians always had. The 4th century would see many changes, even the war cry of the Roman Legions, as they went into battle. Now it would be known as the Germanic war cry. Even the battle formations had changed, enter the wedge formation that the northern Warriors made famous.

The Romans of the government were not very happy at what was happening, but there was little they could do about it. You see it took the ferocious Germanic Warriors to hold back their fellow tribes, this would be their only chance.

The German greatness in battle was unbelievable, and there was no match for them. The men from the far north were taller and much stronger, then any of the men from the southern realms. Many of the huge Germanic Warriors married into the wealthy families of the Romans. Their beautiful Northern women were much sought-after by the wealthy Roman families. The ways of the Germans were becoming the ways of Rome, and the blood of the Germans, was fast becoming the blood of the empire.

Even though the armies of the empire were Germanic, it could no longer even pretend to hold back the men of Thor and Odin after the 4th century. The Furious Nordic Warriors would not be contained any longer, and the writing was on the wall for all to see.

The skilled Roman diplomats drew up plans where certain tribes would be allowed to enter the territory. Certain tribes would be allowed to resettle and live their lives within the empire. All they would ask, is that they would help defend their new land against Invaders. This way the newly resettled tribes fought for Rome, and their new land, that they so desperately needed to feed their families. In return the tribes had to swear their loyalty, and guard their stretch of the Border. Of all the tribes that were admitted for the defense of the Roman Empire, the Franks would gain the most.The Franks would later in history be known as the French, and the Germans,and in 358 the Franks would settle gaul, in modern Belgium today. The Franks above all the other allies, honored their military obligations, but they needed the help of the empire to do so against the Warriors from the north. The Teutonic Viking tribes from the extreme North were totally invincible, and this is the way it was. Before the days of the rifle and the gun, you really had no chance against the blonde-haired beasts. Make no mistake the Franks were extremely vicious themselves. The Franks were famous for throwing hand axes in battle. The Franks one day would form an Empire that would last a thousand years. But thanks to the influence of the Romans, they learned well the Arts of civilization. France led the world for hundreds of years on culture and basically everything. Paris is still one of the greatest cities in the world, and loved by many. At this time in history the 4th century, the strongest of all the Viking tribes were the Visigoths. It is written that the Romans treated the The Goths so wrong, they lost the chance of gaining the strongest Ally they could have, in their desperate situation in the 4th century. The politics of the whole situation were wrong, but then man is a beast, often given to error, and this error cost them the empire.

The hungry hordes had been crossing the frontier for centuries, in search of food and goods, but in the end they had always gone back North to their home land. In 376 the Visigoths appeared on the borders of the empire. They were massing along the Danube River in full force, and this time they would not go home.

Also the Furious Huns we're on the Rampage again, and history tells us, there was no defense against them. Rome once again would have to commit all her armies to just Defend the Eastern borders, from those blonde haired blue-eyed Warriors. The Chieftains of the Visigoths met with the Roman Commanders, and demanded entrance to the Empire. The deal was they would be allies to Rome against all other Warriors. the Roman armies we're hanging by a thread, and of course the answer was yes.

History Would play a dirty hand to the Visigoths, and this dirty deal would eventually cause the Romans everything they had. It's too bad, the Visigoths had the largest army of all the Viking tribes, and this was a grave mistake. But men are men, and they are doomed to make bad decisions. The frontier Commanders would be the ones to turn the Visigoths against Rome. The shipments of Grain that the huge force of Visigoths needed to stay alive were bad, if they came at all. Starvation was what the families of the Visigoths got in their deal. The commanders of the Frontiers charged such high prices for their unhealthy grain, the warriors were forced to sell their women and children into slavery, just to stay alive. Better to eat and live to fight another day, that is the motto of the winners. Of course their weapons had already been taken from them, or else the story would have been much different.

2 years later the Visigoths would have their revenge on the Romans, and it was sweet and very bloody. In the year 378 the Roman army was destroyed with only a few survivors, and that was the pay back. Rome's treachery had cost them dearly. The Visigoths continued to pillage and plunder the Balkans at will. After just destroying that Roman army, it was back to what they do best, and that was take what they wanted.

After totally pillaging the Balkans, the Visigoths Army was even bigger. They allowed many to live and serve them. Because of all the Looting they had plenty to trade or sell. Rome being the master chess players that they were, gave many of the numerous Barbarian tribes, land in what is today Greece or the Balkans. Then fate Dealt the Visigoths Another blow, in the form of dividing the Empire in half. The Visigoths were exactly midway between the two empires, and therefore caught in the vacuum of both, sometimes being courted and sometimes being attacked.

As new tribes moved into the empire, the earlier tribes were pushed far away from the frontier, and of course this led to constant battle and warfare to survive. Each vicious tribe went Nightly on raids,to rape, pillage, and plunder each other. it's not that they were barbarians, it was survival.

The tribes were all looking for a better way of life, and all of the tribes needed protection from the Huns. It was said throughout many countries The Hun's could not be stopped. The Huns took all their enemies by storm, which is to say they always outnumbered everyone. They always had numbers on their sides.They always swarmed their enemies, and encircled them at the same time. They were excellent Horsemen , and all would pay the price. It was very difficult to deal with the tactics of the Huns. The Huns were no fools, and they too wanted greener grazing lands, more beautiful women, and they would have their part in the wealth of the dying Empire of Rome.

Rome's wealth came in many ways, but mostly from her conquering armies, to the winner went the spoils, and the Romans always took everything. The Conquering armies of Rome for hundreds of years, took the wealth of the known world. This was not a Roman idea, but the way of man, all men. The Fearless Ostrogoths took on the Huns in battle, and because of this they had lost tens of thousands of their own people.

To add insult to injury, or salt to the wounds, there were also major epidemics and droughts at the same time. The tribal populations however continued to multiply, and the Germans would not be denied their share of the riches of the empire. Rome was in her last throes of death, and the lions, and the jackals, were going to Feast upon her, for this is the way of men.

In the Living Spaces for the Viking tribes that came from the north, it was just not enough land to feed even half of them. So invasion was the only choice they really had, and they were men, and they took it. It was survival of the fittest, and the rest had to die. All the Nordic tribes were sure of one thing, the Empire had rich land already under cultivation, and it was going to be theirs.

As the Nordic Warriors multiplied, they naturally begin very aggressive. It was this fact that drove the West into the ground. It strikes everybody with knowledge as funny that our Northern Warriors we're called barbarians or Savages, but they were in fact the glue that held the empire together. The Gladiators at the arena and all the other public spectacles, showed just how Barbaric the Romans really were. When it came to barbarians, it was the kettle calling the other one black, and that this is the way of men too. The Romans were very barbaric, however it was a very cruel world, and the cruelest rose to the top. These were the years the Roman Empire was unraveling, all things Roman were suddenly becoming undone, and the death rattle for Rome was shaking. Even the Roman economy was unraveling like an old rug. The production of the great Roman Estates was at its lowest point since the beginning of Rome, and trade was draining the Western Empire of all its gold. The gold reserves Were almost empty. In the 4th century the Western treasury was empty, broke, and trade had gone back to the barter system. Some districts salaries and taxes were paid by the barter system. Money was scarce, and most times was just not there. The farmers were the worst off, and could not even pay their taxes, which led to selling their own land, and working himself, to the large land owner he had sold out to. This was a loss of a way of life, and also a loss of personal Liberty. The price of not paying your taxes, was hard punishment, and that made many of the farmers leave their land and take off with the roving bands of Thieves.

Even the tax collectors themselves were put into a horrible bind, that left them no way out. In Roman law, the tax collector paid out of his own pocket, for every head he collected from. To make matters worse, they could not quit their jobs, for their work was inherited. The tax collectors became known as more terrible than the enemy. The tax collectors made it so rough on the citizens, many ran away to live under the rule of Barbarian kings. As history does repeat , the words of ancient Rome rang true as they do now. Those who live at the expense of the public funds, are more, than those that provide them.

The government that made Rome the great power she was, was now the source of her problems, with greed and Corruption, leading the way.

As the 5th Century came to the Western Empire, perhaps the greatest Barbarian General came to power. Stilicho led the armies of Rome against all other barbarians. It was his time, and he was going to take it. The Roman citizens had lost their will to fight, and left barbarians to hold off other barbarians. For 10 years this great leader, held off The Barbarians, and he saved the empire, By His Brilliant strategy in Warfare. This great General was a Vandal, and they were ferocious too.

But fate would have the final word, and the Vandals luck would run out. the Visigoths never forgot the way the Romans had treated them, and waited to drive a final nail into the coffin of Rome.

At last the Visigoths did come, because they were just tired all together, with pillaging and plundering the Balkans or Greece. The Spoils of War in Greece had become tired, and now the Visigoths would be on the move. the Visigoths were thirsting for the blood of Rome.

It was at this time in history that Rome made its last stand, but it did no good. The land called Italy from now on would belong to the Visigoths. The people who had come to Rome for protection, and land, now came as conquerors, to pay back Rome for the loss of their families and their pride. You know it's funny, the mightiest Army on Earth the Viking Visigoths, came to the Empire for land, and willing to protect Rome, and Rome ripped them off. The moral to this story is, be very careful of all the decisions you make, because some of them might just come back, and bite you in the ass. The Barbarians had always fought Rome's Wars for them, this had been going on for hundreds of years, and Rome played One Tribe against the other. But believe me, those with Viking Blood went to the front lines to fight, the most Furious Warriors in the world.They kept the line for all the Viking tribes wishing only for land to feed their families, so let's not pretend Rome held off the world with her Roman soldiers. Remember serpents and Dragons, when Jesus laid dying on the cross, and Mary Matalin was collecting blood in what would be the Holy Grail, it was a German that thrust the spear into the side of Christ.A Wise man once said every square inch of Europe, has at least one gallon of blood spilled on it. Now you know the truth, and you also know what it really was.The huge Viking Nation the Goths would of course take the best land to grow crops in Italy, but they would also take whatever else they wanted. The Visigoths were Champions of the world, Not just champions from where they came. They knew no such thing as losses in combat, only small setbacks. Rome thought they were invincible because they had Viking blood flowing through the veins of most of their soldiers. Cream does Rise to the top, and Rome's days were numbered. The Goths would go all the way through Europe until they hit the Atlantic Ocean. Later in History the Goths would be even better known for their architecture. All of the beautiful cathedrals and churches in Europe that came to a point, that was considered a new style, and that was Gothic.

In fact the Gothic Nation was so huge, that when they swarmed all of Rome's defenses, it was an easy victory. Many of Rome's soldiers who were actually German, said hell no we won't fight against the Goths, or the Vandals, and in fact many switched over to the other side during The Invasion of Rome. One thing Is certain, never again would man consider Europe the Roman Empire, and I mean never. It would be hushed up quite a great deal in American history, but what you're looking at was the German Empire, taking over. Like I said the Goths would go all the way to the Atlantic Ocean, which would be Spain, and then they would bring the Viking ships and say what's next. The Roman Empire had never seen such desire and ability to take the world, but believe me grasshoppers, they would do it.

I think I've said it before That when Christopher Columbus 1000 years later sailed for America, or the gold. In that area, he had Maps. Many maps of all the lands he would find, even Atlantis. History has a way of telling you ,what they want you do know, and the rest you have to find out for yourself. But that is what this book is for, and I hope the dragons and the Serpent's that read this, will take this to another level.

The dragons and the Serpent's, had been the insignia for wisdom and knowledge for many thousands of years. That's why in the Catholic Church, the serpent was considered the devil or evil itself. In this way, all the European nations that went in Discovery of the world, would smash all things with serpents and dragons on them. Whole libraries would be burned, by men that didn't have the faintest idea of what they were burning, they just wanted to go to the Eternal heaven. In this way the Catholic Church kept total control over men's Minds and future generations too. But of course what the Catholic Church really wanted was all the gold, and believe me they got their share. Religious zeal and fury is real, and All Nations know the power. The Catholic Church with a thousand ships, invaded the gold nations of the world and took it,in combat.

You know it's funny, tribe after tribe crossed the Rhine River in Germany. As soon as word got out, there are no longer any Defenders along the Rhine River, they all came. It is estimated that up to a million barbarians and Vikings crushed the Roman Empire, but they did take it for their own. The new blood and the new Fury would help create the greatest civilization in the world. It would be this new European Civilization that would be looked at with envy. As far away as Great Britain The Outposts of Rome would be stripped of soldiers, all coming back for the defense of Rome. By the time that they made it back, Rome was actually Viking owned. It was too little too late, and on New Year's Eve in the year 406 the rest of the Germanic tribes swarmed across the Rhine River. Fate would have it that the Vandals led the assault. The Roman Empire in the West Was now Barbarian Europe.

The invasions of Roman territory kept up for 150 years. Let's don't forget they had no trucks, cars, and airplanes, and many just walked. The Germanic invasions kept up, one after the other for 150 years, for all wanted in the luxuries of the empire, and the good ground to grow their food. Many of the invading Germanic tribes had brief moments of Glory, only to be wiped out by the next wave of Invaders.The Tribal wars, we're very brutal, and very bloody, and nobody took prisoners. The Viking Wars, tribe against tribe were to Brutal to record, and history does Passover this time Quickly. Some say it was just too nightmarish, blood and guts, and who knows what else.

These were the days of Great Adventure for all the Nordic Warriors, and they were very violent and bloody, and they were Scandinavia's best. Some historians refer to this time, as the great Viking heroic age. The tribes from the north, would settle down in the new lands that they took for their own. It was at this time, that the cultures mingled. In the old Western Empire Romans were everywhere, especially in Gaul. The majority of the Gauls were not Roman but instead we're romanized citizens. Gaul would one Day become the nation's of France, Belgium, and Germany. As Time marched on, the Franks from Frankfurt Germany area, would take all of France and part of Belgium too. The Franks were extremely warlike, and no invading Army, ever went through their Nation. As the Germanic tribes mingled with the roman populations, a new Society began to take shape. All of Western Europe was now ruled by Germanic Kings, germanic blood ruled from the North Sea to the Atlantic Ocean. The greatest of the Germanic Warriors, took the largest Farms in the Western Empire, and instantly became wealthy landowners, their day had come.

The great social order that Rome had started, remained the same except for the positions of power. The Germanic Kings kept the peasants, and the slaves, just like the Romans did before them.

The Viking warriors had the greatest respect, for all things Roman. They wanted to share in the riches of Rome, and they would, of course. The roads, the buildings, the fountains, the churches, all things Roman where the greatest in man's achievements. The Viking warriors from all the Teutonic tribes, sat in awe of what was theirs now.

The Germanic Kings let the Roman officials function, as they had always done, except now it was for a different master. A great writer once said, to the Victor go the spoils, and that's exactly how it was.

The pages of History tell us the average Germanic King thought of himself as rightful heir to the throne, and the invincible Empire of Rome. It would of course now be carved up, into literally hundreds of Kingdoms. It must have been a hardship, for the newly crowned Kings, when they found themselves as powerful leaders. A bigger population than they had ever dreamed about. Someday their countries would literally have millions of subjects, but it was up to them to figure out how to survive. Make no mistake, boundaries for kingdoms and Nations are not set in stone. New so-called boundaries or borders would literally change thousands of times, and always they would be sealed in rivers of blood. Great things do not come easy. By the 6th century, or the years 500 on, the old Empire of the West, was trying to take shape. The ruthless violence of hundreds of Viking tribes would have to play out, for this is the way of men. The Ostrogoths kingdom included all of Italy and Greece, or the Balkans. While the Visigoths fought their way, with rivers of blood all the way to Spain. It was in Spain that the Visigoths would stake their claim, and they would never be ran out. This is the day before guns, and cannons , and jet airplanes, these were the days of Mortal combat, and the Viking Nations would not fall to anyone. In the north of Spain another Viking tribe the Sueves would take the north part of Spain for their own, and I'm sure the Visigoths, realized they would need allies at some time in the future. The Furious Burgundian Kingdom was between Italy and France, some of the greatest growing soil in the world. Of course you could grow anything, future Generations would love it.

The Anglo-Saxon By the 6th century, had taken all the land from the Rhine River in Germany, all the way to Jute Land, and by this time, had also invaded England. The Saxons are from Saxony Germany, although we think of them as the British, if we are not educated enough. This is the purpose of my work. I am in the 4th quarter of my life, and there are many things I want to pass on To those behind me. I wish to make it much easier for only those that seek the truth, in a world of Lies, propaganda, and fabricated stories. The truth is Stranger than any lie, especially when you talk about the top secret knowledge, but it is very inspiring, and very addicting. Knowledge is power, and I wish to leave behind as much as possible for the real serpents and Dragons, those seeking the ultimate truths.

Getting back to the Vikings from the north of Germany the Anglo-Saxons, there is of course a lot of information misdirected on them too. The Angles were a very fierce tribe and they ended up owning a bigger part of England than even the Saxons.The Angles is the correct name, not Anglos, just another goddamn lie, of thousands to misdirect and Confuse. At one time thousands of years ago, many thousands of years ago, the wise man of the Saxons directed The Angles and the Saxons to cut down the biggest trees, to hollow them out, and to make paddles to row with. It was only then that the dream of crossing the English Channel became reality. But make no mistake when they landed in England, they were met on the beaches, and sometimes Met even in the water up to their knees, with weapons. The Celtics the Picts, and probably hundreds of other tribes, met every invader on the beaches. The Saxons knew they had to attack with lightning raids, steal whatever they could, and kill many and just wait to come back and do it again. These attacks on Great Britain were extremely bloody, and extremely ruthless, but this is the way of men.

The kingdom of the Franks went from the mountains of Spain, all the way to the Rhine River in Germany. The Franks were always an enormous Army, they never gave ground.The Franks were all the tribes from the Frankfort Germany area,they were wise to come together.

The Vandals with their Navy, had taken the grain producing areas of North Africa, that the Romans had squeezed for food and wealth. The Vandals also took Sicily,Sardinia, and Corsica into their Kingdom. The Bavarians from Germany had already staked their claim to the same area it is today, they loved it and took it. The Lombards were to the east of Bavaria, and the Alemans to their West. This was the early 6th century, or the years 500 to 600.

The Franks and the Saxons were serious Northern tribes who held Their Kingdoms in the North. These two powerhouses were slow to develop, but Their Kingdoms would last longer than all the rest.

The Franks, Saxons, Goths, Vandals, and Burgundians, all came from the same common Germanic Homeland. It's called Scandinavia, land of the nature's Best. You know it's funny, although all these Furious enormous tribes from Scandinavia, all carved out their own Empires within the old Western Roman Empire, they all traveled different routes to forge their new kingdoms. The Franks who had founded France, had the advantage of having close contact with the Roman culture ever since the year 300. This was the same time the Franks had settled into Belgium from Scandinavia. Belgium was close enough to Roman Gaul, for the Franks to be influenced by all things Roman and also to strike, because they were close enough. In the 5th Century,. the Franks expanded into Gaul, and kept it for their own. The Franks were wise and took very small pieces of the empire, until the time was right to take huge chunks. In the sixth century they wrote a preamble to their tribal laws and it is as follows.

The Glorious people, wise in Council, Noble in body, radiant in health, excelling in Beauty, daring, quick, and hardened, this is the people that shook the cruel handcuffs from the Romans off their necks. The yoke had been broken, and would never be put back on.

It took this kind of pride to make the best, the best they could be. The Franks who named their Realm France would take the lead, and they were to become the most important Germanic Realm. The Angles and the Saxons, and the Jutes, well this is a whole different story. Odin and Thor were the only gods, terrifying Warriors ever new, and this is all they would know for a long long time. The Angles the Saxons,and the Jutes we're all Kin, or basically they were all family, cousins and all that. They always shared in their Conquest and Britain would be in their sights. The Angles, Saxons, and Jutes, were Savage Warriors, who for thousands of years, had always taken what they wanted, and they did not go to church on Sunday and beg for forgiveness.This is the way of men. The Savage Warriors had never been exposed to Roman laws or any other laws, except tribal laws. The Angles, and Saxons, and Jutes, planned for centuries how they would dominate The Island called England, across the English Channel. They knew in their hearts the island would be just what they needed, and what they dreamed about, and an isolated Little Empire. They would have to divide it several ways, but then they always did, they were blood kin. You know it's funny in the land of the Britons, Roman culture had never really Penetrated. It was the fifth century that Rome's survival called for the evacuation of all Roman troops back to Rome. The Roman forts in Great Britain were stripped of their Warriors but the end was in sight for Rome. In the 5th Century the residents of the magical Island of England, quickly went right back to their Celtic language and their Celtic tribal ways. Of course they did, for these had served them well for thousands of years. They only pretended to be romanized. The Angles, Saxons, and jutes, many historians say, where the most terrifying of all the Scandinavian tribes. But like I said earlier The Angles, Saxons, and Jutes, would never take the Celtics land easily.

The Celtics were extremely vicious themselves, and their warriors were very Valiant, and looked upon as great Heroes, and they were. There are a few records of the actual invasions and many Maps with many X's on them for places of invasion. The Legends and the sagas that come down to us speaking of the actual invasions, tell an incredible story of the savagery and the bloodletting, and the Cutting off of the arms, legs, and heads, with their swords. Their battle sites looked like a horror movie. Once the full-scale invasion started they would not stop, with each new hundred ships of battle-hardened veterans, their Kingdom would grow.This was a large-scale battle for the right to live, and to care for your families. This was survival of the tribes. The small lands of Scandinavia could no longer hold the tribes or feed them, so invasion was the order of the day,and invasion it was.

The Britons of course held their own. Fresh reinforcements kept arriving from Scandinavia for the next 100 years. The more they killed, double that amount would come, and it was time for some political thinking. The Britons had to give ground eventually and they knew it. Many of the

British tribes saw the writing on the wall, and migrated in masses across the English Channel into what is now the Brittany peninsula. Those Britons that remained were forced into wales, And Cornwall. These were the dark days for the Britons, and from these dark days came a truly great warrior named Arthur. Arthur would rally his Knights in Southwestern England. Arthur and his Knights of the Round Table could not hope to win forever, they started making plans. In the year 577 King Arthur and his Knights of the Round Table could hold them back no longer, and they suffered a tremendous loss in the battle of Durham.

It is here that the Angles,Saxons, and Jutes decided to cut out there Kingdoms. Instead of making one huge Kingdom, many smaller kingdoms emerged. I suppose each of the truly great warriors wanted his own kingdom, and I suppose that's just the way it should be. There were many shot callers, and each one deserved his own domain. The names of some of these kingdoms are still with us today. Only now they are used as the names of regions. The best known of these would be West Sax, which was known as the land of the West Saxons. The Mighty Kingdom of the Jutes was Kent. Most of the land was conquered by the Angles. All the land began to be known as Angle land or England. it was the Angles they gave their name to this great island of England.

It was England the Germanic Warriors forced their language on, more than anywhere else in the old Roman Empire, it was England or Angleland.The Roman Church, was almost entirely wiped from the memories of the local population. The Angles, Saxons, and Jutes were certainly not loved by the local population, but this did not matter to them. For it was they who were the Masters of the Battlefield. Of course they always received the respect no matter what. As we shall see later, the great mixture of Viking Blood, would not stop here, for the Gods were not done creating the Englishmen.The Viking attacks on England started as small raids,for centuries I must add.They turned into full scale invasions.The English fought like lions,however fate was not on their side. No land on earth could stop the Viking tribes,and all would fall.The tribes of Scandinavia would of course in the 9th century fight along with the Great Danes,and together they would smash all opposing forces.Together they would be called the Vikings.As the Vikings ships went from small paddle boats that raided up all the rivers,to large Dragonships with huge sails,the game changed quickly.Now everyone would fear the wrath of the Vikings.Even Paris and London would be robbed more time than you could count.However they were great warriors,and they always gave the cities the option to buy them off,or fight.Paris and London chose to pay many times.

The lessons of History are hard and brutal, but if we forget to learn from them, we are doomed to repeat them. The fall of the Roman Empire, and the beginning of the German domination of all of Europe, was just beginning, and it is a very difficult time to digest. So, we will take Great Lengths to observe the lessons of History, that would plant the seed for all future Generations. These were the days of action, and these were the days of Adventure. Let us not forget as we become historians of all the Viking tribes, the greatest and most powerful of all Scandinavian tribes Were the Goths. The Goths of course were powerful enough to change the course of history, and they did. The Goths originally started in Sweden, and the Goths roamed and wandered, and lived for centuries and probably thousands of years this way. These were the centuries that most tribes were wandering,for at this time in man's development, this was considered normal. The story of the Goths is confusing like so many things are from that era, but once you sort it all out, everything can be fully appreciated.

The sheer numbers of the Visigoths always made them a great Factor to the empires of the east and west. Some historians say the Goths had 100,000 Warriors some say 200,000 Warriors. As their long list of victories Grew, they might have had half a million. Whatever the final tally, they were a huge Force to reckon with. They could not be ignored, and they could not be dismissed. All the major decisions in the Empire, for centuries always had to consider the power of the Visigoths. They were the strongest allies, that Rome ever had, or ever would have. These were the soldiers that backed the Roman Empire. No matter how Bloody the combat was, the Goths never ever ran. The Emperors of Rome used the Visigoths Nation as a huge chess piece in the game that Rome played. Rome always bit off more than she could chew, but with the Scandinavian Warriors behind you, I guess you could do anything.

But getting back to the original thought, The Visigoths were the greatest allies that Rome ever had. Rome knew it would always be this way, and they played their hand accordingly. The Visigoths being Rome's greatest allies, were given plenty of land to grow their crops for their huge tribe. Throughout the Roman Empire word went out, of Rome strong allies. The Visigoths could have their cake and eat it too.

Because of their enormous numbers, and their fantastic strength, the Visigoths had to be watched constantly. True, they were Rome's trusted allies, but when wealth is at stake everyone must be watched. Many said the Goths were becoming more Roman everyday, but those that knew men well, knew they probably hadn't changed a bit. The Goths were probably the same barbarians they were when they crossed the frontier centuries before. In the end it was this group, that did more to tear the strength of the Empire down, and grind it down, than any other Force.They marched to their own drummer,this is true,they were nobodies patsys.

The Goths had fun, side by side, back to back, with the Roman armies for centuries, and they prove their loyalty with blood.

The Greatest Warrior the Goths ever had was Alaric the Bold, and he is given credit for sacking Rome. They say Alaric was more than just bold, he was a champion, amongst champions. They say Alaric in battle was probably the greatest Warrior the world would ever see.

It was King Alaric that marched from the Balkans seeking food and land for his people. The Goths lined up and fought with the Roman army many times on their hungry March. This was the greatest invasion that Rome they would ever see, and they were terrified. This is where the Romans sent a barbarian General named Stilicho to command their troops.

This Barbarian General was actually born a Vandal, another great Scandinavian tribe. The armies of the world, say there was no better General than the Vandal. He rose to the ranks, and knew no better. He was baptized in blood, as all good commanders are. At every Clash between the generals, the Roman West was Victorious. But make no mistake the Visigoths killed many.History has it that the greatest warriors Scandinavia ever produced, begged the Roman Emperor for land, for his starving people. All he wanted was for his vast population, was to settle in North Italy. In exchange he gave his word and his honor, that his huge Army would forever be loyal to Rome. He was well aware of the fact that the Roman Empire, was constantly being attacked. He told the Roman Emperor our two peoples can merge together as one, and make both people stronger.

This was a year 408, and this year will be remembered by historians till the end of time. It was in 408 the Empire would explode, never to be the same. The emperor of the Roman Empire of the West had his number one General Stilicho executed. He was the best battle-hardened Commander the Roman Empire had, and he was born a vandal. The emperor said he had his Barbarian General executed, because he believed the Vandal General was plotting to kill the emperor. The emperor knew he was about to be assassinated, and he struck first.

It must be noted here, if it makes any difference at all,that the Barbarian General always Took the side of the barbarians, when arguing for more from the emperor. The Romans were barbarians themselves in the way they treated anyone, and in the end they would learn the hard way. The Barbarian vandal Commander did come up the hard way, but his heart and sympathies were always with his own people.

True he made it to the top, but he's still realized that the Barbarian families needed much more. With the exploding populations of the Germanic tribes, most were still starving to death. All they really wanted was good soil to grow the food for themselves, and their herds of animals. The only bargaining tool, they had, was the Barbarian vandal.

But now that he was dead. The blood of the Teutonic tribes began to boil again. Plus with the best General of the Western Empire Dead, there was no stopping the Visigoths.This time they marched all the way to downtown Rome.

This time there would be no asking, or pleading for help of any kind. This time they would only be demanding. Alaric the bold and his Goths began a furious campaign against the capital city, and before it was half done, the Romans were starving to death. Now that Rome knew what hungry was all about, they reconsidered, possibly because there was no other way. After the vandal Commander was killed, the Roman Emperor commanded his Legions to mass murder all the families of the Barbarian troops that settled in the north of Italy. Remembering this, Alaric and his Warriors were relentless in their attacks on the Romans, and we're not about to accept any of there earlier commands.

What caused a major shift in Barbarian troops, tens of thousands of mercenaries switched over immediately To the Goths, and eventually even the slaves of Rome soon joined the ranks of the Goths. The Gothic Army swelled in size, and swelled in fury, and the world belonged to them. The Butchery of the Barbarian families would be a death sentence to the Empire. At a time so crucial as this, when the Empire needed the Barbarian strengths to hold the empire together, this fatal mistake was made.

As the ranks of the Goths swelled with Germanic Warriors, the terms of the Peace swelled too. Before the Goths would agree to leave, Alaric the bold negotiated a hell of a deal. The terms were as follows. 5,000 lb of gold, 30,000 lb of silver, 3,000 lb of pepper and 4,000 silk tunics.

Alaric the Bold kept his word, and left the city, but he would be back as soon as he was done ending the oppression of Rome elsewhere. In the Roman provinces of Spain and Gaul, the Germanic tribes were welcomed as liberators.As they swept through the land the people rose in rebellions, and revolts, and many flocked to the armies of The Barbarians.

One year later, reconsidering all that it happened, the Goths and all their Germanic Mercenaries were once again at the gates of Rome. In the year 409 the Goths raided The Granary at the city of Portus, and this was a great move. The grain of Rome was kept here in enormous warehouses. Again the Romans had no choice but to buy off the Goths, and again it was gold and silver, and food that the Warriors wanted, and the Warriors Got.

One more year would pass and it would be 410. This time the full Wrath of the Goths met at the gates of Rome, and this time, They would write their own ticket, or another words, they would

take everything, like they should have done the first time. This time there would be no bargaining, and this time all would be theirs.

For three days and three nights, Rome would be pillaged and plundered. In the year 410 Alaric the Bold, proved to the world, just who he was, and sacked Rome,and shocked the whole world. It sent Tremors through the Civilized world. You know it's funny, after living the dream that Alaric had for his entire lifetime, he died several months after he sacked Rome. Cream does rise to the top, and Alaric found his place.He lived to see his dream come true.

One King Rises and another one Falls, this is the order of things. Alaric's successor was a great Chieftain named Ataulf, and he had earned his way to the top. The new Chieftain realized the situation the empire was in, and told the emperor if he wanted peace, there was only one way.

The new Viking king demanded the emperor's sister in marriage. He said that if this happened, he would Ally his Goths to Rome. Knowing how desperately the Empire needed him and his Warriors, he asked for a little bit more. He asked to be next in line for the throne of the Roman Empire. It was considered a Cunning move, and it showed that he was not so barbaric after all, for he too desired it all. The emperor of Rome flatly said no, but his sister had designs of her own of course.

The emperor's sister accepted the marriage to the strongest man in power, anywhere in the world. The Viking king was the future power in Europe, and he had no equals. Believe it or not, in the year 414 the wedding took place. There was no way around it, the world was changing, and if Rome was to survive, she had to change too.

To show that he was a man of his word, Ataulf The Gothic Leader, made a deal to send tens of thousands of his Gothic Warriors all the way to Spain to back up the Roman Legions in battle. There was always a battle for Spain, always. Spain was like a jewel in the crown, for she was littered with Gold and Silver Mines, and I mean plenty of them. These mines were the biggest gold producers in the world. The Romans built aqueducts to bring water to these hills and mountains of Spain. It took years to build these aqueducts, but they did produce greatly. The war in Spain went well of course with the Gothic gladiators fighting side-by-side with the Romans against everybody. Soon there was no one else to even kill, the war went well.

The most important Gold and Silver Mines of Spain we're back in the hands of the Roman Empire, they deserved them, and they got them. The Romans and the Goths Allied together were totally invincible and unbeatable. There was no power on Earth that could change this fact. The Goths were heavily rewarded for their loyalty in battle, and soon they were granted a nice prize. The Goths would receive in the year 418 their own spot within the empire, their Domain was granted. The new Homeland of the Visigoths would be Southwestern Gaul. This would be the new Homeland, and they deserved it, and they received it. As it turns out, that is exactly where the Goths had been settling for years. It was the best of the best, and they deserved it period.

Then when all was perfect, the hand of fate touched the lives of the Nations again. Before the new Gothic leader could father a child with his new Roman wife, he was killed in single combat, by one of his own, oh the hands of fate.

Panic quickly shook the Goths and the Romans, but things worked out just fine, at least this time. The Visigoths prospered greatly as the allies of Rome, and their domain in southern Gaul began to grow, and it was great. The Visigoths where a major power, and their leaders were men with vision.

Of course Gaul had been populated for centuries, and of course there were problems with everyone agreeing to the new Arrangements. But make no mistake, might makes right, and things would have to be worked out, like it or not. The population that lived in Gaul for centuries would have to learn to adjust to survive, because now it was the Gothic way, or it was the

highway.Southern Gaul had always been a dreamland,and the Gothic warriors deserved it.It was a
 fantastic fertile land that all others yearned for, however it would go to the Gothic Warriors, who had fought side-by-side with their Roman allies.

It is written in the pages of History that the Goths made huge territorial claims,
And of course it was their right to do so. An old Roman law stated, that to the military Protectors of the land, went 1/3 to 2/3 of the land, and two thirds of the produce from these lands. When one thinks about it, not too high a price to pay for protection in those violent times. The Visigoths having the largest population, of course took the best farming Lands. The richest of the farming lands belonged to only a few of the great landowners and their slaves. In this way the rich lost out, and the poor lost absolutely nothing, but gained the protection of the Goths. Everyone was happy with the new arrangement, and life would go on.

To all the parties except the great landlords, nothing was lost at all, and much was gained. The Visigoths knew how to make a peace.Like staking their claim to their 2/3, the great warriors of the Goths distributed themselves throughout Southern Gaul. Like most Barbarian tribes, the Goths left the duties of administration to the Romans. Since the Goths spread themselves out throughout Southern Gaul, the Romans and The Barbarians had contact everywhere, and they began to merge as a civilization. They were in close contact with one another, and a mutual respect developed.

The Goths had to learn the methods of farming in the new region, and this they did quickly. The old saying, when in Rome do as the Romans do, applied here, and the Goths prospered greatly and quickly. In fact the Goths learned to speak Latin quickly, and their German language was forgotten within 3 generations. It was definitely a melting of these two people, because the Goths and Romans admired each other. The Gallo Romans Even changed themselves, forgetting the Roman togas, and began wearing the breeches of The Barbarians. The men and women of Gaul even began to wear the famous Gothic jewelry, and it became quite the fashion. In fact although the law was against mixed marriages, they were common everywhere in Gaul. The Gallo Romans and the Goths would have merged totally as one, if it had not been for their religious views. The Goths were Aryans, and the Gallo Romans were Roman Catholics.

The difference is it in their beliefs on the Divinity of Christ, caused violence even to the end. The Arian religion, although Christian, said Jesus was a man. That's what's the difference with the Roman Catholics was. Even in Spain the final homeland of the Goths , there were outbreaks of violence over the real nature of Jesus Christ. It was this difference in religion that would plague Europe for well over 1,000 years. Religion was the unifier supposedly, but was also a major divider.

When the Goths were locked in combat, fighting for their land in Gaul, the Vandals were already in Spain. All the world knew Spain belonged to the Vandals. Most of Spain was definitely their territory. But the Goths and the Romans Kept pouring into Spain by the tens of thousands. The extremely violent Vandals could read the writing on the wall. So they decided it was time for a major move.

The Vandal King and his Chieftains decided to take the extremely rich provinces of North Africa. The Germanic tribes had already swarmed over every inch of Roman territory in the Western Empire, and it was time to take the rest. The Vandal Chiefs knew they could have it all, and they went for it, and they took it. In the year 428, all The Vandals assembled in Spain to pick a new King. It would be the honor of the new Vandal King to lead the invasion of North Africa. They would strike at the very heart of what was the breadbasket of the entire Roman Empire, North Africa. With their Mediterranean climate, this area could produce grain for Millions, and they did, always. To lead this Motley Crue, the Warriors chose Gaiseric. Here was a great story, the new king was in fact the crippled son of a Slave, and now he would try to make the Romans slaves. An eye for an eye I believe is how it goes. The pages of History tell us the Vandal Warriors could not have made a better choice. This was a Monumental decision, and they chose well. he was a ruthless King, but all power is rooted in tyranny, many wise men have said. Gaiseric drove a hard bargain for 50 years, and he made the Vandals feared, in every camp in the world. Historians tell us, that the new King was a genius at making political treaties, all ways to the advantage of the Vandals. The Vandals would crossover to Africa from Spain. It was from here in North Africa as the vandals swarmed to the east, they followed the Mediterranean, and they took everything. The Vandals swarmed, and no one could deny them. It was here in North Africa all along the Mediterranean Coast,that the grain was grown, for the Roman Empire for 800 years. All along this Mediterranean Coast, the Romans built beautiful cities, and they also built beautiful granaries to crush and store the grain of Rome .

At the city called Hippo, the Romans made a magnificent stand, saying the Vandals will go no further. But Hippo, like all others, would fall to the battle-hardened and hungry Vandals. The siege of Hippo was brutal, and took 14 months to complete. Hippo was conquered and the Grain Supply of the Roman Empire was now in the hands of the Vandals. The tides had changed, but nothing Remains the Same for very long in this world that we live in. It was here that Gaiseric took advantage of his great situation. He used the Tradesman, the builders of North Africa to build him a powerful Fleet. Now not only did the people of North Africa have to fear Him and the Vandals, but all shipping in the Mediterranean was now at the mercy of the Scandinavian overlords. The Vandals like the Goths took their two thirds of the land,and stretched out there Warriors all over the domain that they called home. Now it would be the Vandals who lived amongst the Romans. Again like the Goths in Gaul, arguments erupted over the religion for the same reason, the divinity of Jesus Christ. The Vandals were no Roman Catholics, brainwashed thoroughly. They were the leaders of men and of religion, and no one was going to force anything down their throats. The Vandals like their kin, were Aryans too.Gaiseric Held the Non-Aryans in check with his ruthless Vandal Warriors, and you know it's funny, religion was always a problem, especially when it came to the Divinity of Jesus Christ. That would always be a problem, and I believe it was designed that way, to make war amongst the victors for centuries. A brilliant plan it all was, and only today, looking back, can we see, just how grand, It was.

These were all great and powerful men,who bowed to no one.They worshiped their gods of war,and they were very close to them.They believed they were the chosen ones,and the battlefield proved it.Jesus was a man of peace,who lived in a world of war.

In Northern Africa, Which was now in the hands of the mighty Vandals, the Roman Catholics were the majority, but make no mistake, their lives and their beliefs were second to their own. What one group of people could not take by the sword, they took by the Bible. Students of History, this is the hardest lesson to learn, and some die never knowing the truth. I will not explain myself any further, I think you know what I mean. Of course the pages of History and the Catholic writers spin a lot of grim tales about the persecution of the Catholics, But didn't they persecute Millions. I think that's like the kettle calling the skillet black. But this is the way of man, he is such a cunning, lying, hypocrite. In most cases it is only his greed that spurs him on. The Vandals would not let the Roman Catholics try to take over, and force was met with many times more. You know it's funny, the Vandals grew fat and lazy, just like the Romans did after centuries, and they became totally seduced by living in luxury. Just like Rome they became corrupt, and this led to the unraveling of the carpet. It was in the year 533 that the Vandals North African Empire fell. A little over a century, and luxury had ruined them. They had rose from nothing to Greatness, and they could not handle it.This is the way of man.

The Vandals will be known for many things to the pages of History, but they will be known most for their invasion of the Roman Empire. In the years 406 to 409 It was then that they swarmed across the Rhine River, and raped, pillaged, and plundered all the way through Europe, and all the way through Spain. It was at this time because of the Vandals, that the Empire lost control of its far away provinces. After the frontier forts were stripped of Defenders, as far away as Britain, it opened The Floodgates for numerous Germanic tribes to pour in, and pour over Roman territory.

Among the tribes that benefited the most from the Vandal invasion, where the Franks, the Angles, and the Saxons. The same can be said of the Vandal invasion over North Africa, for this was another crippling blow. As the Vandals conquered North Africa, the vital food supply of Rome was terminated,it now belonged to the Vandals and their Allies.

What This did in the larger picture was cause food shortages throughout the Roman Empire. It also stopped cold the armies of Rome, as they planned military campaigns. Napoleon could not have said it better when he said, An army marches on its stomach.

By cutting the grain Supply to Rome, many of the Roman counter attacks were called off, and because of this, the Germanic tribes were free to swarm over Western Europe. If this wasn't enough the Vandal Fleet of pirates were ruining the shipping. This made resupply of the army impossible.

Now we will look at the double-dealing at the hands of the Romans, Vandals, and the Huns. History is so confusing, but it is so fascinating. In the year 434 Gaiseric was King of the

Vandals, and he and all other Germanic Kings of their tribes, would find themselves locked into a bitter backstabbing deal with Aetius. He was a great Roman Commander, and like all Roman Commanders, for centuries had played 1 Germanic tribe, against the other. They said it was for the overall good of the empire, but I'd be willing to bet it was just greed. Aetius was given the reins of power for the Roman Empire. The new Roman Commander sitting on the throne would rule how he saw fit, and that was the only way he knew how to rule, no different than the so-called barbarians.

Once the new Roman Commander had given a whole province to the Vandals, so that he could keep his many huge Estates inside Gaul. He fought many battles against the Germanic tribes, and it was he that brought the Huns into Warfare, inside the Western provinces. The Roman Commanders we're all playing chess moves in people's lives, like they were chess pieces in a game. They were just chess pieces in a game, and the game was called life. The Huns would never let the Roman Commander down, for they were ruthless, but Aren't they all. The new powerful Roman Commander knew the Huns very well, for in his youth, he spent a lot of time with them, as a hostage. He learned their ways well, and his eyes and ears took it all in. This group of Barbarians were from Asia with a yellow streak in their blood. The leader of the Huns, and the leader of the Roman Legions, trusted each other, for they knew each other's ways very well. All Aetius Had to do to get the Furious tribesmen, was to pay them in gold, and that is the way of men, all men. A Roman Commander took a small wagon of gold to talk to the Huns, cuz he had a lot for them to do. First the Roman Commander would bring the Huns in to crush a slave revolt in Western Gaul. The Huns got everybody by surprise as they stormed the situation, and soon the results of the revolt where exactly what they wanted.

Other Roman Commanders loved using all the Barbarian tribes against one another, and this they did for centuries. The Warriors did it For the Love of gold, that's it. The Roman Commander also sent the huge Asian Barbarian Force against the Germanic Burgundians. The Burgundians were swelling their numbers along the Rhine River, getting ready to launch an attack on the empire, and the Roman Commander sent the Huns to stop them.

The Huns were victorious in most of their battles, for they used the surprise attack better than most. They also had a massive amount of soldiers on horseback, in the days where soldiers were on foot. This was a major advantage. Attila was the king of the Huns and he took every opportunity to collect the gold from Rome. Against any army, just like the Vikings, they went to war for gold only, everything else didn't mean anything. Attila, King of the Huns was always cutting deals with the Roman top brass, and his Mercenaries we're eager to collect Rome's gold. As the Visigoths we're making huge advances into Gaul, The Hun's once again we're paid in gold to stop them.

In the year 451 Attila brought his Huns to Gaul, and I mean all of them, some say 60,000 to 200,000. This time Attila had dreams of invasion on his mind. Attila and his soldiers were among the best at rape, pillage, and plunder, but in the world at that time, it was the order of the day. Every time his Warriors entered Gaul, shockwaves and tremors were in the hearts of all.

Always before Attila had been summoned to fight Rome's battles, but this time it was a real invasion, and the Huns took everything for their own.

The Goths and the Romans had no choice but to join forces, and hope they could win against the Warriors of Attila. This Asian nightmare had stabbed Rome in the back, but then they were all good at that. Besides the Huns, Attila had many other Warriors. He had Mercenaries from all the other tribes, that the Huns had already defeated in combat. There was no need to slay everyone, only those that resisted, or thought they could win. There was never a reason to kill everyone, because that means you had thousands of soldiers and thousands of slaves. It is written in the pages of History, deep in the pages of History, that the Ostrogoths even had warriors fighting on the side of the Huns, I guess gold Knows No Boundaries. Under the command of the Visigoths their were the Franks, and the Celtics ,the Saxons, and The Burgundian Warriors.

This fighting Force would have struck Terror in the hearts of even the meanest Warriors, and only time would tell who would be victorious. What history was about to witness, was the clash of the two mightiest armies the world would ever see. The fighting would be close and bloody, and it would be a battle like history had never seen before. The Visigoths had a historian with them that recorded the battle for future Generations, and he wrote well.

Hand-to-hand, that clashed in battle, and the fight grew Furious, confused, monstrous, and unrelenting, a fight who's like, no ancient time has ever recorded. This truly was The Clash of the Titans. But make no mistake both these armies we're fighting for the future control of the world, please make no mistake. There such Deeds were done, that a brave man who missed the marvelous fight could not hope to see anything so mighty In all his life.

All agree, there are really no words that could have explained the horrors of this battle. Wise men say enough blood to fill a small Lake, was spilled that day, for the opportunity to rule the world. Like the song says, Everybody Wants to Rule the World.Historians say,this was the battle for Paris ,and it was,however it would be one of many.France or Gaul would be fought for many times in the future,and millions would die,and she was worth it.

The historians estimate of the deaths on this one day of battle were 165,000 dead. One cannot even imagine how many were wounded, a half a million Maybe. By far the bloodiest day in the history of the world, the battle was truly fought for the greatest real estate in the world. And you know what's funny, the greatest day of battle, bloody battle, was fought to a draw, with both sides taking heavy losses.

The great lessons were learned that day, that would never be forgotten. Attila the Hun was so shaken, by the enormous losses of the Huns, that he took his army and retreated all the way across Gaul, stopping on the far side of the Rhine River. He left the battlefield completely, and didn't stop until he had left the empire on the far side of the Rhine River which is Germany. The pages of History tell us Attila the Hun knew at this moment, there was no hope of taking the Western Empire. When it was United, it was impossible. Like I said great lessons were learned this day, and these lessons must never be forgotten. United we stand, divided we fall. The Huns had never received such a bloody loss, it was like Napoleon's Waterloo. But time and fate have a way of handing out the proper punishments when they are due. But make no mistake Attila knew at this time, because he told his Commanders, the West could never be captured with the Viking warriors fighting at their full strength, this could not happen.

That's amazing though 165,000 Huns and Romans, and Goths dead in a matter of 10 hours, definitely one of the bloodiest spectacles ever. I wonder if Mother Nature smiled upon the situation.All that blood that watered the soil.

In the year 452, Attila was back again, to take the empire. His Huns invaded Italy, and this time they drove all the way to Rome, instead of Paris like they tried before. As they swarmed around the gates of Rome, the Huns screamed they wanted to be paid to leave. The Western Roman Empire with all their gold, agreed to pay the Huns in gold.

Soon after they left, Attila the Hun died. As so often always happens, once deprived of their great leader, the Huns were never a threat again. the story does not end here, except for Attila. For now it was time for the Fate of the powerful commander of the Rome's Legions. Valentinian could read the writing on the wall, and he was commanding from the Eastern Roman Empire.

Valentinian knew the Western Empire was still in the hands of Aetius. This leader was a hero in the West by his own hand.The order was given to assassinate the ruler of the Western Empire, and so it was done, and that was the way of Rome. Being the way of Rome, one assassination Spurs on another assassination, this is the way it went, and soon Valentinian was too. Rome's greatest General in the West Was Dead, and Rome's emperor in the East was dead, and now Rome had another great mess.

With the great leaders gone in the west and the east, the world knew Rome's enemies would return quickly.

The Vandals would come first, and they would be brought by their huge Fleet, because the Vandals were also a major sea power, Vikings. The Vandals and their allies, did not beat around the bush. They landed their Fleet close to Rome. They marched in and they sacked Rome, and To the victor go the spoils. The sacking of Rome was beginning to be normal for all the Teutonic tribes. They had held them off for centuries, but they would hold them off no more. Between the years 410,to 563, Rome was sacked 8 times.

The once unheard-of idea of Rome falling to its enemies, was now the norm, and Rome was for sure in decline, and it's true she was going down fast. The Viking tribes were relentless, and showed no mercy, much like the Romans had showed them in the past.

After the Vandals had their fill, and filled all their ships completely full of treasure, they decided it was time to go. The Vandals vandalized Rome, and this is where they got their name. To vandalize in English meant to just tear things up. This is where the word vandalize came into being.

Word quickly spread like wildfire that the empire was on her knees, and everyone wanted a piece of the mighty Cult of Rome. The whole peninsula of Italy, was next to fall. The Barbarian Mercenaries who served in the army of Rome, now decided they wanted all the spoils For themselves. They just didn't want what was left of Rome, they wanted the whole peninsula that Rome sat on. The Barbarian Mercenaries then ruled, Emperor, after Emperor for 20 years, and the outside world was fooled, that all was well.

Then upon the stage of Rome, entered a strong man, to grab the reins of power. His name was Odoacer. He sent the puppet emperor packing, and The Barbarians did not put a successor on the throne.

This is the event that history calls the fall of the Roman Empire. Any real student of History knows the Germans already controlled the entire Western Empire, lock , stock and Barrel. Those that lived after the fall of the Roman Empire, lived with the ghost over their shoulder. Although the Western Empire was all Germanic kingdoms, ruled of course by Germans, no one wanted to challenge the Byzantine emperor, or the emperor of the Eastern Empire.The armies of the east were real strong and powerful,and would remain that way for another thousand years.

Next to take the spotlight on the stage of world politics, would be the king of the Ostrogoths. Eastern emperors tried to make a deal to take both Empires, but of course this didn't work. In the long run no matter who won the battle for Italy, both armies of Germanic Warriors would be crippled, for Germanic Warriors preferred death to surrender. Next from the Eastern Empire in the year 489, was King Theodoric. King of the Ostrogoths would now invade Italy. The Clash was very gory and very bloody, and the battles went on for four long years. Finally there was a meeting, between the two great Barbarian leaders, and the warlord's Met at Ravena. Like all Viking get-togethers, it was a huge feast, with plenty of drinks, and the warlord's agreed to rule Italy.

Of course everyone agreed, but everyone knew things would not go as smoothly as the leaders said they would. Theodoric King of the Ostrogoths, killed his rival with his own sword, and his huge bodyguard of furious Goths, wiped out all the other Warriors from the other side. This is how things are really done, and all through the pages of history, there is proof. But this is the way of men, and it is man we're talking about. In the 1930s Adolf Hitler Would say, all kingdoms are rooted in tyranny, but for thousands of years all wise men knew that anyway.

Even though it was an underhanded move, killing his opponent after just making a deal with them. He was sitting squarely on the throne, and you know that's really all that matters isn't it. And you know it's really funny, the pages of History tell us, that' Theodoric was perhaps the best ruler Italy had had in centuries. Theodoric attempted to restore Roman Life to the West, and some historians say he attempted to restore all things Roman to the to the West. Theodoric did try to restore the Roman way, instead of let everything go to The Barbarians, however this did not work. Theodoric attempted and gave back administrative duties to the Romans, and even gave back many of their titles. It was this one great German Theodoric that gave back all the great Public Works that Rome was famous for, and yes had made the world so jealous of, the real Rome. Theodoric ordered that all the seaports be rebuilt on the same scale of old. He also set up repairing all the Roman aqueducts, which gave the Romans the cleanest supply of water in the world. They weren't about ready to give up all things Roman, because Rome had a lot of the great things, and they were Roman. This one great leader of men, Theodoric gave plenty of gold to every kind of cultural activity, so then once again all men and women would be proud to be Romans. There was only one thing wrong, if let to decay, it would be, centuries before anything else could even attempt to replace her .

Theodoric chose Ravenna as his new capital, and it was here that he built a beautiful palace. The rest of the world set in awe of this glorious building. Theodoric had the Beautiful Marble Columns of Rome transported all the way to his Palace. Also Theodoric kept in touch with the high command in Constantinople, the Eastern Roman Empire. He sent letters to the emperor of the East, letting him know that he was trying hard to be a great imitation of the greatest Empire on Earth. Theodoric was quite the Statesman, but then politicians are all the same, like actors on a stage. Theodoric Kept the Catholics and the Aryans in line, but to do this, he made them live in separate communities. Remember the Aryans and and Catholic thoughts we're actually 2 Separate ways. It was the Aryans of which gives us Arianism, another major religion of the time. It said Christ was a prophet not God himself, or the son of God, or whatever story you believe. That was the main difference between the Catholics and Arianism. It always ended in vicious arguments, and major bloodshed, because this is the way of men. Although Theodoric was smart to keep them separated, which was good for him, because now everybody could pay taxes.

In the year 526 the new leader Theodoric of the West died. As often happens, after a great leader passes away, all hell broke loose. When caught in the vacuum of a powerful leader, many strive to fill that vacuum. But the western Roman Empire did have the luxury of having Theodoric rule them for 35 years. The West Was certainly upgraded. But after his death, disorder was now the rule of the land.

In Constantinople the eastern half of the Roman Empire , the high command was really happy, for now the emperor Justinian had every reason now to invade. They could now take Italy back into the orbit of the Eastern Empire. Without King Theodoric to lead the Ostrogoths into battle, Constantinople knew a victory would be quick and easy. Emperor Justinian not only wanted to reconquer Italy, he also had designs on all the Roman Empire. It is said that Justinian wanted to reconquer all the land all the way around the complete Mediterranean, which was once all Rome's. The command for the assault on the western Empire would be led by Belisarius, and it was decided it would be an invasion by sea.

The General was certainly the man for the job, for it was he that commanded the attack on the Vandals, in North Africa in the year 533. Because of his leadership it was always a short campaign, and in the end it saved many lives. For he was a great Commander.

The general had many Vandal victories in North Africa, and he landed his army in Sicily, and Marched North to Naples, and then marched on Rome. But when the time was right, the German gods produced a warrior king, that stopped the Eastern Empire in their tracks.

The gravity of the times was enormous, but the Germanic Warriors were up for the fight once again. It was a new Ferocious Germanic Chieftain. The Germans would flock to the toughest Warrior of all Soon. Tortilla had an army that needed a King, that they could follow in battle anywhere, and they got one.

The Ostrogoths elected the massive Tortilla King. The Warriors of the Goths once again lit on fire, and the memory in their blood was on fire. The forces they would now confront and battle,were 5000 warriors on horseback, and 10,000 on foot. These were the best 15,000 Warriors the Eastern Roman Empire could Assemble. Both sides were well aware, this was a battle to the death, and there would be 0 prisoners taken. As usual even the wounded Would be cut to pieces. For 20 years the battles would be fought, and at times both sides were reinforced, cuz this was for all the marbles so to speak. The pages of History, were bloody and gruesome, however this is the way of men.

In 563 the Ostrogoths had been beaten, and Italy was once again in the Roman Empire, at least on paper it all looked so good. Even bragging rights, must have made them feel a lot better, but the whole empire was basically ruled by Germanic blood. North Africa after the Eastern Roman Empire Invasion now belonged to them also. The Vandals had been beaten and were in retreat, so that they could come and fight another day. But anyway the Vandal war was over, and the Romans once again owned the Bread Basket of North Africa. She still grew millions of pounds of barley ,wheat, and other Grains each year. There would be no Hungry Mouths and stomachs in the land that owned North Africa. The southern coast of Spain with all the bloodshed now belonged to the Empire once again.

The Germanic gods would not allow these victories to stand, and soon fresh Germanic Warriors were arriving from Eastern Europe ready for battle. This time it would be the Lombards, and it would be right here, that they regained their reputation that would never go away. The Lombards were extremely Furious, like most Viking tribes, and they pushed on Yelling Thor's name, and victory did come again. They drove the Eastern Empires forces out of Northern Italy by the year 572. They also took much of southern Italy all the way down to the Po River, which flows to Rome. At the same time, their cousins in Spain the Visigoths, began an unrelenting attack on the Empire's forces that held their coastline.The Visigoths pushed all the Invader forces, with much blood on them, back into the ocean. When the battle was done in fact, the Roman Legions were driven from Spain, and they suffered terrible losses at the hands of the Viking tribes.

All this bloodshed in the battle for Spain was well worth it, because Spain had the biggest gold mines at that time. The fight was on, and the Viking tribes won again. At this time the Roman Empire of the East, gave up their designs on reconquering the old west. The writing was on the wall, and it belonged to the German tribes forever. Any Roman knew for sure there was no possible chance of ever owning the West again. They found out the same way that Attila the Hun found out, their armies were beaten badly,and lucky to have any soldiers left.

In the long run the Germanic tribes learned very well their lessons, and realized they were truly on their own. Even though their military abilities gave them the right to rule, they realized they would never be accepted, because they weren't Roman Catholics. The German tribes had a Christian religion called Arianism and their belief was that Jesus was a man, and a prophet, and the Roman Catholics believed that Jesus was God on Earth. It was quite a difference, much like the Protestants that would come later, but there would always be problems with the different religious ideas. Maybe that's the way it was intended to be, since so many different religions did spring from Christianity. The high command in Germany in the 40s said it was for this reason the Jews were ordered to write the Bible, to divide the mightiest military power in the history of the world, the white race from Europe and Scandinavia. As things turned out that's exactly what happened,a couple thousand years of war between Catholics, Arianism, Protestants. The high command of Germany, in World War 11 Had many discussions on this very subject. It was rumored that it was the Persian King, the strongest power in that part of the world for thousands of years, ordered this done, under penalty of death if it wasn't. It really makes one wonder doesn't it, and the writers of the Bible make no mistake, were all Jewish writers, and they produced the Bible. They don't even celebrate Christmas, cuz they say Jesus was only a man. It's a very deep subject of which we will get to the bottom of, as the history book goes on, and we get to the Days of Thunder and World War II.

That was just a little knowledge to sprinkle the mind, but like I said we will get back to it later on. Even the Germanic Warriors in the times of the collapse of the Roman Empire, many were baptized in the Roman faith, and this was done for political reasons. The tribes for thousands of years worshiped Thor, Odin, Frey, and their Gods never deserted them. It would have been an insult for most of them to Dessert their gods now.

The Roman citizens of the West also learned their lessons, and were shocked at what they found. The soldiers and administrators from Constantinople treated them worse then the Germans ever did. They also realized they were a world apart from their Greek speaking, Greek Church, of the East.

In fact the Romans of the West, were soon to realize, they had much more in common with the Germanic soldiers, then the Greeks from the East.

The Roman citizens of the West, and the Germanic tribes, learned they were on their own. They had no choice but to pull together, and rule themselves. If they were to survive in a hostile world, this was their only choice. Survival of the fittest, it's the story of Europe, and the fittest we're still alive.

The Romans of the West and the Germanic tribes, had spent centuries together already. In the good times, and their sufferings, nothing was left, but for that these two people to merge together, with the Germanic Chieftains leading the way. The New Order of the Western Empire, was in the making, and no longer would the Eastern empire be looked upon for leadership. Those days were gone, and would never return. The West now was in an infant state, knew they were on their own, which means they were in excellent hands. They knew the ropes, and they learned the lessons of History, and now it was time, to apply these lessons.

The West would still be Influenced by the East, because of her traditions, and her institutions. The Eastern Empire would shine forever, or so they thought .They would be forced to rebuild the West on their own.

In retrospect the last 500 years the Roman Empire had been infused with energy, with vigor, and the blood of the Germanic tribes. This had brought the empire to Great Heights. It would be this new Force the Germanic tribes, that would make the strongest Empire the world would ever see. It would be this new force of energy, molded together with the Roman traditions of the past, that would build the greatest Powerhouse of the world, Europe. It would be Thor, and Odin, in the blood in these great warriors, and this is their story.

The problems of changing beliefs to other gods,was a problem the empire,and millions never really did.It was a war of mind control,or was it something bigger on all sides. In 285 a.d. The commanders of Rome called for a mass assembly of their armies at Le Valais .There was to be a huge pagan sacrifice,to secure the favor from the Roman gods.The Theban legion had been called back from Egypt.The Roman leader Maximian wanted justice on the commander of the Theban legion,and he threatened to
Execute the Christian Commander of that Legion,while all the armies were watching. As his final gesture to loving the Christian faith the Commander of the legion knelt before his troops on one knee. It was then his head was cut off,the leaders of Rome,had no choice but to try to snuff out the belief in any other god or gods.They could not show any weakness,and they would not,with the Roman gods watching, this was their payback.This sacrifice was a hard thing to do,however they had to.
The Theban legion chose to follow the example of their leader,and they all knelt too.They refused to worship the Roman gods any longer,and offered to display their nerve.The commander not to be out done,ordered every tenth man to lose their heads also.This did nothing to change the hearts and minds of the warriors. Maximian next made the decision to kill everyone in this battle hardened legion.All heads did roll for all to see.In all

666 Roman warriors died that day.

The biggest slaughter and sacrifice in history.

666 for the man who has wisdom>

THE MASTERPIECE

CHAPTER 7

The Aryans, are not the name of a tribe, it is a name of a civilization. The civilization lived in Sweden, Norway, Greenland, Iceland, Russia, Northern Asia, and basically stretched from the North Pole countries, all the way to ancient India. India means land of the Aryans, Iran means land of the Aryans, I think you get the picture. Parts of Scandinavia are still Rising by hundreds of feet each year, and over millions of years, whole countries will emerge. A good comet strike, or meteor, could speed the process up quite a bit.Also the North Pole Shifting could also speed the process up. All over the area known as the Pacific Rim, Lands are being born as I write. All around the Pacific Rim there are underwater volcanoes that are erupting constantly, and they create new land daily.

This is the never-ending creative power of nature, and the other side of the coin is, Nature's Never Ending destructive powers. Mountains over millions of years, will be grinded to dust, and new Mountains will rise up. This is the awesome balance of nature. It is a known fact today, by modern scientists, that many of the lands around the North Pole, inside the Arctic Circle where at one time very different than they are today. In fact the coldest region in the world today, a million years ago was hot and tropical. The scientists have drilled down through the ice, to see just how life was in the past. Of course it is only theories, on how long ago that was, no one really knows the truth, how could they. The great Ice Age that covered most of the Earth , was said to have had its maximum melting about 13,000 years ago. There are deserts in the world like the Sahara and the Gobi, that in ancient times were covered by the oceans.Most of ancient Egypt including the spots, where the pyramids and all the temples are, are completely covered with sand. When the outer casing Stones were still on the pyramid, there was a high water mark, that went almost all the way up. For miles and miles and miles nothing but sand, and they say the Sphinx was even partially covered. Sea shells can still be found in enormous quantities in all these Sandy spots including ancient Egypt. Change is the order of the universe, and things will continue to change. Just like the song says nothing Remains the Same. All ancient civilizations like the Egyptians, the Babylonians, the Incas, and Aztecs, were formed under the religious Doctrine, that the serpent,and the snake, were the symbol of Eternity, and of course wisdom. It is only with the Jewish writers of the Bible that the serpent or snake was written in as being the devil, or evil. In this way whenever the Christian Soldiers would see these symbols, they would smash them, and burn their libraries. What a beautiful plan when you think about it, the Jews were Masters at dominating the hearts and Minds of others.They were masters at lying,but terrible on the battlefield.They spent most of their lifetimes as slaves to all nations in their part of the world.They lost their nation around the time of Christs death.

The oldest information that we have, come from The Aryan Hindus of ancient India, and of course all the ancient writings or hieroglyphics are on all the ancient Egyptian temples. The secret passages were loaded with writings, and possibly even books. But of course we can't expect to be ever told the truth,because knowledge is power, and they want to keep all they can.

One must remember that Archaeology is basically a new science, and man has been at it for a couple hundred years. That is not a very long time to piece together everything. Not only did Modern Man have to sift through all the debris, he had the catalog information and break the codes of all the ancient symbols. This was not an easy task, for the ancients were very brilliant, and they were also brilliant at hiding things. Modern Man is just beginning to understand the real truth as he sees through a mountain of Lies and deception. The initiates of Egypt, Greece, Aryan India, wrote only for their wise men, not for the masses, of which most couldn't read anyway, or even understand.
Ancient knowledge is basically secret knowledge, and can be very dangerous in the wrong hands. Sometimes in the ancient scriptures of all the nations, the truth is concealed from all. The dates and events we're confused intentionally, so that no one could follow. This was done to preserve the real knowledge .But most of all to make it unreadable to All Foreign Nations.

Knowledge definitely is power, and all the initiates will cling to it, it was really better than gold. The modern scientists agree to disagree, so that the truth remains and only in selected Circles of power.

It was really in the 1800s, that archaeology really took off. The ancient cities of Assyria and Babylonia were being dug up, and gone through thoroughly. These were some of the oldest civilizations on Earth, that we are told of. The Assyrian and Babylonian libraries written in stone were excavated and the wisdom of the western world grew quickly. This was the age of discovery, and man would learn a great deal.

These ancient cultures Were on the shores of the Persian Gulf. It was here at the mighty City of Eridu , was built some 6000 years ago. This is one of the many holy sites on Earth, and it was also the earliest of Chaldaean Civilization. In the story of EA the god of wisdom, the Legends tell us of the Half Man, half fish, who brought the knowledge to the Babylonians. The half man, half fish instructed the Babylonians in all the Arts, and all the Sciences.

The Bible Clams this city is only 3500 years old, because then this would fit perfectly into their timetable of world history. In fact it is much older than that, maybe twice as old, but they have to continue to run their own game, where they are top dog. What in fact the half man, half fish really symbolizes, is that the god of wisdom came from the sea. This is one of the many Legends that is directly linked to the flood waters over Atlantis, for this is where the man God came from. This is what the symbolic meaning of the half man, half fish, is really all about. Only the most highly educated understood, and that's just the way they wanted it.

This is exactly what is meant by symbolic language, that the ancient historians used. Remember true knowledge must be kept away from all their rivals and their enemies.

The ancient world of Egypt, India, and the Sinai Peninsula, we're firmly tied together, with trade and intellectual knowledge. They had been bonded together for thousands of years, and it would remain so. The French, under Napoleon would comb through the ruins of the Egyptians, knowing full well that they were the Masters of the ancient world. Napoleon with his savants, would comb through the tombs and ruins that were available to them. Remember only 20% of the ruins and temples are above ground to be combed over. 80% still lay underneath the Sands of the desert. That's how ancient This area is. Ancient Egypt was above ground before the great flood of many thousands of years ago, this we are certain of.

In the ruins of Telloh, the French scientists found statues made of Diorite, which is one of the hardest and most beautiful stones in the world. On the statues of the ancient ruins, the French scientists found inscriptions. It said the green stones of Diorite had been cut from Megan in the Sinai Peninsula. The whole peninsula Was ruled by the Pharaohs of Egypt, and the French dated the statues to 6000 years ago. There was a special teak wood from India, that have been found at all the excavation sites, even at Ur , the first city built after the great flood. The teak wood is special only to India, and the Babylonian records tell us that's where they got it. The Babylonian records tell of all the clothing and special cloth that were received from India.There was much trade between Egypt and India, and don't forget they were colonies of the ancient civilization of Atlantis. Atlantis was a World Civilization, and they were thousands of years ahead of anybody else.

Getting back to the symbol of the serpent or dragon, there was a time long before the Christians and long before the Jews, long before the Muslims and Muhammad and the Koran, when the world was so different. The Serpent and the Dragon were held in the highest levels for wisdom, and also for immortality. It is the snake that sheds its skin each year, and receives a new body that makes him so different than all other creatures. I'm sure the ancients looked at it as a form of reincarnation, for the snake receives a new body. That is why the ancients we're so taken by this creature. For tens of thousands of years temples were built on all The lands to the serpent and to the Sun. The Cult of the Sun, and the cult of the Dragon, where the very Foundation, that all civilizations were built upon. Now these Cults of man, have lost much of their power, but still remain strong in China and Japan. Other Buddhist countries the serpent has been from day one, the emblem of wisdom, immortality, and secret knowledge to the Cults of Egypt, India, and Babylon.

It is most interesting to note that the Egyptians called their vast Underground Network of tunnels snake holes, so you see the snake had many different meanings. The Syrian high priest also referred to themselves as the sons of the Dragon. The legends of dragons did not evolve to Great Britain, but in ancient days, thousands of years ago, The Druids belonged to the cult of snakes. The pages of History tell us The Druids of Britain were famous for saying, I am a serpent, I am a druid. Remember the Egyptians and The Druids were one of the same blood, and mind, As obvious with their monuments to a glorious past. In the Valley of the Kings, which is where they were buried, or entombed, Ramses II was finally located. They said his hair had grown all the way down to his knees, as hair continues to grow even after death.

Ramses II hair was definitely Aryan because it was red. This piece of knowledge will cement together all thoughts about the bloodline connection. Ramses II is credited at least with building more monuments of ancient Egypt than anyone before him or after him. I found it quite interesting when the truth came out on the hair color, of possibly the greatest pharaoh that Egypt had ever seen. The Serpent's or the wise men of Britain, India, and Egypt, and the Americas, also had the titles of builders and architects. This they earned with their enormous monuments that lay in Ruins today.

The Knights of the Middle Ages we're all initiates, and they called this the search for the Grail, but like most things Grail has several meanings. The Grail is, what is called the Philosopher's Stone at its highest level. The Philosopher's Stone is what all men seek to activate. Modern Man calls this the pineal gland which is located in the head. It is this gland that will provide spiritual vision if it can be activated. This pineal gland is actually what wise men have been calling the third eye for thousands of years. It is there and it can be activated. Of course just like with everything else the world tries to tell you the do's and the don'ts. The left hand way, the right hand way, the good way, and The evil way.Make your own decision,it is your life,and your vision.

You have not seen anything until the third eye is open.

In the world we live in today, a million different people want to tell you the right way, the wrong way, their opinions, and sometimes even their mommy or Daddy's opinion. Gather together all the information you can, and make your own decisions. But of course, go to the source, and try to find the truth, Know This,all will be revealed..

But getting back to certainly one of the most important things in life, the search for the Grail is exactly where we will Go now. It is this little Organ the size of an almond, situated at the base of the skull, that wise men and women have tried to activate for thousands of years. We only get a glimpse in the power of the so-called philosopher's stone, when we realize it is the pineal gland that allows us to see in our dreams. The pineal gland or philosopher's stone, is the ultimate vision, and must be sought after by everyone seeking true knowledge. I will give you in the following pages all the ways I know to activate the pineal gland. First we'll start with the most difficult and almost impossible way. A lot of the wise men from all religions, from all Races have chosen this way, because it is considered the one true way. Students of this way include millions that have tried, and we'll never know how many have succeeded. But this is the safest way and the path for people that fear a lot. Men on spiritual paths have for many generations remained very quiet on the road to starvation. It is known to the wise men that a fast is more than just a day or two without food. To get Earth shattering results one must fast almost to the point of starvation and death. But this path will take you to the Matrix and this is for sure. All science knows is before death of starvation your life will be shown to you. We will get glimpses of the past, and possibly glimpses of the future, but locks will be opened. And combinations will click. Many of the Great Seekers of the truth would go up to caves, or to the wilderness to do this, and as they did this, would wait for Nature's answer. Religious men like Gandhi of India were skin and bones, but it was well worth it to them, to see what they saw. There's only one way to get to the truth, and it will be difficult, but do it with others just in case. This is the truth, I know to reach spiritual vision, because before you die, the heart will secrete some chemicals to activate the pineal gland while you're awake. Only then can you see with the vision of the Gods, and truly be reborn. This is the search for the Grail, and this is one way to do it, but it's not the only way.

The other option that the true Initiate would have, would be the way that Millions have taken in the long history of civilization. Initially this knowledge was in small circles, but it was kept by all. From the mountain tops of the Himalayas, to the jungles of Brazil and Peru it was done. From the Indians in North and South America, to the Asians, the path was the same. All Egyptian High priests, and of course royalty were confronted with the choice to see all, or just wear blinders through life. At this point I must warn all Initiates, and seekers of the truth, they must be prepared for it. The high priests of Egypt had many studies to take, before they were allowed the vision of the Gods. This way they could not harm themselves mentally, and they would realize exactly what they were seeing .

I can only add that all the high priests or the scientists of ancient times, used the most powerful drugs to reach the Unseen forces, behind the veil that stands before us. In the Himalayas they say the goddess Soma is there. Soma are the magic mushrooms and peyote that grow there always. These hallucinogenic drugs have grown there a million years, and this is one reason why countries like Tibet have led the way with gurus and religious minded people for thousands of years. It is a guaranteed fact that only Soma, peyote, mescaline, and mushrooms can bring you to the higher state that all serpents and Dragons reach for.

Be careful on your trips to the Sun, remember the legend of Icarus who flew too close to the Sun, and it melted his wax wings. Remember too, especially with your mind, traveling past the speed of sound, you're likely to get burned.

The plants named Chuchuhuasi and Ayahuasca are also used in the occult learning process for higher development. Occult meaning Supernatural, of which this is, should be considered highly dangerous for some. These two plants are for Earthly Serpents and Dragons, that wish to experience flying or astral projection. Only the strongest Minds should Journey down this road, 4 bizarre creatures Will be seen. Remember these trips are not for the weak of heart, but if you do search for the Grail, you will find it. In fact you cannot miss it,it is easier than you think.

It must be noted that on the mountain tops of Peru there are beautiful temples that stretch for almost a hundred miles along the Andes. Peru has several hundred of them, but they do go on. The Spanish conquistadors wrote back to Spain about them, but after they were looted for their gold, no one cared about them in the least bit. Of course many explorers have come since then to steal whatever they could sell, to museums or private collectors. Remember that the ruins of South America are among the oldest anywhere in the world, and the European conquerors call this the new world . But of course it was the ancient world. To give you something to think about, when one thinks of the ancient ruins of South America, remember the Indian said that white men built them. The indians said the builders of all these structures had red hair,and some were blonde haired.

Once one of the most glorious civilizations on Earth was in Peru, but the Incas wiped them out, and with them the high civilization they left behind, decayed and was lost.

You know it's funny , we will end this chapter soon, and it has been one of the most enlightening chapters in the masterpiece. We cannot go on without saying a few words about the most intriguing way to activate the pineal gland, or philosopher's stone. Most serpents and Dragons wish to call it by its oldest name, the third eye. The search for the Grail is about opening this third eye, and being able to see, with the vision of the Gods.

All the ancient civilizations From the Egyptians, to the Persians, to the pyramid Builders of Mexico, and South America, all worshiped the Sun. Sun Cults are as old as man himself. The sun is the bringer of light, and warms life. Jesus and all the Many religious leaders of the world spoke often of the powers of the light, as well as they should have. There would be no life on this planet if there was no sunlight. The high Priests of the Mayans, and Incas, and the Egyptians all used the power of the sun to their own advantage. All the wise men, of all the world's civilizations, kept Eternal fires burning in their temples. In this way they kept the togetherness with the solar being, don't forget the sun is alive too. The secret occult powers of the college's of high priests, were known to only their initiate's. The powers of the sun god were known to only those in the ruling class.

Modern researchers tell us that dragons and serpents knew how to reach out to the controlling forces of the Sun. From the tops of the pyramids long before the points were put on, the high priests gathered at sunrise and sunset to view the Sun. It was at sunrise and sunset when the sun had lost its main power for the day. It seems the high priests were able to gather it's rays in to the eyes, and then let it flow into their nervous system. It's Not only fasting, peyote, mushrooms, and Soma that activate the pineal gland, sunlight could also expand the mind. This is secret knowledge, and not much is known, except it was done when the Rays at sunrise and sunset were at their weakest point of the day.

It Was Written that sunlight could activate the pineal gland, and sunlight could also expand the mind. It is not known how long the wise men open their inner workings to the Rays, but what is known in certain circles, is that they did it with good results. It is not known either if they looked at the Sun, or maybe at the light, but it is known the high Priests of the Egyptians developed mysterious powers in sight.

To put you on the path to the true knowledge I can only say read a book called Project X. The search for the secrets of immortality, by Gene Savoy. Gene is a modern serpent and perhaps the greatest Explorer in modern times.

Gene and his expeditions to Peru and Brazil uncovered over 25 unknown cities in the jungles, and the mountain tops. These cities were like all the rest of the ancient monuments, built of huge stone blocks with perfect precision.

I will only say that South American civilizations were built by a race of white men that the Indians called Viracochas . The Incas conquered the Viracochas and killed them all, and perhaps even sacrificed a few. This is why the cities were left abandoned, and for the jungle to grow over them. The temple cities are Outside, are built at almost 10,000 feet above sea level, on the peaks of mountains, and inside the same mountains are networks of tunnels the lead to the tombs of their ancestors. It seems that all the big mountains of South America and Mexico, on the insides are catacombed with huge tunnel systems that lead into the interior of the Earth. Not much has been said about these tens of thousands of tunnels, or even who made them, and for what reason. I guess they don't like to talk about them, because they do not want to start a stampede to the tunnel systems inside the Earth. Let's face it, whoever runs the show here on Earth would certainly be inside the Earth, if just a little way down. The bad weather and winds would have no effect on those underneath the surface. Meteor strikes and comet strikes would have no effect on those that live below. Underground Air Force Bases with nuclear missiles are under mountains, and cannot be touched by bombs, even if they are atomic.

All those hidden cities Probably got it so nice down there, they will never return to the surface. One of the oldest countries on Earth, Tibet, they speak of the underground communities of Shamballa and Agartha, which have been there for thousands of years. I imagine all the underground communities have been there for at least a few thousand years, and if anyone was going to survive the ice ages, they would have no choice but to go underground, I believe it's right here that it all starts.

It's funny how the Indian civilizations of the Americas, are hooked together mentally with the other ancient civilizations of the surface of the Earth. The great buildings called pyramids are on all continents, and we must not forget the continents were hooked together as 1. This is one reason why many of the ancient stories like the great flood are everywhere, passed down from father to son, Chieftain to tribe.

Of course In the modern world, scientists with all their theories, about the continents Breaking Up millions of years ago. How the hell do they know that, it's just a theory. They tell us so many things, we have to begin to think for ourselves. The water from the melting of the last ice age,drowned many lands,and separated the continents too.

I've written about the three meteor strike in the Bermuda Triangle, and the huge meteor or comet strike in Canada, and that huge meteor strike in Mexico at some time in our ancient past. I would think that these huge explosions would really jolt the land masses, and spread them apart rather quickly. The continents could have been together thousands of years ago, instead of Millions, nobody really knows. But as they drifted apart, the positions pretty much stayed the same. Science and their theories have been wrong so many times. Remember when they told us the Earth was flat, and the world believed it, or so we're told.
 Theories often are nothing but made up lies, to soothe the population. Just like the drifting apart of the continents are theories. So are many of the theories of the Ice Age. Science tells us the Ice Age lasted millions of years, and that the melting of that ice age ended approximately 13,000 years ago. The melting of that ice age for sure added to the great flood, added with the comet strike, and the meteors. Between these three things the Earth was flooded, almost completely. The great Ice Age took a heavy toll of all kinds, and because of the extreme cold, the lack of sunshine, and the shrinking food supply, nature produced creatures smaller. Self preservation is the first law of nature. If man had not lived before the Ice Age, he most certainly would not have drawn pictures of the animals he saw, and fought with for survival. The gigantic flying reptile that many remember in the Hollywood movie Rodan, the Pterodactyl is a magnificent example. The Pterodactyls pictures are all over China, and Japan, the Americas, and even Europe. All over the world, Legends of the gigantic animals are well-preserved in our museums. In the caves men scratched and drew these beasts worldwide.

He left his drawings as a record for the following Generations. When it comes to Giant men, science says the land of the giant men are covered in ice today, and believe me they are drilling through the ice. Some of us have to know. Of course much will end up in private collections for a whole lot of money, for this is the way of man.

There's still plenty of land at the bottom of the ocean to investigate also. Certainly under the North Pole and the Arctic Circle we will find at least many bones of those that lived there before us.The south pole will show us everything,from ancient civilizations,frozen in ice,and technology Frozen in 3 miles of ice.
Granted, there have been times that men have been excited,like in Lichen, in France,in 1613 when enormous bones were found. They turned out to be those of dinosaurs. But there have been times that they were not, and the Catholic Church and the government lied. This was done they said, for the good of the masses, so as not to upset the status quo.

However history does not lie, when the White Aryan Warriors tell it, for to them lying is a tool of the cowards and the losers. Let us now enter the world of the Giants we know about. The great warrior Chieftain of the unbeatable Teutons won many victories for the Viking Blood before the Roman warrior Marius, defeated and killed him. If you read your history books the Teutons were totally invincible in the days before the gun. The great leader of the Teutons was measured at death, and he was well over 9 foot tall almost 10 ft tall. Another Roman Emperor Maximus was almost eight foot tall, but that was with his helmet on. In his bare feet he measured 7 foot 6, how's that for some facts. In 1850 there was a Hungarian they put on display. he measured 9 ft tall. The Mantra Negron Dinello was 8 foot 7. It was Darwin that said when races of people are crossbred, there is a tendency to revert back to the original type. What I guess I'm saying here, had there been no Giants in ancient times, there would be none today.

It 1858 when science was taking off like a rocket, in the age of discovery, men traveled to the four corners of the Earth, to search and find all things not known. With the church executing Scientists for a thousand years, not much was known. They told you, you could fall off the edge of the Earth that's how much they knew. But misery loves company and the church wanted only power over your life, your mind, and even your soul for eternity. They played a hard game, but it worked for a long, long time, with no books too.Before the age of discovery,there was a thousand years of ignorance.

In the year 1858 a find at Carthage, which is the old Phoenicia, stunned the world. It was reported in All the major newspapers. What the wise men found was a sarcophagus of giants, or a sealed tomb, and giant human skeletons were found. This was hushed up as quickly as possible and carefully too. So much of the ancient records were destroyed by the Catholic Church, and the rest went to the secret libraries, and the secret societies. However some of the Pagan writers said they were from the church, and their work resurfaced centuries later. The ancient Pagan writers tell of a giant human skeleton 22 cubits long. Historians up until the time that the ancient city of Troy was dug up, laughed at the silliness of the legend. Once the site of Troy was excavated, they chuckled no more.

It is a fact when the long bloody war at Troy was being Fought, a massive giant was killed in battle by the warrior Apollo. The dead giant was paraded before the entire Army for all to see. Another great Pagan writer whose work survives to this day, wrote a book on the volcanoes of Greece. In this great work Abde Pegues tells us on the mystical island of Thera there were enormous giant skulls laid out, as offerings to the Gods. The truth Waits outside your religion, and there's still plenty of time to learn. It is interesting to note that in the city of Troy, the world was stunned when the swastika was found in all the temples of the fabled city. Not only at Troy, but almost all of the ancient cities dug up, used this mysterious emblem. In ancient India the temples had swastikas on their walls, and it was considered an Indian sacred symbol. The swastika to the old minds, also is the symbol for reincarnation,the wheel of life,then death,then life again.

The world is full of deceivers, and full of liars. It matters not how you play the game, but only if you win or lose. The Jews got their account of the great flood from the Chaldeans, and Babylonians. The Jews mysterious number 7 comes from the Aryan Legends. In fact, they stole all their Legends from the Aryans, when they were the slaves. If you lost the war, you were the slaves.

All over the world in many countries were also stories of Noah's Ark, although Christians think the Jews were the only ones to write about it. But when children grow up, and their brains mature we find the truth, even if we don't look for it. As a civilization we are no longer blinded by the church or their books. Man looks now for the truth, and that will even be harder to find. With the help of the historians the truth will be known, completely. A new age of discovery begins soon.

Before moving on to the many interesting subjects this Masterpiece will discuss, I cannot leave without saying a few words about Noah's Ark. The Ark is probably the 1 story outside of the flood, that the bible really Cashes in on.Christians believe that the Jewish writers of the Bible, have the inside track to all the knowledge of the ancient world. I mean they had everything figured out, including the first man and woman and so on.The day the Catholic Church began losing complete power over the lives of everyone, science did progress, even if it was slow at first. But as the brilliant archaeologist descended upon the ancient world, the stories would soon change. All men would find out that every race of people considered themselves God's chosen people, even though they didn't have A Bible to put together. The Bible is just a collection of many books, and many stories, and it will be read forever.

The knowledge I wanted to pass on to the serpents and the dragons reading the masterpiece, concerns Noah's Ark. With the story of Noah's Ark, millions of Minds were captured. Can you imagine As they began to put together all the pieces, of all civilizations. This was not supposed to happen, whole libraries were dug up from the Babylonians, and the Sumerians. It was time for men to begin to understand the old Legends from the old histories. I'm sure the church was Furious, when they learned of the chaldean Noah, or the Hindu Noah, were found. So after all the brainwashing by the Jewish writers of the Bible, we learned we were duped. We were played like a child would play a game.We stared at ignorance in the mirror,but we learned.

It seemed that every single civilization in the world, had the story of Noah's Ark, and even had many of the stories in the Bible. Even far away places like ancient India had stories of the flood, and even had a very similar story to Moses floating down the river. When all the stories of the world were put together, they were pretty much the same. I guess if it was excellent mind control in one place, it would be excellent mind control anywhere.

I hate to repeat this because I know I've mentioned it several times before, but that's just how valuable it is, and I don't want anyone to miss it. If you can't understand that, I mean because you're an extra fast person, that's just too bad. I want to make sure everyone goes along for the ride. I think it's very ironic, that it was through the legends of all the Aryan tribes, and the pagans, that the Jewish writers received all their knowledge. It was only then after assembling all the great stories, that the Jewish writers of the Bible, wrote that the men of the knowledge were evil and had to be killed. You either believed things their way, are you were considered a heretic which is Punishable by Death.Hundreds of thousands were tortured or burned to the stake,some only had a page out of a book.

Always it amazes me how the Jewish consequence called Christianity took over the minds of the empire. One has only to ask any Arab or Islamic Warrior about the Jews, and they have all taken a blood oath To Kill Them All. They will tell you they are the great deceivers of mankind, and that they had no real history, so they had no choice but to steal everyone else's.

You know it's so funny how the Jews traveled the roads of the Catholic Church, in their command positions.They had the Catholic church in their pockets. Learning was forbidden for over a thousand years, and all books were confiscated. There was no education allowed. If there was a school,they taught the bible. The Only learned men lived outside the empire,or traveled in and out for business.The jews went out alot,and stayed the wise men.

This is the only reason why Christianity took over In Europe, and it is also the Jewish Blueprint to power. It took a long time for the Europeans to wake up, but when they did, all hell broke loose. The wheels of karma would spin quickly. In Europe money could buy you almost any position in the church,no matter where you came from,it was all about the money,like it always is.

After sending Christian Soldiers to go out and conquer the world, in the name of the church of course, the fat rats in the Robes of the church, became even more powerful. As the thousands of ships came back to Europe, fully loaded with gold, the Bishops, the Kings, and all royalty, in fact became extremely wealthy. It was a fantastic plan And it worked. The Jews were in an extremely powerful position, since no one in Europe was educated for a thousand years, they truly were the keepers of all knowledge. It worked so well, until the cloak of the church was cast off, and the power came down on them. I'm getting way ahead of my world history but I want the serpents and dragons, the wise ones, to know it all.

You know With the invasions of North and South America, the Christian Warriors fleets of ships,were supposed to be going to spread the word of Christ to the Far Corners of the Earth. What in fact did happen, was the rape, pillage, and plunder of several continents. Never before in man's long history has any group of people known such wealth. Just out of Mexico and Peru, The Catholic Church made enough gold to fill many fort knox's. The Spanish conquistadors took it all in South America, not just Peru. The Conquistadors traveled through many jungles to get to even the hidden spots, and they also searched all the temples on all the mountains. The Serpent and dragon idols were smashed, and all evidence of their civilization was destroyed. I realize that money makes the world go round, and I'd rather have it than be without it, but the church sent Christian armies To get their gold.

This is the deal that the Jewish wise men made, to the courts and followings of every Kingdom in Europe. Every group of royalty, in the hundreds of Kingdoms of Europe, had their Jewish advisors. The Jewish advisors to the Thrones of Europe, we're the only ones that realized the international affairs that had been going on for thousands of years. The Jewish advisors were well aware of the gold in Mexico and South America, and the Jewish advisors knew the Phoenicians had been coming to South America for gold for thousands of years. Only because of our satellite mapping, and our special cameras that see through the jungles, were we able to locate pyramid complexes on the jungle floors. The British ended up sending archaeologists and soldiers of course up the Amazon River all the way to its beginning, at the bottom of the Andes Mountains. It was there they discovered the pyramids, and met with the Indian tribes to find out who built those. The Indian tribes only called them the ancient ones, and said they had been there long before the tribes even existed at that location. They also told the British archaeologist That there were lights coming from these pyramid complex for centuries. Ships came up the Amazon River, and all along the banks of the Amazon, where ruins of some ancient civilization. The British scientists were quick to realize, this was Phoenician writing. Of course they took back to Europe, some of the inscriptions, but the writing was on the wall, and everybody knew.

The Phoenicians are mentioned in the Bible several times, and All civilizations have known about them. Of course for the masses we only get part of the story, cuz this is the way of men.

You know it's funny, the historians have always told us, that it was the Phoenicians that brought us the alphabet, and this was their contribution to civilization. So that man could learn to read and write, and Converse with each other. No one ever told us the truth, that it was the Phoenicians that were bringing back the gold from the Americas.

So the only knowledge we really have about the Phoenicians, is what is mentioned in the Bible, but it was also mentioned a lot by the Roman Army and Navy. The Phoenicians were their rivals, and they fought major Wars for the wealth. But let us not forget the Phoenicians were sailing the open oceans, going Intercontinental back before the time of Christ, thousands of years ago. Of course they never said a word about it, but who would have. It is work like this, that makes the Masterpiece special, because like the satellites that orbit the Earth taking pictures, we try to open up new areas of Interest, and New Roads to old places.

Some of the Wise men say, Phoenicians were related to the Jews, and they were, of this I am certain. It makes one Wonder how much the Jews actually knew about the golden South America, and the trips that the Phoenicians made.

I'm sure that the royalty all over Europe made deals with the Jewish so-called advisors to get the gold, of this I am sure also. It was only a matter of time before plans we're Drawing up to go get the gold for themselves. The Jewish advisors of Europe's kingdoms had a very high place right from the start. The Jews were not welcome in any other country in the world, but in Europe they made these poor kingdoms power houses. Because let's not forget the Golden Rule, he who has the gold makes the rules. The gold hunting hungry Europeans would never forget the lessons that the Jewish advisors gave them, and they would forever cement there high place in Europe because of this.

The Jewish Blueprint to power would only work in Europe. Europe was the powerhouse of the world, and of course Europe was great enough for a people that had no country for thousands of years. Not only would we find many Jewish advisors to the crowns of hundreds of Kingdoms in Europe, and advisors to Kings and Queens. We also found them hidden in the robes of the church. It was a brilliant plan, and it worked. That's the Jewish consequence. Christianity, slowly took over the empire that was once Rome. Of course there was a jockeying 4 positions of power. It is no secret today, but a lot of gold could buy you a position of power. Especially if you were from the rich families. Many a Cardinal and many a Bishops office was paid for in gold.Nothing was more powerful than gold,and of course it paid for position and prestige.

Like a huge chess game, As the advisors rose up in ranks and wealth, they became even more powerful. They played the kings and queens and their armies and navies, to their own advantage. And of course all the hundreds of rulers of the Kingdom's paid their advisors for knowledge, to their own advantage. For they were playing a chess game too. These two Powers emerged, German Royalty and Jewish Advisors, and they ran a master plan on the entire world, and brought Europe to its pinnacle of power.

How masterful and how daring this plan really was.It is so great and masterfull that no one even noticed, and no one was able to put together this plan for over a thousand years. Remember that anyone in Europe that had an education was exiled, and no one else would receive one. All the books were confiscated, and went to the catacombs of the Vatican, where they were never seen again. The elite or ruling class of Europe we're only two ready to form this Alliance between the royal families of Europe, and the Jewish advisors and financiers.Let us not forget thousands of years ago, when the Jewish homeland had Solomon and many other wealthy and Powerful leaders, that the Jewish people had great wealth. The trade routes of the entire world traveled through there, and the merchants and salesman and Traders became extremely wealthy, trading with every country from India and China, all the way to Europe. All Nations Caravans came through ancient Israel, and that is why that land was so valuable. Of course the Roman Legions dispersed The entire population after the death of Jesus on the cross. There were many other reasons, but Jesus was the final straw that broke the camel's back. Now all of that money that did flow through the so-called land of milk and honey, now went into many others pockets.

I'm sure the Jewish leaders after settling in Eastern Europe, began to plan for how they were going to be a major Force in Europe. They planned centuries ahead, and they planned well. I bet they couldn't wait to talk to the leaders of all the kingdoms. After all they were Jewish and shared the same blood that's Jesus Christ had. They were according to them, God's chosen people, and if you wanted to go to heaven for eternity, then they believed it. One has to wonder if they truly went for just the gold, cuz they're certainly was a lot to be had. I'm sure when the Jewish advisors began Consulting with the kings of the many kingdoms, that the talk soon led to subjects like, where did the Jewish kings and Families bury their gold. Solomon's Temple was said to have had tons of gold and precious stones underneath it. Where was the Ark of Covenant buried. The wise men said that was buried somewhere on Temple Mountain too.

All the treasures,were buried on Temple Mountain somewhere, there was plenty of room, networks of underground tunnels, and just plenty of places to hide the wealth. I'm sure the Jews told the kings and queens they knew exactly where everything was, including the spear that went into Christ when he was on the cross, and the actual cross itself. The Jews also told the kings and queens they knew exactly where the Ark of Covenant was, their most treasured relic. Of course they Told of the extreme wealth of King Solomon, who did Bury it all on Temple Mount. The Jewish advisors and financers did have all the knowledge of where everything was back in their ancient Homeland, especially around Jerusalem.

The black spiders weave a tangled web, but of course they know how to navigate it.The Jews were no different. Imagine how it really was. The Jewish historians that were now in Europe had the ears of all the rulers, because after all, doesn't everyone want to get rich. What an alliance they formed. The Jews had no Homeland for thousands of years, but they're Treasures were still deeply buried on Temple Mount or close by. Eventually of course the rulers of hundreds of Kingdoms in Europe called together each other for special celebrations. You might ask yourself what were they celebrating, and the answer would be, they were celebrating all of Solomon's gold that they were going to bring home.By them I don't mean the kings and queens of Europe, but I mean their armies and their navies. I'm sure they had hundreds of lightning raids, but of course this was going to take a great deal more. Crusades Eventually were organized, my favorite Crusade had over 30,000 of Europe finest Knights. These 30,000 knights were the baddest Warriors in the world at that time, and it was one of the biggest armies the world had ever seen. Especially when you take into consideration, they all were heavily armed with heavy metal helmets and breastplates. All vital areas of the blood flow were also covered, even behind the knees. The feet were also armored, so were The Arms and the hands. The Viking warriors from Europe would be heavily armed to the teeth and no one, no one could stand in their way. This was the first crusade, and the religious zeal was strong. The holy Warriors were told they were going to get the Holy Grail, the cup that Jesus and his disciples drank out of at the Last Supper. This was the same cup, that Mary Matalin held up to the bloody body of Jesus When he was on the cross. Jesus was nailed to the cross, hands and feet, and they were held there by spikes. The blood that came from them, was collected in the Holy Grail by Mary Matalin. This cup the Holy Grail, men would fight Wars for, and this is the power of the Holy Warriors and their religion.

The 30,000 knights we're told they would also be blessed with the cross that Jesus was crucified on, and they would fight for it, and return it to Rome, and this they did. The Knights were also told they had a good chance of digging up Solomon's gold and diamonds, that were hidden on Temple mount somewhere, and the Jews would tell them where to dig.

Make no mistake, the Knights knew only too well, that part of the riches of the Middle East would be theirs. Many said nothing, but raised their swords and battle-axes to the holy war. This is the way of men, and I'm sure it was well thought out, but they were all hoping to get rich too. I'm sorry for the religious Fanatics,that might be reading this book, but many of the Holy Warriors went for the chance to get rich, quick. that's it.

You know it's funny, the Jewish Blueprint to power was awesome In Design, in the hundreds of Kingdoms inside Europe. They were usually and greatly influenced. But make no mistake, it was that it was the chance to create wealth like they had never known before.The Viking tribes that ruled and owned every inch of western europe,were on a mission,that would pave the road ,for them to become the most powerful nations on earth.This is politics at the highest level.

The Ark was found,and so was the Grail,and the Cross,the spear was found. The Knights Templer's looked for 9 years,and found everything at their fortress on Temple Mountain.

Make no mistake please,The Knights took home enough gold,silver,and jewels,for several countries,plus of course whatever they could stash away from all the others.The plan worked so well,and most never caught on.

PART 2, OF THE MASTERPIECE   BY GERALD JOHNSON

In the masterpiece, I have spoken of all the Teutonic tribes. We will talk at Great length about the Angles and the Saxons, from the Vandals to the Celtics. We will talk about the Jutes and the Norseman, and we will talk about the Goths, Great Danes, and the Franks. I have gone to Great Lengths to talk about the lands that became theirs, by the trial of combat. Nothing belongs to anyone in this world unless you can hold it militarily, this is the way of man. There were so many tribes in the Roman Empire, and of course, we have only touched upon them, but If this is the masterpiece, it will be the only great book written, telling the truth about the blonde, brown, and red-haired tribes, that basically conquered the world. In the land area, all these tribes came from, it's only about 5% of the total of the Earth. These were magical people, with magical weapons, and ships. There will never be another book written like the Masterpiece that is for sure. So I'm taking the time to research all the Viking histories, and haven't missed any really. I have researched these great warriors for 40 years, to collect all the right information.

I wanted to write something to make everyone reflect on just who they are, and from what tribes they came from. All the Viking countries have contributed greatly to this thing we call civilization. All Viking countries whether it was Ireland, Britain, France, or Spain, or 20 other countries, were basically interconnected. In that time a thousand years ago, there were no thoughts of belonging to a world situation. The Viking tribes from whichever country in northern Europe, only northern Europe, assembled every 9 years at the greatest of all temples, Uppsala, in Sweden. In earlier chapters, we went into the blood cult where 9 Vikings are sacrificed, and the Sacred Groves, where horses and dogs are also sacrificed to Odin and Thor. I went into detail about the solid gold chain that you can see from 50 miles away, that the Vikings had stretched out on the mountain tops. This was their sacred land. The name Sweden has the word Eden in it, and believe me this was considered their Garden of Eden. This was the number one Pagan site that produced the world's number one Warriors. The Goths led, they were the strongest tribe, since the days of them leaving Atlantis. That was the original homeland of the Aryans. Before they were done, it would go all the way to Tibet and India. Enjoy the complete history, of a fantastic group of tribes. Many wise men say under the ice of the north, part of Atlantis awaits us. The ice age, and also the massive melting of the thick ice drove all the tribes out.

The reason we're talking about the great temple of Uppsala again is to explain, the power of these people. But also to explain the Pagan religion and thought. We will talk more about the Swedes because when you talk about the best of the best, you have to talk about The Warriors from Sweden. History calls them the Goths. They were the best of the best, even though their country today is so small in the Affairs of the world today. It wasn't then, but of course, when the Goths crushed Rome they brought along all the Scandinavian tribes. You know it's funny, Sweden is a fairly large country, but most of it it's covered with ice. It is only along the southernmost areas that the population ever was. But when the Swedes were ready to roll, with sails up, all the other Vikings in the area wanted to go for the sheer adventure of it all. I really don't think there's anything I can say, to make you realize how great this Viking Nation was,because all other Viking tribes wanted to be just like them, and they were. They all intermingled and partied together, sometimes all through the winter months. They all made a lot of cash with the Goths, and they were the leaders. It was their time to collect great wealth and every one of them did.

The Viking Blood from Sweden was extremely magical, and their Warriors were extremely large and brutal. The battle axes were there best friends. Let me say now how it was before the Christians, the average Viking had 40 wives, or 40 concubines, sexual old ladies. The average Viking since the beginning of time had approximately 50 children if he was not killed in battle. The Christians way of life stole this awesome way of life, from the greatest warriors in the history of the world. What their enemies could not take in battle, they took away with the bible.

This is the way it really was, it gave the Vikings an army that was their own. This is one reason they were totally Invincible in battle, it was a family affair. Our Viking history has been denied us but not anymore.

 In the country of Islam the world knows they had many women in their harems, but just how many people know, the Vikings had three times as many. You know it sure is funny the Vikings made it to the very top and called the shots for the old Roman Empire, which was all of Europe. The Viking history was soon to be taken from them piece by piece. For that truly is also the way of men, jealousy is a very strong power. If you tell somebody something enough they're going to believe it.

I've mentioned several times in the masterpiece about the 26,000-year cycle. Where the star constellations that make up the zodiac, one by one take their place in our skies. When the 26,000-year cycle is completed, the poles of the earth North and South become inverted, the water of the Earth Becomes highly active, and great floods happen. Modern scientists tell us there are also at this time heavy volcanic action under the oceans and earthquakes, and the world changes dramatically. The ancient civilizations of the Aryans and the Egyptians have left behind a roadmap for us to follow, but only the wisest and most studied are able to read it. This is why we have the secret societies. The Treasure of the ancient knowledge must be guarded, from those that would destroy it, or keep it for their own. The Catholics, the Persians, the Hindus, the Jews, and all other religions, or races, Talk about the ice ages. No one really knows, not even today, how long they really lasted. All we know is when it got cold enough all the northern countries, especially the Viking countries migrated. Odin led his tribe out of Atlantis. Some men say Atlantis sank overnight, Other say it broke up into pieces over a million years. This is what we're dealing with when we talk of ancient history. Because the ancient Library of Alexandria was destroyed, and the Hall of Records from Egypt never saw the light of day, we are left guessing, and in the dark. Because of historians like myself, we will construct man's long history. But my favorite part, of course, is the Vikings, and the contributions they made to this world, it' still lives with us today. The hall of records of the Egyptians, and Alexandria, and the 500,000 books destroyed, and many fires hid our awesome history from us. They think we are stupid, and they tell lie after lie to cover their tracks. Someday they must be pressured to show us everything. We must demand, or we will never know the truth.

Some Wise men turn to the east, with their ancient civilizations, that go back even further than ours. We come to a place high in the Himalayas between the two tallest mountains.This is where paradise was supposed to have been. This is where man's recorded history was found.

There was a man Sturluson, in his time was the greatest Of the historians. He chose to specialize in the Voyages and The Wanderings of God's chosen tribe, the Aryans. In Sturluson's sagas, the Aryans came from the northern lands, where the sun shines for 6 months straight. These were the sons of Light with their long blonde and red hair.

Their story starts in the land of Atlantis, And the old Viking records say it was Odin that led them out of it, to Sweden, Norway, and Denmark. Odin and his followers the Aryans, drove as far as the Don River, which is in modern Russia. Is it any coincidence, that white men are called Caucasians, for these mountains are the region that Odin and his followers settled in. They followed the mighty Odin from Sweden, and Frey, another of the Viking gods. Frey has another name that is more known to historians as Yngve. From the north, he founded the ancient Kingdom at Uppsala. It was this great Viking that started a long line of Kings right there.

The Goths who were also called Gotar, were the tribes that were the backbone of the Teutonic invasions of Rome. The Viking Army spread across the world, they conquered all the way to India. The Goths sacked Rome, and along the way, Sacked everybody else. India would be known as the land of the Aryans. Much later in Europe these stories would all come alive in the operas of the 19th and 20th century.No one was even aware of their ancient history, but when the age of discovery came, they were shocked.

You know it's really funny, we speak about this 26,000-year cycle, that the Egyptians told the rest of the world about, but we forget to say how the hell did they know about it. The governments of the world and the churches have hidden from us, our ancient past, and allow us to know absolutely nothing, so that they may rule in confidence. They tell us the oldest civilizations were between 4,000 years, and 6,000 years. All of our recorded history they only let us know about, 4 to 6000 years of our history. And then they tell us it was Adam and Eve, the creation in the Garden of Eden, they're lying. The only way they can stay in power, is they keep the nation's so doped up, the people don't even think about it.

The ancient Library, and perhaps the biggest library, the world will ever know was in Alexandria, ancient Egypt. Do you think there was anything they didn't know? Someone set fire to this building or Library, and 500,000 books. That's a half a million books destroyed, or so they say. I wonder where all the good books went, Probably to the Vatican. That was 500,000 books of the world's ancient history, and once gone, any ruler could make up whatever he wanted to, as long as he knew where all the gold was. It took even the Viking Nations A Thousand Years to cast off the chains of our minds from the Catholic Church. We were allowed to know nothing, just what they told us. But today we are no longer enslaved at all, and around the globe, people are waking up, and an ancient world is being discovered. To some of us, that's a great thing, it's very exciting, and we will not stop until we know it all, or at least most of it.

Inside of the Great Pyramid in Egypt, was supposed to have been the Hall of Records. The Hall of Records were the records of man's history since he was human enough to remember it. In the Hall of Records, everything was recorded, and this is why once the Europeans broke in, they said there was nothing there. But then they sent thousands of ships to North and South America to take the gold, the Indian civilizations had been collecting for thousands of years. Of course, they wanted no one else to know, but modern wise men are piecing it altogether believe me. Underneath all the pyramids whether it's Egypt, Middle America, or South America, were many passageways, with many secret rooms. They don't bother to tell us about one thing they ever found, of course, unless it didn't mean anything at all. There's a new light burning in the minds of men, and because of books like this, all will be revealed, and those that don't like that, they know what they can do with it. All these pyramids all over the world, and they want us to believe it was so they can see The Stars better. The pyramids performed many functions, from power plants to vaults for the gold.

 All those underground passageways that link up all the pyramids together are also hooked up to a big tunnel system, that goes into the Earth, to underground ancient civilizations. You know it's funny, all the thousands of ancient markings and hieroglyphics all over the walls Of the pyramids, and all the secret passageways Underground, no one ever let us know. It was Napoleon who found the Rosetta Stone, and with this one stone, his savants or geniuses, we're allowed to break the code of the Egyptians, and I mean the ancient Egyptians, of which no one knows too much about. Let's thank the historians though, because the deck is stacked against them, and of course we must remember, that archaeology and the rest of History's tools are only a few centuries old. We tend to think it's been going on for thousands of years, and the sad truth is, it hasn't. But in today's world, the people do want to know, and believe me I will do my part.

Man is very much like all other animals in nature, and every spring, the male animals meet, to see who has the right to rule, and the create babies. This is the law of nature, like it or not. and it's also the philosophy of the human tribes.

Science admits to the great ice ages, that once covered most of the land masses. It is a fact that Sweden, Norway, Canada, the northern United States, most of Europe, to name just a few were covered with huge ice sheets. Modern scientists Tell us that the melting of the ice ages started About 50,000 to 13,000 years ago. As much harm as the ice age did, it also created many great things. It is from these gigantic icebergs and glaciers, on the tops of the highest mountains, that the rivers of the world begin. So it seems that nature, or the spirit of the Earth, has a great plan and scheme for her ways. Mother earth is the oldest deity on earth, and she has been worshiped as long as man has been here.

It is most interesting to note that Plato and Herodotus both believed that Sweden and her Islands were part of Atlantis. They were not the only great thinkers that believed this, thousands more agree. As Sweden was covered with ice, and the Ice Age kept moving across the land mass, the tribes of Sweden migrated all the way to Asia and further. Once the ice started melting, it never stopped, it only grew stronger and stronger, until it became dangerous and deadly. The rivers of water were many times more powerful than anything on earth today. The melting of the ice from the Ice Age created the biggest floods in the history of the world. Tibet and India were the only safe places to settle. They were considered the rooftop of the world, and they were.

Many of the tribes went into India, perhaps the oldest civilization on Earth. It's hard to call it at this point, but I promise someday we'll know exactly. When the ice finally stopped receding, there was another migration of many Teutonic tribes, back to their Homeland. The pages of History, tell us that the ice did not melt in even stages, and in the middle of Sweden, was the very last to melt. The scientists can tell this by close examination of the mud and the clay Earth that was left behind. Even in the north of America, there are distinctive marks left like mounds of giant boulders the stretch for Endless miles. This to the geologist is proof exactly where the ice age stopped.

It is calculated by the Best Western Minds, that on a sunny year, the ice of the Ice Age, would melt 2000 yards. The markings left on the Earth by the great mass of ice, show the melting started in the southernmost part of Skane or Scania. Scandia gives its name to Scandinavia of modern man.

The greatest minds of the geologists and historians tell us that the southern part of Sweden and Norway were submerged beneath the ice for thousands of years. But finally, Sweden became an island in a big sea. As the years went on, the rest of Sweden came out of the water, and Norway too. Historians say the east of Sweden was the last to come out, she Looked like an island. At this time in man's history, Ostergotland and Upland together formed only a small strip of land in the icy ocean. Though in the south of Sweden and Norway they did rise, they found themselves connected to Denmark, and of course the rest of Europe then. This made travel between the countries easy and the tribes did mix. It was at this time due to the great upheaval of land, that the Baltic became an Inland Sea. Whereas before she had been the ocean. This area and age is gone, It's nothing like it is today. Today it is divided into the Three Kingdoms of Sweden, Norway, and Denmark. In those thousands of years, Scandinavia was one land and remained that way until the battles of the night century.

When Charlemagne was setting up his Empire, over the old Roman Empire, the other tribes fought for their own kingdoms. Man is a predatory animal, and he like the others, marks out his own kingdom.

Historians have found human settlements that date back to 6000 BC or 8000 years ago. These first so-called settlements were found in the south of Sweden. There have also been found ancient traces of settlements in the uppermost North of Scandinavia all along the coast. The Viking scientists said the Ancient Settlements were there even though the glacial periods. The rest of Scandinavia, along the coast, stayed free. This must have kept the ancient Vikings real happy, to have their homeland along the coast. Then all they had to do, was push one of their ships into the water, and it was on again.

It is interesting to note that these Scandinavian tribes endured much like the Eskimos on the coast of Greenland. It should have been named Iceland, for Greenland is covered with ice, except along the coast. But the names were reversed on purpose, so that the settlers would all go to Greenland. This is a fact, the tangled webs we weave. Once again the traces of ancient civilization have been found in the extreme North of Scandinavia in Lapland. No date has been given, and I wonder why. Extremely Interesting to note that iron or Steel would rust and crumble to dust in 7,000 years, so of course only traces of man can be found in places that are older. This region of the world has been grossly ignored, and I ask myself what are they trying to conceal.

Not much is known of Sweden and Norway, except by Greek explorers. It wasn't until 1939 Viking Chieftains were found buried in their ships. It is not known what year the Aryans came out of Scandinavia, and began their long migration to the Highlands of the Himalayas. But what is known, is they had no choice. The total Destruction of the northern continent and freezing temperatures at Scandinavia drove the tribes to Central Asia. The legend says that Odin led the tribes through Asia. The floods kept them going until they reached the rooftop of the world which is Tibet. It is here the Aryans lived and died until the waters receded far enough to see countries below them. In India today as one digs through the layers of dirt, one can easily find the traces of the great flood. They can also find the traces of enormous earthquakes. As they dig through the layers of dirt, one can find houses that are flattened with families caught inside. Many of the bones of the skeletons were broken from falling objects. There is no sign of battle or War, only of mass destruction. Because of the work of the modern archaeologist, we know that natural disasters even changed the course of India's Mighty River, the Indus. It is from the bringer of

Life the Indus, that India gets her name. We now know that once the waters had receded, the Aryans moved north, and some of the tribes moved into the extremely fertile lands of Northern India. Legend says it was here, that the Aryans would call home. In modern times as the world looked through the Sanskrit writings, they discovered that Sanskrit was the mother tongue of All European languages. By putting them all up against one another, it was easy to see that even Greek and Latin, had come from Sanskrit.

As the great historians sifted through the legends, they found that the enormous Aryan tribes had gone their own way. Now as modern historians look back, they realize that the Aryan tribes were the ancient ancestors of Rome, Greece, Germany, England, the Persians, and many other nations. When the Aryan tribes split, When the ice was gone, most of the Aryan tribes headed back to what is Europe today. They founded great civilizations, just like they always did. A lot of the Aryans tribes that were still in the highlands, went over the mountains, into India. When the Aryan tribes split and went in different directions, it opened up a new chapter in the history of Europe, and of course Tibet, and India, especially India.

The Aryans for thousands, and maybe tens of thousands of years, had driven their herds of cattle, sheep, and goats wherever they went. The Vikings were great meat eaters, as most strong men are, and their favorite meal, of course, was a huge steak. A few of the tribes settled around Anatolia, and their civilization flourished. Other tribes traveled all the way to the beautiful and Lush lands of Persia, which is Iran today. Way back then that whole area was green and not sand. Today Persia is called Iran which is a word made from Aryan, or other words they were family. When the Mongols and the other Asian tribes centuries later came, the blood was mixed thoroughly. And this is the reason why the Iranians today have a different complexion, due to the mixture of their blood. The Indo-Iranian language is strongly related to the Indo-European languages of modern Europe. Like a mighty river that breaks up into smaller streams and tributaries, the Aryan blood was the source of many civilizations.To the historian, this is a big deal, to the seekers of the truth it will be too. It was the Greek historian Plato that explained that the Aryans built the pyramids, and of course, the natives claimed them after they moved on. In Plato's Day, he called the people of Egypt, Ethiopians. The seeds of Aryan civilization

were planted into the soils of Rome, Sparta, Athens, Babylon, and many civilizations. In the mass migration from Europe, to the highlands of the Himalayas, in the great flood, even the Jewish tribe went along, it was a mass Exodus for survival. The pages of History tell us that among the tribes that crossed the Himalayas into India, the Jews went with them. But they were always outcasts just like they were in most places, and they did not remain in India for very long.

They started their Journey Back, after the great flood Waters we're gone. Back to the area around Egypt, this is what the secret society's say. The Jews were enslaved by many people, the Egyptians, Babylon, and several other countries. This is where the Jews got there Stories of the great flood, Noah's Ark and many more. They stole them from those that had enslaved them, put them in a book, and took credit for everything. This is the reason why all the Arab Nations Are at war with Israel and have taken a blood oath to destroy them. The Arabs have screamed for centuries that the Jews stole their history, and claim it as their own, and they truly did. But this is part of their blueprint to power, and all men struggle for power, so that doesn't make them a bad group. The Jews are actually an Arab tribe and share the same father, Abraham. The Masterpiece will force all to learn.

The Indo Iranians lived for the longest of time in the land of Persia, but like man always does, the tribes split again. It was at this time in history, that the tribes that had pushed into the Hindu Kush mountains, realized they had picked a dream Homeland, and they deserved it, and they got it. Seek and you will find, and if you don't, keep looking. It was here That the Aryans finally found their Homeland. It was everything they ever wanted, for raising their families and living the good life. The grassy hillsides were heaven on Earth to their flocks of sheep, and their herds of cattle.

This is not to say that India did not have people when the huge group arrived, because they certainly did, but most of the population of India was in the south. India's Legends tell of gigantic earthquakes, and title waves, and floods. Wise men say that India had once been part of the Great continent of Lemuria and that ancient continent went from India to the Americas.Unlike Atlantis where most is covered in ice today, which was water, before it turned to ice, it was flooded. The rest of Atlantis would be on the ocean floor buried in 500 feet Of dirt. The only remains of the ancient civilization the great historians call Lemuria are the south sea Islands and Australia.

To understand the evolution of the races, one must first understand all the writings of all the major religions. And I mean all the major religions. A wise man once said, sometimes one must go outside his own religion, to understand everything.

If your mind is consumed by only the Christian Bible, one's intelligence will only grow so far. The Jewish Doctrine speaks slowly, and symbolically. The real light of learning comes from the Persian teachings, and also the Hindu Aryans. For the real secret of the complete truth, one must go to the Secret Doctrine of the Hindu Aryans, for those are much older.

The Secret Doctrine of Tibet and the other nations that gather along the Himalayas, go back as far as 60,000 years, and this comes from the secret societies. All wise men from Buddha to Jesus spent a lot of time in this area, talking to those that quite possibly know everything.

The Aryans drink the flowers of the Himalayas, and the plant is called Soma. The spiritual vision that comes only with Soma, separates the men from the boys. When under the influence of the magical Soma, one has the vision of the Gods, and all is revealed. One is truly Reborn when he sees His Body As Only A Shell, and he sees it from a distance. The mystical drink of Soma was never given to the population, or even to the lower ranks of the priests. Many of the lower ranks Fast for days on end with only water to drink, and after anywhere between 7 and 14 days, the Spiritual Vision will come. This is why great spiritual leaders like Gandhi from India, and many others were so thin. 14 days is the usual time for visions, wise men say it always works.This is one way, there are better ways.

Hitler from Germany, when he became initiated to the higher workings of life, chose the black magic shortcut, Soma. Some say it is a flower that you find on a certain cactus, and some say you find it on the hilltops, and Timothy Leary made it himself, love special delivery, or LSD.

Soma is the secret knowledge of the Serpent's or wise men, and when swallowed the Cosmic Chronicles are viewed. Everything that has ever happened on Earth, has left an imprint like a footprint, of which can be viewed, and the high priests call this the Cosmic Chronicles.

Now all the wisdom has been presented to the serpents and Dragons, those that have to know, and those that will know. I am in the 4th quarter of my life, of which I have enjoyed tremendously. I have chosen this time to give up all the secrets that I have because they were passed down to me by great men and women. This is the way it is done, and this is the ancient way. I have told you the to paths that one can travel, the choice is yours. Thousands of books have been written about how to open the third eye, and how to expand your consciousness, and now you have it all before you. There is no more, you have arrived. This is the search for the Grail. there are two paths, the choice is yours as it is with every great person.

ONE MUST BE REBORN TO ENTER HEAVEN>

THE ONE REAL TRUTH

THE MASTERPIECE LIVES,

You know it's funny, not much of Ancient India was known to the outside world, until the British came and made war with India. The British knew that in India's ancient history Northern India was the land of the Aryans. Like so many other things, all European nations knew nothing about their histories, especially the ancient history. Their rulers thought it might be safer to not let them know anything, because you can control the masses, the stupider they are. But the British were always brilliant, since the days of The Druids. There was always a certain group of men that had to know everything. but it was a long road back for the British, just like it was for every other European nation. To have to start all over with nothing, and the church holding back all science, it's a wonder we still know anything. Western minds are extremely powerful, and could not be brainwashed forever. Creme does rise to the top, always.

But the British had to know everything about their ancient past, so eventually the military was strong enough to search anywhere they so desired. The British came to India, and once they realized just how rich with gold and precious stones India was. They said I think we're going to stay a while, and they did for centuries. India became the jewel in the crown, for the British Empire. The wise men from Britain also decoded everything, and they decoded the ancient Sanskrit language and discovered to their amazement the root of all European languages.

From that point on European language became known as Indo-European. The British were not the only ones, for every Invader into the history of the world, wanted to unlock the Mysteries of this nation. For all nations knew, their secret knowledge of Northern India, was the settlement of the ancient Aryans. All through history, Every Nation wanted desperately to trade for the riches of India, and they had many. The diamonds, the gems, the rubies, the silk, the spices And countless other products. India had always been a wealthy Nation. The Aryans would hold on to this diamond in the Sun, until World War II, but they still control the riches, not the government.

One must remember that although well-educated now, this was not always the case. For the power of the Catholic church had held Europe from knowledge for 10 centuries. It was an evil plan, where only a few, the church, and royalty, made out like bandits.

The Dark Ages are what they called these dark periods, and only the priesthood, held the truth and Power. The knowledge of the priests was unbelievable, and they recorded their knowledge, in what they called their books of knowledge. These books also go by the name of the Vedas. The Aryan books of knowledge were passed down for thousands of years, orally from person to person. Sometimes they sat in great circles and retold Time After Time the history of their people. Let no man or no book put dates on anything Aryan, where they cannot prove them. Modern historians sometimes kept the knowledge in small circles, because it is power and wealth.

The oldest of the books of knowledge are the most sacred of course, and they are called the Rig Veda. This means the verses of knowledge. The Rig Veda is a long and mystical work and has 1017 Aryan poems in it. I guess it was a custom for the Aryans to love to tell of their heroes in Poems. Many of the treasured poems went to there sacred Aryan gods, and many others were to the best of their blood. As a matter of fact, this gigantic collection of work was the world's first literature. It is not possible to tell when the first Aryans arrived, for their homes were built out of light wood and bamboo. They built no false Idols of stone, for they believed their gods were very close, and watching them. The Aryans lived in The Villages of their tribes and kept themselves surrounded by their cattle, goats, and sheep. The archaeologists who hate the Aryans say the dark people were civilized first, but this is a damn I lie. The Aryans made slaves of the entire black race in India, and call them Dasas, which meant Slave.

In 1921 an Archaeologist dug up the famous Mountains of the Dead in India. The British had seen these mountains for hundreds of years but cared less what was in them. Little piles of dark skins and the diggers found baked bricks. This is the reason they say they had an advanced civilization, bricks. The dark people of India are still to this day making homes of big bricks, they crumble and kill tens of thousands every earthquake. so really this shows absolutely no intelligence at all if you ask an intelligent person.

The British after finding the bricks, we're tickled as hell. They used them for ballasts for over a hundred miles of railroad tracks. so they did come in handy eventually.

It is most interesting to note, that in the Dig they found a statue of a bearded man, who had a robe on, with the emblem of a Cloverleaf, that the Irish love so much. At Mohenjo-Daro, there were no temples or places of worship. And it was noted that they too divided themselves into castes, Or classes of people, as the Aryans would do to them also. The excavators did find a statue of a dancing girl, who became known as the dancing girl of Mohenjo-Daro.

Some of the other sites dug up, we find higher civilization, but we also find statues of horses, of which the Aryan brought to India. It was said that the Aryans taught the Stone Age Savages of India quite a great deal. The truth is the truth, and there's no need to sugar-coat anything.

The most Mystic find was about 500 miles south Of Mohenjo-Daro, and we find the double Graves. Each grave has one male and one female, but this is the ancient Hindu custom where the woman goes to the grave

with her husband. It is interesting to note that this practice still goes on, and sometimes the wives are burned at the stake. In the western world this would seem barbaric, however, it was their custom, and so it was done, period.

The Aryans build no walls around their settlements, but Mohenjo-Daro had done this with bricks. In the Aryan Legends, it often speaks of the desire for no fences or walls. For they had no fear of other men, and with many generations of great warriors, why should they.

After Atlantis last Island was drowning they came to India on horses, with chariots and weapons of bronze. It is interesting to note when the cities were dug up, so where the battle axes. Of course, these were the years before guns and gunpowder, and the Aryan Warriors had no fear whatsoever. They had sliced their way from the Arctic regions to the Himalaya Mountains, and further with those battle axes, and believe me they were Legends. The battle axes we're only one of the favorite weapons of the Aryans. The long bows and arrows were also found at all the ancient excavation sites. On their long journey to India, the Aryan Warriors had encountered all the hardships of nature, and they were very brutal. They certainly had no fear of the men they met, to do battle with, for their land.

In the Legends of the Rig Veda, it tells of the storming of the positions of the dark ones. It also tells of their victories in battle against them. They Call themselves The Fair skins, and them the dark. The Rig Vedas go back at least 6000 years, maybe a lot further, for the Legends were passed down father to son for many generations. The north of India was where the Great farming and grazing lands were, and the Aryans took them in the battle against the dark skins. At Mohenjo-Daro, there is a huge mound of dirt, and under the dirt are the dark skins that dared to go into battle against the Aryan Warriors. The Veda Legends are still told today by the Aryan Hindus, for those who seek the most sacred knowledge. The Rig Veda is a masterpiece of information, and their knowledge and Magic come all the way from ancient Atlantis. When the last of Atlantis was being submerged, the Scandinavian lands, especially Sweden were spared. It must be noted that the continents of Atlantis and Lemuria we're both huge, and overlapped each other. It must also be noted that all the continents were hooked together into one called Pangea, and how they broke up, and when they broke up, is really anybody's guess.

The Rig Vedas go much further into the history of the Aryans. Historians cannot agree on the years of the conquest, because the facts are still being gathered. It is such a tedious process. To fit into the scheme set by the Bible, the historians claim the Aryan civilization was only 5,000 years old. Some wise men say, it was many times multiplied older, but one thing is for sure they came, they saw, And they conquered. In reality, when Odin came with the Aryans from Atlantis, it was at least 13,000 years. I'm sure they came in waves many times, science tells us there were mini ice ages, usually after comet or meteor strikes.

We Do know however quite a bit about the Aryan religion, for the high priest always kept great records. The Aryan name is for the family of tribes, but it has another meaning, that meant Noble or the highborn. It is true that the Aryan tribes, fought against each other occasionally, but they always United against their dark enemies, as well as they should have. The ruling Aryan tribe in India was named Bharata and their King was called Rajah. Even today thousands of years later, the Indians call their kings Raja out of respect to the best of the best. The Sanskrit name of India even today is Bharat, after the Fearless and greatest of the ancient tribes.

Another of the famous Legends Goes by the name of Mahabharata, which means the Great Bharata. The king and his cousins, they became the Royal Family. It goes into great detail, of the battles between the Nobles, and gives us great insight into their lifestyles. It seems each separate Aryan tribe had their own high priests, and it was left to them to memorize the great Legends. It was also up to the high priests, after they drink their Soma, to watch over the animal and human sacrifices.

The Aryan tribes were all beef eaters, and their cattle were worth as much as gold. In fact, The Aryan tribes used their cattle as money. The high priests were paid in cattle to watch over the sacrifices and make sure all went well. The Aryan warriors were also the first to drink wine, and it was the Aryans and Vikings that invented beer and whiskey. You can just imagine how many people would run up to the ships, when they saw the Vikings coming, knowing they had whiskey beer and wine, and no one else did at the time. The Vikings could trade all this for anything, and this made them great Traders. The Aryans treated their cattle, with so much importance, it was no wonder that the non-Aryans, the dark skins, worship them as gods. Today in India the cattle are still worshiped, and in that starving Nation, it is estimated there are 10 million cattle.
The Aryans brought civilization to India and took Northern India with the battle ax.The Aryans brought civilization to India, as well as the rest of the world. The custom was the father rules over the family, like the raja rule over the tribe. Today the custom is still firmly in place in India, as well as many of the other Aryan ways. In the Legends of the Vedas, the poems called for Sons to be manly and heroic. The sons were Treasures to the Aryans, to watch out over the cattle, but most important, to bring honor to their family, and tribe in battle. All Aryan men were expected to be heroic Warriors, and all of them usually were. The daughters of the Aryans had little value except as a vehicle for the Warriors to enter the world. This is why dowries were attached to the women, so the new husband would start with a little wealth. If she was not pure on her wedding night there were problems. If she was not a virgin, she brought great shame to her family.

If her vagina did not bleed it was the husband's Duty to kill her. This may seem kind of harsh, but there were no tramps like the 20th century produces. And of course there was no venereal disease, it did not exist in the Kingdom of the Aryans. These were the days when men were men and women were women, and women were only the vehicle for future Generations, not vehicles of lust at the single bars. The laws of the Aryans might seem harsh to the women of today, but because of these laws, Aryan Society prospered greatly. These were the laws of the Aryans and they brought mankind out of Darkness. The women then we're like the women today in the Arab world, they were kept out of the Limelight, and in the kitchen. The women remained at home to rear the children, and the women were not allowed to partake in business Arrangements. The world is so messed up today, however, this is the world we know.

The women were not allowed to be present at the human sacrifices. Only the sons could inherit the property of the fathers, and only the sons fought for it. The American women of today would be shocked at how things were, for they have been granted total freedom, and the American dream is being ripped apart, because of it. American women now go to the highest bidder even if it is another woman. By loosening the controls on the women, the American families are falling apart, and the sacred blood it's been mixed with everyone. In America, the middle class is going to hell, and soon it will become a third world nation possibly.

In the great Vedas, there is no mention of child marriages, but they have them today in Modern India. When Aryan civilization was at its height in India, it was in the northern part called Punjab. It is here that the five Great Rivers of Punjab flow into the great Indus River. It is because of all these ancient Rivers, that the land is exceptionally rich and fertile. The great Himalayas for years went over the mountain passes, then the secret passages were opened. Instead of going over the top of the highest mountains in the world, the passes were found at ground level, which made everything especially easy. Knowledge changes everything doesn't it.

The most famous of the mountain passes is the Khyber Pass, and everyone in that section of the world knows exactly where it's at. It is through the Khyber Pass that many armies have swept into India. The Aryans had it made in Northern India for thousands of years, and they were content to live in their little Garden of Eden. All the Aryan family's Warriors stayed in Punjab, because of the excellent farming, and they stayed, and we're happy for 500 years. At the same time, all the pretty women were getting pregnant every year having many children, and that meant plenty more mouths to feed. No longer could the Aryan Warriors and Families survive just on the Punjab section of Northern India, so they conquered new lands To the east. This time they set up their huge camps around the Ganges River, another of the super important growing areas, that the Bluffs country of India offered to the world. It is only in the last few books of the Vedas, that the Ganges River is mentioned and that is the reason.

The great tribal structure that the Aryans were built on, began its transformation as the Warriors conquered beyond the Ganges River. The warrior in their blood was beginning to boil, and the battle axes were being sharpened, and turning a bright red...

The great tribal structure that the Aryans had built, began its transformation as the Warriors conquered beyond the Ganja river. Just like when Rome conquered too much territory, it proved to be more problems than it was worth. The long list of Conquests of the Aryan Warriors brought many new people and problems under their rulers and laws. But it was here that the Aryan government was born. The ruling Raja required a lot of help from his Noble Warriors. The ruling King now formed the council of the elders and gave them power over their tribes. Of course, this was not done in a democratic Style, for the power belonged to those that dared to take it. The most powerful warriors, of course, received the right to rule, and govern, and the best of them served as the king's bodyguards. Times they were changing, and necessity is the mother of invention. In other words, if you need something, you will invent it.

The king would first go to his priests, and it was there from the high priest's, that he would get the help that he needed. The high priest would help the king in any way he could, in all matters religious or political.

The Aryans gave their civilization, great books, that became the foundation of All European nations. In the 10th book of the Rig Veda, lay the groundwork for the four classes of people, there would be in their society. Keep in mind these four classes of people, and this whole thought process would last for thousands of years.

In the Vedas, gold is the metal most often mentioned, and it was used in their rituals and their sacrifices. India was the land of precious stones and gold, to this very day, there are still open gold and Diamond Mines in India, that the Aryans started thousands of years ago.

By 1000 BC the use of iron, the heaviest metal had moved to Persia from India. The Persians made great use of the iron, for their weapons of war, but also for the metal pins in the harness of the horses, that helped so much the advance of the war chariots. The Aryans that had settled in what is now called Iran were brilliant, and they also led the way in war, and they feared no Nation.

In 1950 the ancient Aryan City of Hastinapura was dug up by the modern scientists, and the archaeologists were thrilled to no end. To the men of wisdom, this was the most powerful city of the Aryan Legends, and now they had proved it was real. In truth, science has had only several centuries to dig up things and places, for it wasn't long ago that they called it the age of discovery. Science now was beginning to have the power, that they had always dreamed of. No longer could the church hold everybody down, and say everything you need to know is in the Bible. But keep in mind these are the same people, that told you the world was flat, what the hell did they know, or were they just lying. The further they dug, the more weapons they found, all of Aryan make and before 1500 BC. There was a whole lot going on in this world Thousands of years before Christ, but the church would have you believe different. In the Rig Veda the Aryan Legend, it is obvious that the Aryans we're being transformed from just the greatest herders of cattle, into agricultural people too. In the Rig Veda barley, wheat, and rice are mentioned, and also lions, and elephants, remember this was India. The Sanskrit name for elephant, translated means Beast with a hand, meaning the trunk.

The leading sport for the Aryans was Chariot racing, just like in Rome, Greece, and Britain. The Aryan poems of magic were chanted not Sung. In the Rig Veda the Aryans never tire of speaking of War, wine, music, gambling, sounds a little like the modern man.

The Aryans also had poems that were put to music and the singing. The musical instruments of the Aryans where the drums, the flutes, and the Lutz. It was from the Aryan race that the slaves learned, and in later centuries, the Indians put song and dance to their worship of the Gods. Nowhere in India today can one find a temple, that does not have dancing girls. But as for the favorite drink of the Aryans, it was Soma with the sweet nectar of the Gods. Soma was drunk by The Warriors and high priests, to prove the existence of the spirit world, with which the eye cannot see. The high priests and those that know a lot about the effects of Soma kept this Secret from the world For thousands of years. It was only in the 1960s in America that men broke through to the other side, once again, and found out just what was on the other side. The Aryan race was not lead by The Blind Faith of Christianity. Soma had shown them thousands of years before Christ, the spirit world. They needed no one to show them the way. Later on, as time went on, thousands of years later, the Aryans were converted to Christianity by the sword, and many great warriors fought and died for their true religion. It is most interesting to note, that Soma Grows All Over the foothills of the Himalayas, of which the Aryans traveled through, and I bet they took their time. It was here in the Himalayas that the Aryans received their true knowledge, and here that they realized they were immortal. The mysteries of Life become quite clear when the powers of Soma are within you. The effects of Soma, we're so powerful and enlightening that peyote the beautiful flower was worshipped, as it should have been.

The biggest celebration of the year was the day of the Soma sacrifice. It was then that the Aryans became one of the Gods himself. Yes, the beautiful flower of Soma helped the Aryans to rip off the chains of Illusion, and break through to the spirit world, and some say the real world. While feeling the effects of Soma, one might even be outside time itself, and astral projection becomes a reality, if one knows how to focus, the power in the right direction. The biggest gift that the Eastern World gave to the West, Was the knowledge of astral projection, when the spirit can fly Beyond the Earthly realms, and on that day alone man is Reborn.

THE SEARCH FOR THE GRAIL IS OVER< IT HAS BEEN FOUND BY MANY, GET YOURS. <

In India, the changes were coming, and India would be much better off than they ever dreamed possible. The height of their civilization was when the Aryans arrived and took it to its Pinnacle of power. Most wars especially in ancient days, one side fought until they had wiped out the other side. This is not what the Aryan armies wanted for India, and the so-called dark skins were allowed to survive. The Aryans taught and instructed them well in, all the jobs that they were assigned to. Those jobs included Carpenters, tanners of the cattle skins, Weavers, and blacksmiths. This was a caste system or a class structure, and it worked well for India for a long, long time. The Aryans by law, forbid the races to mix, and they kept the true knowledge in the hands of their own tribes. As a wise man once said 1 day, to the victor go the spoils and this is how it will always be, till the end of time.

Only the Aryans were permitted to be initiated with Soma, into their Spirit domain, and of course, this was fair. They called themselves the twice-born class, and they most certainly were. It was only the twice-born that could even read or hear the Vedas, and this was a great idea, to keep their own history in their own hands. Many religions and nationalities around the world do the same thing, this is just good common sense.

It is interesting to note, that the Aryans worshiped a network of higher spirits. There were 33 named in the Vedas. Of these, there were four that ruled, and they were Indra, Varuna, Agni, and Soma. Indra was perhaps my favorite, Indra was the God of War, and obviously, the Aryans had a close relationship with Indra, for they were the Masters of War. Wherever they went on the face of the Earth, They were the chosen tribe and proved it on the battlefield.

Indra like Thor In Germanic Legends, also had his Thunderbolts, just like the ones on the throats of the SS soldiers for the high command later in history. Just so everyone does know, on the throats, right at the jugular veins, the SS bodyguards wore the lightning bolts of Thor. That's not the letters, as written on their uniform. Those are lightning bolts.

It was just like Thor, who had power over the Skies. Indra was also the god of storms and had supreme power over the Waters of the Earth. Indras power is greater than the great floods, and the Great Rivers, that brought death and destruction to the World on several occasions. In man's long history, every time a comet, or a meteorite hit the Earth, it sent 600-foot waves around the planet, and drowned all Coastal communities worldwide. Sometimes the tidal waves went inland for hundreds of miles.

Indra was the first great conqueror of the Aryans, and since they were so Greatly Victorious he deserved their worship, and he got it. Never forget those that take care of you, for the list is really rather small. On the night of the Soma sacrifices all looked for Indra to appear, and with everybody's third eye opened by the nectar of the Gods, I'm sure some of them saw Indra. It is written, that Indra drank his Soma in 3 giant gulps every day. It is written that Indra did this to do battle with the Demons of the darkness. I got news for him, The demons are in the daylight too. Indra was the main god for this tribe, that fought all the way from Sweden to the highest mountains in the world, the Himalayas. The Viking tribes would not desert Indra. It is written in the pages of The Vedas, that it is the Thunderbolts piercing the darkness, that releases the Dawn and the light every day.

Varuna is the Aryan God of universal order, and it is Varuna that puts strength into the cattle, and the horses, that the Aryans brought to the rest of the world. It is also Varuna that puts fire in the waters, and the willpower in the hearts. It is Varuna That puts the magical Soma on the mountains. There is a dual Connection in Varuna, for Varuna was much later to become Shiva, who is the highest with the later Hindus.

Agni was the god of fire, and also the spirit of the Sun. Agni's presence was needed for all sacrifices. For Earthly fire was the mirror of the great fire, the Sun. The spirit of Agni was very powerful, and Agni had the power to heal and also destroy all things. Perhaps this is why the surgeon holds heats to the knife before surgery, and this has been going on a long long time. Agni was the power of light, the extreme opposite of Darkness, and on the sacred altars, Agni was the spirit that looked over all rituals. The Aryans were extremely loyal to the spirits around them, and sometimes in them. Because of this one fact of loyalty, is perhaps the biggest reason that they conquered the world. Only after the false religion of Christianity, were the Aryans divided in Mind and Spirit. I'm sure that's exactly why the Jews wrote the Bible so that the Aryans would be enslaved mentally, and every other way. They took their gods from them, so they could try to climb to the top in the Aryan civilization, and they did pretty well until the Germans woke up. Still many in Europe like King Louie the 14th went with all the ancient beliefs, and all the ancient rituals. These beliefs are what pushed the Aryan Nations to the top. King Louie the 14th, was always talking to the wise men of Europe about deserting their ancient gods, to take up a belief in a carpenter from Israel, who did nothing to help the cause of the Aryans. Many great minds believe, that the Jewish Doctrine called Christianity, was brought into play to let the air out of the balloon so to speak. For hundreds of years, the Christian nations fought each other over the divinity of Jesus Christ. Some said he was God, some said he was just a prophet, like all the others. But either way, you had hundreds of battles to settle the score, and every time the enemies of the Aryans laughed At them. Imagine that the Jews wrote in the Jewish Bible that they were the chosen people, and they didn't even have a country for 2,000 years. But because Christianity was brought to Europe, they have the Europeans do their fighting for them, for eternity it still goes on.

But either way you look at it, the population of Europe was in total darkness for 1,000 years, and these were called the Dark Ages, the light of learning was turned off. If it had not been for Napoleon, and then Hitler, the Jewish Doctrine, and the Roman Catholic Church would still have total control over Europe. Turning the Nations away from their gods, actually put them in spiritual slavery. The Jewish Blueprint to power was a great chess game, however, science would end their game, and the Germans loved games too.   CHECKMATE

PART THREE   OF THE MASTERPIECE

 Like Led Zeppelin said, in one of the greatest songs ever written, all things will be revealed. When I began the Masterpiece this is it exactly what I had in mind. Were probably halfway through the Masterpiece, and I've only began to tell my story. It is written in the pages of history, that Churchill and Roosevelt in World War II who made the agreement, that Hitler's knowledge would never reach the light of day, but those two old men are dead, and the complete story is before you. There is no reason for propaganda, however there is a major reason for the truth. A very wise man once said, that the truth is much Stranger, than any lies could ever be. Just for the sake of knowledge, Let it be known that it was Eckhart, that initiated Hitler, and took him to the higher levels, where he needed to be. Eckhart was a member of the secret society of Germany, and this Branch was called the Thule Group. The secret societies with their secret libraries taught the New German leader,all he would need to know.

Last, but certainly not least was the god Soma. Soma was the god of immortality, and the pathway to it. The nectar of the flower was said to be sweet and glorious, and that it's drops brought freedom to man, and protected his body from disease. Here is the message the ancient Aryans chanted. ' May we enjoy with an enlightened spirit, the juice that gives us ancestral riches. O Soma, king, Prolong our existence, favor us and make us prosper. For thou has settled in every joint. O Soma the search for the grail is over,the keys like in Egypt,are in your hands.

Make no mistake the Aryans also we're great nature worshippers, as well as worshippers of the cosmic powers. The Aryans also believed that they were the instruments of the Gods above, and that each was there to help the other, in keeping the balance of all. The Aryans believed that Gods and Men each had their duties to perform, and that it all fit fitted perfectly into the grand scheme of things. The Aryans believed that only when the Gods and man, behaved as they should, that the Universe would properly function, as it was designed to do.

The Aryans knew that truth could always be diluted by illusions. Their high priests chanted their magical chants Around the Clock. The Aryans gave daily sacrifices to the Gods. The high priests said there was Darkness, hidden by Darkness at the beginning, this was an illuminated flood. The first which was hidden by a shell, that one, was born to the power of its own heat.

The writers of these words were initiate's, and masters of wisdom, and with their origin of creation, modern scientists are blown away. Let Me Shine the Light Of Truth once more on the high Priests of the Aryans, for they like the high Priests of all ancient civilizations, held all the knowledge. We call them priests, but they were the scientists of the ancient world. Oh, what a tangled web man weaves. You know it's funny, the ancient Mysteries were knowledge for the ancients. The high priests also said desire, which many centuries later, became known as love, was the force behind creation. Love is the opening door, and love is what we came here for, John Lennon said it the best.

One must also remember when reading the Aryan Vedas, the Bible, the Quran, that their religious writings are written symbolically. Remember the Legends are history in the written form, but the meaning is concealed always. This is why even in the secret societies of Freemasons, there are many degrees, or levels of understanding. Only after the student has reached the higher levels, are the doors of knowledge opened to him. The final indoctrination is made when the initiate is given the sweet drops of Soma, and then all is revealed. It is however not necessary to go through the levels of perception.

Just like the movie said, welcome to the Matrix,and Soma will definitely show you the Matrix, There is no guessing. It's amazing how Soma, and the other mind-expanding drugs were kept from the populations, but I guess knowledge is power, and why share it if you don't have to.

I think the most important part of the Soma experience is the higher levels that men and women are exposed to, and if the initiate has not prepared himself for the grand tour of the cosmos, he will most certainly not understand what is happening to him. This can be

extremely dangerous or deadly to the person who has become experienced, like Jimi Hendrix said. The battle between light and darkness will be conceived by the uninitiated as only a great light show, of Shadows and Light. The Many Colors of the spectrum of light will become a Psychedelic show for the young or the unlearned. If taken before the time is right, the person will have no understanding of what is going on, or what he is seeing. If taken in large doses, the results can be ugly, for most minds are not ready to even consider, the constructions of life and space, and time itself. The building blocks of life,and the patterns that make them up, are there for the initiate to view.The veil of knowledge is lifted for all to see.

The unlearned mind will not be able to understand his views of past lives, and will only be able to consider them a dream. There is no way the unlearned mind can deal with the Raw building blocks of nature, and most will become terrified, when one loses control, and most do.

If shown before their time, this can have serious damages, and sometimes permanent mental problems develop. The long and Winding Road is where one can become aware gradually, and be able to fully enjoy that experience. The shortcut can be taken also,

and this is called black magic, And this is extremely dangerous. One must remember that while under the influence of the magical Soma, when one is exposed to Worlds or levels of perception, that he never dreamed possible. There is spirits of all things, there to confront

you. All things do have spirits, it is just the Good and evil spirits, it is just a matter of your perception. If you see the spirits come to try to take you away, like at death, this can be viewed two ways.One that the spirits are evil, because they are trying to take your life, or that they are good spirits, trying to free your spirit from the prison of the body. It only it is a matter of perception, and perception can only be taught to the initiate through a gradual Process. Grail has a second meaning, in that it does mean gradual. The search for the Grail should be a gradual process, and not a earth-shattering one. This is why in the 1960's in America, it was a spiritual rebirth with the hippies, and the government wanted to stop it at all costs. They enjoyed their population thoroughly brainwashed, and set in their ways. The hippies were not initiated and they viewed their Glimpse at immortality,as only a trip, The masses were told that everything they saw were hallucination, and that was a huge lie.

The hippies of San Francisco opened the doors of perception, and Jim Morrison named his band The Doors after the book, The Doors of perception.f The whole rock and roll movement, was right on time, and they were the pulse of a Nation. The hippies were no more able to deal with the forces they encountered on their Journeys, then Hiroshima was able to deal with the A-bomb.

But in reality,they were the same, for the spirit world Hit the unprepared with the power of a nuclear explosion. Only this one was an inner explosion. As Jimi Hendrix Played in the 60s, are you experienced, this is what he meant.

Jim Morrison of the doors in San Francisco kept it going with Break on through to the other side. You know night destroys the day, the day destroys the night, try to run, try to hide, Break On Through To The Other Side.Telling like it was,and many knew what he was talking about.

A whole generation was tuned into the lyrics of their self-appointed gurus, and they were Enchanted beyond belief. Music became the mystical Pied Piper of an entire generation, and the generation thought, lived, and experienced as one, if only for a while,it was a beautiful thing.

There was a song written about Woodstock, that told of the generations thinking.Hundreds of thousands of hippies descended on New York, for the greatest rock and roll concert in history.

By the time the concert started there were 500,000 hippies that had assembled, and the Army and the state police were called to block the freeways and keep the rest away,it was so out of control.

America was experiencing a spiritual rebirth with the drops of Soma, or its relative. The Cult of a generation was born. Never before in the history of our country, or probably the world,has a generation been so caught up was just loving each other, and it was a truly beautiful experience.

 A whole generation call themselves brother, and sister, and never in the history of the world was there such love between just Everyday People. At the large gatherings, it was Heaven on Earth, it was truly Magical, and there was a secret power in the air. At Woodstock an entire generation came together at least in spirit, and songs were written to talk about it. One song that clearly states the dream, I'm going to camp out on the land, and try and set my soul free.To the initiate of the 1960s, It meant taking a little LSD, or Love Special Delivery. There were countless other songs recorded about spiritual enlightenment, but the press said they were just sex crazed drug addicts, but that was only part of what they really were.

It was the most beautiful age in the history of the western world, and like All Things Great and small, it ended. When Charles Manson and his hippie cult committed very bloody murders of the rich class in Los Angeles and Hollywood, the beginning of the end was in motion. This was 1969 and the world would change fast against the long-haired hippies. For the actions of one , the entire movement suffered. But this is what the government had been waiting for, and they got it.They turned all the short haired people,against the long haired hippies,who were experiencing spirit things no generation ever had.The government was hoping for something like the Manson Murders,and they got it.Manson the hippie Guru,had sent his hippie girls to commit vicious bloody murders,and now the whole country looked at the hippies in a new light.The hippie movement would suffer greatly,and the innocence of the hippie movement,had turned into a nightmare.

The 1960s were a very powerful time, not just the millions of hippies in America, but also the endless, enormous Vietnam War. Vietnam was extremely bloody, and extremely violent and brutal. 500,000 troops or soldiers kept the war effort going in Vietnam for 10 years.

The US government Did not want a generation who thought for themselves, and we're totally unlike the generations before them, who were totally brainwashed. We had no reason to be in Vietnam, but we had a reason to stay, to keep making enormous amounts of money. Never before in the history of the United States of America, did every member on the stock market rise and multiply their money on a daily basis for 10 years. Trillions of dollars in bombs, missiles, airplanes, tanks, artillery shells, and just the everyday War, and bullets for half a million soldiers. It's staggers the imagination to think how much did this cost, but it didn't matter. All that did matter, was how much money the top 10% were making. They weren't the only ones making all the cash. The Employment section in the newspapers sometimes filled 15 pages full of jobs, so the American population could make good money too. The war went on and on and on, it seemed like it would never end. Everyday starting at dinner time, you turn on the television, and it would show you all the army helicopters swarm in Vietnam, picking up the wounded. They also always showed the attack Jets firing away at the enemy,and the U.S.air force bombing complete areas of that nation,it was extremely vicious.

Soon the entire Young Nation was protesting the war, saying hell no, we won't go. The television at night would show hundreds of young people burning their draft cards, and clashes between the police,and long haired men, smoking pot. The nation was exploding inward.Families were picking sides against each other,and they would never be the same.

It was the first time in American history the demonstrations became so large, we're talking in the millions of people, chanting stop the war. There were millions of hippies around all the monuments in Washington DC, including the Pentagon. They were pitching tents, and partying like young people do. The cops would storm the campgrounds with horses,and smash the tents right in front of the White House. This was America too, and if you weren't there, you would never believe it. These Million Man demonstrations we're not drug craze mental patients, they were Americans.

The demonstrations also surrounded the Congress building everyday, and hundreds volunteered to slash their tires, everyday. The freeways coming in and out of Washington DC we're completely stopped, by tens of thousands of protesters, making human chains across the freeways. It was really something to see, hell I had to catch me an airplane, and go back to Washington DC, and I did. Not only Washington DC, but all across America millions of people protested daily. Groups like The Weathermen exploded bombs in government buildings as often as they could. It was obvious to the whole world, that the demonstrations were only getting bigger and more violent. And of course the news reported every single night for years. And there was always talk of when are we going to end the war, and on TV every night we saw dead American soldiers and body bags, and everybody knew this had to end. The police across America killed about 20, and this only made the demonstrations intensify. The power of an entire generation was too much for the government to handle, and the US ended their involvement in Southeast Asia. I know big business hated To end that war, because they made tens of Millions a day. You know it's funny, when the last of the American soldiers were pull out of Vietnam, the hippie movement slowly fizzled out, and they needed that, everybody needed that. The war in Vietnam,that brought a generation together to protest the violence, was over, so much of the strength of the so-called Revolution was gone.

At the end of the Vietnam War, we left so quickly, that we didn't even bother loading up at all of our weapons. I'm talking the best artillery pieces in the world we left behind. Tanks and jeeps, and everything else the Army has, was left behind. It was an unbelievable shock to watch this on television, but everybody wanted the war over, and they ended it, God damn it.

Here's a little-known fact that only 1% of the people alive know about Vietnam, we left behind enough equipment to make the North Vietnamese one of the strongest armies in the world. They took that equipment and massacred everybody that were friends of the United States. There was a movie and a book written on The Killing Fields of Cambodia, and millions were killed, with weapons the US left behind. They killed Millions of our allies, but when you grow up, you see that's just the way it goes.Thing are not always so pretty,and politics is a nasty game.

I must say something for all the brave, tough, American boys that fought in that war. They fought well. Never before in history had a group of young men, been asked to do so much, for no reason, but to make money, but that's the way capitalism goes sometimes. But getting back to them tough American boys they grew up on the beaches, and other nice places, that America had to offer, in just a couple months time, they were taken from the places they grew up, and thrown into the darkest, deepest jungles in the world. The enemy had been fighting for 175 years straight, Against several Nations, to maintain their enormous supply of heroin, and Thai weed, and everything else they dealt in. Underneath the ground in all of Vietnam were tunnels, that the enemy moved freely in.

So they were underneath you, they were in the trees, and the jungle that you couldn't even see 10 feet in front of you.The 18 year old kids from America, were thrown into hell. In the neighborhood of 80,000, that was the number that died. What they never tell you, is there was between 1 and 2 million American soldiers wounded. Only because of our fantastic support,for the wounded, that 1 million did not die.It was the bloodiest war in u.s. History,and it tore the nation apart.The addiction problem that followed the soldiers home,was something this nation had never seen or dealt with before.When the war started it was beer and terrible pot from mexico.When it was over it was Opium and the hard stuff. The country would never be the same,how could it.

   That way it sounds so much better. If the mash units, the surgical units, had not been so close to the action, there would have been over 1 million men killed. But because of new technology and brave doctors and nurses, they kept the dead down to 80,000. Without the doctors and the nurses and the new technology, there are estimates we would have had 1 million dead,maybe two million.The wounded were mangled,and many would have preferred death,but they were still proud. TELL THEM YOU LOVE < PLEASE
THEM
But I cannot close this part of the book, without telling you the truth, that I doubt no one else will, American kids were all terrified, But they fought so God damn well, estimates say in the Vietnam War we killed between 5 and 10 million.

And you talk about the young American soldiers, they never ran, like the kids at home might have. In fact the American Army in Vietnam for 10 years never once, and I mean never once, lost a full-scale battle against the enemy,they fought greater than them all.
Thank you all the vets, you did great,thank you so damn much.some of us loved you dearly,and still do.

Getting back to the most important subject in the world, on how to open up the third eye. In this book you have both pathways explained in great detail, on how to do that. This grasshoppers, is the search for the Grail, take it if you want it. It is there for those that dare to take the step forward. But beware, do not go alone, the experience, it's like taking off in a gigantic rocket, with

3 million pounds of fuel underneath you. Take a friend, or someone that has been experienced, like Jimi Hendrix said.

I hope those seeking the ultimate wisdom will gain it, for that is what life is truly all about. Putting the pieces of the puzzle together, forming the big picture.The Vikings loved their trips through the Matrix, to wherever they might end up, including the presence of the universal mind, where all things are answered.I am firmly convinced most inventions and knowledge come from right there,there can be no doubt.

The Aryans before Rome was even a thought, had built fabulous cities in India. We have the great Legend the Mahabharata Written in the times, when the Aryans conquered the area of India around the Ganges river. When the Aryans busted into India, they found the greatest fertile land in the world, and it was here they would build their thousands of farms, and add to their gigantic herds of cattle and sheep.

Northern India was the first to be conquered, because the Aryans came from Tibet, the rooftop of the world. But of course having beautiful women, the population of the Viking tribes swelled. Soon they were looking for another place to plow thousands of farms, and feed tens of thousands of cattle, and build cities. This would forever be known as the land of the Aryans, and some wise men say that it was always there Homeland. Of course you have many so-called wise men Having different opinions, on if the Aryans were truly from there. That really makes no difference, it has been theirs for thousands of years. They took India and their civilization to new heights. One thing is for sure, regardless of different opinions, the Aryans took as much of India as they wanted. They had been on a migration for thousands of miles, over many, many years, and they weren't about to go home ever, it was theirs, and they milked it. The Indian epic was written about between 6000 BC and 1000 BC, no one knows for sure, because all legends were passed from the high priests to the population, or from father and son. There were Legends written of the great area, and Conquest of Northern India, and also the plains of the Ganges river, which was very fertile. You know it's funny, in the modern world, we're all caught up with our automobiles,and our places to live, and our technology, but for these massive groups of warriors and their families, it was about eating, simply eating. And of course they needed grassy areas for their tens of thousands of cattle, sheep, and goats. This is what Conquest was all about. The Vikings are seen in the Ice Age coming from the northern lands, and they lost many of their families to the ice, and they migrated thousands of miles to their new Homeland in India.You know it's funny, when you date the year that the Aryans busted into India, or when they took the area around the Ganges river, it might have been thousands of years before the date that archaeologists give, cuz the truth is, nobody really knows, and the truth really is, it doesn't matter. The truth is they came, they saw, and they conquered, and they never gave it up, this is the way of the Aryan tribes.

When the Viking tribes found The Ganges river, they found this area Lush and beautiful, and of course they called it home. Going centuries of sometimes hardly any food at all, they now had it all, and it was their Homeland for thousands of years. The complete conquest of their new area, required stronger metals for heavy plows, and stronger metals for cutting down the forests.They had them,and if they needed stronger,their great minds would invent them.

The Aryan tribes however were Masters, and well before 1000 BC, the Aryans had iron. It is not known, if the Aryans in North India, or their cousins in Persia, discovered it first. It is known however that in their Iranian land, their cousins had iron plows, and iron axes, that were used to clear the ground and the forest. The ancient tools of stone, copper, and bronze would no longer be good enough, and they probably would not have held up on the plains of Ganges anyway. It was very rugged land, with deep forest. Aryans with their Superior weapons, size, and strength, the dark skins were no contest for the great Aryan Warriors. The Aryan tribes fought bloody battles in India, as well as the rest of the world. The Indian legend the Mahabharata reminds one of the Middle Ages in Europe, when European nations slaughtered each other, or like the Aryan Nations did in World War I and World War II.

Some historians like to equate the Mahabharata with the famous works from Greece, for both are filled with Tales of bloodshed between the Royal cousins. But this is the way of man, like Cain and Abel,first two kids of Adam and Eve, one killed the other one, nothing is ever changed.

The Indian legends talk about the story between family tribes, and the great Slaughter for Supremacy. The fighting is between the Royal cousins for the Aryan Empire of India.The story is very Savage, and very bloody, but combat always is. The noble Warrior Bhima is perhaps the most colorful of all the combatants. It says in the legend, that he howled like a wolf, as he danced around the battlefield. And he did this after he drank the blood from one of his dead cousins, sounds pretty intense. In the legend there are other Heroes that have human problems like addiction, and gambling. It must be noted here that chess and dice were the favorite games of the Aryans, and that they did originate in Aryan India.In one of the legends, the king loses at dice, and everything he owns,even his kingdom and his wife.

Gambling has always been a big thing with many groups of people, remember the story of the Roman soldiers, gambling at dice for Jesus's robe, and whatever else was his, on the day of his crucifixion. Please never forget there were miles of people being crucified,it was the Roman way of execution. In all, tens of thousands of people were crucified. The Christians like to pretend it was just Jesus and a couple more. It makes it so much more dramatic that way.He preached against the jewish leaders,and he was dealt with accordingly.In that part of the world,they will kill you,if you even speak out against their beliefs.

It was also at this time in ancient India, that the Aryan tribes were breaking up into kingdoms. In 1000 BC it states that the gods were losing their battles against the demons, but once they chose Indra as their King things were reversed. It was the leadership of Indra that would lead the Aryans too many victories. In The Vedas it tells of Aging Kings, that received their youth back by drinking the Soma, and then entering into chariot races which were really fixed, to let the old monarchs win. The Kings became common in India, they no longer worshipped the title of Raja, which meant King. They wanted to be called Maharaja or great king. The Aryans by this time in history had made the transformation, from Chieftains of tribal villages to kings of major cities, and the gods were spinning their mysterious web. Thousands of years before Christ, the Aryans had already figured Heaven and Hell below, and basically everything else. There are literally hundreds of great stories and legends but space will not allow me to go into great detail about them.

I have already explained several times the difference between taking the long and Winding Road like the Beatles said, or the shortcut, black magic. They achieve the same results on your search For the Grail. The Mystic wise men, the sages of Asia, knew exactly the right way to view immortality, and that is the gradual process of learning and understanding what you have learned. Although one may prepare for years and still not get the blinding flash of reality, we all seek. For the wise men of Asia say, to learn the mysteries of life, to understand, it's harder than walking barefoot on The Razor's Edge. The wise men or sages of Asia, developed a method called yoga to bring them closer to the spirit world. Yoga is physical, as well as mental exercises. It is fact that the most knowledgeable gurus can achieve limits that the Mind cannot believe. There have been many Gurus from the sacred land of the Himalayas, that can hold their breath underwater for over an hour. They have total control of their bodies, and their minds. The Gurus are also able to slow their heart beats down to where all body functions cannot be felt or measured by doctors. The Gurus of Tibet have shown the world over and over demonstrations of their power, and although real they are still unbelievable. There are Gurus that can stop the flow of blood in their bodies, and prove it by sticking narrow knives deep inside them, or sometimes through them, in the case of an arm. The limits of the Mind we don't even know, although we think we know so much, we don't. The initiate saying is, all things are possible, and the longer I live I believe it's true. The Ancients have a great saying will power , a so anything is possible.

The sages of India where as many, as the stars in the heavens, but they truly have the answers to life's mysteries. The sages of India we're too smart. They realized that they were part of an endless cycle of existence. Man would be reborn and die, and be reborn again, until he learned the mysteries of life and death. The only way man could end this cycle was to escape to the knowledge of his true identity, and be reborn with Soma, and view his former lives. Before man could stop returning to this plane of existence, he had to realize the Dual nature inside himself. In other words man could be like God, and see with his own eyes, the organ of vision the Pineal Gland. This is the search for the Grail. The Christian Bible says, you reap what you sow, and sow what you reap, but the Himalayan knowledge which was Tens of thousands of years ahead of the Jewish writers of the Bible, knew a whole lot more. Like I've said several times in the Masterpiece, the Jews stole every bit of knowledge they had from one Aryan Nation or another. To the Aryans this was law . The Ancients and the modern Hindus believed that every action, good or evil is answered by the same. Our grand total of our earlier Karma, determines our present state, and our present Karma, will influence our future lives, this is the law of karma.

I could write all day and all night on the religious doctrines of all Nations, but to the Aryans it was the law of karma, other words you make your bed you sleep in it.

At the time when Rome was starting to stir, the Aryan civilization in north and East India, we're already fully developed. The great Aryan tribes added kingdoms in modern Iran, and Bengal, and as far as Afghanistan. The Aryans kept their famous capital at the foothills of the Himalayas. It is not far from there that the great Buddha was born in 563 BC.Buddha was from a tribe in the Hills that sat at the bottom of the mountain chain that history calls the rooftop of the world. Of course we're talking about the Beautiful Himalayas. Buddha was known as the sage of the Sakyas, and his name meant the enlightened one.
Buddha was born into a complete life of luxury,very much like Moses had been.Instead of living it out,he
Left his life of luxury at 30 years old, and wandered for 6 years through the forest, meeting and talking with the Sages, or Wiseman. Buddha had been a tribal Prince and had everything he had ever wanted, but still he had an empty spot in his heart and his soul. After 6 years of traveling in the woods, And talking with the Sages, and the Hermits, Buddha found what he had been looking for, and that was his destiny. It is interesting to note that Buddha and the story of Moses are too similar to dismiss.Soon he was ready to give his first great sermon, and this would be the core of what would be called Buddhism. In the sermon Buddha revealed His Four Noble Truths. The first Noble Truth was suffering, of which everyone's life would be full of. The second Noble Truth was ignorance, and ignorance was a basic cause of suffering. It was the ignorance of reality, that caused people to suffer, and the two were bound together. Buddha said in his sermon, had we the wisdom to understand realities, we would be able to elude Suffering, or at least lesson it. Since our will to exist would weaken, as with the Passions of our sense organs, or eagerness for contact, sensation, clinging, and birth, all of which chain us to the Wicked Wheel of suffering, rebirth, and death again. Buddha's third Noble Truth was that any ill, which was understood, could be in fact cured. The 4th truth was that Buddha was the 8 step path to enlightenment, of which was to hold on and practice, and follow the right views. Right aspirations, right speech, right conduct, right livelihood, right effort, right mindfulness, and right meditation. Buddha told his followers if they stuck to this 8 step path, they would reach their Narvana, which meant the blowing out of the flame. Nirvana was the same state that the Hindus called Moksha, a paradise of Escape rather than pleasure. Buddha was telling his disciples to take the long and Winding Road, instead of the shortcut Soma. The Buddha preached for the next 45 years about his 8 step path to enlightenment, and the numbers of his followers grew everyday just like Jesus, but this was India and the Himalaya Mountains. The numbers of his disciples were so large, that they were already considered a monastic order or church, of which the disciples were forever growing. It was a power that one man started, that was destined to be taken to all of Asia and Europe after the death of Buddha. Buddha like Jesus became famous far from home. It just goes to show you, traveling can be everything. Men that entered the order of Buddha had to take a vow of Chastity, which of course meant no sex. Also a vow of nonviolence, and of poverty. The Christians copied again. Make no mistake Buddha was a Hindu Sage, but as the religion spread to China and Japan they were called Buddhists.

Right before he died, nuns were admitted to the order, but Buddha was always worried about the men being tempted by the women. Buddha wanted his monks to be free of the temptation of lust. When Buddha's first disciple asked him what to do, to best behave around women, Buddha said do not see them. Buddha's disciple said, but what if I happened to see them, Buddha replied do not speak to them. But suppose you can't avoid speaking to them, the disciple asked, Buddha answered, then keep alert. The monks of Buddha's order had to break off communication with their families. They also had to beg daily for their food. Whoever put rice in their bowls, Buddha ordered his followers to praise them, and this in India became a virtue instead of Shame.

The Disciples of Buddha marched across the plain of the Ganges with their head shaved, and bare feet, and their message. The great Buddha did however have many followers in Europe of his style of monasteries. This is why India is considered the motherland of all religions. Not only did the Christians, Chinese, and Japanese follow the tradition Of the monks, but they also borrowed much from The Cult of Buddha.
Although the cult of Buddha swept the hearts and Minds of China and Japan, most of the Southeast Asia, and India, it never achieved the power and wealth in the other countries.

THE MASTERPIECE

PART 3 CONTINUES

The Cults of the Aryans of Northern India, Persia, Rome, Greece, Norway, Sweden, France, Germany, and Britain, are the Cults of the Warriors. It is written the gods of this Earth love the ritual that man calls combat. Even in the animal kingdom, the lion rules his world, and all animals have to fight for the right to live, and mate, and sometimes just to make it through another day.

The animal kingdom is nothing but a reflection of man's Kingdom, for man has to War for the same reasons. Never forget that once the warrior cults had secured Their Kingdoms, or countries, only then could the non-violent peaceful people have a say at all.

In other words it is manly and expected, for the sons of man to become Warriors. For without War, or at least the threat of War, there could be no peace. In the violent World in which we live, the meek shall inherit only the graves. It is only because of strong Warriors guarding the borders, that philosophers and Priests are allowed the freedom to speak and preach, and this is the way of man. Without the manly heroic Warriors there can be no civilization, and sometimes one must die, so the stronger can live, and this is the first law of nature. It has always been that way, and it will remain that way. What would the Masterpiece be without writing about Buddha or any of the other great men, that have left a major impression on the world. But Buddha was a man of peace, and certainly no Warrior. But that is one of the main things in life that we have to do,is find Our Place in this world. But most of all, we must be true to ourselves. Just like no two snowflakes are alike, no two people are either, and that's the way it was intended to be. In the Buddhist records, there are some interesting texts, we will now review. There is a text the Tells of a great king, they went into the forest looking for the great Buddha, who was living in a Grove of trees. Buddha had over 1250 disciples living with him, of which he preached to daily. As the king entered the tree Grove, where Buddha and his 1250 disciples were, he became frightened, because he heard no noise, not even one noise, not even a cough. The king was so sure he was entering a trap, because he could hear no sound coming from all this mass of people. But no it was no trap, it was just the strict discipline of the cult of Buddha. He was 80 in the year of his death, and the year was 483 years before Christ. At the time of Buddha's death, he was being worshipped as a living God by all his disciples. Buddhist Sages asked how are they to act when Buddha was dead, and Buddha answered, you must be your own lamps, be your own refugees. Take refuge in nothing outside yourselves, and hold firm to the truth. Whoever amongst my monks, does this will reach the summit. Buddha had come from a life of luxury, and he had been a prince for his early life, much like the story of Moses. Next he had to break away from the teachings of the Vedas and the power of the high priests.He was born in the year 540 BC.

This has been an extremely long chapter, filled with enormous amounts of information, and I'd like to end this chapter, where I started. At one time in ancient history Sweden came up out of the ice, of the Ice Age, and looked to be a beautiful Island. It is those days that I choose to go back to right now. The Ice Age lasted over a million years, some scientists say several million, no one really knows for sure. Once again science says the major melting of the ice sheets from the Ice Age happened between 13,000 and 20,000 years ago. This is also the time that meteorites hit the Earth and caused worldwide destruction. Some say the Meteorites we're fragments from a Comet that historians have nicknamed Typhoon. Geologists With the help of satellites mapping, can point to the very spot that Typhoon hit. This jolt from the Comet Typhoon would have certainly knocked the Earth off its axis, and change the rotation of the Earth forever. Mathematicians say that Typhoon had the explosive force of over 200,000 atomic bombs. Many of the wise men, say this was the Great Deluge or the big flood worldwide. Of course there were volcanoes erupting,and earthquakes around the world. Enough dirt and dust, and debris, was thrown into the atmosphere to blot out the sun light for a long, long time. Historians and geologists say this would have caused a mini ice age. The fact is The ice age is still going on, and icebergs are melting every single day. There is nothing new Under the Sun when it comes to The Melting of the ice. Huge sheets of ice sit on major mountain tops, and the melting of these ice sheets are what makes our modern Rivers. Life on earth needs the cycle of life, and all living things need water. In the last million years of ice ages, coming and going, out of Scandinavia to the North Pole, migrations of tribes have come and gone thousands of times, this is what they call history. It is not exact at what time and year, the northern tribes left on their long travel to the Himalaya Mountains. My guess would be, at the height of the flooding from the Ice Age, and the impact of Typhoon at the same moment, this is the worldwide disaster that most religions talk about, only they say it was God. No it wasn't, it was the ice age, and the Comet Typhoon, that caused it. There's a reason for everything, and you have the reason for the major disaster,and this was a worldwide disaster.

Some wise men say Sweden was part of Atlantis, and the Vikings say the second part of Sweden, the word would be Eden, the Garden of Eden. But Sweden is a very ancient country with Mysteries, and will try to get to the answers of those Mysteries. Sweden called the shots for all the Viking tribes for tens of thousands of years. It was only in the modern ninth century the borders were drawn, and countries were separated. For 10,000 years they all were one. In ancient Sweden, your number one export to the world were there Lush Furs and animal skins. The Vikings were the biggest traders on Earth, and they were always ready to cut a good deal. They took the Furs from several continents, and exchanged them, where they had never been seen before, to bring a much higher profit. The Vikings were the greatest at it, and they sank the other ships, that might have been involved in there lucrative trade. The Vikings also were the first men to invent and drink whiskey and beer, and of course this turned out to be a major product, that the whole world wanted, and could not get enough of. The House Of Holies in Sweden was at Old Uppsala. It was here that the ancient Vikings buried their dead Chieftains in their ships, and they covered them in huge amounts of Earth. Uppsala was the greatest of all Viking Temples, and there was only one. There was an also an ancient site at Vendal, and the Viking chieftains were buried the same way in their ships. The ancient Vikings had many burial grounds for ships and Chieftains, but many were looted, and I imagine they could have named their own price to the collectors. The Viking Lords were buried with their Treasures, much like King Tut of Egypt. In the book called Beowulf, it tells of the ancient Wars between the Danes from Denmark and the Goths from Sweden. Of course they were fighting for Supremacy overall the tribal lands and their possessions. It is from the ancient work of the Viking Raiders, that man has learned the fabulous history of the Viking tribes.

 Beowulf is a must for the students of the truth and the Viking Legends. The Swedish tribes where the Masters Of The Seas, and the land. They were the greatest trading merchants the world will ever know. When many of the writers, tell of them, it's always about the rape, pillage, and plunder. the Viking way of life, was a lot more. They were Master businessman, who traveled the complete Earth, to take products to places that had never seen them. In this way the Vikings could charge whatever price they wanted, because it's about supply and demand. If you don't have it, the price comes up. To think that all the Vikings did was make war on each other, day and night, it's ridiculous. Many of the Viking fleets we're loaded with many valuables, when they left the Homeland, and Many Viking fleets came back loaded to the brim with new products. This is the way of the Vikings, and they were great businessman, and would travel any amount of miles to make that great sale and enrich themselves. All the trading spots where the Viking Fleets pulled into, got a chance to see the worlds best things, and the newest products on the market. This is the way it was done, and many of the Vikings goals was to make a million bucks, not kill a million people. Those that are jealous of the Vikings, and there are many, just love to talk a lot of nonsense.THEY ARE ALWAYS JEALOUS OF THE BEST.

Only listen to those that truly love the Vikings. There are still going to be plenty of opinions, but only one truth. Not only did the Vikings travel all the oceans of the world, but they also went up Many of the rivers, that emptied into the ocean. By traveling up these Rivers, the Vikings found, Paris, London, and hundreds of cities and communities. Every major river in Europe and Asia, were home to the Vikings. Their ships were small and highly maneuverable. The Swedish tribes were master shipbuilders and they learned to build great ships. The rollers could be attached too, so that they could pull them over the land When they needed to, like when it was necessary to go around the Rapids of the Great Rivers. The Vikings would get out, when they came to the Rapids and attach the rollers, and pull the small ships until there were no rapids no more. You would take the wheels off, Put the ship back in the water, and start back up the river. This is how it was done. If a Viking fell in battle on the rivers of Russia or Germany, special Graves were made. Actually it was just stacking a bunch of big boulders over the dead body, so the wild animals couldn't get to it.They put some huge Stones up with markings on them, To say who had died. They called these markings Runes.These mounds of boulders, or Viking Graves were found throughout Russia, and most of the other lands that the Vikings traveled through. But please don't get me wrong, even though the Vikings were superb businessman, they were of course also Master Pirates, and master Warriors, and their long history says exactly that.

It must be also noted that before the divisions of Scandinavia in the 9th century, the Viking tribes of Sweden ,Norway, and Denmark fought and sailed together. The mighty Swedes Carved out Kingdoms in Russia, Iceland and England, and it was from there they traveled to the coast of America. In 1000 ad. the Roman Emperors of Constantinople, had many Swedish bodyguards. Their strength and their Fury, where unmatched by mortal men. The Vikings took many slaves in their conquest of Europe, and sold them on the open markets around the world. They were Master businessman, and they sold everything for gold. The Christian Missionaries had a difficult time, Because they were just too damn different. The missionaries appeared to be so civilized, actually quite feminine would be more like it, and of course our Vikings were so barbaric to them. In reality the entire world was very violent, this is the way of men. The real Bible of Scandinavia is called the Edda, it should be read by all those of Viking Blood.

When Christianity began to take hold in Europe, and Scandinavia, the wise men of the Pagans talked to each other. It was agreed they would take most of the images of their gods, and bury them. They were smart enough to realize that things were changing, and all the Pagan Nations would become brainwashed, and the brainwashing would be complete and thorough.

The Ancient Ones Talked about this for quite some time, and developed things to hide the Pagan ways. It was agreed the days of the week would hide the names of the Pagan Gods, like

Thor's day was Thursday, and Tuesday was for the Teutonic Warriors of Scandinavia. Wednesday would be named after Woden. The wise men of the Pagans knew that someday in the future, the blood in the Veins of the Vikings would stir, and the Vikings would find their way back to their ancient past. They knew this would happen someday. They knew that someday in the future, the Pagans would dig up the images of their gods, and become whole again. To the warrior that needs to know, they dug up those images In the 1930s and 1940s. On the throats where the jugular vein goes, the Germans would wear the lightning bolts, on both sides. Intelligent people think that is SS, no those are Thor's lightning bolts. All Aryan Nations love Thor above all other gods, even India, where they change Thor's name to Indra. The Scandinavians worship the same spirits of nature, that their cousin's did in Aryan India. In-early 1070 , much was written by the Germans about their blood in the North. The center of Pagan Worship had always been the mysterious but great Uppsala Temple. It was here that the Viking gods would be in spirit, and it was said you could feel them, and with Soma you could see them. The Temple was covered in gold, and inside the temple, the pagans worshiped three gods. Thor is the mightiest, and his throne is in the center. The God Odin is on one side, and Frey is on the other. Thor rules over the Thunder and the lightning, and also over the rain that falls so everyone can eat, yes Thor ruled over the farmers.
Odin,
Which means Madness, is the God of War. Odin had always been the God of War, and the Vikings had gained tremendous kingdoms believing in him. It was to Odin that the Warriors prayed for strength , and they prayed to Odin to make them treacherous in the face of their enemies. Frey was the God of Peace, and also the god of sexual pleasures. The statue of Frey in the temple is shown with an enormous penis, of which some of us Vikings do you have. Odin Is shown in the temple covered in armor. Thor is shown in the temple, covered with his scepter, which is the symbol of Thor's hammer. Each God has his own priests, that offer sacrifices to them. Sacrifices are offered to Thor if there is disease or poor crops. If war is threatening, sacrifices are made to Odin. So once again We have the Holy Trinity, just like your Christians, the 3 Viking gods, had the greatest Kingdoms in the world, and carved them out in blood.

SEARCH FOR THE GRAIL<NO MORE>

PART3
CHAPTER 9
Charlemagne,   THE SONG OF ROLAND

This is chapter 9 , which is the Viking number. Now we will talk at length about the Viking tribes, and we will examine them, and see just how they did create the greatest Empire on the face of the Earth, which would be Europe. The whole world has so much to be thankful for to Europe. Why don't we talk about three things. It was Clovis, Charles Martel, and The Greatest Warrior Charlemagne. These three men we're like gods to Europe, because without them Europe would never be. It was because of these three great men, that Europe definitely had a chance to survive, and that's all she asked for, was the chance to survive. German metal would do the rest. Charles Martel, Charlemagne, and Clovis, were definitely the greatest warriors in the history of the world. But then this was what the world was asking for at that time, and this is exactly what she got. The Frankish Empire would produce great warriors and keep producing great warriors, for they were the backbone of Europe. It was Charles Martel that turned back the race war with Islam. But that race war was far from over, and battle would be bloody and vicious for hundreds of years. The Empire of Rome had fallen, and the whole world knew. They would all come to see what they could take, if anything at all. Clovis was a giant of a warrior, and tens of thousands of men worshipped the skills this man had in combat. Clovis had been the biggest unifying force, for the German tribes, that historians today call the Franks. Most of these tribes moved west into modern-day France, and that is why they call their money Frank's. Most of these tribes came from the area of Frankfurt Germany, and this is why they go by the name of the Franks.In 768 a greater man named Charlemagne would sit on the throne. Before his life was over Charlemagne would lengthen the Empire of the Franks, to the modern-day Elbe River in Germany, and all the land in between of course ,he took by force. Charlemagne was a gifted ruler, who ruled for 46 years, but his greatest gift was his sword, for he was from the old school.All historians agree on one point, this Champion Warrior was the greatest leader of Europe, above everyone else. Some historians call Charlemagne the father of Europe. It was because of his Conquests, that this one great ruler had their hearts and minds of the Germanic countries. And it was because of Charlemagne that the Europeans began thinking of the term Europe. Charlemagne laid the foundation for a common culture,

among the Germanic tribes, that Western Europe has been adding to ever since. The ancient Greeks had only dreamed of this concept, when they gave the name of their goddess Europa to the great land mass. To the Greeks they were only part of Europe, and all the landmass west of the Don River, in modern-day Russia to the Atlantic Ocean, would forever be called Europe. The Greeks gave the name Europe a thousand years before the Empire of the Franks, but they had traveled as far as Britain, and some say even Sweden. The Greeks like many other great cultures and Empires were very adventurous. The Greeks were well aware of the Don River in Russia, and they also knew the great distance to the Atlantic Ocean, and they insisted that Europa would be the name. The goddess Europa was of course a pagan name, and the Greeks like the Romans were pagan. The church in the 5th Century would spin their web, and set the stage according to their brainwashing methods. The churchmen of that era pretended they had everything figured out, a story was invented to cover the land masses.

Of course our church fathers used the biblical story of Noah and his three sons, to explain it. Asia was said to be the homeland of Shem and the Jews, while Africa was the land of ham and his kin, while Japheth was the first settler of Europe. This was the the lie they would tell all the little sheep, of the Christian church. By the year 700 all this made much more sense to the people of the Early Middle Ages, for the world was actually divided into three spheres.

It was only one problem, the three zones were changing rapidly, and they always would, because this is the way of men. After the fall of the Roman Empire, and the spread of the Germanic tribes across Europe, the military power of Islam grew rapidly. In the years that followed 700 AD, Islam had conquered all of North Africa, and much of Western Asia.

Not to be satisfied, the armies Of Islam crossed the Strait of Gibraltar from Africa, and began pouring into what today is Spain. They came by the tens of thousands, fully armed with their most modern weapons, and they also came with the lust of the European women. Remember it was rape, pillage, and plunder, and you can believe it definitely was in their hearts. Right after the year 700 AD, Islam was invading every square inch of Europe, because Islam did not have to worry about the mighty armies of Rome, and therefore she thought it was going to be easy.

Even the mighty Byzantine Empire, or the Eastern Roman Empire as it was called, had lost many precious tracts of land to the invading armies of Islam, but of course she would definitely fight on. Islam conquered much of that whole area of the world, because now they had their religion to fight for, and Muhammad himself was one of the greatest warriors of Islam. Make no mistake Muhammad was a great warrior, that killed thousands, like any great warrior did, and he was no man of peace, like the so-called Messiah of the Christians. Try to nail him on a cross, and I bet his Warriors of course would have nothing to do with that. So what you see in the land of Islam, was to make everyone Warriors for the cause, and then call it a holy war. Good plan, it worked, but then they ran into the white guys in France. In that part of the world, all that was left was Germanic Europe, and make no mistake Europe belonged to the Germanic tribes for thousands of years. No one, no matter the size of their armies, would ever take it from them, and I mean never. They say that every square inch of Europe, is soaked in a gallon of blood, and this is no lie.

The threat of Islam Did more to Unify the West than all other things combined. In their Unity, was their concept of Christendom , or really Christian Europe. I guess the rulers knew after watching The Fury of the Holy Warriors of Islam, that the only thing that might beat them was Christ. This is where the Knights Templar started, thousands of knights from all over Europe, and believe me, all suited up in their armor and weapons. You certainly wouldn't want to meet up with them. Of course the leaders of the church wanted to conquer the world, as did the Kings and their armies, but Islam had plans of Their Own, or basically the same idea. Each religion of course Centered on spreading their faith and religion to the four corners of the world.

I'm sure all the holy Warriors went for that idea, especially if they could get a percentage, as small as it might be, of the booty and the treasure. Remember even holy Warriors got to be paid in treasure. The Catholic church and Islam both cleverly designed their schemes of military conquest. By spreading their message around the world, of course they could pick up all the wealth as they went, Simple Plan , but it works really well. Both the Christian and the Muslim armies fought with Fury, and a fever that was 10 times what it normally was, and both leaderships we're well aware of this.

Charlemagne the first of the Germanic Kings was the very first of the great warriors to also have a thirst for learning, and this is what made him so great. Those that knew him the best said, that his Lust For Learning, even surpassed his desire for Combat and for Conquest. Charlemagne many said was the father of all Europe, and millions claimed he was their ancestor.

Charlemagne was the first of the Germanic Kings to place extreme value on ideas and learning. After seeing what the Romans had built, and the Greeks before them, he realized he had to pick up where they left off. If it wouldn't have been for Charlemagne, there might have not been a Europe. Charlemagne was a great War leader, but nothing like the Tactical genius his grandfather was. The grandfather was none other Than the famous Hammer who was of course Charles Martel. The best trait that Charlemagne had was his unrelenting Drive, and his determination to succeed in his plans. History tells us that Charlemagne also had an uncanny gift for realigning his troops, at just the right time. Charlemagne fought over 60 major Wars,yes he was a great warrior,and yes it did run in the family.

And all 60 Wars he held the The Spear of Destiny in his hand, as he led his armies into battle. You might remember, the Spear of Destiny was the spear that went into Jesus Christ when he hung on the cross. Longinus the spear man, the Centurion on the White Horse, thrust the spear underneath the ribs of Jesus Christ, to show that he was dead, and then the Jews that were marching up the hills with clubs, could not break him to pieces. This one act that the Roman Centurion did, allowed Jesus to fulfill the final prophecy, not a single bone shall be broken. Of course Mary Matalin had the Holy Grail in her hand, collecting the blood as it came down Jesus leg, and this is the way it was, not a single bone was broken, end of story.

Charlemagne fought with the Holy lance in his hand, above his head, and waived it for all his troops to see.The Holy Lance would Spur Warriors on to fight on against any odds, and for any length of time. The power of Christianity was real, and was probably the biggest Force that united the so-called barbarians. For over 30 years, Charlemagne waived the Spear of Christ in his hand, and in Europe he would be known for it. For some strange reason, that truth never was told in America.30 long bloody years Charlemagne carved out, or I should say enlarged the Empire of the Franks. Many times in those 30 years, Charlemagne had his Germanic Warriors fight many battles at the same time, on different fronts, and with several different enemies at the same time. The world knew the Roman Empire was gone, and so was the strength of Rome, and they all came to pick up the pieces. But what they found instead was a much fiercer Army, that would put them in their graves. One Germanic writer wrote, Charlemagne just got more powerful with each passing War, and he was one of the greatest heroes, and Military strategists the world would ever see.

The Eastern Front had always been a place of hostility, and the Barbarian tribes from Asia, we're always threatening the peace. The fighting wild Horseman from Asia caught the attention of Charlemagne. This hoard from Asia was raping ,pillaging, and plundering wherever they went. Charlemagne ordered his Germanic Warriors into battle with them, and gave them something to think about. The army of Charlemagne crushed the army of the nomadic Avars, and they would never again be a threat, to Charlemagne's plan of enlarging his Empire to the east. In reality the Great War leader Charlemagne was fighting for the land that one day, men would call Austria. To make sure the invaders would never threaten the Franks again, Charlemagne set up two provinces of troops to guard and hold the Eastern Frontier right there. Charlamagne knew his holy Warriors would never fall, on the Eastern Front, at the places men called marches or marks. These Marks or Eastern Forts did Hold the Line, and became a great military power years later. The German blood in the veins of the Austrians, made them one of the most feared groups in the world, and they earned that honor. But like men always do, soon they would be tested again of course. This was the period of History called the great migrations, when all the tribes from all the continents, we're scrambling for living space, and most often new homelands too. The Avars we're going no further west, for Germanic Steel would stop them right in their tracks. And they knew deep in their hearts, that there would be many thousands of Germanic warriors to back up them. This was a time when major race Wars were being fought, and history was disguising them as religious wars. The battle for Supremacy was being waged, and the men of color were bleeding all over the Germanic West. The blood of the Avars had been spilt, and now Charlamagne looked for new opponents and more Empire. Next Charlemagne invaded Spain, for he knew that he must secure this land, and that Islam was fighting for it to. Charlemagne had dealt with the Islamic Warriors, and so had his grandfather Charles Martel. But it was a Growing Power that only grew stronger by the day. Charlemagne had learned from his Grandfather the Hammer, that he must take the fight to them, or else they would have to be dealt with outside Paris again.Charles Martel and his army of vicious Frank's had cut the Islamic forces to the Bone, and now it would be Charlemagne's turn. Yes the race war was on, and Islam would have to be defeated once again outside Paris. only this time it was the Franks that attacked in force.

In 778 Charlemagne attacked across the Pyrenees Mountains into Spain, and he came with more Christian holy Warriors than his enemies could count. In this huge Force, Charlemagne had an army of Frankish Knights. The Frankish Knights fought ruthlessly, and soon all Islamic Warriors were cut in half. Some of them were cut into 10 pieces, cuz this is the way race Wars go, they are extremely bloody. No longer with the threat of Islam to France or Spain, the Frankish Knights we're fighting for their home now, with their backs against the wall, and they wiped them out. It was a fantastic victory and extremely bloody , but then that's just the way they wanted it.

For seven years Frankish Knights fought all the armies they met, and they sent them all to the promised land. Roland was the champion of the Franks, and it was said that Roland killed thousands. I mean this Warrior was very good. They said in the biggest battle that the Frankish Knights fought, that Roland killed a thousand in 4 days. Roland had a huge dose of the Magic in his blood from the Vikings, and he showed it every time the battle came. No Knight of Islam could withstand the fury of Roland, and he also had the luxury of Frankish Knights fighting on his left and his right.

Roland and the Frankish Knights fought for 7 years through these vicious race Wars, with the dark ones from Islam, but this is the way nations are born, or die. The race Wars with Islam would go on for over a thousand years, but the question would be, do you fight them there, or fight them here. The savagery of the Holy Warriors from both sides, would be something that would settle the issue, of who owns what. The army of Charlemagne and Roland knew nothing but victory, and their swords, Spears, and battle-axes were red for 7 years. Of course

Charlemagne and Roland also had the best of the German Knights fighting with them for all 7 years, and they were carving out their homelands. In this world no one gave you nothing, you took it, or you had nothing. The armies of Charlemagne fought their way all through France and Spain , and soon there was one Spanish Town left. This was the Mighty Fortress of King Marcella. It was said in the song of Roland, that King Marcella served the gods of stone. The stone idols were brought from the shores of Arabia to excite the troops. When the Great king of Spain saw that his territory was lost to the Invincible Franks, he pleaded for a treaty. The king of Spain sent many precious gifts to Charlemagne such as camels, bears, Falcons, and many mules loaded down with gold. In the song of Roland, we are told that the presents the king of Spain sent, to Charlemagne would fill over 50 wagons. The king spared nothing, for the Frankish warriors were massed outside his Fortress, and it took 50 wagons full of riches, and also a promise the war would be over. The King said his kingdom would submit to the laws of the Franks, and that they could change their faith to Christianity.

 While his count talked with the King of Spain, a treacherous plan was hatched. The count talked with the King of Spain, and told the king that Charlamagne would Tire of the war quickly if his champion of combat Roland was killed. The king said that his Knights had died by the thousands trying to kill Roland, first Knight of the Franks. Thousands would charge Roland in battle, only to die at the same time. The king had watched way too many of his best knights, get cut to pieces by the great one Roland.If one was to add up all the knights killed in combat by the champion Roland, it would literally be in the tens of thousands, if not a hundred thousand. This one great knight of the Franks, who carved out their empire, and now they were going for more, Spain. The backstabbing plot to kill Roland was simple. The plan was that Count Ganelon Would tell Charlemagne to leave the rear guard in the hands of Roland.As the Army winded through the mountain passes, the forces of the king of Spain, would swarm down on Roland and the rear guard. They would swarm down like an ant pile, headed for the honey, if they could take him. Make no mistake the count was no friend of Roland's, and in fact he hated him. For he was extremely jealous of his power, and his skills in combat. If the plan worked, the count would become wealthy himself, paid handsomely by the king of Spain. That's all the count cared about, was his own power, cuz this is the way of men. Yes he dreamed of the day when his power would increase, and Roland would be out of the picture.

The count went back To Charlemagne and told him the king of Spain was now his vassal, and that the war was over. He also told Charlemagne the king of Spain had surrendered completely, and now his country would be completely under the influence of the Franks till the end of time. The story of Roland goes on, to tell us as the main body of Frankish Knights, began winding their way through the Hills back to France. In the meantime the king of Spain had sent Riders to the four corners of Spain,gathering Warriors for one more great battle, the battle against First Knight Roland. The fighting men of Spain were gathered from every town, and every mountain top, even from the furthest parts of Spain. It was at the King's stronghold at Saragosa that they all came together and assembled. It was there also that they became Traitors to their own words, and hoisted their God of stone, and prayed, and asked for victory. When all was right, they Rode to the mountain passes and waited.

As the Rear Guard of the Franks filed through the mountain passes, the Warriors attacked in waves. The battle raged full and Wild and much blood did flow, and the armor did Shine. The sword that Roland fought with on his last day was named Durand, and his sword had the fury of Demons, and had killed tens of thousands of the Franks enemies.

Roland and his rear guard we're heavily outnumbered, and as his fellow Knights fell one by one, Roland did not fall. Still the waves of Muslim Warriors attacked, and not to take anything from them they fought well, they always did, there was so much honor in battle on both sides. The first battles of that day went well, and Roland and his sword Durand, we're both covered in blood. It is written that in Wrath, the Franks fought on, and with Durand, he sliced their flesh. The Germanic gods of Odin and Thor where in Durand all that day, and all that Roland met in combat, lived no longer. Beneath the Muslims Coats of mail, Roland found the Flesh and Bones of his enemies. According to the song of Roland, the number of Muslim Warriors, that came down the hills that day for him, was over 14,000. The Muslims knew they had to kill Roland to win this war, and if Roland died, all the Frankish Knights would go back to France. The pages of History tell us, the Franks fought like they were truly Gods themselves. But the rear guard of the Frankish Army we're too small in numbers to hold back the knights from Islam on that day.

When Roland had only a few Knights left fighting with him against 14,000, Roland blew his Viking horn, as a signal to Charlemagne, and the main body of knights. When Charlemagne heard the Horn of Roland he cried. and all the other knights hung their heads in shame, because they were not with him.

Now the drama unfolded, for the Muslims knew that the main force of Frankish Knights we're hurrying back to Roland and his magical sword. The king of Spain told the Muslim Warriors, if Roland lives, we lose Spain, and if he dies Charlemagne will Tire of the War. Especially with his Champion Roland dead. The king of Spain sent the 400 greatest knights of Islam in Spain, to charge Roland at the same time. Roland saw them coming, and he met them, and in this charge the song tells us Roland dealt Many death blows To Islam. In the charge of 400 knights Roland was wounded, and he felt the warmblood run down his leg, and he felt death near. The song of Roland, says Roland laid under a pine tree, and thought of all the lands he had conquered, and he saw the great Charles who was like his father. Roland stood one last time and took his magical sword Durend and tried to break it on a big piece of marble. The quivering Stone rang loud but the weapon did not break. At this time he raised his horn, and blew 1 last time, And he blue it ever so quietly.

Charlemagne, And his Gallant frankish knights heard the feeble sound of the Horn of Roland, and they all knew it was too late to save him, for they were still far away. The song of Roland tells us, the Knights of Charlemagne gave flight into Spain, and caught up with the Spanish King's Army. This time there will be no deals, it would be a fight to the death, and I mean everybody's death. There would be no peace for anyone, and all Muslim knights would die. As for the traitor the Count Ganalon, he would be tried in a court, and then ripped apart with horses, limb by limb. He died a horrible death, but so did Roland. But the count got what was coming to him, and he died a traitor's death.

As for Roland , the song of Roland tells us the angels came on wings of gold, to take his soul to God. The only constellation for Charlemagne was he got a view of the battlefield. On Rolands final day roland killed 500 knights, and they were scattered all over the countryside. Roland did fantastic, but now he was dead.It was a heavy loss for France and the Frankish Knights, but France would go on, and now owned Spain. It must be noted here that Spain had some of the biggest gold mines in that area of the world, and was certainly Worth Fighting For. The gold mines of Spain had been heavily mined, and millions of dollars in gold were taking out each year, by the Roman slaves, or those who lost in battle. The reputation of Spanish gold was worldwide. There was so much gold in Spain the Romans built aqueducts 100 miles long to bring water to the hills and mountains. In this way they washed them away, breaking them apart, and of course they were there to pick up the pieces. You might say Spain was worth its weight in gold many times over, and now it was time for the Franks to own everything in Spain. They would never ever give it up, to any army, at any time. Not to mention the heavy grasslands of Spain , and Spain's Earth was as fertile and beautiful as any land on the face of the Earth. Mediterranean Spain, the coast line was fantastic and beautiful at the same time. Spain was a treasure in anybody's eye. The Frankish Knights fought for it, and now it belong to them. With the race Wars over with Islam, Spain would be enjoyed for thousands of years.

BOTTOM LINE THE GERMANIC BLOOD WOULD DEFEAT THEIR ENEMIES WHENEVER

THEY SHOWED UP, ANYWHERE IN THE WORLD

PART3

TAKING ITALY FOR THE GERMAN TRIBES

Now that matters were settled in Spain, the Frankish Knights cleaned the blood off their weapons and their armor. The attention of Charlemagne with his Knights, would be focused on Italy. Italy have been a problem ever since the days of Rome falling, and problems were

Brewing there once again. in 771 the Lombards had grown tired of sharing power in Italy, And they decided to go for it all. The Lombards attacked the Papal States, which meant States belonging to the Pope. Soon they were ready for the grand prize, and the Lombards descended on Rome itself, with the fury of the Germanic Warriors. It was at this time Charlemagne said enough is enough, and attacked with his Frankish Knights, and he brought a lot of them with him. Charlemagne's Knights, And the Knights of the Lombards, engaged in battle for Italy. The Lombards where as ferocious as many of the other Germanic tribes, and this would be no easy victory, and Charlemagne knew it. This time the war would be fought for Supremacy of the Italian peninsula, and it would be A winner-take-all war. The Lombards had once again broken their treaty, and the lands that belong to the Catholic Church, they attacked. The lands that the Catholic Church owned were very wealthy, and the Lombards had to have them. After long years of vicious battles, the war waged back and forth between the Lombards and the Franks. Once again the Earth of Italy was fertilized by the blood of the Germanic Warriors. By 774 the Warriors of the Franks,had finished off the Lombards, and the war was all but over. In 774 the Frankish Warriors now had possession of Italy, as far south as the ancient city of Naples. The remaining Warriors of the Lombards would never threaten Rome again, Charlemagne crowned himself king of all Italy, which of course was the thing to do. The power of Charlemagne and the Franks was increasing with every war, and this is how it was done.This is how it had been done in ancient times, and this is how it would always be done. To the Victor go the spoils. You know it's funny, in most wars some of the losing side would be spared death, and that way the Victor side would actually grow in strength, this is the way it was done. Although sometimes after heavy losses, you kill everybody, and that way they knew they would never have to fight them again.Charlemagne this time showed he had political ambition, for this time he did not return the ground the Lombards had taken from the Pope. This made Pope Adrian extremely Furious, but then, what was he really going to do about it, this is politics. Charlemagne was Nobody's Fool, and by this action in Italy, he stopped the spread of power of the church.

In reality this was a matter of church against state, and the state won. Even though these very lands his father, Pepin had granted to the Papal States, Charlemagne overruled. Charlemagne King of the Mighty Franks, Treated the popes of Rome with due respect, but he left no doubt, who was going to control things. Many years Charlemagne extended the rule of the Franks, with the Holy Spirit of the crucifixion, in his hand, to show he had Authority from God. His bloodiest Wars were fought on the east side of the Rhine River in Germany. On the east side of the Rhine River Charlemagne's Frankish Knights took on all tribes. Like I said He fought 60 Wars extending the Empire of the Franks, which became known as the Holy Roman Empire. It was neither Holy nor was it Roman, it was German. It seems the battle for Supremacy, would be fought thousands of times, In many different race Wars, but also amongst themselves. The rivers of blood spilled by the Germanic tribes were spilled by Germanic tribes alone. But everybody wants to fight for the best, and you can't blame them one bit. As Charlemagne was fighting his 60 Wars against all comers, he fought under the disguise of Christianity, you know spreading the faith, when in reality he was spreading the German steel. This is how the Pagan lands really began Christian. They did not switch from paganism to Christianity because they wanted to, they switched because most of their army have been slaughtered, and to live they had to swear to their gods, and their ancestors, that they would change. Like I said anywhere it took over because of cold German steel. All the Germanic tribes were fantastic at making long Broadswords, and of course my favorite, the battle axe. And of course as Charlemagne was spreading Christianity all through the Germanic lands, he was in fact extending his Empire of the Franks, and that would be from Frankfurt Germany. The army of Charlemagne spent many years in this area, it is now the west of Germany on today's Maps. The Franks were extremely brutal in combat, and most people tried to stay clear of them. The Franks did however win control over all the lands in the Holy Roman Empire, which were actually modern-day Germany, France, and Belgium. To the north of them were their cousins the Teutonic tribes of Scandinavia. The Franks spent years on both sides of the Rhine River. They spilled rivers of blood, but history tells us the Rhine River on both sides, has been soaked in blood for thousands of years, Cuz this is the way of men. The Frankish Knights fought extremely bloody battles, for control over what is now Bavaria, Germany. All who knew of the Frankish Charlemagne, knew that his baptism was by fire and Blood. All were baptized in the blood of Conquest, or defeat, however it went.

But however you look at it, the Eastern lands all fell to the might of the Frankish Knights, and they knew no equals. To them it was like taking candy from a baby. The greatest of all the victories of Charlemagne, were his Wars against the pagan Saxons. In the northeast corner of present-day Germany, the Franks and the Saxons fought heavy battles for 30 years. It was only then that the Victor was crowned. In reality the Saxon tribes were heavily outnumbered for most of the Saxons had Their Kingdoms across the English Channel in modern England. This is why they call the English Anglo-Saxons. That's really 2 tribes, the Angles, and the Saxons. Because the Saxons and the Angle's had been invading England for a long time, most of their power had left Germany, by the time Charlemagne made war with them.

Because the Saxons were so heavily outnumbered, it was only a matter of time and blood, before they would probably lose the war against the larger forces of Charlemagne and the Franks. but still they fought on. The Saxons would not surrender, they were fighting for their own land, that it been theirs for thousands of years. The Saxons of course were too proud to surrender, and they fought the overwhelming force of the Franks for 30 years. Charlemagne wrote down he could not believe these ferocious Warriors kept fighting, with no hope of winning. After 1 battle, he slaughtered 5000 of those that have been taken prisoner.

This may sound cruel To the goodie Goods, that do not understand the war mentality, but they could not let the Ferocious Saxons, live and maybe fight another day, and take many of their lives.

It was a bloody and a gruesome battle every single time the Franks and the Saxon fought. Historians from the Second World War, tell us that Hitler's eyes filled with tears, when he thought about the great Saxon Warriors that fought to the death in these wars. I just thought I'd throw that little tidbit of information in there for you, so that the secrets of the true knowledge, can be known.

Charlemagne seeing the qualities of the small tribes he slaughtered, rethought his actions, and many times resettled these Warriors, with the hearts of lions on the western side of the Rhine River. Charlemagne had one time transported 10,000 Saxon Warriors to the Frankish lands west of the Rhine. It would have been actually pretty ignorant to waste such great warriors. because like everybody knows, in the future will be more armies coming . It might as well let them fight them first. It's hard to believe but for Supremacy , the Saxons did fight the Franks 30 years of vicious combat, and then they began to submit to Christianity, because their numbers were growing much smaller.For 600 years the saxons had been attacking England,one invasion after another.The tribes already there had fought like huge lions,and repelled most attacks.However,many times their were Saxon victories,and they stayed. Saxon power in Germany,was growing weaker by the decade,and the Franks saw the opening.

Many of the Saxons never really became Christians, but they pretended to, and that was good enough. The pages of History tell us that the Pagan Saxons buried the true images of their gods, and left them buried until Hitler ordered them dug up in the 1930s for the Third Reich.

Many of the blonde and brown haired Warriors, could not, and would not, pretend to Desert their gods, and they instead fought to the death, just like the Great Roland. The Frankish soldiers and the Frankish Church, tried
 to occupy the Saxon land and people, and battles broke out again. The Saxon Warriors would not submit to the authority of the Franks, or any other man or Army. Charlemagne was forced to release his tight grip on them. As the Frankish forces pulled out, the Saxons agreed to stand with them against all enemies, and trouble stopped.

From these lands Charlemagne invaded to the east. He launched enormous attacks on all the tribes of the Slavs. In the east the Frankish Knights invaded what is today Modern Day Poland, and once again rivers of blood did Flow. After fighting the Saxons for 30 years, let me tell you the Poles were not going to be a picnic either. The Poles were extremely vicious.Their old legends say, that a pole was born with a sword in one hand, and a brick in the other.

What that meant was, either he was always fighting, just to preserve his land, or he was rebuilding, because he just fought a horrible War.This is the way of men, and this is the way it was around the world, and nothing was easy. What is amazing, and totally unbelievable, is how the Franks fought one battle after another, and one war after another. These were some of the most battle-hardened Warriors the world has ever produced, and now they were going up against the Warriors from Poland, and believe me the Poles were extremely vicious. The Poles we're constantly locked in battle on all sides, like many countries were. In those days, War went for Generations, and sometimes centuries, just to have a living space. It was a struggle just for survival, and the Franks and the Poles survived thousands of years Of combat.

All the nations east of Germany, we're considered Slavic, or the land of the Slavs. The Slavic Nations were well known for their Furious Warriors, and the Franks had launched attacks many times towards the lands of the Slavs. The Slavic women were beautiful, and were taken for slaves for centuries. The land of Poland had great wealth, and of course everybody else was always trying to take it. There were no easy Wars, and now the Frankish Knights would battle with the Polish Knights in a battle for Supremacy, and To the victor go the spoils.

Whenever the armies of the Franks went to the east to fight with a Slavic Nation, these were always bloody battles, and many were killed and wounded. Even though the Germanic tribes attacked for centuries, the Slavic Nations held their own, and Poland truly was carved out in blood. At one point the armies of the Franks we're almost over extended, for the Slavic tribes were more numerous than the Franks, and they were deep.

The Frankish Warriors fight on and on, wherever Charlamagne ordered them, and they fought with the fury of lions. By the time the Frankish warriors were fighting in Poland, the Frankish Empire had doubled in size. The Slavs had watched, As the armies of Charlemagne, had rained death and destruction on the Saxons. For 30 years the Slavs watched the Franks and Saxons locked in combat, with heavy losses on both sides. At this point in history the Polish Warriors agreed that the Franks would be there overlords, and they agreed to let them take power. In this way, they could preserve their Nation. Most interesting to note, that the clash between the Saxons and the Franks, although temporarily over, would flare again in the 20th century. The work of Charlemagne was done in the northeast corner of Germany, when the Furious North Sea Coast Frisians attacked. The Franks had launched invasions there for 50 years, and the fighting was brutal. The Frisians like the Saxons, had fleets or a Navy at their disposal. With these fleets the Germanic tribes raided all of the north of Europe.

The Frisians were just as ruthless as the Saxons, and they were a vicious Viking tribe. Both of their names traveled thousands of miles, and all feared that they would have to deal with them someday. Just like the Saxons, the Frisians would have no part in converting to Christianity, and they would have to be baptized in the blood of battle, instead of the water of the church.
In the violent world they lived in, had nothing to do with a jewish carpenter.
To expect anything different would have been insane, for like the Saxons, they were leaders of men, not followers. Then again like the Saxons, the overall strength of the Frankish Empire eventually Whittled them down. They consented to the overlordship of the Franks because they really had no choice. There was not much sense in fighting to the last man, when one could fight with an even stronger Army, and become more wealthier. It is written in the pages of Germanic history, That they were never really Christians, and their hearts and Minds never deserted Odin, Thor, and Frey. Luckily for the Franks, the Saxons and the Frisians never United against them, or else history would have been written quite different. But a wise man once said strength is in numbers, and so it was.

Before Charlemagne was done, the world would see the Empire of the Franks double in size. Charlemagne and his Frankish Warriors had United many different people under the flag of the Franks. What in fact Charles the Great had done, was give the culture of the Franks to all the peoples, and tribes he had conquered, and laid the foundation for all of Europe. Charlemagne was the father of Europe, and Europe was forged, and baptized in blood of battle. In fact only the British Isles and Spain, had populations of Christians, that Charlemagne had not gotten to.

On Christmas Day in the year 800, Charlemagne was crowned Emperor of the Holy Roman Empire. It is interesting to note, that in the hand of Charlemagne on that day, was the Holy Lance, the Spear of Destiny, from Jesus Crucifixion. The point of the spear had pierced the side of Christ, and his blood was on it. This made it one of the most powerful religious relics in the history of the world, and Charlemagne had it.

This was the Holy Lance, that had inspired hundreds of thousands of converted Christian troops. For the veterans that gave them a special meaning, and then also gave them an intensity in battle, that all religious relics always provide.

It was Pope Leo of the Catholic Church, that placed the crown on Charlemagne's head on Christmas Day 800 ad. The king of the Franks on that day, became the First Emperor of the West in centuries. It was at Saint Peter's Church on that day, that all witnessed the coronation. the Pope Leo, down on one knee, and prostrated himself before the great Charlemagne. Until this time in history this act of prostrating to the King by the Pope, had been done to the Emperors of Rome, many centuries ago. It had also been done to the Emperor of Byzantine or the Eastern Roman Empire, which stood much longer than the Western Empire. The Eastern Roman Empire was very rich and it was Greek speaking, and it stood until the 15th century.

But in the West, this act had not been taking place for many centuries, but now it was done. Charlemagne was Emperor and he loved it. It was because of Charlemagne and the ruthless Frank's, that he had been able to unite the Western Empire, and they would be going on to become the strongest power in the history of the world, Europe. This one act of the coronation of Charlemagne, confuses historians to this day. It was only reserved for Roman or Byzantine emperors exclusively.

The Title belonged to Rome, and only the pope could give the coronation or crown. What this did in reality, was make the Pope the strongest man in the West. Because without the blessings of the Pope, there could be no ceremony. This would be the marriage of convenience for church and state, and now they were destined to be tied together.

It is ironic that for 25 years Charlemagne had tried to make things legal, and he offered to marry a princess from the Eastern Roman Empire. The Byzantine Empire of the East would have no part of this. The Eastern Empire of the Romans still hoped and prayed for a military miracle, that would enable them to take back Rome and Italy, and someday the entire West.

But Dreams Are For Fools, and man does have his limits, even the greatest conquerors. Like a Master Chess Game, the pieces were moving, and the game was changing, and it was so interesting. There's a very wise saying that goes back for thousands of years, if wishes were horses, Beggars would ride.

In reality politics is a shrewd game of power, and everyone who plays, plays to win. What Pope Leo did on Christmas Day, he did for his own power, and also for the Church of Rome. The church in the west was Roman Catholic, and in the Greek speaking Byzantine Empire of the

East, it was Greek Orthodox. Both churches had the Supreme power, and Pope Leo was not to be denied. By crowning Charlemagne on Christmas Day, he made the Frankish King the Supreme New Roman emperor of the West, and Charlamagne definitely deserved it. The other half of the coin is, Pope Leo made the power of the Pope, the greatest and strongest power on the face of the Earth, it also showed Christian Europe, that the gift of title of Emperor, belonged exclusively to the Pope.

The Eastern Roman Empire argued, was Charlemagne right, over the legality of the crowning. But in reality Charlemagne was the strongest man in Europe for centuries, many centuries.

And the truth of the matter is, Charlemagne wanted total control of the Western Empire, and had laid the foundation, for some of the strongest Powers the world would ever see. Charlemagne ruled just as all Germanic rulers always had, with men with ties of personal loyalty.

Charlemagne made few changes in the ways that the government in the west had been run, since his father Pepin, or his grandfather Charles The Hammer Martel. Charlemagne however would take the institutions his family had left to him, and make them work even better. He tightened the reins, he shortened the leash that his officials were on, and Corruption stopped.

The government of Charlemagne was ruled by 2 forces, the Bishop's, and the Counts. Both of these arms of Charlemagne's power were separate from each other, and both were equal in power. Both Powers swore loyalty to the crown, and Charlemagne sent out inspectors to check on all of them. Each district had their own two man teams, that checked and reported on all the officials. All of the officials were rated on their performances, and Corruption was nowhere to be found. The way Charlemagne did business kept everything above board, Charlemagne demanded loyalty. The bishop, the counts, and inspectors, were positions of Charlemagne's government. All Charlemagne demanded was loyalty, for this was all it would take to make his dream on Europe come true. Charlemagne broke down all the other walls of tribal prejudice, and social classes, and he hired from them all. For the first time in the history of the West, Bavarians, Frank's, Saxons, and Lombards shared equally in the power and Prestige of Charlemagne's empire.

The rich were not favored over the poor, in fact all the posts were open to the men Charlemagne could trust. People from all over the Empire we're changing locations, and meeting and mixing, like they had never done before. Many of the Bishops, Counts, and Inspectors were given high posts in lands they had never seen before. Times were changing , especially in Europe, and it was all because of Charles the Great. This did more to unify the empire, then anything else could have. So that no one would get taken advantage of in business deals, Charlemagne reformed the economics of his enormous population. The great Emperor fixed the prices, on what merchants could charge for grain bought in bulk. He also forbid Shady deals from happening, by making business deals happen in daylight hours, and forbid transactions at night. This was a great leader, with great vision. Charlemagne was definitely the father of Europe, and he tried so desperately to create an Empire that would rival the ancient Roman Empire.

The long arm Of Charlemagne, tried to reach into every crack and cranny, and tie up all Loose Ends of the empire. Charlemagne knew very well of the Titanic power base, that he was Emperor over. The rivers of blood that have been spilt to create the empire, would not be spilled in vain, and Charlemagne knew the Germanic Empire, would one day divided up the entire Earth as their own. Charlemagne made sure the Empire he forged in blood, would become the most dominant power in that region, and he took great care of all the issues. Knowing full well, that a chain is only as strong as its weakest link, he made great plans. Charlemagne missed nothing in his reforms, and he even fixed the price a Baker could charge for a loaf of bread. At all levels Charlemagne oiled the wheels of society and government. With real order in the Germanic West, Trade began to return. The Mediterranean was now in the hands of the Muslim Fleet, and would remain that way for some time. The Muslims held the whole north of Africa, Spain, and they raided Italy, and Sicily, and also the Southern Coastline of modern-day France. It was a free-for-all, but then it always is. It was Charlemagne that extended protection to the Jewish merchants, for they claimed they were neither Christian or members of Islam. History would paint a different picture of course, and the Jew would be seen as a collaborator, and a spy for Islam and the Turks. But this was not known at the time, and Charlemagne had no way of knowing this, but he would learn.

The empires of Islam and the Christians of Europe would remain hostile to each other, and this is the way it had always been, and it's still is that way even today. Hostile to each other, each was a dangerous threat to the very existence of the other. Islam had already stormed into the empire, and had been defeated, but of course bigger invasions were still to come. At this moment of Charlemagne's power, he did Grant legal protection to the Jews, but they in turn filled a vital role. the Jews served as a middleman for the east and west, and trade and money still flowed. Of course the Jews that their hands all over it. They were always quick to position themselves to get some money.

The Jewish merchants Made trade Again respectable, and in time a new Merchant class developed in Europe. The people as a whole we're much better off. In the days of Charlemagne, the spices and silks, and other luxury items for the from the East, once again poured into Europe. If the money was right, the Caravans would start in China to bring everything that the Europeans might want, and as long as they could pay for it, it went on. This is not to say that business was usual, because it wasn't. In the Early Middle Ages, Medieval Europe was an agricultural state, and in Charlemagne's rule, things really progressed.

The science of agriculture, was only now becoming well-known to all the Germanic tribes, and the progress of all, was fantastic. Inventions, such as the water wheel, and the heavy plow, we're changing the face of the West forever. The labor of men and animals, could double the crops of 30 years before, and this meant that Europeans had security. This also meant that everyone that grew crops, could share in the wealth. The biggest single reason for the jump and output, was better management. The farmers now used the three field system, where one field lay empty, every third year. What that did was make the empty field Healthier as manure was spread, and it gave it time to recharge. In the long run, the three field system, allowed the Farmers to get a much higher yield per acre.

Seeing the new excessive crops, the herds grew much larger, and so did the population. The greatest Estates however belonged to Charlemagne and the church. If one can believe it, Charlemagne had 1615 Estates of his own. The Royal Estates were well managed by local and capable men, and all under Charlemagne prospered greatly. In fact the stewards ran the richest state so well, that Charlemagne did not even have to tax his subjects. This was truly a magical time, and the magic of the Germanic blood was awesome. The only change in Charlemagne's empire, was a small percentage of the produce grown, went directly to the church.

Of course there were free men that lived in groups of villages, and that also prospered in this wonderful time. With a large group of crops grown, the farmers no longer had to slaughter the part of the heard they could not feed. Now the herds were growing steadily, and the herders had something to trade, and they got over like fat rats.

All levels of Germanic Society prospered, and with the larger Grain production, it led to more being made and consumed. Forests were also being cleared, for now that production was up, so were people's dreams. The poor men and women or peasants, saw their standard of living rise dramatically, just like everyone else. The Army that Charlemagne and his Germanic Warriors had conquered in the east, now opened up for the peasants. Charlemagne had dreams for the territories in the Eastern lands, and soon they would be filled and cultivated by Germanic farmers. The empire was steadily growing, and what had been taken by the sword, was now producing food for the entire Germanic population.

There were still plagues in the days of Charlemagne, and they killed tens of thousands, but doctors were very Scarce. Medicine was almost non-existent, however, the numbers of Europe would never fall again. For the first time in centuries gone by, there was peace and order at home for periods of hundreds of years. After the fall of the Roman Empire, there had been a great Slaughter, in the battle for Supremacy. But those days are past, and with Charlemagne at the helm, all Europe would prosper. Of course there would always be Wars, but Charlemagne wanted the wars fought on the borders or frontiers of the empire. To all the large landowners, and to all the men of letters, these were the days, they had all dreamed of, and the future looked so bright.

Charlemagne was a Gifted ruler, with a vision for the future. As his Conquest grew, so did the need for men who knew how to read and write. It was Charlemagne that took a deep interest in the well-being of his people's future, and he started what historians call the Renaissance. It was because of the Renaissance, that the culture of the empire grew, to Such Great Heights. It was the son of the nobleman that would be the first to be educated, for his nobles were well trusted, loyal agents of the empire. It was the sons of the nobles, that in the future would have the hold on the administrative positions of the empire, and it would be to them that they would be entrusted.

This may sound to the modern man or woman, like a Monumental problem. In those days, you could count on your fingers and toes, the men or women you could really read or write. The whole mindset of the people of that age, and before them, was survival in a hostile world. This is all they ever thought about, but now they had a chance to come up, and they took it. A man in any of the ages before modern times, had better be skilled in the Arts of combat, because you could not hope to kill your enemies with a book.

Even the church men of the Holy Roman Empire, We're Not educated men. However the light of knowledge in Ireland And England, was due to the religious zeal of the Irish missionaries. Make no mistake, the German west of Europe, had to be taught from the ground up, so that the officials could be educated. Even after the fall of Rome for many centuries Europe had been in turmoil. All the wars, raids, and pillaging, and plunder, the framework of Education had been totally destroyed. Many of the great works of the Greek and Roman writers had been lost forever, and it would take a long time to regain their perspective on the world. Luckily the monks carried many Works away, to translate at later times. In this way the monks help preserve the intelligence, that it took so very long to get.

The biggest obstacle to learning in Charlemagne's empire, was the language differences of the regions. Charlemagne was faced with his own Tower of Babel story, just way too many languages. Charlemagne had grown up in the Rhineland, and spoke the language of the Eastern Franks. The dialect of the West was totally different. The Western Franks spoke with Latin dialects, it seemed like a second language, to all who spoke, or heard it.

Charlamagne once said, he had to study the Latin dialect of the western Franks, just to be able to understand them. It was the same Western dialects, that eventually developed into the French, Spanish, Italian, and Portuguese languages. The Latin that men called Roman, was already dead as a tongue, but if one desired to know it, they had no choice, but to learn it in a classroom, it was dead. Charlamagne Above All Odds, did transform the Barbarian minds. To do this he offered cash rewards to teachers, and to all learned men.That's all he had to do, was offer the cash, and they were standing in line to educate the ignorant Barbarian. But please don't forget, it was the ignorant Barbarian, that forged out this Empire, in the blood of its enemies. From Italy came a flood of teachers, by the thousands they say. Italy was the only place in Europe where there were too many wise men. Yes they came by the thousands to teach, and of course get paid well. The famous historian Paul the deacon came, and so did Peter of Pisa, and they both taught writing. Roman music teachers came to teach the art of singing, and also the playing of musical instruments. Culture was being transformed into Germanic Europe, and all would benefit.

The famous poet of the Visigoths Theodulf, became a Bishop at Orleans. Charlemagne assembled the best Collective Minds in the whole of Europe, and those were handsomely rewarded. Charlemagne's most trusted advisor Eginhard , came to study with Charlemagne, and taught him all he knew of History. Hordes of Scholars came from Ireland, to spread their understanding and knowledge, and England sent their men of wisdom too. The greatest addition to Charlemagne's Revival of learning, was an Anglo-Saxon named Alcuim. In this one man,

Charlemagne had the greatest of organizers, a leading man of the studies, and also a tireless worker. He also had been the director of studies at the Cathedral School at York in England. This school at York, at this time in history, was famous for being the West's greatest center of learning. This great man of wisdom was Chief advisor to Charlemagne on every matter from political affairs to religious affairs.

Charlemagne trusted this one man, the future of the empire, when he made him the director of the royal educational program, and director of cultural activities. He was without a doubt the glue they kept it all together.

The Anglo-Saxon Calcium was a man that did like to get right to the heart of the matter, so first he started right at the heart, in Charlemagne's capital Aachen. It was here that Charlemagne had the palace School, and it had been there since the days of Charles Martel in 714. The palace school of the German kings, was in reality a school that taught The Art of War, little else. Under the guidance of the Anglo-Saxon, it became much more. For the sons of nobleman, and the future teachers, and Scholars, the curriculum covered all the subjects they would need on their road to their careers. The Palace School taught all seven of the liberal arts, and it covered a wide range of subjects. There was Basic Arithmetic, and Geometry, Music, Grammar, and Logic. To those that had a love for it, there was also Astronomy. All the learning from the Greeks went to waste, for there were no translations yet, and it didn't look like there would be any anytime soon. The study of Greek was unheard of in the West, because the West Was one hundred percent Germanic.

Also to the pupils of the great palace School, was the introduction to Latin, and how it was used in the powerful literature from Rome. This program of learning was awesome, and too much for the early minds of the West, for it was intellectually starved. Like the Romans and the Greeks of old, the German students loved Broad discussions. The pages of History tell us that even Charlemagne attended the Palace School. Whenever he wasn't fighting his Wars he often jumped into the Lively discussions. Their leader, ignited like an atomic bomb, and soon their capital was called the second Rome, or the second Athens.

Education of the Germanic peoples was like a great marriage, that would last forever. It was not a matter of choice, it was Charlemagne's command. Soon Charlemagne commanded the freedom of villages, and the largest states, to teach the people all they knew, and school was free. Charlemagne's Palace School at Aachen lead the way to education. The other regions soon picked up the art of learning too. It was the Visigoth Theodulf that was the first to make public education totally free for the local population,And for this he will be remembered. Soon all the high placed Churchman went to Charlemagne's capital asking how they could upgrade their Cathedral schools, and also they asked guidance in the subjects that should be taught. In reality what the Palace School at Aachen did, was Secure the future for the German Empire. The German Empire now had educated people, who could become officials of the church and state. Also the Palace School produced the greatest teachers for the coming generations of Germans. A few of the students from the Palace School rose to the top, and soon began to write poetry, that was compared to the best of the Romans or the Greeks. The most startling knowledge that came out of the Palace School was his scientific work, that said that the Earth is round. It was at this time in the German World, that it was taught the world was round, and it would be Taught from then on, so much for Christopher Columbus. This wisdom shock the world, but somebody's got to lead the way. Who knows for how long those with knowledge, had actually kept the secret.

The reality of the education at the Palace School, was that most Scholars devoted most of their time to the study of the Bible of course, and other books by the church fathers too. The biggest contribution the students made, was in the changes they made in handwriting. Handwriting had always been done with large Roman letters, and it always had been written on the Egyptian material called papyrus. But after the fall of Rome, the Mediterranean fell into the hands of the Muslim Pirates, and the shipping from Egypt and Lebanon, could not get through. And because of the Muslim Pirates cutting off their supply of papyrus, other materials were sought and found. Of course the price of writing material in the German West went Sky High, and they were forced to condense the letters, and save writing space.

Ireland and England jumped into the game, with the same thing in mind, and quickly developed small letters themselves. The Franks not to be left out, developed their own compact writing, that was also much easier to write. The Franks were now so easy to read and write ,it quickly came into use, throughout the entire Empire. It must also be noted, that the scholars of Charlemagne, rediscovered, and preserved many of the past great works of art. All the precious ancient Works were recopied, for future Generations. There were dozens of Scholars who worked for months for just one great work, and dozens worked year-round. By the end of the 9th century, many of the monasteries had libraries with hundreds of books. It's amazing but we all have much to thank the scholars for, for if they did not copy, we would not have the writings of Caesar Cacatuas, and many of the other authors who wrote the classics of Roman times.

In the field of Art, the Palace School brought the Biblical Figures, to the covers of their sacred books, and on their instruments that poured their wine, water, and beer. As the culture grew, it was of course more easy to explain things. It is true, that a picture says a thousand words, and more important, it made the Warriors minds stop and think. The new culture was adding so much to a people that were once only Brute Barbaric Heathens. The artists and the many Craftsman added so much to Western Art, and in the future they dominated it. The architecture in the days of Charlemagne changed for the better also.

The church architecture was dynamic, and brilliant, as it was new, and in Charlemagne's Capital Aachen it was breathtaking. The Palace was the greatest example, for the chapel was given an eight sided Dome over it, that inspired all, in the eye, that saw it. The palace Chapel had Roman columns to support arches, and all who saw it, claimed it was a masterpiece.

Bishop Theodulf not to be outdone, Built a masterpiece outside Orleans. In the architectural masterpiece, a Byzantine mosaic was in it, and Moorish arches were built in. The Moorish arches were in fact an invention of the Visigoths. From one end of the empire, to the other, magnificent changes were happening, even if many were just Roman Imitations. In reality what they were proving was a new religious spirit was alive. The child was growing fast and maturing, and Europe was definitely on the right Road. Germanic Europe was being transformed into the greater Europe, gathering the best ideas from the four corners of the empire.

The Final Act for Charlemagne's life took place at his favorite Palace Chapel. On January 28th , 814 at the age of 72, Charlemagne died. He was buried sitting straight up on the throne, that he had ruled from. In 1095 Pope Urban preached the First Crusade to attack the Holy Land, and boy did he preach well, and he laid it on real thick. Each new Christian Warrior knew we must regain the land that Jesus walked. He asked only one thing from the Christian Warriors of Europe. To do their Duty as worthy Sons of Charles the Great.

In reality if only for a moment,the Warriors from Islam had been attacking Europe for hundreds of years.They had raped, pillaged and plundered for many centuries.Many of the thousands of attacks on Europe went extremely well,and much wealth was taken.Much land in Spain,Southern France,and Southern Italy was taken,and many women were taken as slaves.It was a constant bloody war,and at times it even looked as though,western europe would be lost completely.The Teutonic Knights allways rose to every invasion,to drive the invaders away.

The Crusades changed all this, because we took the war to them.And believe me they were very sorry when the armed Knights arrived. We have never let up,to this day it still goes on, this is the way of men.

You fight them there, or you fight them here,it is an easy choice.

Spain had some of the largest gold mines in that part of the world,and everyone wanted them.

ISLAM WAS OUR GREATEST ENEMY<THE JEWS SPIED FOR THEM MANY TIMES>

PART 3
Chapter 10 of the Viking attacks on England, Ireland, and Europe.

 The Emperor Charlemagne was dead, and the Empire he had conquered and United under the Franks, would now get the real test.Europe would be bothered by the ancient Germanic custom, subdividing among all Sons, the property fathers held. The most interesting part of medieval history, was the slow but certain advance of Germanic civilization, and with it the spread of Christianity. The empire to the furthest limits, on the East, the Border had been drawn between the Germans or Teutons, and the Slavs, and the Tartars. This line between the three people's were established to be permanent, because the Slavs and Asians were not German, nor were they Christian.

If one remembers, the German tribes at one time had gone all the way to the Rhine, and the Danube as barriers. These two Mighty Rivers had been their borders for thousands of years, and no man dared cross. It was almost a Deja Vu experience, but this time they sought, to keep out the Barbarian tribes, and it was they who were the makers or the keepers of civilization . It was utterly amazing that Charlemagne and his Valiant Frank's had conquered all the Germanic tribes, and they had them all under their political control.

The list of Conquest reads quite impressive. Among the Conquests were the Alemany, the Visigoths, the Burgundians, the Lombards, the Bavarians, the Saxons, and the Frisians.

It was only the military genius, and administrative skill of Charlemagne, that made it all happen. In the end he had made his dream come true, and the Empire was held together firmly by Blood and religion. In many ways Charlemagne was perhaps the greatest conqueror of all, for he knew when to stop. Others in his position, would have been tempted to be the Conqueror of the rest of the world too. Charlemagne's dream was different, he wanted to secure the Germanic races on his continent, and to forge them into a great Christian Empire. Like the Great Pyramid in Egypt the Empire of Charlemagne Rested on 3 points. The Christian religion, Germanic blood, and the leadership of the Franks. These were Charlemagne's three points. Several key points must be noted before we can proceed into the Middle Ages, for they are powerful as they are interesting.

The power of Charlemagne was an Imperial Power, long before he was called Emperor. He conquered all the Germanic Nations, and for sure was known as more than just a king, he was almost a god. One of Charlemagne's first general laws was everyone in his whole Realm, whether he was a clergyman Or soldier, should renew to him as emperor the vow of loyalty.

It was the same vow that Charlemagne's subjects had taken to him as their King, but now he wanted them to take the vow, to him as their Emperor. He further stated in his law, that all the boys even down to the age of 12, shall take the same vow.
Charlemagne believed that God entered into the Affairs of man on a daily basis, and that in reality this vow was made to God. In the mind of Charlemagne his life had been to fulfill God's will on Earth.He was doing that by spreading Christianity clear across Europe. No one man was more responsible, for Christianizing Europe than Charlemagne. He had spent his life defeating the Pagans and Heathen tribes, and because he had a righteous life, he had a long life.It had been very prosperous.

In 806 Charlemagne for 6 years, according to Legal Minds, drew up the paperwork for the division of the empire, between his Three Sons

The three sons of Charlemagne, at the time, in different parts of the empire, knew which part they would receive, if they in fact outlived the father. In the Record Charlamagne says, with the help of God, defend the boundaries of the Kingdom, to Louis the youngest son, he gave Providence, most of burgundy, Glasgowny, and Aquitaine. To Pepin went Italy, Bavaria, Alemany, south of the Danube, and most of the Alpine Country.

The oldest son Charles received all the rest. Charles would receive the Frankish territory and even Saxony, and the land of the Furious Frisians. To the educated this would mean, that Charles got the largest share, and he would also get the most important lands. In this work of art, Charlemagne left out nothing, and he provided answers to all the problems that might come up. He begged the Sons to respect each other, and their boundaries, and above all else, to help each other defeat their enemies, foreign and domestic.

Judging by the careful wording of the document, Charlamagne feared that the selfishness of men would ruin the structure he had taken such great pains to build. But this document meant nothing, because two of the three sons died before the father. The two oldest sons died, Charles and Pepin, before the great father, and this left the entire Empire to Louis. The Final Act in Charlemagne's life, was to see his son take the crown. in 813 ad on the 11th day of September, Louis was crowned in the Church of St Mary. Another account says that Louis placed the crown on his own head, which I probably would have done myself. In reality, it doesn't matter if Charlemagne or Louis Placed the crown on the head. The point is the Pope didn't get a chance to do it, and could be left out of it all together. It is best when you have a separation of church and state anyway.

The church leaders were men of narrow vision. They would have you believe that it was necessary for the Pope to do the honors. The strong family of Charlemagne knew there must be a separation of powers of church and state, and one must never give the ultimate authority to the church or anybody else. The simple fact was, at this time in history, the connection of the Pope and the Empire really wasn't there yet.

4 months after the crown of gold was placed on the head of Louis, Charlemagne was dead. Charlemagne had ruled for 47 years as king of the Franks, and 14 years as Emperor of all Germanic tribes. Louis would go down in history as Louis the Pious, and enjoy the beautiful right of ruling as sole ruler of the Frankish Empire. But power is a strange thing, and Louis and Charlemagne where as different as night and day. Charlemagne had built his power, by the raw force of his character, and Louis had just been at the right place at the right time.

Unlike the government of Rome, Charlemagne's empire had been built on the strength of one man, and therefore would unravel more quickly when he was dead. Louis had lived most of his life In in modern-day France, and never really experienced the grinding wheels of government. It is said by those that knew him best, that Louis was influenced easily, and often changed sides quickly, to be influenced again. Charlemagne was cut from another cloth, with very fixed thoughts, which had always been prompt, with vigorous action.

The pages of History tell us that Louis was gentle, and his advisers could go on their own way, and then get the uncertain Louis to go along with them. The pages of History tell us, that in a crisis, when personality was all important, the personality of Louis failed to meet the great demands of his time. The biggest issue that Louis wrestled with, is when he died, how would the empire be divided amongst his Three Sons. Louis sons names were Lothar, Pippin, and Ludwig. They were all filled with the energy of their youth.

Louis however was the new ruler, and he made heads spin at some of his decisions. He was not satisfied with the loose moral of the Court, and he set out to purify it. In fact Louis made many enemies with the court of Charlemagne. All his father's friends and trusted advisors were banished from their High held offices, for Louis didn't want to live in the shadow of his father forever. Before he even had his feet wet, he had made many enemies amongst the rich and Powerful of the Franks. He would learn later, that this has been a major mistake, for although there was Heavy partying, and a whole lot of womanizing, these friends of Charlemagne knew how The Empire was run.

Two of Charlemagne's cousins who had been the most trusted of Charlemagne's Advisors were stripped of their posts, and sent into Exile outside the empire. Bernhard, was called in from Italy, and made to swear loyalty in the presence of Louis, and many say he was put on a short leash, and was given no power to make decisions. After King Pepin of Italy died, Bernhard was crowned in his place.

Louis also called his Palace Aachen, with 3 brothers that were the illegitimate Sons of Charlemagne. It was at this time that he showed them there was ice water in his veins. The three brothers were forced by Emperor Louis to become monks, and the secret was kept from the people.

There was also the case of the Five Sisters who partied with the court of Charlemagne for years, and they had been the talk of the Frankish Aristocracy. These five sisters who had seen the best living, and the greatest parties of Charlemagne and his crowd, were promptly exiled to the world of the nuns. Emperor Louis was making waves, and many of the coveted Inner Circle were getting wet, and some were even drowning. These choices that Louis was making, were to serve notice to an Empire, that there was now a break in the traditions of those before himself. Only on one point did he follow the example of Charlemagne, and that is he divided the empire with his sons. The oldest son Lothar was to rule Bavaria, And Pippen got Aquitaine.

The third son and the youngest, Ludwig was Much Too Young To Rule at this point in time, but he would have his day. The first 2 years Of The Emperor's Rule, took him to the Eastern Frontier, and he took a strong hand in the military operations. In 816 the plot begins to thicken, for Pope Leo the third had died. He was replaced by Pope Stephen the 4th. The Third had been the Pope who crowned Charlemagne in the year 800 ad. He was also the pope who had said nothing when Louis crowned himself. The first move Steven 4th made, ways to announce to Louis, he made a visit to the court of the Franks. Pope Stephen the 4th was Nobody's Fool, and his first and most concern, was to establish good relations with the Frankish Empire. The pages of History tell us the newly elected Pope spent his first few days at Rheims, negotiating the rights of the Pope, and finding out exactly what his boundaries were. The biggest political move

Pope Stephen the 4th made, was the crowning of Louis, and he did it with such style. Pope Steven 4th showed great respect to Emperor Louis, by crowning him with the same crown that Constantine had worn. To make things perfect Emperor Louis received his crown in the ancient Church of St Mary. The pages of History tell us the same church was the spot where the ferocious Clovis was baptized. The bells of ancient history were ringing, and everybody danced to the music. Louis in the eyes of the Pope and Rome was now the Emperor, but in reality Louis have been signing his name,since his father Charlemagne died.

It is interesting to note that Louis was the name of later kings of France, there was a long line of them. All the way to Napoleon, it was the same blood in their veins. France had always had a thing for Royal Blood, and they always would. It must be noted that Louis would have continued to be the Emperor without his recruiting by the Pope, but he did need to strengthen his own alliance with the Pope, and the power seekers in Rome.

817 ad. Louis called together the most powerful Brokers of the Frankish Empire at his Imperial Palace. It was the duty of Louis to overhaul the monastic system, for his great Ally the church, was the moral and social Guardian of his people. The great assembly at the Palace was called the Diet of 817 ad. It was here that the great Empire of the Franks would be divided again. Louis was a man of great vision, and he knew that if the Empire kept being divided by the sons of The Emperor's, the Empire would not remain the great power that it was. It was decided by Louis that there would be one sole heir to Emperor Louis, with the approval by those in attendance, Lothair was crowned future successor to his father. Emperor Louis gave his other son Pippin, Aquitaine, also the frontier of Toulouse, Glasscony, And a few large Estates in Burgundy. Of course with these future gifts, also would be the crown of King, and also the title. Ludwig got a few of the frontier lands nearby. Lothair besides getting the Title and Crown of Emperor, was also to receive all the remaining land. The young Kings were given a free hand in their own kingdoms, to manage Affairs as they wanted. The Kings were not to go to war against their foreign enemies alone, or without permission of the Emperor. They also were not to choose wives from foreign Nations, and this was a must. If one of the Kings would die, his kingdom was not to be be divided amongst his sons, it was to stay intact, in the hands of the one son, that the people chose. There was always a clause for any of the illegitimate children that the Royal studs had left behind. It always was something simple, like deal gently with any illegitimate children. The German Warriors had always been great womanizers, and many had dozens of children.

Pippin and Ludwig the younger Sons, of course hated the new arrangement, that gave them the smaller shares, and of course made them subject to their older brother. From the very first day they were United in their effort to get the new plan recalled, but the Proper party was always on the side of Lothair. Trouble is always Brewing because of the divisions of the empire, and now the growing interest of many new nationalities were trying to make further divisions. Especially the kingdoms of Ludwig and Pippin, which had ancient and uniform populations. The people of the kingdom of Ludwig and Pippen would have backed their King in any decision he had made. all through the lifetime of Louis the Emperor, there were countless arguments over what should happen upon his death, and when he did die, the battlefield would decide the future.

The issue of succession, returned to a bloody issue, and on the great battlefields, everything would be decided. It was time in 817 For the grandson of Charlemagne, Bernard, to make his play. Bernard had been King of Italy since 812, and the deal called for his kingdom to go to Lothair. Bernard was now to be only a subject King and mainly an advisor. He thought it was his time to rise to Supremacy. Many other voices of revolt joined his hastily thrown-together Force, but not the kingdom as a whole. Louis upon hearing of the Revolt was quick to lead an Army south. In fact he took the Alpine passes so quickly, that the rebels just surrendered, with not a drop of blood spent.

Bernard and his advisers were brought before the assembly at the Capitol Aachen. The verdict from his advisors was harsh, but the Emperor, changed the verdict at the last second to a lesser sentence, which was that Bernard was to be blinded. Bernhard had such brute force and cruelty,on him that he died a few days later anyway, so Justice was done. There would still be many attempts, and new divisions of the empire. Because of the Family Feud's,the division of Empire, would be a curse on the Germanic Empire, and the blood rivalries would plague Europe all the way to, and including the 20th century.

Between the years 817 and 840 the divisions of the Empire would happen 6 times. In 824 the division of the Empire would be shaken, by the birth of another son. The son was none other than the future famous Charles the bald. This particular son had come from the second marriage of the Emperor, and he was Destined to make a huge mark.

The second wife of Emperor Louis was named Judith, and she too was of noble blood. Judith belonged to the famous house of Welf, which also would make their mark high on history. The famous House of Welf centuries later would produce the great and famous Queen Victoria of Great Britain. Like the great Queen Victoria many centuries later, Judith herself was beautiful, and also a political genius.

The junior Emperor Lothair, traveled from his kingdom in Italy, to proclaim himself Godfather to the new arrival to the Royal Family. The future Emperor Lothair took a vow to defend the child with his own life, and would honor his father Louis decision, when it was decided, what part of the empire the child would receive. Emperor Louis believed the vow his son Lothair had taken. Emperor Louis carved out a slice of the rich and powerful Duchy Alemania or Swabia. Also the new child, Charles the bald, would receive a slice of Burgundy , and several other large pieces of property. The beautiful slice of the Kingdom that the newest royal had received, made Lothair furious, because all this land and Power, came out of his portion of the empire. Lothair became so Furious, that Emperor Louis confined Lothair to Italy, and cut him right out of all the functions of the empire.

The documents of History tell us that in 831 a new document was added to the building pile. The new alignment went as follows, Lothair was to stay in Italy, while the rest of the empire went to Pippin, Ludwig, and Charles. Charles the Bald was to get Burgundy, while Ludwig was to receive almost all of Germany, and Pippin was to take Gaul. Burgundy was to go to Charles,and is the land between modern-day France and Germany. In reality the new plan, was the old plan of Charlemagne in 806. The new plan was never set in motion, but it did show The Growing Power of Charles, and his mother. Lothair was not to be denied, and he quickly made plans for Revenge. The pope and the Frankish church we're behind Lothair, and soon the two brothers were too. The stage was set, and all the players armed, and the field of combat would be called the field of Lies.

Emperor Louis was beaten and imprisoned, and now the Emperor was forced to make concessions, so in 833, there would be more division. This time Judith and her son would be ruined, and now the tables had turned again. Charles the bald was now to get nothing, Ludwig this time would receive all the German-Speaking races of the empire. Pippen would receive all the western territories, and Lothair would get all of Italy, and all the middle part of the Empire known as Burgundy. Lothair loved this arrangement, for it gave him exactly what he wanted. Now the ancient Frankish land of Asturias with Aachen as the capital, would be his private domain.

The Wheel of Fortune and Faith however was not done spinning, and a new web was almost to be spun. Exactly one year after his imprisonment, Emperor Louis had revenge on his deal, for once again his forces had been gathered. Lothair was once again retired to Italy, and in 837 Charles the bald would once again be brought into the picture. Once again there was another assembly called at The Imperial Capital at Aachen. At this assembly, Charles was given another slice of the empire. Pippen was consulted before the slice was given, and he of course gave his approval. This time Charles would be given a new piece of territory, in the very heart of the Frankish lands. Along the beautiful Seine River the kingdom of Charles would be, and as a bonus, the gorgeous and Powerful City of Paris what also be his.

Ludwig lost the lower Seine River and they were given to Charles the bald. In 838 fate would play its hand again, and Pippin would die at the Diet or Assembly of Worms in 839. All the land that was to have been Pippins, now belonged to Charles. The Assembly of Worms gave their legal consent, to Charles the bald, having the entire Western half of the Holy Roman Empire.

Ludwig the German would remain in power only in Bavaria, and the eastern part of the entire Empire would now belong to Lothair. The hand of Fate was ready to touch the lives of mortal man again, and Ludwig arched to confront the Aged Louis.

The death of Emperor Louis was the signal to all successors to the throne, to be ready for battle. The last Act of Emperor Louis, had been to send the Imperial Crown, and all other Royal Insignia of the Emperor, to his successor Lothair. Now the Sacred Holy Lance, the Spear of Destiny, would be in the hands, of the next Germanic Emperor. Power was changing hands once again, and the Holy Lance would be in the hand, of all that sat on that throne.

Going there at once, he began his journey from Italy, to stake his claim. Ludwig the German had plans of his own, and at once gathered all the forces from the eastern half of the empire, and sped to the ancient Holy Ground of the Franks in Franconia. Charles the bald, was busy putting down a Revolt in his kingdom of Aquitaine, and the threat was from his nephew Pippin, who had Designs of his own.

So halfway through the year of 841, we find the Germanic Warriors, armed and ready to Spill the blood, for the cult of power. Ludwig the German, and Charles the bald, Allied their forces together, while Lothair and the rebellious nephew Pimpin did the same. In fact at the site of Fontenay the great armies would Clash, and the future of the German Empire would be decided once and for all. The battlefield was in Burgundy, and the fields in Burgundy would be baptized in blood once again.

This had grown to be such a mess, all the splitting and dividing Of the empire, was getting to be a big pain in the ass.Lothair wanted desperately to be Emperor, and would not listen to anybody. Of course Ludwig and Charles sent one last message, that is that God would have the final word, and it would be trial by combat.

On the following day,they were locked in combat again, and when the last drops Of German blood were spilled, Lothair and his Warriors had been beaten decisively. This battle would be remembered till the end of Europe, because it was more than just brother against brother, and their armies.

In reality it wasn't even Frank against Frank, and was a battle in the big picture of Roman against Teuton. The forces of Lothair in reality were pure Roman forces, while Ludwig was fighting with loyal German blood at his side. The battles of Germans against Romans, have been going on for over 600 years, and this my friend, was just one more episode.

Above all else the violent Clash brought out the forces and spirit of nationality. In 842 Ludwig the German. and Charles the bald, would meet in Strasbourg, and take up against their older brother Lothair.Basically this is how the individual countries that made up the old Holy Roman Empire developed, there's an old saying, too many cooks spoil the broth, and that certainly is no lie. There must be one leader, and history has certainly proved it to us. When people share power, because man is just an educated animal, he will stab anyone in the back to rise up in the ranks, this is the way of men. Many times even in the Catholic Church, we had popes and Bishops do the same thing. There's an old saying that power corrupts, and absolute power Corrupts absolutely. You almost need a scorecard to see who's running what section of the Empire between the sons of Charlemagne. I guess what I'm getting to, is to create an empire, and keeping it going, is an extremely difficult thing. For the sake of all free men everywhere, it was the German tribes, that fought for all men's freedom for Thousands years. If this long and bitter struggle to create an empire, would not have been waged, we would all be slaves and in prison. The host of Strasbourg in 842 is as follows.This was the oath everyone took!

For the love of God, for the sake of our peoples, as of ourselves, I promise from this day forth, as God shall grant me wisdom and strength, I will treat this my brother , like i ought to be treated, Provided that he shall do the same by me. Ludwig gave the first oath, and Charles took the 2nd oath, then the Warriors of King Ludwig and King Charles followed.

The Warriors of King Ludwig, and King Charles,took it each in their own language. In reality this taught everyone that the Empire must not be divided again, or risk losing everything. The treaty was signed between the brothers, and a river of blood was saved, and did not flow on that day.

The treaty in many ways looked like the plan of 817. All agreed that Italy, Bavaria, and Aquitaine were the three most sought-after areas of the empire, and each of the Kings already had one. Ludwig had Bavaria, Lothair had Italy and Charles had Aquitaine. These three places for many years had been permanent governments, and neither of the men would have considered changing it. It took no genius to figure out the enormous length of Lothaire's portion would be hard to defend. The people were a Motley Crue, the Germans, the Romans, and the Frisians. These differences were bound to come to a boil in the future at some time. The people of Lothair's portion had really nothing in common, not even a Common Language. To make matters worse, the Vikings at this time, we're beginning to make raids along the boundaries of the empire. The Frankish Empire was about to be tested again, but this is nothing new, they would be tested all the way up to World War II. Ludwig the German added Bavaria, and all the lands North from the Southern Slope of the Elks, to The Far Side of the Rhine. Ludwig would get basically whatever he wanted in that area. Charles the bald remained King of the West, and kept as his Capital Aquitaine.

Although the empire was still intact, it was only in theory. In reality the empire was split up into three kingdoms, and each would grow along its own path. After all that it happened, the coveted Title of Emperor was an empty title. The three kings,ruled with an iron fist. In reality with all the drama for the last century, the kingdom of Charles would soon become the kingdom of France. And the kingdom of Louis, in 45 more years, would become the kingdom of Germany. The kingdom of Lothair in 888, would be cut up, and several more kingdoms would merge. The huge Frankish Empire that Charlemagne had United, was now beginning to unravel. In 888 the only kingdoms that would enjoy the test of time, would be France and Germany. Each time the empire was divided, it meant that the empire was in reality dying. In reality after Emperor Louis, the men that followed, engaged in petty squabbles, inflamed by jealousy, and greed, for more land. As the sons took more power and more land, their dukes and their counts, took even more from them. A great Empire was dying slowly, or so it seemed, the rest fell easy prey to the Vikings.

Across the English Channel, the Danish attacks Had started in 835, and by 845 they turned into full-scale invasions. The attacks of the Vikings on the empire would be massive, almost like the Germans on France in World War II. The Danes, who were the same blood as the Germans, feared nothing, and nothing would stop they're battle axes and swords from carving out an Empire that they desired. The continent of Europe was to feel the full force of the Viking tribes, and the greatest warriors the world has ever seen.

Just 2 Generations after the great Charlemagne, the full force of the Nordic Warriors fell on them. They came from the Scandinavian North, the Norseman or men from the north. The

Vikings came from exactly the same original Homeland of the earlier Germanic tribes, that had conquered Rome.

The Germanic tribes found a crumbling Empire in Rome, and took complete advantage of the situation. This time the crumbling Empire was the Empire of the Franks, tamed by Christian beliefs. The Bavarian Vikings who attacked England and France, brought with them the old tactics, of rape, pillage, and plunder.

The Vikings brought to the continent, a wild orgy of robbery and killing, like the Franks had never known. It was Deja Vu once again, and the church men screamed, that it was because of their sins, that god had brought the Wrath of the northmen. It had been the same Reason that the Romans had said for their invasion of their lands, from the German tribes. They tried to tell their people it was because they no longer lived the Roman way, and that their civilization was decaying, and that the invasion was actually God's will to punish them.

In reality, the Roman Legions had kept extending their frontiers of the empire, and they finally met their match, the Germans. The same can be said of the Eastern wars that Charlemagne had fought, for 30 years with his armies of the Franks. He had held bloody and gruesome battles with the Saxons, and in reality they were their cousins. The Northman who were the cousins of all the Germanic tribes had come for their Revenge. In 771 Charlemagne was the soul King of the Franks. Thanks to the territorial Ambitions of Charlemagne, the light of History would shine bright on the Northern countries. It was Charlemagne alone that turned on the fantastic bright light that lit up in Northern Nations, and allowed them to go on and rule. It brought the king of the Great Danes, Siegfried into the Limelight, and in the near future King Godfried. For thousands of years the Vikings had been Trading with all the empires of the Earth, but now thanks to the Frankish writers, the Viking Blood and arms entered into recorded history. Do not think for one moment that this is where there worldwide Commerce started, it have been going on for thousands of years. And the Vikings besides being the greatest fighters in the history of the world, we're also the greatest businessman. They dealt with 4 continents, bringing Goods to each continent, that they never had, or had ever even seen before. In this way the Vikings stacked enough gold to fill a couple fort knox's, and I mean all the way to the top with gold. The Vikings must be remembered as businessman, not just for attacking, and raping, and pillaging, and plundering. The Viking fleets traveled the world, and did business with all, to their own advantage, and of course their bank accounts. Of course they were great warriors, many nations had those, but they were International businessman, in a Time, that most men and women never traveled over 50 miles from home in their entire life. While the Vikings were quite different, of this there can be no doubt, I step up to tell you the complete truth.

In 772 Charlamagne attacked the homeland of the Saxons, and for 30 years the battles raged back and forth, at some time it had to be over. I mean, both sides were just as ruthless, and would not surrender, so the bloody battles waged on for 30 years. One day bloody fighting, some days assassin's. But all days were extremely brutal, and extremely bloody. It took every every day of those 30 years for the Saxons to be defeated, for history had never seen a more warlike people. The homeland of the Saxons had several Rivers as their eastern boundary, and the Rhine was their western boundary. To the north, the boundary ran right up to the land of the Great Danes at the River Eider. On both sides of the river, communities could be seen, and both Banks were lined with large villages.

The East, West, and Northern boundaries were set in cement you might say. Nature and her Rivers had defined exactly, where these boundaries would be. To the South, the boundary of Saxony was less Defined, and the Saxons and the Franks would gladly fight for it. In fact ever since the days of the hammer, Charles Martel, the battles and skirmishes had taken place.

The Pages of History, tell us that Charlemagne would start where Charles Martel had fought.Both wanted to be overlords of the Saxons. Many of the greatest Saxons for centuries had gone off to England to conquer and to raid. The Saxons with their Viking ships, had taken England by storm. Some of the great historians say the Saxons from Germany attacked England for 600 years. They were vicious Warriors in every country, they had the magic blood in their veins. The war god Thor had been with them obviously, and wherever they fought, they did extremely well. The Viking invasions for 600 years of Great Britain were relentless, and they would not stop for many generations. The Saxons from Germany, would own at least part of Great Britain someday, even if they had to fight for a thousand years, they would not be denied.

In the bigger picture, what this cross-channel Invasion had done, was drain the mother country of tens of thousands, if not hundreds of thousands of Saxon Warriors. This is the reason, the war went on with the Franks for 30 years. If the Saxon Vikings would not have sailed to Great Britain, I believe they would have easily defeated the Frankish Empire, but if is a very big word. Just to show you how big those two letters really are, if, my aunt had balls, she'd be my uncle.

But still small in numbers The Valor of the Saxons would not be denied, and for 30 years on a daily basis, there was intertribal war with the Franks. Most historians assure us that this was an extremely vicious and bloody conflict. What else could it be with the Earth's Best, and most Fearless Warriors doing the fighting. The Saxons were blonde, and brown haired, fearless and dominating Warriors, who had never known defeat, and in single combat, they never would. The strength is in numbers, unless you have atomic bombs, and the collective armies of the Franks were Victorious eventually.The Saxons were heathen, and Thor and Woden were in their hearts and their minds, and of course in their weapons.

In France they were pagans also, but they pretended to convert to Christianity, and they fought with the Holy Lance that pierced the side of Jesus on the cross. The spreading of the Empire and the conquest, we're always spurred on by the forces of greed, and the hope of improving their wealth, power, and luxury. As a token for good service, loyalty, and Valor in combat, all Shared the booty, Wealth and land.

As one reflects on the Conquering of the Saxons, one must remember that they would not submit to the Domination by the Franks, even at the end. They also would not allow the Franks to occupy Saxony, Germany. In fact it became difficult to the Frankish Empire after a while, to tell the difference between tribal resistance, and outright acts of rebellion. The writers from the

Frankish Church would have us believe it was a religious War, and that it was spreading of Christianity that was the mission. This is a shameful lie, and it was for the reasons of greater power and wealth that drove the conquest.

The so-called conversion of the Saxons, was in reality a shameful and brutal Massacre, but the numbers were on the sides of the Franks and their allies. The dirty little minds of men, they waited for the opportunity To catch the Saxons with only half their strength. Like I said before, the Viking Saxons and fleets, had been attacking and Robbing England for 600 years. Many had came home with the beautiful women they snatched up, and the precious metals, and everything else of worth, but many had stayed. Possibly 100,000, there's no real way of knowing. Every Province or area that has the word sax in it, was conquered and settled by the Saxons. That would be most of the areas like West sax, and hundreds of others. But not trying to get off the point, the Saxon Warriors have been invading England for 600 years, and it couldn't help but sap them of some of their strength. The Franks knew it, and that's when they invaded the land of the Saxons. The Saxons had never known defeat, in any war, against any people. But against the Franks and all their allies, they were outnumbered greatly. They fought for 30 years day and night, and even at the end, they wanted to fight on, cuz they had many thousands of Warriors left. But the Franks too, were getting very tired of this 30 year vicious War, against the most vicious German tribe, and they did come to a good arrangement. The leader of the Franks agreed to take many of the tens of thousands of great Saxon warriors, and resettle them into places that would help him out. They would become barriers to all invading armies, cuz there was no way to win against the Saxons. Even if you cut through part of their land, their Warriors would take a toll on your army, believe that. In the end everything worked out okay, the Franks ended up with France, and the Saxons ended up with most of Germany, and part of Great Britain.

The pages of History tell us this great Saxon war would be replayed in World War I and world War 11 . The 30-year bloody war were talking about right now, was started when the Frankish church destroyed the Saxon Monument to their gods. The Saxons called it the world pillar, or the column of the universe. It was this pillar the Saxon said, that held up all things sacred to the Saxon Nation. After the Franks took enormous casualties fighting against The Saxons, the emperor and his advisers agreed, to come to a solution to stop this war. They said every square inch of Saxony now, had a bucket of blood spilled on it, and both sides we're doing the bleeding.

After many separate invasions against the Saxons for 30 years, there was really no other way out, but to work out some type of agreement. The odds were staggering against them, and there was no Hope of Victory, the differences in the strength of the two forces grew larger.

The largest of the Frankish victories was at the site of Verdun in 782. It was at this same site that history would see the greatest amount of blood spilt, even in World War I, and World War II. Led Zeppelin said it the best, The Song Remains the Same. This site saw the bloodiest battles in the history of the world, between the Germans and the French once again, and boy did they bleed. In this case history really does repeat itself, and sometimes it don't. Historians call the big battle in 782 the massacre. After that every third Saxon, was taken from his native soil, and resettled by the Franks to their benefit of course. But of course this was much better than getting slaughtered, and I guess that's just the bottom line. At times whole settlements and communities moved. Charlemagne was a man of his words, and for every Saxon that converted to Christianity, or even pretended to convert, he spared his life.

However Charlemagne was Making Waves with all the northern tribes, and the Conquering of the Saxons was watched by their neighbors from the north, the Great Danes. The Saxon Chieftain had gone North in 777 to seek an alliance with the king of Denmark, the land of the Great Danes. The pages of History tell us the leader of the Great Danes Siegfried died in the year 800, and the Ferocious Godfried assumed the throne. The King was brilliant and fearless, and he concentrated on the Saxon Conquest to the South. He realized the gravity of the situation, and realized that the forces of the Franks and their allies, had designs on his power to. He realized that the same time, they were after his position, and his Extreme wealth also.

Charlemagne had showed how determined he was to rule this section of the world. The wealth of the entire world, also traveled right through here. Since the Mediterranean was now a hotbed, of Muslim Pirates, the trade of Europe traveled along the North Sea Coast, to the tip of Jutland which is today Denmark. The king controlled the most viable trade route in the world, cuz it controlled the trade of Europe, and at the same time, controlled the wealth of the world, that traveled through it on a monthly basis.

Charlemagne in the far north, made a military alliance with a huge Slavic Tribe the Abodrits. He encouraged his strong military allies to move into the area of East Holstein. It was at this time that the Danish King showed Charlemagne, that he was well aware of his intentions, and set the stage for war.

In the year 800 King Godfried gathered together all the champions from all the northern tribes, and he assembled and enormous Fleet. It was at the site between his Kingdom of the Great Danes and Saxony that the huge battle would take place. All the massive Warriors and the fleet were ready for war, and it was definitely a threat to the Franks, and they would not go any further north. The Franks saw the enormous Army and Fleet assembled against them, and lost all hope of securing the victory. Charlemagne and his advisers talked peace, back and forth for years, and war did not come to these parties. Both sides knew that if they fought, that both sides would probably lose half their power. In 808 the King Of Denmark acted more decisively than before. He stormed his troops across the border, and inflicted terrible losses on Charlemagne's allies, the Slavs. The great Viking warriors from the north took the war straight to the homeland of the slavs, and inflicted horrible losses upon them. There was much death and destruction, and this tribe was never the same.

The Chieftain of the Slavs sued for peace, and begged for their lives, and the lives of their Nation. King Godfried of the Great Danes allowed the Slavs to live, only because from now on they would be paying tribute to him, which means money,and money charms. The Slavs were better off alive, even if they were going to be paying for the right to live.

The terms were very stiff, but they still lived. The Ferocious Viking Chieftain Drosuk took The entire wealth of that Slavic tribe. The Slavic Town Of Rearick was put to the torch, and thoroughly destroyed, as well as it should have been. This one act of Viking warriors Would burn in the memory of the Slavs, and they would learn their lesson well.

The great Chieftain of the Great Danes, and the Viking Army, did not stop with this victory, for the Slavs had made their Alliance with the Franks, and now they were going to pay for it. History teaches us many lessons, and this is one of them.

In fact the Viking warriors used their swords and battle-axes, many times before the war campaigns ended. One Slav Community after another, fell to the force and weapons of the Vikings. The Slavs would regret their alliance with the Franks, and before it was over the Slavs would lose everything on the south Baltic Coast. To add insult to injury, all the slavic tribes from this point on, would pay tribute to the Great Danes. This major blunder of Charlemagne would haunt the Empire of the Franks for centuries, but who can blame him, he rolled the dice and he lost. Plus now the Vikings knew fully well, that the Franks had designs on their major trade route, and these were to be guarded to the last man.

In fact the Danes had enjoyed their position in the North for thousands of years, and they would continue to do the same. The king of Denmark was not about to gamble the wealth and goods that trade in Jutland offered. So next he set about strengthening his hold on his kingdom. King Godfried ordered a fortified rampart to be built, that stretched clear across the peninsula. In reality the barrier separated the Great Danes and the Saxons, and was a massive defensive system of Earthworks, that would keep all would be Invaders out. This massive buildup Of Earthworks for protection, was built so good, it is still in use today. You know it's funny, the earth works that stretched across the entire peninsula of Denmark, did more to secure Denmark, than even their great Fleet. This work of Wonder is exactly why King Godfried is known to historians as the most farsighted ruler in the history of the North.

To understand the weight of this Great Wall, first we must understand that most of the trade and goods, traveled Overland through Denmark.The shipping would not have to chance the perilous Journey around the North of Denmark. That area of the world has the greatest tides and currents in the world, and boulders that stick out of the ocean the size of major cities. Thousands of ships have been sunk on the rocks through the years, and it was just plain common sense to take it across on foot with horses and wagons. This is why the small piece of land, was one of the most powerful areas in the world, and the wealth was unbelievable. This is why the greatest warriors in the world, were there to begin with, and this is why they would never leave.

Because the wealth of the world went through Denmark, all the major powers would want to get their hands on it. But because the Great Danes were the baddest Boys in town, that was not going to happen..They didn't call them the Great Danes for nothing, and before it was all over, every European capital would pay tribute to the Great Danes dozens of times.

Charlamagne of course was extremely Furious at the thought of the small Northern kingdoms throwing dirt in the face of the Emperor, of the mightiest Kingdom. But he was forced to swallow his pride. Charlamagne at this time was commanding Wars in Spain and Italy and had his own problems at home. The next move would be King Godfried, when in 810 he assembled a huge Viking Fleet and raided all along the coast of Frisia, which of course was the land of the Franks. The fleet of Vikings were victorious on all their assaults, and there were many all along the Frisian Coast, and the Warriors came home with much booty, or wealth.

The Danish Kingdom was now showing the Franks, that they feared them not. The pages of History tell us, after these victories on The Frisian Coast, the head of King Godfried swelled with pride. With each Victory he grew stronger, and soon he began openly talking about conquering all of Germany. The way the king from the Viking Land saw it, Saxony and Frisia we're already provinces of Denmark, and the Great Danes would love them and their women. After word had reached the ears of Charlemagne of the talk of the Danish King, the Emperor at once gave orders to build his own huge Fleet. Also Charlemagne ordered all the defenses along the North Sea Coast to be strengthened, and I mean work was started quickly.

By 811 the empire had their huge Fleet together and ready to sail, but it never did for events changed the situation. In 810 King Godfried had been murdered, and his nephew Hemming took the crown. King Hemming agreed to a peace between the Franks and the Great Danes, and the border of Denmark would be set at the Eider River. King Hemming ruled for only one year, and the sons of King Godfried returned from Sweden, of course to claim the throne that they knew was theirs. In 813 Charlemagne died, and Louis assembled an army and attacked Jute land. The Frankish Army drove right through the huge Earth Works and proceeded up the peninsula. The sons of Godfried withdrew their forces to the island of Fyn, and as an impregnable barrier, the Viking Fleet was placed between them and the Franks.

The Frankish Army withdrew South, the Dane Army attacked.

The Frankish Army made their stand North of the Elbe River. Neither side was victorious, and the Danes went back North into their own Realm. It is important to note that although we speak of the Danish Kingdom, and King Godfried, many historians believe Denmark was not yet United under one king, and there was no real Royal Danish power yet. King Godfried was in fact the strongest and the best known Viking and against this there is no argument. But in reality the Viking kingdoms have not been forged In Cold Blood. Any Invader must still have to deal with the Earth's Best warriors, and that just was no easy thing to do. I believe the pages of History, no Army won against the blonde and brown hair vikings from that time. Historians however do not agree at what point Danish Royal Blood was United, but everyone agrees King Godfried acted like a great King when he attacked the Slavs, and subjected them to Tribute, or payment, monthly or yearly.

No historians dispute the supreme authority that the great king had when he ordered the Earthworks built, and once again when war was waged along the coast of frisia, King Godfried acted with supreme authority, when he ordered the defense of the Sacred trade routes. For he knew all too well, the destiny of his Nation, and its future, depended on the fact that the trade routes would be in their hands forever.

The Eastern trade route, ran from the Baltic to the Oder River, to the Danube, to North Italy, and all the way to the Balkans. The Western trade route went by the Rhine River to the North Sea, and this trade route only grew in importance as the centuries unfolded. From the mouth of the river to Jutland was extremely important, because of the wealth that they generated. Please remember the Golden Rule, Whoever has the gold, makes the rules. These trade routes were extremely profitable, and highly prized, for the future of Denmark and the Great Danes depended on them. The Great Danes did not want to spend the rest of their history living in a forest, they wanted to rule. They also wanted to be the elite, ready to fight and die so that this would be so. What else the leadership of King Godfried allowed, was that the mighty Saxons would be allowed to come into his realm, and they only made him so much stronger, maybe even invincible. The Saxons were treated with great respect, and they merged with the Great Danes. So as we examine the great king Godfried, it is natural to assume his actions were certainly not Those of a minor King. King Godfried kept Communications open with Charlemagne all the time he was on the throne, and Time After Time he openly challenged the power of the Franks. He was a master Statesman, and he took great care in watching for the interests of his people.

To further check the situation of power in Denmark, we must see what the German and Frankish writers speak of when they write of Denmark in this time. It is agreed that all the German and Frankish writers speak of Denmark as an extremely strong Kingdom.

After the lines of King Godfried and Hemming, there was a long pause in the known history of Denmark. Although outside Denmark, in the chronicles of foreign lands, the Danes were frequently mentioned. All the writers of the foreign Nations spoke openly about the wisdom and the great strength of the Great Danes. In Germany, France, England, and Ireland, the Danes were all well-known. The records were kept only by Christian writers, because they were the only men of letters at that time.

Knowing the true way of men, we certainly realize there must have been Wars between the descendants of King Godfried and those of Harold. We know of two such Sons of Harold, Klack son of Harold, and Horik. These two fought for Supremacy on more than one occasion. In fact we know from Frankish sources, that in 826, the son of Harold was paid a large sum of money, and given land in Frisia. The very first recorded Christian Mission to the Great Danes, took place early in the 8th century.

It seems very unlikely that The Norseman forced there Christian Slavs to pick a Norse god for their own. It was Charlemagne who brought Christianity really to the Danes, for he left it right at their border. His son Louis in 823 ordered the second Christian Mission to the land of the Great Danes, and only a few heathens were converted. It was Archbishop Ebo in 826 that made Herod's son, and 400 of his followers Christians.

Very few of the Danes loved Harold, for they felt him a traitor to their way of life, and some called him the Emperor's man. The next tale of a mission to the Heathens is a journey to Sweden with a certain Whitmar.They were attacked by the Vikings, and their holy books were taken from them. In 844 the Empire became a Battleground for the Three Sons, and they did fight for Supremacy. The Danes in the north, were only too happy to watch the wars, and the empire, and hope they would all die. While the heirs were fighting amongst themselves, the northern defense took a backseat in the scheme of things. As the defenses were let down, the Great Danes wasted no time and attacked everything along the North Coast. Hundreds of invasions were launched, and tens of thousands were killed.

In 845 the Empire was embarrassed, when Hamburg was sacked by the Vikings. The Vikings had waited for the right moment to strike, and when the time came, they launched over 600 Dragon ships, or warships. I would have said a 600 ship Fleet, but this was like the Spanish Armada, I mean no one had a chance, to do battle with such a force of Vikings, they truly were invincible. The Vikings left Hamburg, Germany in Ruins. And the school, library, and especially the church were destroyed. The whole city was looted and sacked, and much of it was put to the torch. The Vikings were making their move, and all across Europe would soon begin to pray to their Christian God, save us from the fury of the Norsemen, and of course they wouldn't.

The Vikings once threatened by the Frankish Empire, we're now on the attack, and among the towns that would fall to the Vikings would be London, Paris, and many more. The Vikings attacked everywhere at the same time, and captured everything. Once again they took all the gold they can get their hands on, and the most beautiful women, cuz this is the way of men. The Viking warriors burned the capital of the Empire at Aachen, and they also burned and sacked Cologne. Between the years 852 and 904 the Vikings raped, pillage, and plundered the great city of Tours 6 times. All through the Empire, prayers were made to Christ to stop the Vikings, but nothing could, and nothing would. God save us from the Vikings, was the prayer of the Good Men.

To follow the hundreds or perhaps thousands of Viking raids on Europe in the 9th century, one would need a road map, and one would still get lost in the confusion of it all. What follows is an outline on the major attacks of Britain, Frankish Empire, and the Mediterranean, and the study of how their culture, added to that, that already existed. The fusion of the Germanic race was not through, and the Germanic nations of the extreme North, had not yet played their hand. In reality Europe was in its infant stage, and much more was needed to create the civilization that we enjoy today. As you will see Hitler was right when he said civilization as we know it, is Germanic and the Germanic North known as Scandinavia was the Fatherland.

Before the days of the crowning of Charlemagne in the year 800, the coast of Ireland had known the fury of the Norsemen. The first raid that was recorded in Ireland was at Lambie in 795. After the first raid the Vikings made many more, and many went inland to rape, pillage, and plunder. In the writings of Ulster in the year 820, the Irish wrote the sea spewed forth floods of foreigners over Ireland so that no stronghold, no Fort, might be found, but it was submerged by waves of

Vikings and Pirates. To the reader it is obvious that nothing could stand in the Furious onslaught of the Vikings. However by all accounts, it appears the Vikings did not stay, but instead robbery was the order of the day. By the year 840, the famous Turgeis Of Norway had landed, and the alarm of the church was sounded.

The prayers of the normal ones, saved nothing, and they could not be saved, because the power of Steel once again owned the day. The Vikings from Norway commanded a huge Fleet, and many warriors, and when they landed, they did come to stay. The Vikings would never ever leave Ireland, because they loved it, and their women and wealth, and it became their new home. As each new Invasion came from Norway, they immediately Allied themselves with all the Norwegians that were already there, but make no mistake it was their land now. At the time in Northern Ireland, the priest king of Munster, have been involved in a civil war, and it played into the hands of the Vikings. It was at this time in history that the Viking Chieftain and his armed followers spread their domain throughout Ulster. Ulster was in the northern region, and could be gotten too easily. When the Vikings unloaded their ships,it was on.The Viking capture of Ulster Was perhaps the greatest of all the Viking victories in Ireland, because it was the very core of Ireland, and was also one of the holy places of the western Christians. It is because of this one great victory, that the Viking Chieftain became so famous. At the holy place the Viking Chieftain became extremely wealthy, and the power he wielded, would give him a place in the history of Ireland forever. the Vikings came as Raiders, and stayed as colonizers, and greatly improved the power and Prestige of the island nation.

They did more than War, they build great cities, and great harbors, that made Ireland wealthy and Powerful. The Norwegian and his Warriors built harbors at Dublin, Cork, Limerick, and Waterford, and because of these, Ireland's place in the history of the Europe was secured. This great transfusion of blood and energy from Norway truly made the Irish Nation very powerful.

Not to mention, the Vikings from Norway also brought the red hair all the way to Ireland, and they definitely mixed, cuz the Irish women we're beautiful. Once the north was settled, and in Viking hands, the Vikings raided to the South parts of Ireland. The Vikings Raided and sacked most of southern Ireland, and the Riches were collected. As soon as the Vikings attacked a few towns in the south, many of the Irish joined with them, and adopted the ways of Thor's men. Many of the new Warriors were the foreign Irish, or the foreign Keltics or Gauls. The Viking Chieftain the Norwegian at once, cleared the monks again, and set up Worship in the new Heathen temples. The war of the minds of men was still going on, and the Vikings would do all they could to keep their gods. The Vikings hated the Christians and their ways, for they saw with their own eyes, how it Tamed the men, and made them weak. Turn the other cheek, was not an option to Nature's Best and greatest Beasts. The Norwegian Chieftain made history when he expelled,the monks and sat down himself in the abbey, as the Heathen high priest.

These Warriors had the Magic in their blood, and history proves it. This race or blood, would go on to conquer the world one day, as proof of the Magic in their blood,and in their weapons.

This is the way of the Vikings, their high priest chanted the Heathen spells, and consulted the oracles. The Norwegian chieftain also performed sacrifices, for the guarantee of good crops and Good Seasons. This was how the Norwegians did it, and this is how it would be done from now on. In 845 the Norwegian would be taken prisoner, and he would be drowned by the king's henchman. After the death of the Ferocious Norwegian, it was downhill, and although raids were still conducted, the armies of the Norsemen were defeated many times, in the fields of Ireland. In reality what this did was reduce the strength of the Vikings, and blemish their record of victories.

Many of the Irish had thrown in with the Victorious Vikings. By 850 they had their own armies, under their own leaders. Many of the Irish were brought up in Norwegian homes, and had learned the way of them. In reality the Celtics and the Vikings were blending together, for there was very many mixed marriages. In the 850s the strength of their armies would be tested, and it would fight both the Norwegians and the Irish. By 860 their power had been broken, but they still inflicted Terror on the island. In Scotland later,There too would be the foreign Scott's.

For a Time, to the Vikings it looked like the Irish we're gaining the upper hand. This time it was the Great Danes, that would come to take the land of Ireland. The Danish Fleet came in at Carlingford, at the point of County Down. The following year they captured the huge Norwegian base at Dublin. Among The Spoils of the battle, the Danes took enormous treasure, and equally important they took the Norwegian women. The pages of History tell us the Irish wished they all would die. In 852 the Norwegians matched their forces, and attacked the Danish Fleet. The slaughter raged for three days and three nights, and when the last battle axe was dripping red, there was only a few Norwegians left. The Great Danes figured the gods favored them, and then rewarded Saint Patrick with enormous sums of silver and gold. The Norwegians were not one to give up easily, and the year 853, saw the great Royal Fleet of Norway make their reentry into the battle scene. The Royal fleet was commanded by Olaf son of the king of Norway. The Ferocious Olaf was the overlord, and was from the same bloodline of Turgeis. The kid of the Norwegian was not about to let the Emerald Island slip away beyond their grasp. Olaf have brought with him the champions of the Norwegians, and from the very first his authority was accepted. Even the Irish could spot who is really King of the Hill, and they paid tribute to him.

The champions of the Great Danes who had no taste for a Norwegian as Overlord, quickly left to the spot they came from, in England. Olaf, Overlord of Ireland, took as his home the Norwegian town of Dublin. After setting the house in order, Olaf left his brother in charge of Ireland and returned to Norway. He Returned to Norway, and in 856 Olaf came back to his kingdom at Dublin, and ruled until 871. In 871 Norway called again for his presence, and he went back home, and he died in battle soon after.
It was all good until 865, they raided the North Coast of England, and for five years, the Norwegians hammered the Picts, and the Welch in Scotland. The pages of History tell us, that the Norwegians raids against the Picts and the Welsh where highly profitable, and the wealth of Norwegians soared.

The Norwegians, besides taking the wealth from the northern tribes of Scotland, also took the opportunity to settle in the northwest corner of England. The Dublin Kingdom in Ireland, kept tabs on the Norwegians in England, but then their Fates and Destiny's were interlocked. The Danes and the Norwegians in the north of England, had many small battles over the turf, and in 877 the Danes attacked the Norwegian Kingdom of Dublin Ireland once again. The attack on Dublin was commanded by HalfDan, and HalfDan was killed in the battle. Most of the Danes lost their lives too. After this vicious battle, of which rivers of blood were spilled, Ireland grew much quieter, and became more Irish.

The reinforcements from Norway Dropped off, and Iceland became the focus of the world's greatest sailors. The attention the Norwegians gave to their settlements in Iceland, Drew from their strength in Ireland, and it 902 the Irish King took Dublin from the Norwegians. For the next 12 years Ireland would have peace, but of course it would not last.

The first Viking raids of England began in the year of 789. and for the next hundred years the Viking raids would not stop, not even for a moment. Whole Generations after Generations would dream about their chance of going into battle, to make their lot in life better. In Ireland the main invasions came from the Norwegians, but in England the Invasion forces were from the Great Danes. The Anglo-Saxon Chronicles, are our best source of information, for in the land of the Teutons, there were many writers. 90% of the raids of the Danish Vikings, where on the east coast of England, or the coast that is turned towards Denmark. The raids numbered in the thousands, and they came as armed robbers. The Anglo-Saxon English referred to Denmark, as the land of the robbers, but then gold is where it's at, and gold is where you find it. Nothing belongs to anyone, unless they can hold it Military. Anyway you look at it, the Great Danes shaped the course of English History, and also the history of the whole continent.

On the mainland of Europe, the Empire of the Franks was of course not spared the Wrath and fury of the awesome conquerors from the north. in 834 Thor's hammer would fall on the Franks, and they waited for their opening. When the sons of Emperor Louis were fighting amongst themselves for larger kingdoms, they were attacked by the Vikings.

The Great Danes with their Fleet, and their unbeatable Warriors, moved quickly on the inhabitants of the North Sea Coast. Frisia in Years Gone by had been a great War like seafaring people, with a fleet, and it held their strategic ground for thousands of years. Charlemagne in his Wars of Conquest, Conquered this land and its people, and in the long run had opened the floodgates for all the Vikings to come and find easy prey. The Danish raids on the Empire of the Franks had begun in the year 820, but they were minor raids, but also probing raids, to test the coastal defenses. The raids of 834 and 835 were more along the lines of temporary invasions and a Sinister plan became obvious. The size of the Danish attacks began growing in strength, and they became more numerous and more frequent. The Viking attacks also became quite violent in England. The huge Viking fleets of the Great Danes, sometimes Allied themselves and concentrated their force on either England or the North European Coast, and sometimes they divided their forces, and attacked both places at the same time.

On many occasions the commander of the fleet, would be fighting on both sides of the English Channel, and have two different attacks going at the same time. The Viking warriors fought with a frenzy, like the Defenders of the coast, and England had never seen. In battle the Scandinavian Warriors displayed a terrifying ferocity, and in fact the word Berserk comes from the word Berserker, which was the name of a class of warriors, that wore strange shirts in the battle. It is written, the warrior Fanatics fought was such a frenzy that they didn't even realize if they had wounds. The Berserkers sometimes fought in the nude just to terrify their enemies. The Vikings had no mercy on those that had turned their backs on Odin and Thor, and the beliefs of the Scandinavian Nations.

The Viking warriors had nicknames to those that showed Mercy to the turncoats. They were called the children's man, because they would not join in with the others in a bizarre custom after the battles. It seems the Vikings had a habit of tossing the babies of Christian enemies into the air, and catching them on the point of a spear. Many times the Viking methods were exaggerated, but it is clear to all that war is hell.

The Viking attacks that started with a few ships, on Lightning Raids, grew larger and larger until the Great Danes attacked in a fleet of 600 ships. They attacked all along the coast of France and England, at the same time. From 836 to 843 the huge Viking Fleet tested the coast of England, and the loyalty of the inhabitants proved quite heroic. The following years saw the east coast of England completely ravaged, but across the channel the fear of onslaught was taking place too. The pages of History tell us that the huge Treasures of England satisfied the Great Danes, and they were enormous.

In 834 the Empire of the Franks took a tremendous blow, because the Vikings came after the biggest Center of Frankish wealth. It was here where the rivers meet in the arm of the Rhine, there was to be found the biggest Market of Northern Europe. The fleet did the most damage of course. It was at this spot that the Vikings knew the Franks had their mint. The coins the Vikings took back home with them, were copied to make Scandinavian money.

The Fortress of the Franks that guarded The Mint, was the most important, and the trading center was utterly destroyed, for an entire generation. The place was looted and sacked. The town was at the mercy of the Great Danes, and it wasn't until nature changed the course of the arm of the Rhine River, that the Vikings left.

The mighty forces of nature took over, and ended what the Vikings had begun, and with the sweeping of the tides in 834, many of the so-called low countries we're now under water. The changing of the course of the Rhine, in reality was a death sentence, for the once-great trading center of Doris Todd. After the pillaging of Doris Todd was over, the next site of the commercial Viking attack, was at the mouth of the Loire river. This was a flourishing Trade Center, and the Vikings Added great wealth to themselves by attacking here. In 841 the Frankish Empire was shocked, when the Vikings Massed a Fleet at the mouth of the Seine River, and quickly headed up River and sacked and looted the flourishing town of Rouen. The Vikings here used their

tactics known to history has the basic blitzkrieg. They would steal horses, and ravage the countryside seeking food or valuables. The Vikings often did this with such speed, by the time the Defenders of the land grouped together, they were gone. Soon the local Lords of the land would again build many fine council's, to protect themselves, from the Vikings, and also against the other Lords. It is interesting to note that the Germanic barbarians of the 5th and 6th century, came for only land, to feed they're exploding populations. These barbarians of the 5th and 6th century, avoided the churches, for their respect for magicians and Magic was enormous.
 The Germanic barbarians quite naturally assumed the priests of the church held Supernatural powers, like those of their own high priest. The Germanic Vikings made straight for the churches, for by their time the church had held the wealth of the empire. Besides having an abundance of gold and silver, the church also had their jeweled sacred objects. The Vikings had no problem unloading this for anything their hearts desired.

It was common knowledge that after the Vikings collected the treasures, they most often set the towns on fire. In 842 with Viking strength growing by the year, England and the coast of the western France, we're once again attacked at the same time. In 842 the world Would see the sack of London, and of Rochester, and this time the Anglo-Saxon writers tell us, the Vikings wiped out the entire population. Directly across from the Strait of Dover stood perhaps the greatest trading rival of Dorestad. The place was famous. It too had a mint, and there was much treasure to be taken there, and of course the alarm Bells went off with the Vikings.

The Vikings came swarming, like bees to the honey. In 842 the Norwegian Vikings also made an appearance off the coast of France. This raid from the Norwegians would be well-documented by The Chronicles of that era, and it would not be easily forgotten.

In all 67 dragonships, full of Norsemen sailed from their base in Iceland, and appeared off the Loire river. As they collected their forces, the Viking Chieftain met with the Count Lambert of the French forces. Although this territory belonged to the Frankish King Charles the Bald, his unloyal count wanted it it for his own, and a deal was struck. The French sea captains guided the 67 dragonships up the rivers, and guided them around the sandbanks, and around the shallow parts. The day was June 24th, John's day, and it was a great celebration and a feast happening.

The town was filled with happy people, for this was the religious celebration of John the Baptist. The Vikings when the bugle blew, pounced on the merry Christians, and once again they were victorious in the Carnage that followed. They met resistance, but like the great warriors they were, outfought it quickly. The Chronicles of France tell us, that this battle was the most brutal they had ever known. The Vikings from Norway slaughtered all day, and in the streets ran Rivers of blood.

The Vikings from Norway went all the way through the church, and the bishop took a blow from a Viking battle axe , I wonder where Jesus and John the Baptist were on that day.

The congregation in the church took blows from the battle axes as the Vikings fought with them. The Christian God once again was nowhere to be found, and all his flock died that day. But at least they all died in church. Maybe they could still go to heaven. Before the Vikings loaded the treasure, on their ships, every sword and everybody was dripping red blood, and I guess that meant a victory once again. The Norsemen Rode their vessels back down stream, and it is written their ships were so weighed down with gold, they almost sunk. The unloyal count received for his act of treachery a little gold. This is all the count wanted, was his share of the gold, he didn't care about anybody, not even his so-called Frankish Lords. He thought only about himself, and this is the way of most men anyway.

The Victorious Norwegians went back to their winter bases. I'm sure they had a great time counting all the wealth they had accumulated from all those people they had encountered. The Norseman had a practice of always securing a winter bass, and it made sense. They could heal their wounds, and count gold over and over and over again, which really makes most men happy. The Norseman from Norway had a perfect winter home, and it was perfect because it was surrounded by the sea. To the Viking the sea was his life.

There's a lot to be said about an island defense, there's no worry about an attack by land. There was no Fleet that can match them on the ocean, they had nothing to worry about. If someone was able to creep up on them, they would be slaughtered when they got to the Norseman. The Norseman from Norway had no equals on the battlefield, but Millions lay underneath the ground, or I mean killed by the Norseman. The island provided shelter for the tired Warriors, and it provided a safe haven for their dragon-headed ships. It also provided a resting place for the wounded until they healed. The Norwegians always took prisoners, and the island would be a safe place to keep them, until they could be sold.

This particular Island was even much more than this, it was the very heart of the salt trade for all of Western Europe. The island had enjoyed a reputation for many years, and Merchants came there in droves. Merchants also came to the island for the good French wine. We all know how good the French wines are, they were good then, and they're good now. The pages of History tell us that this island was the first winter bass for the Vikings, and they came like flies to a big pile of shit. Up until this time the Viking Chieftains had always left Scandinavia in early spring, or early summer, and returned home in autumn. Up until this time the Viking was only seasonal employment, and to travel by land or water was a Hazard in the winter, and that had always been this way. Now the Vikings no longer had to take the long Voyage Home, and father many children, and wait for spring again.

This new way of life became easy for the real Vikings, and they loved the full-time adventure. A new Leaf has been turned over, and now the possibility of becoming rich was very real. The Vikings quickly became aware that the winters down south, were much warmer, and that the Seas never froze.

The land also was extremely fertile, and very rich, and they also knew it was theirs for the taking. The Vikings needed the extra land to grow crops for their families, and for their livestock.

The Viking women were so beautiful that every year, each Fox was pregnant carrying a new child into the world. There will be more mouths to feed every year, and the Vikings would get all the land they needed. They would buy the new land if necessary, or they would take it with their battle axes. By the year 850 the Vikings were farming and staying the winter in France, and in England. The Norwegians had always settled as they sailed West, and they even farmed in Iceland.

Denmark who had much more land for farming then Norway, eventually farmed all of the West too, for their population was exploding . The Vikings attacks came early in the year 850, and till 855. Attacks in the west were becoming much more frequent, and The Fleets had turned into flotillas, or enormous fleets.

But 845 the sack of Germany in modern day Hamburg really shocked the Frankish Empire, and made them shiver down to the bones. The Royal Danish Fleet of Warships totally destroyed Hamburg, and the 600 Dragon headed ships all filled up with gold and anything else of value, including beautiful women.

That year of 845 was the worst year in history for the Franks. For Not only was Hamburg sacked, but the Vikings in the western Frankish Empire, sacked Paris too. Charles the bald sent and army of Franks, to stop the advance of the Vikings up the Seine River.

Charles the bald divided his forces, so each half could dominate One Bank of the same river, which led to Paris. The Viking Chieftain Ragnar was no rookie at rape, pillage, and plunder, and he at once pounded the smaller Force along the banks of the river. The larger force on the opposite Bank, watched as the Vikings clashed with the Franks.

When the last throat had been cut, the Vikings killed all but a hundred and eleven of the Franks, and these got to live because they were their prisoners. To show Christian Franks how real men fought, the Viking Chieftain had 111 prisoners hung in full view of the second division of the Franks. This was another lesson the Christian friends would never forget. They had seen with their own eyes the victory of the Vikings, and it left them shaking in their boots.

The remaining Franks were beaten by the Viking weapons. The Viking battle axes struck Terror in the heart of the Christians. The Frank's at this time were beaten in spirit also, and they did not even try to stop Thor's best.

The great calculating Chieftain Ragnar, just had the perfect timings of the attack by the Vikings at Nantes, on John the Baptist birthday. This strike would fall on Easter Sunday. Thor's hammer was about to fall on Paris, and the Vikings were now 200 miles from the sea. The number of Viking assaults up the rivers of France, had been steadily increasing, and by this time in history, the Vikings were taking over the rich river valleys of both France and England.Make no mistake, these were more than just raids, the Vikings were attacking up every river that France had, and every river, that every country had. In reality what they were doing, was bleeding each Country Dry, taking the power from them, and checking their wealth. Like I said these were more than just raids, these were invasions. And everywhere that the Vikings attacked, they would eventually move into and take over completely, cuz this is the Germanic way. Getting back to the 111 prisoners that the Viking Chieftain hung in full View of the Frankish Army, was another lesson the Christian Franks would never forget.

The Vikings had said that the Christian armies had grown weak anyway, and they were about to show the world exactly what they were talking about. The time for talking was over, and the time for war was on. The Franks had no choice but to watch the Vikings victories one after another, even on their soil.

The remaining Franks who were beating by the Viking battle axes, were also beaten in the spirit, and some did not even try to stop nature's best, because they would have ended up in the ground too, with a little cross over their grave.

The great calculating Chieftain Ragnar sent his dragonships up River, and just like the perfect timing of the attack by the Vikings at Nantes, on John the Baptist birthday, this strike would fall on Easter Sunday. This was a battle that would shake the entire world. No longer were the Vikings going up the rivers attacking communities, there are now attacking London and Paris. There was nothing that any of these lands could do to try to stop Thor's best.

Like I said the hammer was about to fall on Paris, and for once everyone in the beautiful city of Paris was shaking in their boots, they had never known the terror of the Vikings, but they would soon. The Viking invasions Were hitting England everyday on one Coast or another. Wherever the big cities were built, there were rivers that ran through them, and the rivers ran to the ocean, and the Vikings ran up the rivers.

Wherever the rivers ran into the ocean from London and Paris, and many other cities, the Viking generals were building bases. There would be no escaping the fury of the Vikings, unless you were just ready to pay the heavy Ransom that they were asking for. And make no mistake Paris and London paid Ransom to the Great Danes and the Norwegians dozens of times, just so that their cities would not be burned to the ground.

The Viking bases now put the Vikings within Striking Distance of every community, no matter how far Upstream, or no matter how far inland. It was on Easter Sunday that the Vikings encountered the forces of King Charles the bald and his kingdom, in the western Frankish Empire at Paris.

The Vikings being the businessman they really were, negotiated With King Charles, and Charles paid the Vikings 7,000 lb of silver to leave Paris just like they had found it. the Vikings gladly accepted this enormous Ransom for the City of Paris, and they being real Warriors and Men of their word, they left

It is at this point in history that the payments were given the name Danegeld for it meant the Danes money. In reality there was nothing else Charles the bald could do. For the Vikings had always left a path of Destruction behind them, and Paris would have been next. King Charles the bald had other enemies to think about too, for these were very unsettling times. He had a rivalry of his brothers, and their constant pressure, and his counts, and his Nobles we're living for their own selves, to the point where there was open rebellion in all the provinces, and everyone was going for as much power as they could possibly get. Charles could not even count on the spirit of his forces, or the Loyalty of his Counts, who were supposed to lead them.

In reality these were uncertain times, driven by the forces of greed and Power. With a major war looming in the West with the Britons, the payment to the Vikings was the right move. And to put all bullshit aside, they couldn't have stood up to the Vikings anyway. They had no choice but to pay or there would be no Paris anymore. The Vikings were running at full strength now, and there was no possible way to defeat them.

You know it's funny, the Vikings had agreed that this Ransom of Paris for 7,000 pounds of silver, was a one-time event, but history would show a completely different story, of course. The payment to the Vikings bought precious time, that was so desperately needed. In reality the Danegeld lasted for 6 years, and the Vikings once more returned of course. In reality the Danegeld saved France from the fury of the great blonde haired beasts from the north. That is not to say that many of the Great Danes and other Vikings had brown hair, and many had red, this was the team.

On some occasions, Charles paid them out of the money he collected from the taxes. He paid heavy tribute to Thor's best, and I'm sure the Vikings appreciated the new wealth. In France the unbeatable Nordic Warriors were bought off 13 different times, and on these 13 separate invasions, France still was left Alive. These were actually business moves to keep Paris and the other cities functioning, for both sides knew the Vikings could not be defeated in France. France would not be the only country to pay to the Vikings, in fact many of them would, just to save their lives. The Vikings were International businessmen, they wanted the cash, plain and simple. The Vikings Were now known worldwide to be great businessman, and they wanted the world to know they could be bought off, with a lot of silver or gold. In fact the Viking fleets became so huge, and so strong, that it was common for any of the countries to pay their way out.

A lot of the countries were Christian countries, where weakness was taught through their religion. The Christians were told to turn One Cheek, if you get hit on the cheek, well that certainly wasn't a Viking Way, was it. It is a very cold and harsh world, that we live in, and especially in times of War, and the men need to learn to defend themselves, instead of talking about it. The first recorded payment coming from England to the Vikings was in 865. The payment was promised to the Great Danes. In fact the word Danegeld became a common word on both sides of the English Channel. In France and in England. probably the biggest Viking Fleet that tore up the Empire of the Franks, came in the year 886.

This devastation came in an Armada with over 700 ships with 40,000 of the bravest Viking warriors on them. This enormous Armada sailed up the Seine River, and laid Siege to Paris once again. But this time Paris was going to be taking losses like she had never taken before.

This was the largest Viking Fleet the Fantastic City of Paris had ever seen, and those 40,000 Viking warriors must have been a terrible sight, especially for the Christians. Their Jewish god was not going to save them on this day, and they better try to cut a deal, because the Vikings wanted gold and treasure, and would probably agree to a good deal. The fact that they paid to the Vikings last time, 7000 pounds of silver, might get them a whole lot more this time. They were prepared to make a deal, but if they couldn't get it , they were also prepared to take it. But this time they came back bigger and better than ever before.

In England the story was much the same, and the Viking raids that started in 835 would not stop for 100 years.The Vikings were not playing, and eventually they would take as much as they possibly could of England. The forces of the Vikings once, were threatened by the forces of the Franks, and now the tables were turned, and the Franks were being threatened, and this would continue. No more of this eye for an eye, it was more like a thousand eyes for one, and that was the Heathen way, or just plain And simple, the old way.

In England the story was much the same, the invasions continued to get bigger and bigger, and the losses of both France and England we're mounting. When the raids first started, they came in lightning raids of perhaps a dozen ships, and possibly 200 of their best warriors. In the Empire of the Franks, the Great Danes of England, also ravaged the countryside, collecting horses, cattle, and valuables. However the Vikings did not always win in the efforts to rape, pillage, and plunder the rich Countryside of England. At times the Raiders were caught by well-trained Calvary, but that however was not the norm, and it just happened once in awhile. The Danish Vikings in late 840's No longer returned to their Scandinavian homelands, but instead set up as colonists on the islands, that gave them easy access to France, and to England.

By 855 the blonde, red, and brown haired beasts many times attacked London. The Viking ships came up the Thames River, that London sits on. There was just no way to keep the Vikings out, unless you could match them on the water, and their warships, and nobody could.

It was the same islands that became the homes for the Vikings, and it turned them from Raiders into colonizers. For over 30 years the Vikings launched their violent attacks from their Island strongholds, and they increased in size, and in violence every year. The Vikings cut loose more terror than the world has ever seen.

In England the payment to the Vikings was also called, Danegeld which meant the danes money. It increased beyond belief, and it was here, That the Danes saw a great future. In England several of the petty kingdoms, paid the Danish Vikings on a yearly basis, and it became more like tax collecting. It is written that many of the Anglo-Saxons agreed, bye off the spear aimed at your breasts, if you do not wish to feel its point. That sounds like good information to me, if you can't beat him in battle you might as well pay them to leave you alone. The Vikings were unbeatable, and invincible in combat, and these were the days before the gun, so really nobody had a chance against these huge Monsters of the North. By 864 the Viking raids into England, in reality became full-scale invasions. More and more of the Vikings back home saw the treasure come back, and decided they were going on The next Journey too.

In 860 when the Vikings were on the lips of the people on both sides of the English Channel, I have recorded some of the words they wrote about them.

The number of ships increased . The endless line of Vikings never ceased to grow bigger. Everywhere Christ's people were the victims of Massacre, burning, and plunder. The Vikings overrun all that was before them, and no one could withstand them. All the lands of France and Great Britain, and no one could stop them, 100 Years of invasions.

The years of 856, + 857 saw Bjorn Ironside on the Seine River, and some of the Looting, pillaging, and plunder was due to his forces. Ironside and his fellow Vikings took over a base on one of the islands. Finally the Franks came in force with Charles the bald. But once again the nobleman of King Charles stabbed him in the back, for his own advance.

The nobleman invited King Louis the German to enter the kingdom of the West, to help his brother. The two kings joined forces, but then they started fighting amongst themselves. This worked to the advantage of the besieged Vikings. After 12 weeks the Vikings got a reprieve, in that The Siege was halted. The next course of events would show the treachery of the Vikings, because another huge Fleet had just landed.

Charles the bald, no stranger to bribing the Vikings, offered the new Fleet of Vikings 3,000 lb of silver, to take the Viking held Island. Chieftain Weiland who commanded the new Fleet, accepted the offer, but told Charles the bald, he must have the money first. It did take time to collect this enormous amount of 3,000 lb of silver, for Charles the bald was quick to overtax the farms and the landowners. He also leaned heavily on the church, and of course on all the merchants. The Viking Chieftain Weilan not only got his 3,000 lb of silver, but for waiting he received another 2,000 pounds. The Vikings Fleet also received tons of corn and lots of cattle.

Upon receiving his payment in full, Weiland and his Warriors Attacked the Viking held Island for the second time. The Vikings at their Island Fortress had plenty of money, and much love, but their food was running out. We all know that an Army does March on its stomach, so I would think the Vikings were ready to make a deal.The Vikings from both sides would enter into negotiations and Bjorn Agreed to pay Weiland 6,000 lb of silver to get away. Weiland was not the first Viking leader, to fight against fellow Vikings for money, and he would certainly not be the last. The next year saw Weiland and his men make spectacular raids into the south of England, in the land of the West Saxons, that they call the West Sax. Weilan being a businessman that entered the service of Charles the bald, and changed religions, had even got himself baptized. If that isn't a hustler and a player, I don't know what is, but it's all about the money.

Perhaps he was too good of a businessman, and his fellow Vikings lost respect for him, and called him a turncoat. Soon after Weiland entered the service of Charles the bald, he had himself and his family baptized, and he was challenged to a fight, and he was killed by a pagan Viking. All the Vikings were Pagans, and it had been that way for tens of thousands of years.

They had all seen the temple at Uppsala. It was there that the sacrifices to their gods, and the drinking of the Soma, and the drinking of the blood by the high priests, happened.

ALL VIKING FLEETS WERE FILLED WITH WARRIORS FROM ALL VIKING LANDS

Chapter 11

By the year 830 the Vikings had struck Terror in the hearts of all the citizens of Europe, England, and Ireland. All the populations were terrified that the Vikings were coming again, and they knew they were. It was just a question of when, and a question of how many more times they would continue to come. Everyone knew the situation, that the Vikings lived on a day-to-day basis. Although the countries of Norway and Sweden were huge in size, maybe only 10% could ever be used for man and his animals. The rest of course was covered with ice, and had been that way for a million years. Only along the coast of Sweden and Norway, could man possibly live. Because of the warm currents in the water Along the coast, it made the temperature nice. It was a hard life in Sweden and Norway, and the snow and the ice made it extremely difficult. That's why when the ice finally melted in the spring, all the men boarded their ships, and set sail, or Rowed to where they made their money. Every river they ran through Russia, and the Baltic countries saw the Vikings on a yearly basis. The Vikings always tried to trade for everything they needed. The Vikings were the inventors of whiskey and beer, and a lot of times that's what all the people that lived along the rivers wanted. But of course the Vikings had the greatest looking furs in the world, and they loved to wear them too. The Vikings had hundreds of items for trade, and they could always find many things that the buyers had never seen, because they were The Travelers of all seven continents, they truly had seen it all.

By the year 830 the Vikings were ready to roll again, and Europe, England, France, Ireland, we're in their sites again, cuz it was Easy Pickins for the Vikings. Although all the warring parties of the Viking tribes were of the same Germanic blood, it was a battle for Supremacy, and it usually was. When the Vikings attacked the coast of Spain it was different, because there they had to deal with the Nation of Islam, and this was a race war. If you've never seen one of those, you've never seen nothing. The Moors were waiting for them, and the racial wars produced great anger and great bloodletting in their battles. The viciousness of a race war, cannot be understated.

In the western Frankish province of Aquitaine, Charles the bald and Pepin the young son, were involved in the Civil War, over the right to rule that province. The Vikings chose the side of Pepin, and sent a huge Fleet of over 150 Dragon ships down the Garonne river. The Vikings raped, pillaged, and plundered, and took everything that was not nailed down, all the way down to Toulouse. It was not attacked because Pepin and the Vikings had an agreement, and this beautiful town was spared.

The entire fleet of 150 dragonships sailed right by the beautiful city that to be spared, and sailed back out into the North Sea. This enormous fleet was next seen off the coast of Northern Spain, and they headed for the kingdom Asturias . It was here the race war would ignite, and the Vikings took losses on the sea, and on the land. But of course the dark ones took more losses, and the fury of the battle urged the warriors on. When the last Moorish throat was cut, the Viking Fleet left. The Vikings left no living Moor alive, and the battle axes were red, but they usually were when the Vikings were working.

When the Viking Fleet did leave, they headed for Lisbon which is in modern Portugal. To say the Vikings were utterly Victorious, would be a lie, but the fleet did sail for Portugal, and was still huge and it was intact. This would be the first Blood the black and white races would spill, but it would not be the last. At Lisbon the Vikings launched many raids, and their wealth increased on a daily basis. After every village and Trading Post has been attacked and pillaged, the Viking Fleet pressed on up the other rivers. When the time was right, the bugles blew, and The Fearless Vikings stormed the city of Seville, which I believe is in modern Spain. Seville was the stronghold for the Moors, and the race war had just begun. Seville was also a huge trading center with enormous wealth.

The men of Thor and Odin took this city by storm, and in one week it was theirs. The men were all put to the sword, and many felt the blows of the famed Viking battle axe, my favorite. The women and children were taken as The Spoils of War, and they were placed on the Viking base, on the island. Today the same island is named Isla Menor.

Like many of the Viking bases, it was placed at the mouth of a river. From their Island base the Viking warriors raided the complete Countryside for the next two months, and nothing was denied the men of war. The Moorish Kingdom of Spain was much better prepared to deal with the Viking invasion, than was the German Kingdom of Charles The bald. It is true that the Vikings Massed together many Treasures and slaves, at the expense of the Moors. The Vikings had to leave their Island base, to invite attack from the combat hungry Moorish Warriors. Once the period of surprise, and unpreparedness was over, the Moors left the Vikings in a position of peril. The Moors had a fleet of Their Own, and could be counted on, to launch their own attacks. And so it went on this way, blow-by-blow were matched. The Moors even set fire to some of the Viking ships by catapulting the ancient Greek fire on them. The Vikings however, were not to be kept captive, and launched their entire fleet, and attacked the entire Moorish Fleet head on. The racial battle spewed forth the flame of Fury, and the naval battle between the races, ended with the Vikings losing 30 ships.

The Moors and Vikings both took Prisoners, and they endured great torture on both sides. Men of both races, had their throats slit from ear-to-ear, and many were hacked into pieces, and the Vikings fed the pieces to their dogs or Wolves. The Moorish Raiders have told us, the Moors took so many prisoners, they didn't even have enough Gallows for them. All the Moorish leaders ordered the Vikings prisoners to be hung from the palm trees of Seville. The Moorish victory was announced throughout the Moorish world, and the leader sent 200 of the Vikings severed heads to his house in Tangier. The Vikings slowly starving to death , Ransomed their prisoners to the Moors. A deal was struck that there would be no more fighting, and the prisoners worth would be traded for food and not gold. The Vikings had been cut off for some time on their Island base from resupply, and the Moors were laughing as they watched.

We Know from the records of the Moors, the Norseman and the Moors entered into a pact where trade was to flow freely between the two races. The year was 845, and the Moors and the Vikings had their little race war. This is of course not the only time The Vikings and the Moors clashed, but it was only the first of many. Once the blood is spilt and the tempers flare, there must be Revenge, especially when it's Racial. Chieftain Bjorn Had bought their freedom for the Vikings for 6,000 pounds of silver.

The Vikings would encounter the Moorish tribesmen many times, as they ventured out on their spectacular four year Cruise. It took them to the lands of Italy, North Africa, and Spain. The Vikings with their winter bases on the islands in the West, now could strike in new lands that would have been just too far away before. The 62 dragonships of Bjorn Would attack in lightning Raids in their new warm weather Paradise. Off the coast of Spain, the Moorish Fleet would Engage The 62 dragonships in many sea engagements. The pages of Moorish history, tell us that in one sea battle, the Moors captured two ships full of silver and gold. The Moors were ancient Pirates themselves, and they eagerly clashed with the Warriors from the north, cuz they knew they had a lot of cash and treasure. It was more than just the lust for battle, that drove the Moorish warriors on, it was what they hoped to receive, from the blonde, red, and brown haired Beasts. With the light skins, most of the time the Moors would lose. They would cut to pieces each warrior, sometimes he would be cut into hundreds of pieces, and fed to the dogs, cuz this was a Viking custom. Many fleets of the Norsemen pillaged and plundered all through Spain, even the strongholds, and nothing would be denied the Vikings.

Many of the Viking Dragon ships were in the Mediterranean Sea.Once again it was the Viking Chieftain Bjorn That would become famous for his trips into the Mediterranean, because up until then, no one had really gone, not many anyway.The 9th century Was full of Fury, and action for the Vikings, and every race was fighting for Supremacy, and no race won every battle. Armies of every color were attacking the white man stronghold in Europe,and they held.

The Romans had kept them out for centuries, and the Germanic tribes would have to do the same. The race wars were on, and The Many Colored armies were seeking Revenge. Charles Martel would stop the Moorish Warriors, and so had Roland, and Charlemagne, and now they were being attacked. In this extremely violent time, That men call the 9th century, every race was fighting for Supremacy, and like I said no one race won every battle. The Moors of Spain who had once been pouring there knights into France, in reality we're now on the defense, for the Aryan blood was boiling in the Veins of the Vikings. And when the blood was boiling in the Vikings, millions of lives were lost. The Vikings on their way to the Mediterranean, knew the Moors were in Spain,stopped and fought them just for the action.

Spain had always been the land of silver and gold, and their mines Were extremely wealthy. Ever since the days of ancient Greece, the pages of History tell us of the fabulous silver, and the Gold mines of Spain. This was no lie, every race of people, knew about the wealth of the mines in Spain.

The Vikings had always dreamed of pillaging the lands that lined the Mediterranean. They wanted to pillage these lands so bad for the glory, as well as for the wealth.This fleet of Vikings like those before them, made a stop at the Capital city of Seville. Spain was extremely wealthy, and the Vikings wanted their share of the action.

Once again A Viking Fleet would be loaded with the gold and silver of the Moors. Like A wise man once said, a long long time ago, you win some, you lose some. Not long after the Vikings took as much gold and silver from Seville as they could, Thor's Men found themselves passing through the Straits of Gibraltar, and quickly attacked the first Town they came to.

 It was off to the North African Coast, where the defenses of the North African Coast was bad. 60 of the dragonships of men in animal skins, with horns on their heads, panicked the people and they ran. The Vikings once again had used shock to their advantage, and now for two weeks, they rounded up the population for prisoners, for ransom, and for slaves. Some of the prisoners would never be ransomed, like some of the Negroes that they word keep as souvenirs of their voyage. These Negroes were called firgorm, which meant blue men, or black men. Most of the Negroes brought top dollar, for their value as slaves, but also for curiosity reasons.

The men of Ireland we're shocked when they heard of men who looked like apes, and many thought they were apes. The Viking Blood was running hot for the entire length of this spectacular Expedition, due to the adventure of it all. The Vikings were happy as a pig in the mud, when they discovered the Western Mediterranean had no armed Moorish ships. There were many ships there, but none with arms to oppose them. Bjorn next attacked the Moors wherever he found them. The men of Thor and Odin took their pleasures. The next Viking attack would feel the fury of Thor's men for the first time. The Viking Fleet felt no resistance nowhere on the Mediterranean, and soon the entire southern coast of France, saw the men from the north, and the finest of the ladies were taken from them, for Thor's best.

All along the coast of the Mediterranean the Vikings attacked every town they could find, and went easy on them, for they had come just for their wealth. Their were many raids and robberies that year in the Mediterranean. The Vikings took a base on an island in the Delta of the Rhone river. The Vikings of this Expedition had seen more in one summer, then most men would see in a complete lifetime. The Great Adventures had sailed by, and rated the kingdoms of the western Franks, and the kingdom of Spain. They had the pleasure in the glory of sailing through the Straits of Gibraltar, and had been amongst the first to behold the new lands that ring the entire Mediterranean. Their treasure was so enormous, some of the ships found it very difficult to even steer. The weight of their treasure slowing them down. But this was okay, this is exactly what the Vikings came for, and it's exactly what they got.

They took many slaves, for their own, and They had showed the new world the dragonships. The dragon ships were ready for more Adventure, and so were the men of Thor. The Warriors became Restless camping out the winter, and waiting for the spring to come. But soon it would be upon them. The Vikings raided up the rivers of France, and I mean every single River, cause the getting was getting good, and France had it all.

The Viking raiding parties in France, went Inland Up to 100 miles from their base. It was there that the Valor of the Franks would be tested, and the Vikings gained a new respect for them. The armored Vikings in full battle dress clashed with the best of the Empire of the Franks. The Vikings Valor was matched blow-for-blow. The Vikings were defeated on the field of battle so soundly, that they moved their Island base in the south. It must be noted that the Viking raids were usually lightning raids, and whenever a force of Frank's could be assembled fast enough, the outcome of the battle, could go to either side.

The Viking raids of that expedition, also took time to Raid the coast of Italy, and among the towns that were sacked was Pisa. The Chronicles of the lands that ring the Mediterranean, tell us stories of warriors with a Lust For Gold, silver, and women. They did not come to check the land, but only the valuables. As far away as Alexandria, the Viking forces would be felt. A complete tour of the entire Mediterranean was in order for the Vikings, and they all grouped together. Never before had a Viking Fleet traveled so far, and became so wealthy. The heads of every Viking in the fleet, must have swelled beyond belief, at the thoughts of The Adventures of the fleet,it must have made them great in the eyes of their God Thor.

This World tour would not have been complete without the conquest of Rome. The now-famous Vikings could not leave without a Raid on Rome. The Viking Commander knew the walls of the great City we're so big, a lightning attack would not work. The Viking Commander sent messages to the city of Rome to explain, that they were good men, expelled from their country, and because of a storm, they landed on their Coast. They further said they had no food and they needed some, and that their Chieftain was dying.

The next time the messages were sent to this town made of Marble, they blanketed the ground with tears for their now-dead Chieftain. They only asked for a Christian burial, and the people gladly agreed to give them one. It was at this time that a long line of Rogue Vikings, followed the casket of their dead leader to the Grave. At the moment when his last rights were being read to the dead man, Hastings rose up in his coffin, and drove his sword right through the bishop, and then the slaughter began.

The Men of Thor and Odin slew all that opposed them, and soon the streets were littered with Corpses. The combat, and the pillaging went on throughout the day, and a few beautiful ladies were added to their harems. Towards the end of the day, the Vikings spread through the city. It became evident that the marble city was not Rome after all, its name was Luna.

At this point the Vikings filled with great anger. Hasting gave orders for the whole town to be torched, and all the men were to be massacred. The men of Thor And Odin had their orders to spare the women. For a fleet of 60 ships could use a little companionship. .Although Hasting and his Warriors never did find Rome, the destruction that they inflicted on Luna will always be remembered. The marble city of Luna added tremendously to The Riches of the Vikings, and many of their ships had a hard time even floating. After this marvelous sack, the Vikings had no choice but to head home, and so they did on their long journey. In 861 the Viking Fleet had just passed through the Straits of Gibraltar, when the Moorish Fleet attacked for some sea combat. They knew the Viking ships were loaded with treasure, and they wanted some. Word did spread throughout the lands that all the Viking ships were loaded up to the maximum with many Treasures, and the Moors wanted them, and we're willing to fight for them. The pages of Moorish history, tell us the Moors this time were victorious, and revenge was theirs. To the victor go the spoils, and the Moors were extremely wealthy. Many of the treasure ships were captured, and then went to the Moors, as did the slave women. The part of the Viking Fleet that disengaged the Moors, sailed off. The next stop for the Viking Fleet was Pamplona, which was captured and plundered. It was here that they grew extremely rich again, for in their possession, they had the princes child. Blood is thicker than water, and his blood Payday was for a very high Ransom to the Vikings.

One year later the Viking Fleet was back at the mouth of the Loire River where they had begun this adventure. When this epoch-making adventure started there were 62 ships, and when it ended there were but 20. but out of these 20, they had enough wealth to live their dreams, and that my friends, is all a man can ask for.

Next our attention must be directed to the same year 862, but to another land, England. We have watched the individual Chieftains on their daring raids. They turned into well organized expeditions. We have watched how the Raiders lived off the countries they invaded. As time went on many of these Invaders would not leave. Now a new change came, that of colonizing. In England it would definitely happen. The men of Thor and Odin from 862 to 865 would begin to land in huge numbers. By 865 they were ready to unfold their plan.

In 865 the Viking Fleet would number over 1000 of the strongest Warriors, from their tribal lands in Scandinavia. The leaders of this Motley Crue were Ivar the Boneless, and HalfDan. The pages of History tell us they came from Ireland, and they came from Scandinavia, and they all assembled in England. These gods of War came for blood, and they came to avenge their blood. The blood was boiling in their veins as they thought of the way their daring father had died. Their father was Ragnar, who we know as the Viking who withdrew from the same river in 845, with a ransom of 7000 lbs of silver. It is written that Ragnar came to England with only two dragonships, and plenty of silver. He had been challenged and defeated by the king of Northumbria. Ragnar Died when he was bitten by the poisonous snakes hundreds of times.

Death by being stung to death, was a horrible way to go, and now his sons were there to avenge this wrong. The first thing the Vikings would need was transportation, and they got horses quickly and began their plan to assault. They were now in the land of East Anglia, or in reality, the land of the East Angles. In 867 the sons of Ragnar attacked York to seek revenge. They were on a mission, and they would not be denied. The men of Thor were spurred on by the Revenge of their father. The kings knew they must unite to drive the Great Danes from the kingdom. The Kings with their armies marched on York, but when they got there, the Great Danes had already captured it.

The stage was set, and the field of battle would decide who would rule the northern kingdom. When the last man had been run through by the Lance, both Kings had died fighting, for a kingdom they could not win. The sons of the Viking Ragnar would not be denied their Revenge, as Thor and Odin as Witnesses, they carved the blood eagle, on both Kings backs.

The blood eagle belonged to The Cult of the warrior God Thor. The blood eagle was carved as a mark of vengeance. The act itself was considered an inhuman Act, but the Vikings believed in his own power, and offered the blood eagle to Thor, as the appropriate sacrifice. In reality the warrior would cut away the victim's ribs, from his spine, and then pull out the lungs, and spread them on the back like wings. Ivar the Boneless took part in this act of Revenge for his father's death, and Thor smiled down on them all.

The blood eagle screamed for revenge

With this Danish Viking victory another kingdom now belonged to the Great Danes. Next, the Great Danes launched their attacks in Mercia, and once again the fury of the Great Danes began. The Great Danes always carried their great Fury with them, and it was Legend throughout the world, about the intensity with which the Great Danes fought. The King of the Kingdom paid the ransom, and peace was restored. The Great Danes were excellent businessman, and they always left you a way out, to save face. They always gave you the opportunity to pay your way out, because in truth the Viking love for money and wealth was what they were all about. In 869 the Danish Vikings we're once again on the attack, and this time the target was East Anglia. This is perhaps the most famous battle, because the Great Danes slaughtered the English Army's that were thrown out them, and I mean they slaughtered them, down to the last man. And then they cut his throat. As the English Army's of East Anglia fell before the Danish Warriors, King Edmund was captured. King Edmund was the backbone of the English, and when his power was gone, there would be none to replace him. The Danes were well aware of the situation, and Edmund was sentenced to a slow death. He was tied with his hands behind his back, and then tied to a tree. The Viking archers were told to riddle the king with as many arrows as possible, and not to let him die an easy death.

King Edmund took over 20 arrows, and this one act of Viking defiance for the English, stuck in the minds of all for many generations. But that's just the way the Great Danes wanted it. They did not want the English to rise up again, and make them prove once again, who was the greatest warriors in the world. After this day, things would never be the same, the power had shifted like it or not.

Nothing now could save East Anglia from falling to the Viking overlords, and now east Anglia and the rest were held by the Vikings. At this point the Great Danes owned the heartland of England.For 76 years the Vikings had assaulted the east coast of England, and now the grand total of all these attacks was obvious, for great chunks of England now belonged to the Great Danes. When he said hungry wolves, that is exactly what was going on in England. The stage was set, in 870 he led his ferocious Vikings into the lands of the western Saxons. The battle was furious, and bloody, and full of carnage, but when the last guts of the combatants, had been ripped out, the Danish Vikings had won again. The Danish Warriors beat the Saxons, and this was a strategic down the Saxons did not want to lose. The Great Danes quickly fortified this place, to stand against any future combat, they wanted to make sure they were ready, and that they would win every single time.

In the year 870 the English soil would be soaked in the blood of the Danes and the Saxons, and in all 9 extremely bloody battles did happen. 9 Furious battles to fight for the right to own England, or the land of the Angles, England. The brave Knights of West Sax won only one of the battles in that year, and they took heavy casualties. Alfred who was the brother of the Dead King Edmund, Rode on many raids against the Great Danes, but in reality, he was just pissing Against the Wind. There was nothing you could do to stop the Great Danes. They were probably the greatest warriors that the Vikings ever produced throughout the world. They only lost a couple battles,in hundreds of years, and they were probably stabbed in the back or betrayed when they lost a couple battles. The Saxons were ferocious, but they were nothing to the Great Danes, the Great Danes were the top of the line, the cream of the crop, and they let the battlefield prove it.

The Western Saxons were probably the toughest of all the Saxons, and their blue blood line went straight back to Saxony Germany. The Saxons had attacked England for 600 years and were vicious too. Even after 600 years of attacks, the Saxons had only carved out about one-third of England, and that was all they were going to get, because those that lived there, could Bend but they were not going to break. The Saxons now found themselves in a very strange position, they were fighting for their very survival, and they were fighting for their Homeland. No one would have ever thought this possible, that the ferocious Saxons would be in this position. the Saxons went into battle, with Thor in their hearts, and Thor in their minds, and Thor was definitely a major part of their everyday life, they were Vikings too.

But the Winds of Change, and the Winds of War we're blowing, and anything could happen, this was a way of life. The Western Saxons Stood their ground, and answered blow with blow. After all the other Vikings were only distant cousins, they were cut from the same cloth. The stakes were now raised in the game of combat, and they were raised in the Force of Arms.

The Great Danes now fought under the control of Guthrum, And he was greatly respected for his talents on the battlefield. The Danish forces were trying to steamroll West Sax, but the Saxons Rose to the occasion with their gleaming battle axes. And on this day they took many lives, and rivers of blood flowed once again. The Great Danes changed their strategy, and in the mid-summer of 878 launched all their forces from their base. This time the Vikings under Guthrum caught the West Saxons totally by surprise, and slashed their way to Victory, and occupied the Saxon town Chippenham. No Saxons came to challenge, for they had been beat up badly, and many other Champions died, beaten by the champions from the other side.

By this time Alfred, brother of the late King Edmund, was running for his very life, with the Vikings hot in Pursuit. The pages of Anglo-Saxon history,tell us the future of all the land of the West Saxons was in doubt, and it looked like they may lose everything. Many of the fighters began surrendering to the Viking leader, and many West Saxons left England altogether, and many of the others crossed the English Channel, headed back home for Saxony Germany. It appeared to be All over but the shouting. Alfred's forces had been whittled down to no more than 150, and the Viking axes never shown, because they were covered in English blood. The Angles, Saxons, and the Jutes, had fun with Valor against the Great Dane Vikings, but they could not win against the wild Warriors from the north.

Although everyone in England was whispering Tales of Thor, the Winds of Change we're blowing. as small as Saxon numbers were. They still met the Danish Vikings in battle, often in nighttime raids. This really struck fear Into the Heart of the Warriors to fight at night, in the pitch blackness, these were seasoned vicious Warriors. However the future was dim, for Alfred and his Warriors, in reality he was circled by hostile forces. As the weeks wore on, Alfred was still fighting. Angles and Saxons from Hampshire and Somerset, added their swords, to his strength. The great warriors although outnumbered, we're willing to make one last gallant stand, for the Magic in their blood, and for their people's future.

In South Wales the Vikings under the chieftain Ubbi Stormed the last Saxon stronghold at Devon, and they were shocked at the fury that faced them, and they were defeated. The Great Danes in this great battle, would learn a new respect for The Warriors of England. In reality what this English victory at done, was break the circle of viking forces around Edmond, and allow him to attack, not to have to worry about a rear guard.

The ring of fire was broken, and now Alfred was free to leave, Shouting at the Great Danes with more Angles, Saxons and Jutes, joining forces. 2 months after Easter, they were strong enough to take on the Great Danes heads up, with all the new reinforcements coming in, they were about ready to show the Great Danes that they were fighting in their Homeland, and ready to reach inside and pull out whatever was left of their super strength.

The Ring of Fire Was broken, and now Alfred was lashing out at the Great Danes. Alfred chose the Battleground Of Eddington, to engage the Heathen forces one last time. The English swords and battle-axes, killed many of the Great Danes in this one heroic charge, and the Danes were defeated once again. With their back to the wall, the English found greater strength, and they followed in Hot Pursuit, the fleeing Danish to the town of Chippenham. It was at that this town of Chippenham, the Danish forces held their ground, for this was now their last stand. The Saxons and the Great Danes, the two greatest Viking armies in the history of the world, we're about ready to fight to the last man, and Thor would be smiling down on them, probably hoping for sacrifices afterwards.

After weeks of bloody battles, and often single combat, a peace was agreed upon. The leaders knew it was time to slice England up, for the Danish Vikings would not leave, and in fact had come to change the course of England, and world history. The biggest issue at stake here, was just how much land were the Danish Vikings asking for. Alfred got his answer when the Great Danes later agreed to pull back their forces, from the lands of the West Saxons. It was agreed amongst the great Viking leaders that Wessex would remain in the hands of the West Saxons. It had been their land for centuries, and nobody was going to take that from the Saxons. If necessary they would call in the Jutes and the Angles. And there was no Army on the face of the Earth that was going to beat these three Germanic tribes. Just like the Great Danes could not beat them all together, neither could anybody else.The Danish Kingdom, would include the east of England, and also the North, and for this Guthrum agreed to be baptized as a Christian.

In reality sometimes in life you do things, that you really don't want to do, But all Guthrum the Viking did, was admit one more God to his own Pantalon. In the big picture, Christianity should be practiced in the Kingdom of the Great Danes. In reality it was a deal, you give a little, to get a lot. The arrangement of the English and the Danes was a great one, and everyone was satisfied. It would be The Chieftains that would take the role in the Christianizing all the Great Danes in England. The Great Danes had lost much in England, and they were here to stay, and they would never ever leave. The conquerors from the land of the Great Danes began spreading out throughout the whole kingdoms of the Angles and the Saxons trying to get every square inch.The Danes decided they were going to take London for their own, and they did. But it would not remain in the hands of the Great Danes, because the Saxons and the Angle's had plans of their own. All of these former English kingdoms that the Great Danes took over, now fell under the power of the Danish Vikings. and all the kingdoms that they did takeover, would never see English rule again. The Danes had now carved out a kingdom in the east of England, and in the south. This was to become the place that the Vikings called the Danelaw. The Danelaw was completely outside the influence of the rest of England, for only the laws of the Great Danes were legal there. It was all the territory of the Great Danes that they had occupied in England. In fact it was Denmark overseas.

And of course it was much different from the rest of England. The laws, the language, and even the names and Customs were different. It was its own country, that was within another country.

Alfred had no choice but to live with the Danelaw, for he was in no position militarily to change it. All he and his successors could do, was try to contain it, for there was no turning back. The Vikings were here to stay.All the tribes had fought for their piece of this great land,and now the great Danes,got theirs.

The pressure the Vikings had been putting on the land of the western Saxons stopped, for West Sax showed the strength and Valor of the Saxon Nation, in cutting thousands of the Vikings to the Bone. The Saxons would yield no more, and that was a fact. Plus, that land of the Western

Saxons would expect now, the Vikings to become settlers. They knew in their hearts, the battles were not over for good, but they also knew, that the conquered lands would take time to settle, and get in order. However it was obvious that the professional Vikings would have to look for new ground to rape, pillage, and plunder.

The main populations of the Vikings, we're far from wanting to beat their swords and battle-axes into plowshares, and their blood still screamed for Conquest and adventure. The Empire of the Franks was in disorder once again, for the Frankish curse of splitting the kingdoms with the Sons, created constant disorder. Charles the bald had died in 877, and his son Louis the 2nd lived only 18 months longer than the father. The Empire was in total chaos, and now the kingdom would have to be divided between the two young Sons.

The empire that have been held together by strings, was dividing even further. A strong Count Bozo of Vienna was crowned the king of Burgundy. Count Bozo"s Kingdom covered a large area of the Holy Roman Empire, and his claim to the throne, his wife, was the daughter of Emperor Louis II. He would spend his life telling his Queen, thanks to the backing of the church, she was now the Queen of Burgundy. The Royal Line of Charlemagne still had five men alive, 3 in the Eastern lands, and 2 in the West. Before Royal Blue Bloods next put down an uprising in Lorraine, they then marched off to Vienna. At the moment of the seige in Vienna, Carl the fat, was named Emperor in Italy, and the attack was halted on the church's friend and Ally in Vienna. Politics is a dirty business, but someone must do it.

To add insult to injury, the Norsemen were attacking the lands of the western Franks. The Eastern Franks said their problem was, there were assaults on that part of the empire. in 882 the Frankish Empire lost their greatest of Heroes, the West Frank, Lewis the Third. It was Louis the 3rd that was loved by the entire Empire, for he commanded the Franks in their victory over the Vikings.The fight for a generation was gone, but then it was the better part of the empire. The Vikings were unraveling the very fiber of the Franks, with hundreds of Raids in the famous 9th century.

In 884 Louis's Only brother died, setting the stage for more chaos. The long line of Charlemagne's now is down to only one, and that was Carl the fat, king of the East Franks. He had been crowned by the pope in 881, and in 885 the Nobles of the West wanted him as their King also. Carl the fat was now the emperor of the Franks, and his enormous Empire was the same as Charlemagne's 80 years ago.

How desperately the Empire needed an emperor with strength, and also the force of personality, to unite the various people. At all costs endorsements had to be stopped, and they needed a leader that could do that. The pages of History Show us a different story, that Emperor Karl the Fat was a coward, and incapable of leadership.

The population of their empire backed their leader out of loyalty to the crown, but Carl changed this himself. Carl the fat signed the treaty with the Vikings, allowing them to openly flood into Burgundy, and begin settling in the richest lands. The pages of History tell us that this was a shameful Act, because the Franks were already fighting for Paris against the Vikings. The stage of politics was set for a real man and a real Warrior, that could lead the Franks into battle. To add salt to the wound, the man would be his nephew ,Arnulf. It was this man that would have to lead, and God knows they needed a leader desperately. To add salt to the wound, the bastard son of Carl raised the banner of revolt, and anyone with any heart at all joined in with them. He was in the prime of his life, and he was well aware of the fact it was he, or no one else. Arnulf had the fortune of having the Nobles of Bavaria in his corner, and he could count on their swords and battle-axes to back his play. Arnulf also had the Nobles from all over behind him, and he gathered the forces of both these powers, and Marched at full strength to the center of the empire.

Everywhere the forces of our new leader marched, the population showed great enthusiasm. They knew they had a new leader, the question was, was he up for the task. He had the political and military backing of all the Eastern Franks, and soon he was declared King of the Franks. The king could have been king of all the Western franks too, but he did not seize the moment. Local Independence, and power was being redistributed between or because of the feudal system of land holding. Now the power was being divided, and the thought of political Unity was disgusting to most. The new thinking was of local power, and an Emperor to rule over all, was thinking for days gone by.

New centers of power were developing, and Burgundy was one. The west would have to deal with Burgundy,and she was extremely strong at this time in history. The fall of Carl the fat, and the revolt, was a signal to all new powers to emerge. So in reality while the new King was waiting to be swept up in the events, many Little Kings were popping up throughout Europe. We must focus on this power shift in the land of the Franks, because as we do it, we see the territorial development of the eastern states. Before, the Throne of the Franks had always been inherited, passed from father to son, and now it was Arnulf's shot at fame.

The complete system of government changed, the day Arnulf was selected by the kingdom of the Eastern Franks. In reality the election of the King was a return to the ancient Germanic tradition of electing the best man to be leader.

The powerful families of France and Italy were also showing signs of nationality. When the two most powerful families began talking politics, it was Berengar that was backed by the Frankish Knights of Italy, and also by the churches of Lombardy. Berengar the man of the moment, declared himself King of Italy, and was crowned at Previa. This was the ancient site of the Lombard Kingdom, and it was well known throughout the lands. We must remember that 100 years before, Charlemagne had ended the kingdom of the Lombards, by conquering them and making himself their ruler. However time waits for no one, and King Berengar was now the man of the moment in Italy. The stage was set now, the new king called a conference with the nobility of Western France, and he would be chosen to be the king of the Western Franks. However fate would have the final word. The army of King Berengar, could not land the final blow, so a truce was declared. The hand of Fate would play this game of Kings and Kingdoms, and in the end the Knights would win a crushing victory over the forces of King Berengar. The endless bloodbaths and battles for power, kept the Frankish Empire torn in pieces, and they often felt easy prey to Invaders, because there was no organization.

In the end Guido was crowned emperor of the Frankish Empire, by the Pope in Rome in 893. In the Frankish Western Empire, the situation was much the same. Odo count of Paris, was the toast of the town, and also the hero of the empire. Odo count of Paris made himself a hero, when he led the Frankish assault on the Vikings as they were warring to 886.

His dakring attacks on the Vikings, awakened strong forces in the hearts of the Frankish Warriors. Odo, and the Long Blades of the Frankish Warriors, had denied the Vikings their victory, and Carl the fat had gambled it away with his shameful treaty. Odo was the right man for the job, and he had the backing of all the people, so he set himself up as King.

The kingdom of France belonged to Odo, its greatest Defender. In the rich province of Aquitaine, the power belonged to the great Duke Randolph. Duke Randolph was perhaps the real power in the Frankish Kingdom, and it's been that way In Aquitaine for years. His Ace in the Hole, his son, was in the future to become Charles the Simple. Between the Kingdom of Italy, and that of the western Franks, they had the kingdom of Provence. This kingdom was important because it held the famous Saint Bernard pass, that entered Italy, or kept Invaders out.

The kingdom of burgundy had their problems too, on where the boundary should be placed, and what family should hold power. It went back and forth for years. Finally Rudolph was crowned King of Burgundy. Rudolph would go on for years, trying to also pull part of the Lorraine into his Realm. The Little Kings were popping up throughout the empire, and one scroll said the Fat had been deposed, and made to give up the throne. Many more popped up all over the empire. The kingdom was broken up in the six independent kingdoms. These were Changing Times where nothing could ever set in stone, and many were shocked at the latest developments. Imagine the person of that time period, seeing only Royal Blood on the throne for centuries, and then seeing Carl the Fat deposed, or fired, and the next legitimate ruler Charles the simple was Passed over.

If that wasn't enough, the person of this period also saw the bastard son of Royal Blood elected to the throne. These however were uncertain times, and they really had been that way for many centuries. In a century that had seen invasions by the Moors in Spain, and invasions by the Vikings .

Yes these were Changing Times, and deaths rattle was shaking away.

The Holy Roman Empire was a mess, and each time a king or Emperor died, everything was divided amongst all the Sons, which added chaos instantly to the situation. The empire of the Franks was unraveling and Arnulf the Great with the sheer power of His personality, held together the unraveling Empire. The emperor's crown and title were tossed around at the whim of the Pope's, and it began to grow into a paper tiger, or without strength. We can thank the Germanic tribes of the Franks for being the first to have elections, and it just caused more problems. There were always those that should inherit the throne, and those who thought there should be the right of Elections. We can thank this long process of government, for preserving the right of Elections, and we do indeed owe western civilization to the Germanic tribes. Only the uneducated could believe anything else.

While the popes were handing out the title, Emperor of the Romans, a real power was forming in the North. The Pope's dreamed of having an Emperor in Rome since the days of ancient Rome. Also they desperately needed power in Italy, since the days of the Roman Empire, Rome had been on its own.

Even in the ninth century the Arabs were making yearly raids all along the coast, and the shipping of Italian cities. In 846 the Moorish Pirates devastated trading towns, and they even had begun even raiding Rome itself. If it had not been for the combined strength of Naples and several other Italian cities, Italy would have been conquered. It is only because of The Fleets of these towns, that the churches, and the Christian relics of Rome were saved. Rome was not the seat of power for the Christian church, it was Constantinople, which was the capital of the Eastern Roman Empire, it stood until 1453.

The Roman Catholic Church tells us a different story of course, but then their power is all they cared about. If it had not been for the alliance between the Church of Rome and the Franks, the Lombards would have taken everything they had. It was Pippin that defeated the Lombards, and then the Pope crowned him. The Catholic Church spent so much time and energy on the tribe of the Franks, because everyone could see it at that time, they were the up-and-coming power. With the new alliance, the Roman Catholic Church could in reality rise up with them, and that's exactly what happened. In fact Charlemagne was in reality of Christ, but not the servant of the Pope. In fact the Frankish church held power over the Pope in Rome, and Charlamagne felt himself the head of it. In fact it was a political deal that made the alliance between the Franks and the Pope in Rome.

The Pope needed help militarily Against all enemies. A deal was struck, and the rest is history. It was Charlemagne in reality, that spread the church amongst the German tribes, not the Pope. The power of the Pope began to grow with Charlemagne, and not centuries earlier, like the Catholic writers have said. In these times The power of the Pope was not there, it developed from the time of Charlemagne. It was a development that would last for 500 years, and continue to grow as the centuries went on.

In the Eastern Roman Empire the Bishops of Rome, we're only bishops of Rome, nothing more. In the west, it was given that the Bishops of Rome, were leaders of the honor of the church, not the authority figures, that later Christian writers said. After the Roman empire was divided into East and West, the seat of government was Constantinople in the east.

In fact the Roman Church made up terrific lies, of which we must investigate to the very end. The Petrine theory it would be called. The theory according to the church was about the founding of the Church of Rome by Peter the Apostle. The Roman Church built their case on the fact that Peter was the chief of the Apostles. The Roman Church said Peter was selected by the master Jesus, to have authority over all the others. The Roman Church went on to say that if Peter founded the Church of Rome, that he received from Jesus a precious tradition. They said that since Peter founded the Church of Rome, and handed this tradition on to his successors, the possession of the tradition, gave to that church, the same kind of authority over all churches, that Peter had over his apostles.

This is the grand total of the lies the church forced on the minds of those with no education. The church knew its propaganda, and enforced it, and developed it for their own gain of course. By the time of Leo the first, this pile of crap was accepted by almost everyone in the western world, because they didn't know any better. The Germanic invasions of the 5th Century broke apart all the governments of the West, that would never have allowed this to be. The Germanic kingdoms that followed, had no government to oppose. This government clothed in the silk Robes of the church. Their Blueprint 2 power was perfect, and they were going to have it all. As one Germanic Nation after another changed from Arianism to Roman Catholic, the lock on the western thought was achieved. Arianism still believed in Jesus, but they believed that Jesus was a prophet, and that was the religion of most of the Europeans. They knew the truth, but the Roman Catholic Church changed everything. From the time of Pope Gregory the first, to Charlemagne, was 200 years, and Pope Gregory began his conversions with the Lombards in the year of 600. From 600 to 800 it was all the church could do to hold off the Furious Lombards. The Lombards were like any other Germanic tribe, they were ferocious. After Rome officially belonged to the Eastern Roman Empire, they did little to guard against the pressure of the Lombards, and little to help with the Moorish Pirates of the Mediterranean. It was a joke, that was not funny, for Constantinople still taxed Rome, but they offered no defense against Rome's enemies. Only out of desperation did Rome turn to its Germanic conquerors in the West.

The Lombards encircled the Bishops of Rome, and the alliance with the Franks was a matter of survival. As the Franks conquered their neighbors, their leaders used their new religion for the fury of a holy war. It is no coincidence that the lands of the Heretics, were enormous, and very fertile lands. In reality the so-called Holy Wars, we're all about Frankish and Roman Catholic expansion, and of course armed robbery. As the new lands of the Aryans were taken under the banner of the cross, the wealth and power of the Franks and the church grew rapidly. In reality if they would have lived on, there would have been no need for their conversion. I hope the reader sees the truth, I'm trying to bring to light, for with the facts, come the wisdom. In fact,it was a scam in itself.

The scamming song, who better to make it all clear, then the famous and respectable Gregory of Tours. Gregory was the bishop of the Franks, and also a great historian, who wrote books on Charlemagne and other great works. We will let Gregory of Tours tell us in his own words, it would be hard to find in the life of the Frankish people, evidence that Christianity had done much to soften the manners, or to touch the hearts of the nation at large. It is clear that this is worse than barbaric Society. It is a Society of barbarians, suffering the first inevitable evils of contact with a civilization, the meaning of which they could not understand.

They history of the brainwashing of the Franks, is one of the darkest periods of Europe. As the Lombards readied for their conquest of Rome. Rome was deserted by the Byzantine Empire. The church struck an alliance with the all-powerful and combat-ready Franks.

The man with true wisdom does however know that the forces of civilization could be brought to triumph over the dark Forces of Barbarians, only through the church. Charles Martel however was the first to be on good relations with the Catholic Church. The Monrovian Kings took the very same position, that the Eastern Empire Emperors of Constantinople took. Both of these Powers, were in fact church and state, and did not want to give a percentage of the power to the Roman Church. The Monrovian Kings, with the powerful men of their Nation, regulated the Affairs of church and state together. The best that can be said of the Frankish church under the Monrovian Kings,is at a better time, the beginning of great moral forces, would become part of the barbarians mentality.

It must be noted and understood that the power of the popes of Rome, had been light inside the Frankish realm, and under the authority of the Frankish Kings. It must be understood that it was the long thick two edged swords, that supported the power of the Pope in Rome. It must also be understood that the popes of Rome, at the beginning agreed that they were to be under the control of the Frankish Kings. However the Society of the Franks because of their political deal with the Roman Church, allowed the pope to be the authority on religious matters only.

The Act of crowning Charlemagne on Christmas Day in the year 800, in fact merged the beginning of more power for the pope. This one Act contained within it, the germs of religious problems for the next 900 years. Now Church would fight state for the power to rule everything. The popes of Rome and other leaders, had the vision of planning for the far future, and their plotting or planning, cannot be overestimated.

The view of the Pope's in the future would become tied to the coronation by the pope on Charlemagne. Now any Pope would have the right to dictate to the Emperor. It was a big mistake, and like the historians say, it was the downfall of the state, and they uprising of the church.

The Pope's would argue, spiritual power was always higher,\ than Earthly power, and therefore the spiritual power should control the Earthly power. It was a great argument But in reality it was a whole lot of shit, or Politics as it is called.

Any Man of the modern world can look back and realize the game the church played in the minds of everyone. The Emperor's did not get to their position being fools, and understood perfectly the role of themselves, and also the role of the men in the cloth of the church.

The Imperial view was short and simple, whenever the argument was raised. Their view was the Emperor was the successor of those ancient rulers, to whom the Pope's had always been subjects, therefore he had the same right to control the Pope that the ancient rulers had. So to give up power was very wrong.

The battle for the control of the Populations minds and loyalty, would go on as long as men lived in the darkness of ignorance. Only now in the modern world, as we have the past laid before us, can we dissect every move, every angle, and every real intention. But in the centuries gone by, as the ones we are concerned with here, the level of knowledge was slim and none.

So to go back into their world, we must put back on the blinders, and be led down the roads of church and state, both leading to the same place, bullshit. We must remember that Rome had been the most powerful city in the world for centuries, and she would fall. It was quite natural for the men of Rome, to attempt to recreate that situation. This time however it would be done with the holy book, instead of the spear and the sword.

Also the major players were setting out to conquer the minds and hearts of the men and women, and also the land. The plans of the bishop of Rome were simple . Even in the days of Gregory the Great, the power of the lands were beginning to flow to the Pope. Their Blueprint to power was exceptional, and of course it did work. The lands that history call the Papal States, were gifts. The land in these times was perfect, and the popes of Rome had its states scattered all over Italy, but also in Sicily, and Gaul . The administration of these lands were left to the officials of the church, but the money from them went to the Pope in Rome. The pope was an extremely wealthy man, and that's what it was all about, wealth and power.

Here great words of Charlemagne fell on the stage. The lands of the church have become much larger. Of course with their vast Holdings of land, Rome would become the Hub, or Center. It is at this time that men began to call these lands, the states of the church. One could even expect the church to grab all the wealth and power they could, as a rock and roll musician once said, Everybody Wants to Rule the World.

Charlemagne gave his support, and said let the popes of Rome enjoy these lands, and their wealth. The Pope's dated their claim to these lands to a grant from ancient Emperor Constantine. They claim that Constantine granted the lands to the bishop Sylvester centuries ago, when Rome was Supreme. The population swallowed this big lie, all the way down to the 15th century. It took quite some time for men and women to understand all the lies of the men in the church, because they just weren't the sharpest knives in the drawer. Plus there are no records to check, and who would believe that God's representative would lie. This giant lie that would be the basis for power for thousands of years to come, was nothing more than an outright lie, and with the church, there would be plenty more to follow. You know the giant lie was believed until the 15th century, when the popes and the papers we're just shown to be clumsy forgeries. The church for centuries had lied to everyone, and until the 15th century it worked, but then they were exposed.

The very Foundation that the church built its power on was a lie, and a very big one. These men of the cloth enjoyed their power over the minds and lives of everyone. The real truth is Charlemagne gave the Pope the right to hold those lands, and also gave them the land grants, and some were huge. The pappel States grew rapidly, and they did so because they were allowed to.

Charlemagne and Pepin Gave the largest land grants of course to the Roman Catholic Church. They gave the powers of Rome all the lands on the Adriatic Coasts, which up until this time had been in the hands of the leaders in Ravena, who had been appointed by Constantinople. Here is where the powers of the western and Eastern churches would Clash, and these would go on for a thousand years. What these large tracts of land grants did, was give the popes of Rome territory on both sides of the Italian peninsula. This United all the land on both sides of the Adriatic, under control of the Pope.

When Rome fell to the Germanic tribes, it must be noted the Empire Still was intact, in the east Greek speaking lands of the Eastern Roman Empire. The Greeks had been much wealthier than the western half, and they had a much larger population.

The Eastern Roman Empire would still remain for over 1,000 years, and the religious issue would not go away for them. The Greek Christian Church of Constantinople was not about to bow to any Bishop of Rome. The power struggle was on. The Greek eastern empire or the Byzantine Empire, had their own Theory, that the Bishops of Rome were still subjects of the Greek Emperors of the East. The Byzantine Empire of the East would not agree to the theory that there were two Roman Empires.

To the Roman Empire it would take centuries before the Byzantines would relax their Theory. The theory of the Byzantine Empire, being the only Roman Empire, meant that the Bishops of Rome we're under the umbrella of the Byzantines. Perhaps the biggest issue at stake between the Church of the West, and the Church of the East, was in the west the churches of Rome were more filled with pictures, and Idols of stone and wood. To the Church of the East, and Constantinople, these practices were no different than the Barbarian temples, and they all had the flavor of heathenism.

The Eastern Church also hated the Mosaic work and the statues of the West. The early Christians had been totally against statues, and forever in the day, criticized the Romans for praying to Idols of stone. How quickly they forget, once they assume power, and how quickly they in reality, just ran and changed the images being worshipped.

A master plan of deception it was, but the men in the cloth of the church, were perhaps the most educated men in the world. As the years rolled by, the worship of idols and paintings drove the churches of the East and West apart.

The question Of Bulgaria was the cause of major rifts between the churches of the east and west. The Roman Church tried their best to have control of Bulgaria, but fate would have other plans. The Eastern Church would put its foot down, because after all Bulgaria belonged to the Eastern Empire.

The Bishops of Rome would claim, that Constantinople, was only the seat of government, and that Saint Peter's church was the seat of the real Church. That's my friends, was a power play by the men in the cloth of the West, but the men in the cloth of the East, had their own plans on control. In fact the doctrines of the East and West were very different, and this is why, we have the Roman Catholic faith, and the Eastern Greek Orthodox faith.

It was the Western doctrines that in reality divided the churches. The Western doctrine had said that the Holy Ghost proceeded from the father and the son, and in the East it was another story. The western church invented soul-destroying heresy's, such as the celebrity of the previous, dancing on Saturday, and the use of eggs and milk during the first week of Lent. However the biggest division was over the stupid theory that the Holy Ghost proceeded from the father and the son.

In reality the Church of Rome wanted a division, because by their Theory, St. Peter's church in Rome was Supreme. The Church of Rome with its Newfound power and wealth, tried their best to secure their hold on the lands east of the Adriatic. The Roman popes enjoyed their position with the popes states on the Eastern side, but Constantinople blocked their Advance any further.

All this would soon change, when in the seventh century the Barbarian Bulgarians swept into these lands in enormous strength and numbers. The Furious race of the Bulgarians, led them to take a Valley close to the lower Danube. It was at this time in history, the land assumed the name of the warlike people who claimed it. In fact those people are still on the land today, which we call Bulgaria. This land has been called different names from ancient times, but since the days of the enormous migration, it has been known as Bulgaria. In the famous 9th century, the king of this Heathen tribe, had been converted to Christianity, by priests from Constantinople.

Then the priests arrived from Rome telling the king, he had been instructed with the wrong doctrines. Here is where the plot thickens, and then pope Nicholas played his hand. He sent a letter to the king of the Bulgarians.

He told them of the teachings from Constantinople, he said they were totally wrong. And that there would be no salvation, unless they fell into the orbit of the Roman Church. Bold advisors assured the king that Rome was the only true faith.

The Eastern Church grew angry, and sent strong messages to Rome. The Eastern Church explained to the King that since they belong to the Eastern Empire, that they could not be joined to the religion of the western Roman Empire.

As the war of words was fought between east and west, it became obvious to all, there had to be a separation. There of course were different political agendas to consider, as well as the racial makeup of the two lands. In the end, there would be, two different spheres of power and influence.

In the long run this separation would work extremely well for them, and it gave them more time to concentrate on commanding Western thoughts and ideas. The biggest Scandal the Catholic church was involved in, was a Great Collection of Phony Letters the Church called the Decredals.

 It was too late, and their con job had worked for over 700 years. These letters helped mold the church laws, and Molded the Teachings of the Bible However They Saw Fit. These collections of Phony Letters went all the way back to the time of the Roman Empire.

 The Papers Claimed and still claim today, that they are the foundation of Christ himself. Because of this, they claim they are independent of any state Recognition. The letters take us back to the days of Christ and Peter, and give us all the propaganda they can muster, and boy could they throw some lies at you,all for the sake of power.

The modern historian, with the advantage of wisdom today, can see the letters were the fabrication of sly dogs, who capitalized on them for centuries. In fact history has a name for the lies of the church, and calls them the False Decretals. The Roman Catholic Church built its enormous power over the lives of men, on the Phony Documents of the Forged Decretals.

The Roman Catholic church built its enormous power, on the Phony Documents of the Forged Decretals. I said that' twice because it is so important, check that out on the internet, the Forged Decretals.

The Catholic Church claimed it had the Decrees of the Pope's all the way back to Peter, and how they came about is still a mess. Modern Scholars agree in one thing though, it was a perfect plan, to raise the authority of the Bishops and the Pope's, to a height they could not have ever hoped to reach.

It was said Nicholas the first, brought them to light, but modern men say they could have been forged much earlier. One thing is certain, and that is the Decretals Where All Forgeries, not just a few, and today that is admitted by everyone.

The Collection called The Forged decretals, was published under the name of Isidor. It is amazing to what lengths these men of the cloth went to, to grab the minds and hearts of the population. But this was a huge power grab, and to tell you the truth, they did well with all their lies. They took over a major portion of all the power sitting on the face of the Earth.

You know what's the funniest thing about it all, is what they did to the minds and the hearts of the population, was extremely evil, but then they had on the robes of the church.
You know it's funny just like any other government, the power wars were always on with the religious leaders, especially the Catholic Church. Who else in the whole world could promise you everlasting life in heaven, if only you just believed, and gave them 20% of all the money you would ever earn. It's pretty evil when you think about it all, how they took over the minds and hearts and souls of so many millions, but they made so many millions, and that's exactly why

they did it. And you know The Biggest Lie hardly ever told, is when Jesus Christ was instructing all his disciples, he told them several times never to speak outside the Jewish people, about anything he had ever said. I mean Everyone else was considered an unbeliever, and non-believers were no good, it was just that simple. He asked every single one of them to never utter one word of any of his messages outside the Jewish people.

But as soon as he was gone, Peter saw the opportunity to become one of the most famous people in the world, when he took his messages and information, and the Bible to Europe. There, Peter became extremely famous, telling everyone about how he was Jesus number one guy, and explaining everything that Jesus said, and what he really meant by everything he said, this made Paul so powerful. I'm sure that once he thought about it all, about how he could go from basically a bum begging for food, to eating with the kings of Europe, he had to go for it. So you can't take away nothing from Paul, but he was one of the biggest hustlers in the history of the world.

In this world it's truly every man for himself, and it seems that jealousy is probably the strongest power of all the different powers that man possesses or uses. If you remember, it was one of Jesus disciples that turned him into the Romans, for just 33 pieces of silver. He sold out the up-and-coming god, or son of God, depending upon who you listen to . Yeah Judas was a major piece of shit, telling on Jesus, but he committed suicide in the end or so The Story Goes. There is so much deception and lies especially when you're dealing with the men that truly do run it all. I want the reader to understand, the church was not the church we know in America today. The church was the ultimate Authority, with power over your life and death, at any time. They were the power, and As their power grew, Kings and Emperors, were so jealous.

These False decretals we're probably the biggest pile of crap, that any church ever made up. In these False Decretals, the purpose was to Elevate the Priests to Pedestals. To show you the way things had always been done, since the time of Christ. And that way it showed you the rules and regulations were acceptable, and that's the way it always had been done, so of course that's the way it would be done in the future.

The real purpose for these Forgeries was of course to represent the Pope as the one single source of authority in the world. It made little difference to the average man, and most were not even aware of the meaning of the Secret Forgeries. But as time went on and the power of the man in the Purple Cloth increased, it was a different story.

Popes would later go on to assert their right as God's representative on Earth, and even Depose Kings. So you can see the Weight of these Forged Documents, and the charade went on until the 15th Century, A Thousand Years. Having the weight of Saint Peter and Christ on their side, they involved their deceitful rights against local powers, in the church and the state, to win every argument, the Forged Papers were looked at for their Ultimate Authority.

In reality the Pope's and people for centuries would give the Forged Decretals the power of Sacred Relics, even the Holy Grail, the cross that Jesus Christ was crucified on. That is how important these Decretals were, and they were nothing but lies. The people of that era never questioned the authenticity of the papers, for something so Sacred, could not be questioned. For many generations the False decretals would be quoted and taken as the supreme law. And at a later time in history, when men dared to question them, it was perfectly obvious, not only were they Forged, but they were actually very Clumsy Forgeries.

What must be noted to understand the cunning of men in the cloth of the church, is that without the Forgeries, the Pope's would not have enjoyed any power whatsoever. For centuries nothing held so much power and hold over the minds of all of Europe, as the False Decretals.

The basis of church Authority was completely shifted from One Foundation, to the new one. The aim of the men in the cloth of Rome, was to make the words of a Roman Bishop, equally important as the teachings of Jesus. Pope Nicholas the first, died in our famous 9th century, and let things set, so that a strong successor could wield the power, he had only dreamed of. By this time the popes were being elected without the approval of the crown, and this was forbidden.

Because of the strong work of Nicholas the first, Hadrian II, only had to apologize. You see things were a changing and this was the first time an emperor would ever be submissive to a pope,and Louis II was heavily criticized for it. The wheels of world politics were beginning to turn as we examine the next set of events.

At the time that Louis II wrote a letter to the Eastern Emperor of Constantinople. Louis II and his army of Franks had just taken a couple Greek Cities By force, from their enemies the Arabs. The Eastern Empire of the Byzantines was ruled by Emperor Basilius. Louis the 2nd had no right to use the title of Emperor of the Romans. Louis answered that, his uncle the king of France and Germany, did not hesitate to give him the Title of Emperor. Louis II said, the king of the Franks, did not gain this title by chance, but by the will of God, declared by the Pope. He said, no emperor of the Franks, as the Greeks had called him, but Emperor of the Romans sounded better.

He had been called for the defense of Rome several times, and he was a high priest from Rome. His father had given the Title Emperor of the Romans, and he was consecrated by the Pope. He further stated his case to the Greek emperor, of the Byzantine Empire, and proclaimed by his Legions, Yes, the Roman Emperor of the East. Were the Franks less worthy to Bear the Imperial name than the Spanish, or other Roman emperors.

Louis11, was so right when he said the Franks have become the rightful inheritors of the empire, because the Greeks had abandoned Rome and their language. Because they abandoned the Holy Roman City, the people lost their claim to the title. To see the wheels of politics turning, we must look at the statement that the title of emperor was legitimate only, if the pope was there for the coronation. The reality is thinking carries the germs for conflicts, between the church and state, even more through the following centuries.

In reality, he was giving up all the power of His ancestors, of the Pope's, and the church. The early Frankish Kings had made the election of the Pope, meet their approval, even though it was far away in Italy. The wheel was spinning, and the successor of Adrian II, John the 8th, would really change the way things were done. King Arthur II of Lorraine died in 870 to set the stage, with the Limelight. Upon his death there was a mad Scramble for territory among the Royal Family, and also the Dukes and the counts. This mad relining of the empire was called the partition. When the dust has settled in the northern Frankenstein, the Middle Kingdom was gone. Now the power of the entire North was divided between France and Germany. For the first time, the Rivalry between France and Germany for the crown became obvious.

Still wishing the Coveted crown of Emperor, in Germany the players were Ludwig the German and his three sons. Ludwig II had died with no heirs, and For the First Time The Crown was not spoken for, in the rights of succession. For the first time in history the pope made the choice. Charles the bald was chosen by the Pope in Italy, and asked to come to Rome for his coronation. You might remember it was Charles the bald, that had taxed his subjects beyond belief, to pay for the ransom the Vikings that asked for. He bled them dry one more time, and he went to Rome to get his crown.

It is amazing to the historian, the wild change in events. The Roman popes knew now their new Strength, and you can believe, they used it.

As the Pope in Rome with all the False Decretals to the audience, he explained how he had been chosen by God to Crown the next Emperor. Charles the bald said not a word, He allowed himself to be To be crowned king of Italy, and he appointed Count Boso officer in Italian affairs, while Charles slipped back over the Alps. In reality what the pope had done was crown the Emperor, that would stay out of his own business. He had also selected the Emperor who would not challenge his supreme authority. Of the bigger picture, we see here the future germs of a German and Roman rivalry.

It was the politics of John the 8th, that succeeded in organizing Italy into a formidable Force. It was here in Italy that the forces would gather to stop the advance of the Arabs. This John the 8th was in reality, a warrior in the closet for the church. He surprised everyone when he raised a huge Fleet in the waters off Italy, and actually commanded that same Fleet, in a clash with the Arabs. It must be noted that the Popes Fleet thoroughly beat the Arab Pirates. The Arab fleet would go to the bottom of the ocean, and it was waiting for them.

Emperor Charles the Bald, was again summoned by the Pope to Italy, to defend the Holy city once again. John the 8th hailed Charles as the savior of Italy, and he truly was. On his way back to Germany, he was Poisoned by powder given to him by his Jewish physician. and once again, we are faced with who would take the crown. The political powers of Rome were divided upon a new Emperor. Some wanted the Empire to go to a strong man, but then not too strong. They would all have to take a seat in the shadows again, the young German Karlman rushed into Italy, with his Knights, and many in the north of Italy rallied to the German Warrior. A Young German is a matter of politics himself. He rallied the powers that were the enemies of John the 8th. The Pope before he could be pressured by the German forces, left the country, and went to France to discuss politics of the future.

The Pope saw no likely successor in France, for the son of Charles the bald was to young, and to weak. The Pope John the 8th, stayed in France for one year, knowing he had to settle the issue, he had to go back to Italy. At this time, the Three Brothers of Germany were there to force the issue.

The three brothers of Germany, came to the conclusion that Carl the Fat would be the next Emperor, and of course they would be next in line. It was decided, the pope crowned him.

He would not have to wait long, for soon after the crowning Pope John the 8th began begging for help, because the Arab Pirates were attacking Italy again. Men Spin a mysterious web, and Carl this time would be the spider, instead of The Fly. You turn no back on the traitor in the closet, because now he understood the game totally.
With the death of John the 8th,there was a pendulum swing back to the emperor having the final word and the ultimate power. The popes of Rome would learn their lessons the hard way, like all men do, and they would learn they needed a strong Imperial power, so they could succeed in their own control over the Affairs of men.

They would also learn that a weak Empire would leave them the church, easy prey to real enemies.
CHURCH AND STATE,THE STATE MUST REMAIN STRONG<TO DEFEND THE CHURCH>

THE POWER OF STEEL TRUMPS ALL <

CHAPTER 12

We have watched the Germanic tribes take every inch of the Western Roman Empire. The fighting was extremely vicious, but the Germanic tribes had won out. The Viking tribes had slashed the armies of Rome, and Rome was no more. We have watched Charlemagne and his family before and after, take the lead with their Frankish Warriors, and form an Empire of all the Germanic tribes.

The Empire like all others, had been forged in the blood of its rivals, and its enemies. The Royal line of Charlemagne would manage the Affairs of Western Europe, throughout the turbulent ninth century. Make no mistake, Charlemagne and his beloved friends, or Germans, and their Capital at Aachen Stand in modern-day Germany. We also have watched the role the Roman

Catholic Church had played, and watched how their influence helped begin to civilize The Barbarians.

The church took the lead in forming the Empires, Heathens, and Pagans. We have also watched The Bishop's or Popes of Rome, begin their power play, with the Kings and the Emperor's, that would continue into our own modern era. We have seen how the Forged Documents, and would strengthen the grip of the Roman Church, and thrust the popes of Rome, high up on the center stage.

What is important to note, is the Church and State needed each other desperately, and German civilization as we know it today, could not have been produced without these two major political forces. Make no mistake it took both of these powers to round out all the edges, so that we have what we do now. We Begin to watch the other parts of the empire, Begin to wield their power.We watch the part they played in helping to form and preserve the greatest civilization on planet Earth. We have seen the race Wars begin, when the ninth Century opened, with the dreaded Moors invading from Spain. We have seen the German blood produce Champions like Charles Martel to repel them, with of course Champion Warriors at his side.

We have watched again as Roland was needed to teach the Moors a lesson again. In the ninth Century we have watched the Empire struggle, and repel All Foreign Invaders. We watched their baptism by Blood, and their trial of combat.

The lead now would go to the great warrior Arnulf, who had by this time been crowned King of the Eastern Franks. All the little Kings had popped up throughout the empire, ending the hopes of Arnulf to become Emperor over all the Franks. Carl the fat had been deposed, for his act of submission. In 886. there were Turbulent times, and the forces at work where unrelenting, uncertainty was very common. Each of these little Kings, had the approval and support of Arnulf but in reality they did not think of him as a superior. Arnulf had no time to ponder the question, of who was Superior at home, for his work was cut out for him, in trying to secure the Hostile borders of the Eastern Franks. The dream that Charlemagne had materialised was gone, and that was of unifying the empire under one force, or one crown. Italy was the kingdom of Guido, And the kingdom of Charles the simple,changed with every battle.

Providence was the kingdom of Louis, and Burgundy was the Kingdom of Robert, and of course Odo of Paris took whatever he wanted. All the little Kings had their own domains, and these would be the Royal Blood for many centuries into the future, and this would also be the foundation for all the European States.

As all the little Kings, thought only of their own domains, it was on and off, to shoulder the burden of Defense against the enemies, who were approaching the Empire at all times. The Vikings had finally been beaten, in the enormous Battle of the Dyle, which is in the Lorraine. It was more than just a victory for the Warriors of the Empire, it stopped all further Viking advances into the Lorraine. What the battle had shown in the big picture was, if all the German forces would fight together, they could not be beat, and I mean by anyone, at any time, on any day. But that's if the German forces would fight together, they would have course become invincible, and this is what they had to prove to all the Invaders, that thought they could cut a slice, out of what the Germans actually owned.

On the eastern border of the German Empire, a new power was threatening the peace and security of everyone. It was in the Eastern territory, that the huge Moravian Duchy, had been created to stabilize the frontier lands. The Moravian Duchy, or territory, was full of the warlike Poles and the Bohemians, and also many other tribes, that were in fact Slavs, and not Germanic blood.

This is now PART 4 THE concentration of Slavic tribes was now beginning to become independent, and a great power of their own making. In the troubled times before Arnulf, The focus on the Eastern Frontier was slacking, and now in 891, they were a power to reckon with. The Slavs were now well-organized, and vicious, and it was time for them to carve out their own kingdom.

The frontier line that separated Germans from Slavs was the Elbe River, that ran down the Great Plain between the Danube and the Tributaries. The man in charge of the frontier was the Duke, or more commonly called Duke Swat. He did not recognize the fact that King Arnulf was his Overlord. This was a thorn in the side of the Eastern Franks, and the King was the man given the job. Fresh from his enormous victory over the Vikings, King Arnulf wasted no time, when he marched his German Army East, to do battle with the Nation of Moravia. The year was 892, and it was going to be another bloody one. The forces of the Germans encountered no great battle with the Duke, but skirmishes were fought and the countryside was wasted. Two years later another German Army, under the same King, invaded the same place, and this time the Duke was waiting with his forces. The pages of History tell us that the Brave and Bold force of the Bavarians, was wiped out. King Arnulf with a small percentage of his Warriors escaped. The forces of Moravia were great warriors, with a great leader, and if he had lived, history might have been written quite different.

The great Duke would not live to see another year, and the Barbarian forces were closing in on the new Power Moravia. The lands of the great Duke upon his death, were divided amongst his Three Sons. The sons did not know it at the time, but a plague was coming to sweep the land, and the name of it was the Barbaric Hungarians.

The Slavs along the eastern border of Germany, were a serious threat, to the whole German Empire. The Empire was safe however, because to the left of the rivers that held the Slavs, the Saxon Nation lived. The Saxons although losing many Warriors to Charlemagne, and many warriors to the conquest of England, we're still very, very strong. Their Valor in battle was an accepted fact of life. In fact it would be the Saxons blood, and the Saxons Warriors, that would build a great Empire out of the Frankish Empire.

Blood is thicker than water, and the Franks and the Saxons were cousins, so it's only right for the Saxon leaders to add a lot of life to a dying Empire. Just like their Teutonic cousins, they had given new life to the dying Roman Empire, and the Saxons would do the same for the Franks, and the land of the Franks. King Arnulf of the Eastern Franks, knew he had no worries in the east, with the sword's and battle-axes of the vicious Saxons. The king made a stop in Saxony, on his way back from the Viking battle of that year.

But it was just a tour of his kingdom and its defenses. In the west the power of the king would be felt when he made his son King of Lorraine.Lorraine was extremely valuable,and would be fought over for centuries.

The King was a little ahead of his time, for he had the vision of the greatest men, and wanted only to make Lorraine a strong buffer, between the future friends, and the future Germany. This buffer Kingdom of Lorraine, would be fought over in 1860, World War 1 , and World War II, between modern-day friends, and modern-day Germany. Even in that time real man with vision realized that one day France and Germany would be great Rivals, and even then they needed a neutral ground between them.

In reality, Lorraine had been sliced off German territory. When the King died, it was given back to them. When the king died it was given to the little King Ludwig. Of course the sons of the King naturally would fight for the kingdom. But in the battle, the king would be killed. Before they could slice off Lorraine, to give to his bastard son, he was invited to Rome by the Pope to be crowned Emperor. On his way to Rome, he did battle with the Knights of the Lombards on several occasions, and he was even crowned king of Italy. These were vicious times, full of drama, and things weren't about to change. The Pope tried to put several princes on the throne, especially a couple of the tyrants that were in the closet of the Roman Church, but eventually everybody realized the crown must go to Arnulf. He was the most powerful of the Germans, and the only one that could unite them, against all the enemies that would be coming.

In 896 Arnulf was back in Italy, and this time he came with his large army of Swabians, and this time no Lombards wanted battle. This time the Emperor would not be denied entrance to Rome, for the Swabians were known to be excellent with their swords. The local Powers wanted nothing to do with a German King , or with the German army, entering into the politics of Rome, so they closed the gates of the city to him. It became obvious to the German King that he would have to fight for the crown he wanted so desperately. So the battle was on, they would fight, and fight to the end.

The Swabians shone like bright stars in the night sky, and they proved their Valor in combat inside the walls of Rome. They were friends of the German party, and soon the Furious Swabians were inside. Of course it was King Arnulf that led them. Now for the first time in German history there were Two Emperors, and the wheels of politics kept turning. The forces that be, would place their bets, and suddenly Emperor Arnulf became seriously ill. All he could think of, is he didn't want under any circumstances to die any place else but Germany, so back through the Alps once more he went. The first attempt at a German King, to control the politics of Italy, ended badly, but he was still alive. and planned for further expansion.

The biggest problem was the invasion of the horrible and Barbaric Hungarians. The Huns were Extremely vicious, and before the the Huns were done, all parts of the German Empire would be involved. It is ironic that the Emperor who had been the great German Chieftain to save northern Europe. From the fury and the Wrath of the Vikings, rallied all the German forces and produced the great victory. It was this Victory in the 9th century that made him King. It is ironic that this great German Chieftain, was also the man, they would be blamed for the plague, that man called the Hungarians. When the King before he was crowned Emperor, fought his Wars against the Slavs in Moravia, he Enlisted the help of the Furious Hungarians as Allies. It was their help, and their Fury with which they fought, that enabled him to win his crushing victories.

In reality, what the King had done was show these dreaded sons of the steppi's, the wealth and the beauty of the western world. The alliance was needed against the enormous power of German Enemies. But in the end, it brought the Wrath and fury back on them. It was on the minds of these men of the mountains, that if they could penetrate the frontiers of Germany, that they could have the wealth of the West. It would not happen in the life of the Emperor, but his successors would be staggered. The pages of History tell us, the German Emperor was more than just a great warrior, he was also a great lover. Germany's writers tell us, that the Emperor fathered over a dozen children, but only one was legitimate, and that boy was named Ludwig, after the great one. But the most powerful Chief of the Tribes, United Behind The Offspring of their Best.

This definitely shows the progress, in the succession that always followed. But it also Showed the German families loved their Emperor. Because the child was so young, he gave the great German Nobles, the time to build their own systems of power, if you will. It was at this point in German history, that the great Ducal powers were grown, and magnified in intensity. The Stems, or centers of power would become in the future, the very core of German power, and German might. These powers that were building in the Duchies, Would One Day become the strongest powers in the world, and would send Tremors through it. We will examine for the first time in America the exact way it did happen, and to hell with the Non-Germans, or the other races, we must have the truth, and here it is.

The most important part of German history, is all of it, for each piece had its own place in the giant puzzle. To say that one piece was more important would be Wrong, for all joined together. Bavaria is perhaps the best-known, for it had always been in the spotlight. Bavaria had always since the beginning of time, winded across the Beautiful Blue Danube River. The prime location would be the Great Valley. As long as recorded history, that spot had been a Frontier Town for the Roman Empire, and it is situated at the point of the Danube River, where it reaches its northernmost point. Even in the days of the Hammer, Charles Martel, Bavaria was under the control, of the House of Bavaria. This Ducal family had governed since the beginning of time, and had ruled, with their own Fair laws. The House of Bavaria, married the house of Charles Martel, so there would be a blood alliance between the German families.

The House of Bavaria would submit to no other concessions, and refused to be under the control of Frankish law. The Knights of Bavaria, and the Knights of Charlemagne, met on the field of battle, to decide the issue in front of Thor and Odin.

By Shear strength in numbers, and overall Brute Force, the Knights of Charlemagne won, and the soil of Bavaria, was soaked in the blood of both Teutonic armies. In the end of this chapter, the Ducal power of Bavaria Was beaten soundly. But many would live to fight another day, and that's exactly what they did.

Bavaria was made a province of the Frankish state, and Royal officers tried to administer it. After the death of the great Charlemagne, Bavaria became the power, for the King of the Eastern Franks. The Franks of course, found Bavaria not ready to submit on a daily basis to the Franks, so things were slacking. The great Ludwig the German, also took Bavaria as his Center of power, and so did his son Carl Mann, and his son Emperor Arnulf. You can see that Bavaria was indeed the core of German power, and was also the Kingpin of the Eastern Kingdom. Bavaria was the center of power in the east, and it's Mark was made on the frontier. It extended All the Way Beyond, where Vienna Austria stands today.

It is interesting to note, that Adolf Hitler was from a town near Vienna called Linz. It was at this Frontier, that all military operations against the Invaders, would start, and there would be a long list. Bavaria like all parts of the Germanic Empire would be baptized in blood. Bavaria was known throughout the centuries for its Valor, as well as for its Knights. Thor and Odin only smiled as they look down on them, knowing they would need every last one of them.

The fighting Knights of Bavaria would prove on countless fields of combat, that Thor and Odin's men were still going to shape the future of the world, and this they did.

The House of Luitpold was also from Bavaria, and from this family came champions of combat, by the dozens. It was in their genes, God had made them that way, and they were the best they could be. It was from this House of Bavaria that Arnulf gathered his best knights, in the wars he fought, against the Slavs.

That they performed excellent, is of course written in the pages of History. When the Emperor died, the Bavarians placed themselves under the leadership of the bravest and toughest knight, from The Fearless house of Luitpold. In 907 The Fearless Knights of Bavaria would be tested beyond belief, when like a Title Wave, the Wild and barbaric hungarians, forced their way into Germany.

The Great Valley of the Germans, would be totally destroyed, when the full force of the Huns was felt. Knowing that they were outnumbered 200 to 1, The Master Knight Luitpold collected his forces, and set themselves right in the path of the great force of the Hungarians. The Bavarians were totally outnumbered, and when the last German knight had fallen in battle, Victory went to the huge Hungarian Force. In that battle the German blood ran freely on the valley floor, and the master Knight was slain himself. The loss was a terrible blow to the pride of the Bavarians, but the Valor the knights had shown, was incredible. After this battle, with the Bavarians annihilated, the Huns moved up the valley and settled.

It was a force, and a terrible blow for the Bavarians, but when they were ready, the blowing of the bugles would begin again. The boy King, Ludwig the child, was looked after by the powerful forces inside Bavaria, and was given the rank and title of National Duke. The wheels of politics were turning, and at times backwards. They once again became a United Power, within the larger German Kingdom.

For the events that just transpired, it made their local defense, the most important issue of that time. The national problems of the empire, they did not have the luxury of even thinking about, and it was all about self-preservation.One day at a time,and new shiny weapons of steel. With those they had a chance.

Swabia in itself, had a long and glorious history. Swabia was the Ancient Land West of Bavaria, and would later in history be called Switzerland. Swabia, and the Danube, were some of the most treasured real estate in the world. Since the ancient times when the tribes came from Scandinavia,it was known to have been known the place of romance and poetry. Swabia had been under the control of the Franks, for centuries, and the top men on this turf, were the Counts. And of course, those were appointed by the Franks. As often happens in the German lands of the East, they felt insulted by the overlordship of the empire. The nobility of knights had forged this land long ago, and resented the authority over them.

However this is the feeling of all German men, where only Thor or Odin, we're more powerful than they were. It is the spirit of individuality, that created the freedom that we know today. Many times in the history of Swabia, counts would organize revolts, and there were always rebellions because man-to-man, there was no better. At times the revolts worked well, and of course the nobility enjoyed it all, as is the way of man. North of Swabia, and Northwest of Bavaria, we find the Duchy Franconia. It was here in the Duchy of Franconia, that all the Empire looked up to for power, because it was from here, that the Franks ruled.

Since the days Of the mighty Clovis, the Franks had carried their weapons to the east, to the land of the Rhine River. It was here that the richest cities in the empire were, and it was here that they gathered. Also Franconia was the land where the Franks church was all-powerful, and the seats of power for the church were found right here. Franconia in fact is the very Heartland of all the German tribes, and Frankfort was the ancient capital. Bamberg, Worms, and Speir, Are among many historic towns. It is here in Franconia, that we find the most important lines for traffic or trade.

In Franconia there were two families of enormous power, and they were the Bambergers in the east, and The Conrads in the West. The Conrads were the relatives of the famous King Arnulf. After the death of the king, a bloody war broke out amongst the two ruling families.

War devastated the house of the Bambergers, and added great Fame and power to the house of the Conrad's. Going further north we find the ancient Germanic land of the Saxons. Long before recorded history along the rivers elbe, and the Weser, the Saxons had lived and died.

Saxony was the home of the champions of the world. They would carve out Their Kingdoms in England. The land of the Teutons was the homeland of countless Germanic tribes, before the age of migrations.Since the days of the ice ages,the Viking tribes had no choice but to go south into modern day Germany. Migrate they did,and the world was a better place for it.The tribes brought war,but they also brought civilization,however it would be a long and bloody process. Germany housed all the separate tribes with the Aryan blood in their veins. In the famous 9th century the Saxons were converted For political reasons only. As Hitler would say in the 20th century, we still know where the images of our gods are buried, and in his day they retrieved them.

In reality, the Saxons saw the advantage of being converted, but their Ancient Germanic tribes were never conquered. It must be noted that although they were Christianized, they never submitted to the Frankish rulers entirely. In fact the Frankish Emperors, and the Kings of the Eastern Franks, knew not to meddle in the internal affairs of the Saxons. The Saxons feared no man, no beast, and not even death itself. In the pages of History, we read of the Saxon uprisings, against the Franks, when Louis was on the throne. The Franks learned their lesson well, for after that, the Frankish rulers preferred to stay away from the best.

The main reason was that they could count on their loyalty, and they could count on their Warriors, and the wheels of politics demanded it be done this way.

The Saxon leaders loved the arrangement, and they thought of themselves as independent, but still a vital part of the empire.These were the thoughts of the Saxons in the early 10th century. The Saxon people for centuries had governed themselves quite naturally, and in the Saxon system there were two levels or two classes. The nobility were of course the upper class, and to them was entrusted the defense of Saxony, against all enemies. The other class, and perhaps the majority were The Peasants, and their duties included everything else.

The fighting Knights of the nobility, honored their duties, in the defense of the Eastern Frontier, against the violent and ruthless Slavic Warriors. The Knights of Saxony would hold the Eastern Frontier, and the land would be bathed in blood. There were bloody battles fought all along the rivers, and it was here the future of German blood would be decided. Even in the days of Charlemagne, the leading Saxon Families had been smart enough to realize the future of Saxony was mixed with the fate and fortunes of the Franks. This the Saxon houses of nobility took the lead in The Alliance, and also Prospered the greatest. It was the great warrior Ekbert who first struck gold, when he married into the family Of the emperor.

His son Ludolf would increase the influence of the house of Ludolf when he married his daughter to the young King Ludwig. The young King Ludwig, was the son of the all powerful

Ludwig the German. The house of Ludolf would raise its fortunes and worth, when Ludolfs Sons, commanded the Saxon Army, in the great battle against the Vikings in 880. Once again a Saxon leader, would rise to defend the Homeland, against all Invaders. The great Saxon was named Otto The Illustrious, and he rose so rapidly, because he had the consent of all his fellow Saxons. These were desperate times after the death of Arnulf. This great Saxon Otto took the reins of power and did well with them. The Saxons were on their own, but they would show the world the quality of the Saxon blood.

The Saxons took on the hungarians that were invading from the south, and causing enormous destruction. The Bavarian Army had been wiped out, and the enormous Army Of The Barbarians kept moving North. It was a do-or-die situation for all of the German kingdoms, and the rattle of the snake was loud. the Warriors of Thor and Odin, we're more than a match, for the hordes who were the Hun's.

Every battle axe in Saxony was dripping red, and every inch of Saxony was covered in a quart of blood. The hungarians could not believe how invincible the Warriors of Thor actually were, but after they lost two-thirds of their huge Army to the Saxons, it began to Dawn on them. It didn't take long before the Hungarians took flight and ran back to where they came from, to escape the vicious Saxons. The Valor of the Saxons, was established, in the memory of the Hungarians, for they were never to return again. To add salt to the wound, the Eastern Frontier would also be tested, and baptized in the blood Of the Warriors. As is the way of men, the Slavic tribes attacked the Invincible Saxons, only because they figured they had not the strength to hold them off. Losing many warriors to the Hungarians, the Slavs pounced on them. From deep inside, the Saxon Nation, all the knights went to the Eastern Frontier, and thousands of Slavs were slaughtered. With each Invasion the force of the Slavic Warriors became larger, and with each Invasion, there was a horrible slaughter on both sides, but the Slavs were defeated every single time.

The Saxons to the Empire, had proved how extremely valuable they were, and without them, the German states would have been wiped out, and civilization would not exist, not even today. At the death of Ludwig the child, Germany, was divided up into four different states. Lorraine, the bone of contention for a thousand years, was in the hands of the French Royal Line, with Charles the Simple as ruler. At times it seemed that the only remaining blood of Charlemagne, Charles would be asked to reunite the Frankish Empire.

And then, the one French Charles died, the power of the throne would fall to the Germans. It is obvious at this time, that the Germans were beginning to be conscience of themselves, as a separate and unbeatable power. The Germans had saved Europe from the Hungarians, and again from the Slavs, and the Slavs tried so desperately To conquer them. the Empire actually owed the Germans, and they would collect.

The Germans had definitely saved Europe once again, and the magic in their blood was Awakening the truth in these men of Thor. For now they knew, the future was in their hands.

The year was now 911, and the Germans were taking hold of the power in the east, and we're beginning to see themselves as the dominant power in European affairs.

The most powerful, and the most respected man in Germany in 911 was for sure their war hero Otto the Saxon. The German warriors were jealous through the pages of History, that all the German stems or States, would give this heroic figure the Royal Crown, and they offered it to him. It was a free election, of all the stems, and it was decided, Otto the Saxon was the man for the job.

Otto declared he was by then too old for the job, for at this point in his life, it would be an enormous burden. He asked of the princess, only one thing, and that was, they should unite in their choice of his younger rival Conrad of Franconia. This my friends was the first real election of a German King, and all the stems were present. Although let us not be fools, the Saxons and the Franconians help sway the decision of the entire assembly. After the election Conrad was crowned King by the Archbishop of the German Church.

The Pope in Rome was not consulted, or even considered, and the wheels of apologies kept turning. The Roman Empire of the German Nation, was being revised on a German basis. The problems of Conrad's were immense from the start, For no Duke from any stem, would allow Conrad to stick his nose in their affairs. To show that the German King was the supreme authority, Conrad had to step on many powerful toes. He made many powerful enemies.

When push came to shove, Conrad was forced to use his power, and control the Dukes with naked Brute Force of Arms. Even to Henry of Saxony, Force of Arms became an issue, and it was Henry's father that stood aside, and let Conrad take the throne. This is no way it was ever mentioned that Conrad, and he didn't give a damn anyway, was building an empire. In his New Empire, all of the Dukes would be subject to the crown.

In the end when all was done, Conrad had made the Royal Authority felt in all the German stems, and he had also made them hate it. In the end, Conrad had spun the wheel of politics, quite fast. For in reality he made every stem more conscious of its own identity.

He also made the resistance to the crowd stronger than ever. The greatest friends and powers that Conrad made, were the leading minds of the German Church. For the church had always sought one ruler, so they could rule side by side. But then of course, the nobility would be cut out of the picture. The German church was becoming very strong and with its alliance with Conrad, openly lashed out at the Nobles, and so much as called them traitors to the crown. In 916 the German men of the cloth, assembled in Swabia to discuss the future, and the rights of everyone.

All the stems were represented except one, the mighty Saxons. Pope John the 10th sent his words on paper, to warn the Germans that their disorders were ruining the land. The Churchman declared themselves on the side of the king, and demanded his enemies to appear, and called them traitors.

It also warned the German stems to avoid infringing on the rights and property of the church. The church men agreed no priest should be brought before a judge, for judgements on them were reserved for the Pope alone. They also announced that disloyalty to the king, was to be met with the curse of the church, and that the traitors would be the same as Judas who turned in Jesus Christ. Two Of Conrad's enemies gave themselves up to the great assembly, expecting a mild judgment against them. Conrad shocked everyone, and condemned the men to death, and they were beheaded immediately. This time Conrad had stepped over the line, and the forces were building quickly against him, but he died.

On his deathbed he called to his brother, and said to him, Fortune my brother, together with the noblest Spirit, has fallen to the lot of Henry, and the highest hope of the nation is with the Saxons. Take there these Insignia, The Sacred Lance, the Golden Bracelets, the Royal Mantle, and the Sword of the Ancient Kings. Take the Crown, and go with them to Henry.

In 919 Henry the first the Great Saxon was offered the crown.He of course accepted, with the Saxons and the Franconian Princes present. The offer of church sanctioning, of the crowning of Henry was turned down, for Henry Wanted only the Alliance with the Fighting Men of his Empire. Henry was wise Beyond his years, and the mighty Saxons stepped in right behind him. Henry gathered the Warriors of Saxony and Franconia, and set out to force his word on the Dukes, that did not take part in his election. The first stem to see the knights of Saxony and Franconia, was Swabia and the Duke 's ,and they surrendered.

King Henry recognized the Duke as the leader in the Affairs of Swabia. In Bavaria Things did not go so smoothly for the Duke wasn't in the habit of bowing to any Force, no matter the size. The King, called for all the Knights to assemble, and readied themselves for combat. At the last moment the Duke declined and accepted the situation, and recognized Henry the first as his Overlord.

The two rulers came to terms, and the Duke was given the right to appoint the Bishops of Bavaria. Then the question of Lorraine was taken into consideration for since no one actually knew who the ruler was at the time, they knew they could come to some kind of deal. Some say it belonged to the French, some say it was German, and both powers so desperately wanted it. The French King, Charles the simple, had settled the question many times, by saying it belonged to France. However the real forces in that country, rallied around the powerful families, and said they wanted to be part of Germany. The churchmen thought, ask the people to be under the power of the western King. The next course of action would be when Henry the first, met with Charles of France, to negotiate a permanent arrangement.

For 7 years this had been an issue, and finally the politics of Henry the first changed it in one day. Henry the first gave his daughter to marriage with the Duke of Lorraine, and this sealed the alliance, and also brought it into the orbit of Germany. You might say the alliance was sealed in blood, because it was.

After the end of negotiations of Charles of France, and Henry of Germany, it ended up with only one very important issue. Charles of France formally recognized the king of Germany, for the first time in the history of both Nations, Germany was officially legitimate. So in retrospect 6 years after Henry had taken the throne, he was officially the head of the German nation. The selling point to the enormous power that Henry would win, was he recognized the Dukes of the individual duchy's, as the central power in their local affairs. In reality the Dukes were happier than a fly in the Cowshit, because they were basically independent, and there were also Royal officials. The five separate stems, became German states, within the German Kingdom, and this worked to everyone's advantage.

In reality they all needed each other, because it was still a hostile world, and there would be military engagements, of this they could be sure. The first concern of Henry's was to improve his own dukedom, and the military strength it wielded. The eastern Frontier was the hot spot like it usually was, for it was here that the Slavic tribes would do battle with the Germans. In reality the Slavic wars were Wars of necessity for the Slavs, for their lands had been shrinking since the wars of Charlemagne. The German Empire had expanded to the East, and always at the expense of the Slavic people. The further East the German Warriors drove, the more resistance they met. The Elbe river would be the barrier, the Slavs would hold the Germans at. The house of Ludorf had always taken it upon themselves to secure the frontier, and they had done a great job.

Saxony was very independent, with the Enemy close to the borders. Henry Changed the overall,strategy, and because of it, Saxony would be well protected. It was Henry the first that had the Saxons build council's at strategic points in the country. So that even if invaded, the food supply would be well protected. The Fortified places or houses, were also, Places where business could still be conducted.

It was the vision of Henry, that secured a future for Saxony, and all the kingdoms of the Germans. The Fighting Men in the open country would be divided into nine groups, and one group was always to guard the store houses, and Marketplaces. For the rest In this way, if war did come, the Warriors and the population would not be hungry. The large country force was organized into a militia, and we're drilled heavily in the Arts of combat.

Henry the first took great care to organize the fighting men into an effective fighting force, for he knew the enemies of Germany would be back. It wasn't so much the Slavs, he was worried about, but the nomads from the steppes, since Roman times were called The Huns. These Huns or hungarians as they were later called, invaded in swarms more numerous than snowflakes in a winter storm.

The Slavs although not Germanic, we're pretty much like the Germans, but the Hungarians were wild, and ate raw flesh. The Hungarians were a small Asian race with slanted eyes, and not so far removed from being animals themselves. King Arnulf had used their terrifying Force to his advantage, when they fought as allies against the Slavs.

Arnulf had however exposed these Heathen Tribes to the wild and beauty of the German lands. The German lands were everything the Huns had ever dreamed of, because they grazing lands for their herds, these wild men lived off. The Hungarians had taken the same route to Europe, as the Ancient Huns had in the days of the Roman Empire.

Both Invaders had headed west and traveled across the Steppes of Russia, and headed for the Lush lands of the lower Danube. Besides the land, they of course could always get high ransoms for the women they captured, not to speak of their lust. The Frankish writers gave descriptions that sounded exactly like the descriptions the Roman historians had used centuries earlier. The Hungarians were still in The Nomad stage, and their horses and their cattle made them actually wealthy, by the standards of the day. It was not their ability in combat that made them feared, it was their overall numbers, that was difficult to defend against.

They were Masters at attacking in swarms like bees, with their handmade bows, they took many lives. They fit their race perfectly between the Slavic Kingdom In the North, and the Bulgarians in the south. All along the southern route these wild Nomads would find a paradise for their cattle and horses to graze upon.

It was this land the Huns would take, and they gave their name to it, Hungary. In fact the offspring of the wild Nomads are still there today, doing much the same thing their ancestors did. The Hungarians, the Slavs, and the Bulgarians, are one reason eastern and western Europe are two separate worlds.

However It was not the beautiful grazing lands that the hungarians were really after, and the German kingdoms would realize that soon enough. In the summer of 899, Italy would be the first to feel the fury and the Heat of the race war. The Hungarians swept into Lombard Italy in full force, raping, pillaging, and plundering. The pages of History tell us there was great destruction to those who lived on the Great Plain of Lombardy. Wherever they went they stole all the cattle and farm animals, and burned the villages to the ground.

The Men Who defended their homes were killed, and the women and children were taken as The Spoils of War.In the summer of 899, the plain of Lombardy was left in ruin, and the blood was sprinkled over the entire landscape.

King Berengar collected his forces together, and although there was much blood spilled on both sides, the White Army was destroyed. The continuing race war, swing like a pendulum, sometimes favoring one side, sometimes the other. The God of War was worshiped by all, and fate would always have the final word, in the Affairs of man.

After their great raids in the Northern Italy, that men called Lombardy, the Huns threw massive wild parties, and enjoyed the things that they had taken in battle. With the taste of Victory still fresh in their minds, and with the fruits of their Conquest right before them, they now knew that they were the Supreme Warriors.

With the Knights of Lombardy, stripped of their armor and dead on the battlefield, the Huns called out to the spirits for more. I don't care who you are, you can't win them all, and now it was time for the Huns to mass many victories together. The Hungarians we're now spilling the blood of the Invincible Germans, and how quickly things change.

With Lombardy over ran and burned, the enormous force of the Huns was free to roam the lands, looking for whoever dared to match their Fury. The Hun's next opponent would be Bavaria, for they had great walls, and even greater women, and the Huns lusted for it all. The Bavarians met the enormous Army at their border, and rivers of rivers of blood were spilled, and although heavily outnumbered, they stood firm. The Hungarian attacks lasted for a few years, and many battles were fought to the last man, but still reinforcements, filled in from both sides. The race war raged on and on, and still there was no certain Victor, but the Bavarians did not fall.

In the year 906 the Furious Huns Allied themselves with the Slavic tribes that lived along the famous Elbe River. Together they invaded several countries at the same time and burned and totally destroyed everything that came in their path. The wealth of the Slavs and the Huns increased dramatically with this prized Conquest. In 907 we saw a huge German Force assembled to meet the awesome invading Force. The champion of this great Bavarian Army was none other than Mark Graf Leopold. The Invincible Bavarian Army would be annihilated. It became obvious with the loss of an entire Army, the Bavarians would have to let go of the land the Huns had taken for their own.

The greatest of the German stems sent Champions to discuss the future, and the tactics they would need, if they hoped for victory. The future looked quite dim for all the German lands, and many wondered if they could stop them, or even contain them.

For many years the savage Hungarians poured at will over the borders of all the German lands, and they raped, pillaged, and plundered. The fighting men dressed in the armor of Saxony, Swabia, and Bavaria. Many Times they Marched down to Battle the Furious Warriors from Asia, but it was exactly like pissing Against the Wind.

The endless swarms could not be beaten, however the German Knights definitely took their toll on them, and sent many of Asia's best Straight to Hell. These were the years of savage, close combat, and the Saxons, the swabians, and the bavarians, always bloodied their swords and battle-axes. The race war was Furious, and bloody, and the magic in the blood cried out for more.

The Saxons, Swabians, and the Bavarians proved their Valor, but the odds were too big to overcome. The ancient military strength of the Germans under Charlemagne, was not the same strength, the Germans were in 915, but the overall military was great. The upper classes in German lands shouldered the responsibility, for it was their ancestors that had conquered it. In reality, this was the weak Link in the chain. Charlemagne's Knights with the old empire, would have conquered with what he called the old band, which was everyone together, big and small, and this was what the problem was at the moment.

In reality, the German military had lost tremendous power, when it had streamlined The Great force of warriors. In fact the loss of say 75% Veterans, Weakened the defensive power in an emergency. King Henry the first had been the first German leader to speak out against the modern ways, and it was he that changed things.

In 924 Henry the first got his chance, and Thor and Odin answered his request. In 924 the Valley was once again,crawling with Huns, and they drove North, and he switched his tactics. He chose the time, and also chose the place of combat. It was a Horrible Slaughter, on one large body of the Invaders. Thor and Odin were with the Saxons on this day, for among the prisoners was a great Chief of the Hungarians.The Saxons of course would torture,the Chieftain,and soon he would tell them everything.

 Many asked to torture the Heathen, to pay back for the horrors he had brought on their people. The great Chief begged for his life, and the Saxons accepted his plea, and his surrender. The Saxons so desperately needed time, so a deal was struck. Peace would be secured, but the Saxons would pay on a yearly basis, tribute to the Huns. Henry the 1st, was a man of brilliance, accepted the offer,for he had plans of his own. To start building fortified places, and be ready for the next War.The great numbers of the Slavs,added great power to the Huns,they were allies,and almost unbeatable,they would be there in full force.

Year by year, every year improved. But the first few years went by, everyone In Saxony began to wonder, just how effective the New Saxon Army would be. Henry the first was arming,and timing was everything, and he knew when to strike. Thor was in the blood of Henry, and to the Saxons, the occasion would come sooner than later, to prove it. The Slavic warriors soon proved to Henry the 1st, that they would be the test, when they began invading in huge numbers. It was the site that that historians call Lenzen on the river, that the future of both races would be decided. The new Saxon army responded to the Slavic threat, with new shiny armor, with brand new weapons.The clash between these Warriors, was extremely brutal, and the Saxons took light casualties, but the Slavs were destroyed to the last man, and the last man was hacked to pieces, and fed to the German Shepherds.
 The Saxons were resurrected on that day, and the hope and courage of all Germany was inflamed. In 933 word came to Henry, the Hungarians were coming, and Henry called his fighting men together. Henry asked his Warriors if they should fight or pay, and The Messengers of the Huns arrived shortly. We do not know what words were said, but we do know the Huns left empty-handed. When the Hungarians drove down in the valley as they always did, they stopped to get there Slavic allies, before they launched their invasion of Germany. The Slavs answered through the carcass of a fat dog in their camp. The Slavs its obvious, had learned their lesson well, and the Huns were on their own.
 The largest group of German Knights to enter Saxony, were the German Knights of Thuringia, and the Saxons stood arm to arm, or horse to horse, at the border of Saxony. It was here the

Huns felt the full Fury of the Allied knights, and the German battle axes turned red from the blood of those they had destroyed.

With their back against the wall, facing the largest force of Huns ever assembled, The Knights of Germany completely destroyed the one-arm of the Furious invading Force. The other force of Barbaric Huns drove into Germany, and King Henry with all his Knights in their Gleaming Armor, met the force, where the rivers came together. The huge force of the Germanic Knights cut a path of Destruction right through the Asian Calvary, and the thousands of Huns lay wounded on the ground, were finished off by the Infantry. The German Knights charged again in full force, and the Huns took flight. The Knights of Henry chased the invaders for 10 miles, but no more would be caught. The Speedy Warriors outran, the heavily armored Knights, and they were lucky to escape at all. This victory was so desperately needed, and Henry was the toast of all of Civilized Europe. Many times in history one man has made the difference, and King Henry was this one man. Without this man, history would have been quite different, and because of Henry the first, German civilization would go on to this day. The soldiers of the German kingdoms saluted Henry on the Battlefield as the Emperor. Henry was never officially crowned Emperor, but by all standards, he was.

The Hungarians at this time stopped all invasions of German territory, for any others would have been met with total Destruction. The princes of all Europe looked to Henry With Envy, and with loyalty, and for the first time in many years, the Empire had a great leader. Henry the 1st would enjoy his Fame and Fortune for only 3 years, and then he would die and go to Valhalla, the German place reserved for Heroes. Henry a man of vision, was ready for his death, and he had taken the steps to ensure a peaceful transition of power. The Stems he got together, and asked that his son Otto be crowned King. It was 936, and the German stems agreed that Otto would rule. It was the Saxons that has saved the kingdom, and it would be the Saxons that would rule it, and that was understood.

All the German stems agreed in this way, for Thor had shown his favor. The ceremony of Otto, and his Coronation took place at the Majestic Capital of Charlemagnes at Aachen. Henry had been satisfied for only the approval of the Saxons and the Franks, but Otto wanted all the stems of Germany, and also the Western Frank's, to acknowledge his authority. Henry had rejected the coronation by the church, but his son wanted it done traditionally. The ceremony took place in the Church of the Franks, in the Cathedral of Charlemagne, and the Archbishop took a leading role.

Otto took the first step before the high altar, and received from the Archbishop the Insignia of the Kingdom. The Archbishop handed, first the sword of the ancient Kings, and said receive the sword, to drive out all the enemies of Christ, even the evil Christians alike. By the Divine Authority granted to you, for power over the whole Kingdom of the Franks, is giving you by the Divine will, to the lasting peace of all Christians.

It was a beautiful coronation, and the Church of course was gorgeous, and everyone invited was caught up in the moment. The Dukes all took part in it too, and it truly was a glorious event, for they had a great Empire, and their hearts were beating very strongly in their chest. All the German stems were represented on this day, and the Saxon Otto was declared Overlord of all Germans. Now the Empire of Germany was declared, and it was Otto that was given the task of getting it under one ruler. He wanted to be so much more than Duke of Saxons.

 The 14 years were full of petty squabbles and sometimes assassination attempts, and all for power. There are two sides to every story, but the historian does not take sides, he just presents the case. At the end of 14 years, Otto would come out smelling like a rose, but it was a long and bitter battle. His greatest enemy have been his brother Henry, which of course was just jealousy. In the end Henry was given Bavaria. Swabia was given to Ludolf, and his son and his own child with his marriage to Edith, who was the famous daughter of King Edward of England.

Lorraine had been given to Conrad of the House of Franconia, and there's an extra present,he didn't have to give his daughter to Conrad. Saxony and Franconia we're left in the hands of Otto. So in reality after these 14 years of constant squabbling, the duchies of Germany were in the hands of 1 family. For Once the Future looked as bright as the noon sun on a summer day. This great Statesman with great vision, in 14 years United the whole German Nation with a single Bond, his blood. The story of the Church of Germany, and the Church of Rome is a part of Aryan history that must be studied, and also must be learned.

The study of the struggles, offer wisdom and deeper understanding of apologetics, power and Men. The 10th century offered battle, alliances, and invitations, just like the ninth century did. I have Shined the spotlight on the Franks, and the Germans, and now we must not forget the Italians. We must remember that the only thread that held Italy to the Germans was the church. The popes of Rome would use this point to the fullest, for it was real power, the men in the cloth really wanted. Not only did they wish to rule the Empire, but they wished to rule the minds and the lives of all their subjects. As we left the Pope's of Italy at their last mention, they were desperately trying to raise the stakes of handling out the title of emperor.

Emperor Arnulf had been given the Title of Emperor in 896 by the pope, because he had been in the service of the Roman Church, at every turn in the road. However the powerful families of Rome, as being the ones who could advance their own power and prestige, when one pope died another was elected. Sometimes the politics got way out of hand, and almost unbelievable.

Pope Formosus died a few months after the coronation of Arnulf, and the leading families of the nobility could not wait, to fill the void in the local power. A new pope was elected, and he died 30 days later, and another Pope replaced him, and set the stage for a disgusting event. The dead and buried body of Pope Formosus was dug up, and dragged into Saint Peter's Church. For 8 months the corpse had lay buried, and now the scheming nobility wanted a trial. The dead Pope was dressed in the clothes he had worn in life, and placed upon the throne in St Peters.

He was given a spokesperson for his defense. The spokesperson for the new Pope Stephen, next called upon the corpse to explain why he had allowed himself to become Pope, while he was still the Bishop elsewhere. The spokesman for the dead Pope, gave whatever defense he could muster, and then the assembly gave their verdict. They of course were God's voice on Earth, or so they said, and declared the dead Pope, guilty. The clothes of the Dead Pope, were ripped from his body, and three fingers with whom he had given the divine blessing, were cut off.

If that wasn't enough, our good men of the cloth, next dragged the body by the feet to the river, and tossed the dead corpse in. This incident is for sure a great insight into the men of the cloth, and also said something about the morals of the seemingly sacred men of the church. The ninth century was unbelievable from east to west, as well as from north or south.

The next Pope lived only for months, and the leading Powers assembled again to elect another Pope, that lived for just 20 days. By this time the local fishermen had gotten Pope Formosus out of the Tiber River, and buried him in St Peters, with full honors.

Pope John the 9th, saw that the future did not belong to the petty Emperors of Italy, and in 898 the churchmen of Rome agreed, then no Pope selection would be valid without the approval of the Emperor. In other words, if the empire was not going to be in the orbit of the Roman Church, the Roman Church Must realign themselves.

At this time in Aryan history there were in fact two Emperors, and the Roman Church called one only a Barbarian, he was not even taken seriously in Northern Italy. The hopes of the Roman Pope disintegrated when Lambert died suddenly, and his Northern rival Berengar, claimed the vacant throne in person. Berengar was given Lombardy, but he would not get the Empire of Italy. In the boot of Italy, the powerful families make sure Louis of Provence , the son of Boso came in that summer. In 901 Louis was crowned Emperor in Rome. The records of this time are slim, and all we really know is, everyone played their hand for political power, it was almost a free-for-all.

Between the years 896 + 948, many popes sat on the throne at St Peters. and all of them died because of violence, and most often were assassinated. Only one thing in these conflicting times is the house of Tusculum, and they were the richest family in Rome.

Emperor Louis rallied the southern Italian forces, and launched a military campaign against Berengar of Lombardy. The fear is Germanic Lombards easily defeated the forces of the paper Emperor, and Louis was captured, and he was blinded. The new pope John the 10th, was a Sly Fox in the cloth of the church, and one might even say an opportunist, but they all were.

The pope immediately summoned Berengar to Rome, where he was crowned as the next Italian Emperor. The Roman popes wanted so desperately to ride on the coattails of an Italian Emperor, but Thor and Odin had different plans, so everyone else's was just going to have to wait.

The Italian emperor would be tested at once, and it would come from the Arabs. The Arabs still had their stronghold in the south of Italy, and they took this exchange of power, as a weakness. They attacked all the strong princes of Italy, and sent many small armies of warriors, to the race war, for Italy. Even the Byzantine emperor sent a massive Fleet to the coast of Italy, to do battle with the Moors.Germanic blood flowed to the south of Italy, the Army was United and was very strong. The command for the Army went to Berengar, Who was the most powerful man in Roman politics at this time. The Pope was the great power in the shadows, for he had offered all the princes more land, if they went to war.

As the German blood fell upon the dark skinned Moors in combat, there was a racial lust for killing, that spread amongst the Warriors. It was a Savage, racial conflict, that would be decided when the last Moor was dead. The Pope of Rome led his Christian Warriors into the Carnage, and in doing so, lost prestige in the eyes of the good, and the meek, and the weak.

With their holy man leading the race war, the battle was Savage and unrelenting, and when it was all done, the Arab power in southern Italy was over. The Italian affairs were filled with assassinations, and people doing strange things, and it was just strange times,and it was Italy.
In 924 the Empire wanted Berengar in the north. The Nobles of Lombardy sought help from outside their domain, to raise the stakes in the game. The Nobles asked the king from Burgundy to come to Italy, and accept the crown. King Rudolph dreaded a trip over the Alps, because those mountains were extremely high, and extremely dangerous, but he would go because he wanted the crown. King Rudolph could think of nothing else but the glory, and so it was, he went.

Emperor Berengar was accused of inviting into Italy, for his own gain,the Hungarians. After he did this Treacherous Act he was assassinated promptly at Verona. Lower Burgundy, Known as the Kingdom of Arles, was in The Power of One Man Hugo, who was the grandson of King Lothair the second. He desperately wanted the lands his father had held, and more if he could have them. Hugo told Rudolph if he would give up his claim to Italy, that he could have Southern and Northern Burgundy. Rudolph accepted, and by doing so, laid the foundation for a United Kingdom of Burgundy. In reality Rudolph went for a stable Kingdom, for it was common knowledge how uncertain the power structure was in Italian affairs. With the death of Emperor Berengar, the title and position were meaningless for another generation. Italy still had Kings, but they never succeeded in establishing a real Kingdom on the peninsula. The politics of Italy were cunning and ruthless, and in the 10th Century, they were even more so.

King Hugo was a clever and master politician, and when all else failed, The Burgundian took to the field of combat, to decide any issue. On many occasions the German Knights attacked the walled Fortress called Rome, and just as many times, were driven away. Hugo when his military campaigns did not work, he tried his hand at Forming family alliances. Hugo's daughter was extremely beautiful, and he made sure that she would marry well, and advance his power and prestige, and that's just the way it was done. Hugo gave his daughter's hand in marriage to the grandson of Emperor Berengar, and that was a good move. At this time the young Berengar was becoming the most powerful man in the Lombard nobility.

Hugo was a brilliant and a great individual, and I might add he tickles my heart. He quickly arrived there and Married the Widow. This Hugo was a man of ambition obviously, and the magic of his blood was not going to be denied.

The son of Hugo, Lothair would be fixed in marriage to the daughter of the widowed Queen. It's ironic too, Father and Son married a widowed Queen and daughter. How cunning they all really were. Lothairs bride would later become a famous Queen, and also an empress.

Rudolph's son Conrad ,Saw full well what was happening, and knew his days were numbered. King otto from Germany would Place Conrad under his protection, and Hugo would not be permitted to be crowned King of Burgundy. The wheels of politics where turning and Europe was beginning to materialize. The deep-rooted schemes of Hugo did not work, and all his hearts planning had placed many enemies in key positions. By 935 the princes of all Lombardy waited for the opportunity to take down Hugo, and everyone began making alliances with the great German King Otto.In 945 Otto brought his German knights South, and the Princess of Italy welcomed the great power from the north. In the cities, the people welcomed the great power from the north, and they welcomed him with great enthusiasm. The nobility of Lombardy was filled with the excitement of change.

In 945 The Hand of Hugo have been played out, and Hugo gave up all rights to the crown, and offered in his place, his son Lothair. For 5 years the knights fought with the Knights of the young Berengar. But fate would have the final word. Lothair died suddenly, Berengar immediately assumed the crown, and the excitement of change did happen.

The Burgundian power in Italy had come to an end, except for the Widow of Lothair. Berengar had plans to marry his son with another of Italy's power families, but everyone instead looked to the north. Berengar was a crafty Statesman and he would be Be heard from again. Otto was loyal to his friends and his alliances, as he had shown why he defended his father's house in Burgundy. Otto received letters from the pope of Rome, begging for help, it seems Berengar's Army was attacking the papal lands along the coast of Italy. The Pope begged the German to defend the lands and rights of St Peter. Because some had already fallen, to add to the collection of people who begged the German King , we must add members of the nobility of Lombardy. The year was 950 and the wheels of politics were turning as usual.

Otto of Germany was the most powerful man in all of Europe, and no one else was even close.

If the scattered kingdoms were ever going to be United, it was going to be when he was on the throne. The duchy's or stems were all in good hands, so the King was free to settle the business of the unruly South. Of all the German provinces, one was stronger, in its loyalty to the king, and that was Swabia. Ludolf was of course the Duke, his thinking of course was only of glory and

Power. He crossed the Alps with his Order of Knights, and did battle for his father, and for his own Glory.

The Knights of Lombardy with Germanic Blood in their veins, yielded nothing to the son of the German King. He had no other option , than to wait for the German army, for the Lombards had been raised on War, for many generations. In the late summer of 951, the German King and the German Knights, began their Journey over the Alps, in advance to the Famous Brenner Pass. The Lombards were ruthless in battle, but they did not offer combat to the German forces. The Germans marched and rode all the way to the Lombard capital without opposition. Berengar with his forces, did not enter into any combat, and allowed The German King to pass through.

It didn't take Otto long to feel at home, and his Army stayed that winter in the Lombard capital. In The Long Winter base, he began making land grants as presents for his greatest warriors. He also began handing out future positions of privilege, as if he were already king. The Queen and Bride of the powerful leader of that area in 951, was still in the gossip of Italian mouths, and she had many romances in the spotlight of society. In fact the ex - Queen was involved in a scandal with the Bishop.

It seems The Burgundian power in Italy over the course of the last 20 years had multiplied. It was only two powers that could command attention in Italy. One was bribery, and the other was Force. Otto was certainly at home in Italy, where he had proved he could Master both of these. Otto had come a long way, in his stay in Italy, he had married again, and got a new crown. Germany's best was on the scene, and things would never be the same.At this time Otto was more powerful, than anyone could ever hope to be, and he seized the moment. He sent his top spokesman to Rome, to tell the Pope, he was coming for the Imperial Crown. The pope refused because he wanted the upper hand. The Pope and his power base, never would submit to any power, and still had dreams of the number one slot, not number two. Otto did not want to have to march on Rome, so being a master politician, he withdrew from Italy. In reality he also had problems at home, for his Dukes in his absence had gone to war amongst themselves, and tried to capitalize on the royal power.

In fact it was his own son Ludolf that made the most problems, and he would continue to do so. He was jealous of his father's power, and his powerful new bride.He quickly found the other powers inside the German Kingdom, that were not happy with their own power, or their position.

From there it was a simple step to organize a force of opposition. There were so many that wanted to take the crown away, for the power and Prestige of it all. So many people, Duke's and archbishops, we're going to fight for the crown, there was going to be a Civil War in Germany.

After all Germany had been run through, now they must go backwards and fight among themselves. However Otto did rise above It all, and only because of his loyal and ferocious Saxons. The Saxons played their trump card, and Otto did not fall from Power. Henry of Bavaria was also another Major Force in the Civil War of Germany, and it was his Warriors that tipped the scales in favor of Otto. We call this a civil war loosely, because this is the way royal power was built, or destroyed, it's just the way it was.

The biggest problem these battles brought on German Europe, was it showed you all the animators, that the German territories were not United, and that perhaps they were even weakend. At the same time all the many quarrels in Germany, the Huns were waiting and they grew excited, and they waited for the dust to clear.

Ever since King Henry had to destroy the hungarians in The Hun's invasion in 933, the Huns had not dared to try on the Saxons again. They had tried, but the Saxon battle-axes were always wanting for the blood of the Asians. They did not hate them, but if it was going to be a race war, the Asians were going to lose. Every time the Yellow Race would appear, the Saxons would begin to whisper Tales of Thor.

They would not come to see Thor's best in Saxony, for that was a mission of suicide. However they did Roam free on the Northern plain of Italy, below the Danube all the way to the Adriatic.

During the first years of Otto's rule, the Hungarians rode through Bavaria many times. On their raids they drove to the very heart of France. Anything that was not well fortified, vanished in the fury of the Wrath of the Huns. The Huns make no mistake were a serious threat to all civilization, and the tales of their cruelty, and they're viciousness, is well documented in The Chronicles of all the German lands. Orleans and Rheims Have seen tens of thousands of the wild men from Asia right before their walls. These hordes of Warriors and thieves, as they came back from France, even crossed the Alps and stormed through Italy, passed Rome itself, to Capri. All through the chronicles of the Saxon lands we hear Tales of Terror and Horror.

The Huns were nobody fools, and they coordinated their attacks on the regions where the families were warring against each other. Of course then, they could not Mount, any United defense against the Huns, and this is exactly what they wanted

In 954 rumors surfaced throughout the kingdom the Hungarians were on the move again, and this time their numbers were so large, then no one could even begin to count them. Word had it the tens of thousands are headed up to Danube, and Otto called his Saxons to Arms. Otto called for every man who can hold the spear, sword, or battle axe, to join in the defense of the German kingdoms. Before the Army and knights of Saxony could reach them, they turned west, and headed to the lands of France and Lorraine. Ludolf the son, and Conrad, the son-in-law, were now ready to form an alliance and a union, for United they would stand, and divided they would fall.

The winter of 954 saw the most powerful men sit down and Hammer out a new defensive strategy, just for the Huns. All the Dukes that made bad decisions, were stripped of their power, and gave positions they might handle better. Otto's brother Henry could have been totally loyal, was of course given Bavaria. After all the new alignments had been set, the defense of Tours and Odin's best would be secure. It had to be this way the new alignment, because the Huns we're not going to go away, they must be part of the Earth, deep in it, for Germany to go on. The next summer The Hun's Came again stronger than ever recorded. The chronicles of 955 read of the excitement of it all. Many of The Chronicles gave their estimates that the Hungarians this time had fielded a force of over 100,000 Warriors. The Hun's boasted, there's no power on Earth could destroy them. They were so strong and so bold, they took the same route, straight up the Danube. They tore right through Bavaria, and they poured into Swabia, which is modern-day Switzerland. It wasn't Swabia, they swarmed the city of Augsburg, and laid Siege. The city had walls, but was not strongly fortified. The first human Shockwave that assaulted the city was repulsed, but barely. The Huns like the ancient Germanic Warriors hated to attack walled towns and fortified places. The Defenders grew great strength, when they watch the Huns being whipped, so they would attack. When the Defenders saw how scared the Huns were, they began whispering Tales of Thor.

Chapter 13

The fury of the Defenders Of The Fortress increased daily, as their numbers decreased, for this was a race war to the very end. There would be no prisoners, and no future for the losers, except going to the promised land, If there really was one.

Otto at the siege mustard his Saxons, and began the long ride to the defense of the German Blood. Bloods thicker than water, and the Germans we're going to prove this. With the army of the Saxons that Otto was bringing, they could not hope for a complete victory, but they knew in their hearts they could still make a huge difference, and they knew in their hearts, they could still save their Valiant Brothers. They had their prayers answered when they learned they would not be fighting alone.

From every Duchy came a brave Gathering of Knights, and suddenly the German army was a force to be reckoned with. As Otto's Saxons quickly headed for Augsburg, the warriors from the Duchy's streamed into formation. There was a great joy, and it lasted for battle, when everyone realized this battle would decide the future of the races, and which lands these races would own,
Till the end of time.
For the first time a truly German army, was United, and we see here the great Royal Army coming together. The great Royal Army was divided into eight separate columns. 3, where the Armies of the Bavarians. 2, where the Swabians under the command of Count Burchard, and he represented his Franconians. And then Otto with Champions from every single stem, and of course he brought along all his Saxons. The last column was a force of 1000 Bohemians, who had the chance of rear guard. Someone must have the command always of the rear guard, to stop the stab-in-the-back routine. Also for every large Force there was an endless train of baggage and supplies, and of course extra weapons. The Warriors of the Bohemians got the call, and they would stand proud and vicious.

When the Royal Army arrived at the scene of the battle, Otto called for order, so that he could devise the best plan, to bring about the best results. The Hungarians with their enormous Force we're camped out all along the left bank of the River Lech. They were camped out for many many miles, and their camp look like a million lights at night. Otto quickly Ordered his Knights to cross the river, and to kill everyone right on the spot. Neither Commander was a rookie to battle and each had his own plan. At the same time, as the German Knights were crossing the river, and engaging in first combat, a huge force of Huns also cross the river, and completely encircled the Royal Army. The Bohemians were heavily outnumbered, but that mattered little, for Thor was in their blood. The Huns and the Bohemians locked in battle, and blood sprinkled the Earth like rain. It was at this time that Conrad ordered his Masters of Combat, to the rear and once there the calvary charged into the full force of the Huns. Conrad's knights fought with the fury of lions, and a deep hole was torn in the Huns lines.

The Knights of Conrad would not be denied, and Thor and Odin would be proud of them all. The battlefield was covered with thousands of the Fallen enemies. The German Knights fought shoulder-to-shoulder, and they would not fall, or be driven apart, and all the time thinking of Tales of Thor.

King Otto gathered his Saxons, and the rest of the royal Army, and attacked the main force of Huns straight ahead. Many heads would roll on this first charge of the German Knights, and the the ground would turn red, with the blood of that days battle. The Huns show on Horseback, could not deflect the charge of Germany's best, and many of them died in the first hour of combat.

The writers of that day, tell us the Lech River had so much blood in it, that when it ran into the Danube, the color red could still be seen. All along the Danube, the crowds took the bright red color as news of the Hungarian defeat. The Royal Army of Germany had learned from its past mistakes, and this time it would be a war to the Finish. No longer would the Germans let the body of the Huns Force Escape, so that they could return in the future. The Hun's on horseback would not escape the German Horseman this time, and small battles were fought all over the entire landscape.

The Huns were cut down, sometimes in full flight. The German Royal Army took no prisoners, and they slew the Huns where they found them. The Hungarian King was taken prisoner, and so were their Chieftains. All of the prisoners were handed over to Duke Henry, and they were hanged before the eyes of Thor and Odin.

The Royals had proved their Valor in combat, and they had completely annihilated the Huns, who for centuries had caused destruction all over Europe. From this great battle, the Huns never recovered, and they never were a terror to the civilization of Europe again. No one alive could deny the fact, that a United Germany could not be beaten on the battlefield. News from the Battlefield was heard around the world. Especially in the east. For now after centuries of sporadic Warfare, the German East was Secure. The race wars in the East were over, and the German Knights proved their Supremacy, and for this all would benefit. This great victory in the east, was the same as the great victory in the West. They were both were race Wars of survival.With their backs against the wall the German forces United, and then it wasn't even a question of who was going to win, it was just a question of how long it was going to take.The old cliche, united we stand, divided we fall, sure was True to life for Germany. In America we have lost all control contact with our ancient past, and I guess it's because we don't have an ancient past. But for many reasons we have all lost contact with our ancestors ancient past, and it is so glorious, it's really quite a shame. This is one of the main reasons I've written the masterpiece, is 2 reawaken the Magic in the blood. The average American has no concept of real world history, and no concept of what it took to get to the point, of where we're at today. There is no gratitude for what our ancestors did, and there is no love for them either. In America there's such a sense of individualism, but in reality, the times in the past that we grouped together, is where we won everything.

Because of Hitler's mass killings of the Jews in World War II, a dark spot has been placed on Germany that Still Remains. After reading a masterpiece like this everyone realizes now that whole countries of people were wiped out, thousands of times, because this is the way of man. In reality it was the Saxons of Germany, and all the other Germanic tribes, they gave us everything that we hold dear in our civilization today. Also the Saxons in England helped to mold us, as we are today.

The bottom line is Europe including England are Germanic, and civilization as we know it is Germanic. It took the combined strength of the Franks, and the Saxons to forge their Homeland. They did this for all the Scandinavian tribes, or Teutonic tribes, however you want to look at it. We owe much to this one group of people, who had probably over A million Warriors killed, to get what we got today, so let's look take a fresh look at everything.

The Moors and the Hungarians caused tremors in Europe for centuries, but when it was all over, they helped to unite the Ferocious barbaric Germanic race. The Hungarians after they're spectacular loss at the Battle of Leach Field, never were a military threat to Europe again. It proves that Force is The Peacemaker. There must be War, before there can be a true peace. If we do not learn the lessons of History, we are doomed to repeat them.

 The Huns settled down to a life of farming and agriculture, in the beautiful land that man calls Hungary,that is where they stay today. They did not want it this way, But in the end, this is all that was available to them, if they wanted to survive as a race. After two generations the Huns would even become christianized, and they would be absorbed into the family of Europe.

Germany learned Its lesson well, and the war drove it home. If the Germans had spent 1/2 of their energy fighting against the Huns, that they had spent fighting amongst themselves, the 50 years of the Hunnish plunder would have never happened. The other side of that coin would be that greed and Power are most of man's desires. It was this lust for greed, that enabled man to survive,sorry there was no other way.

It was at this time of the great battle between the Germans and the Huns, that men began calling Otto, Otto the Great. Otto was in fact the strongest power in the German land, since Charlemagne.

Now for the first time, Otto could devote himself entirely to his only ambition, and that was the Title of Emperor. It had been the vision and Leadership of this one great German, that had forged an Empire, out of the blood of its enemies. The wheels of politics were turning, and Otto's fate hung in the balance. It seems that one year before Otto the Greats stunning victory along the Danube River, in Italy the Roman leader had finally died, and now a vacuum appeared in Roman affairs. These were prosperous times for Rome and for Italy,and everyone hoped,there would be more.

What this did,to the hearts and minds of the Romans was, it raised all doubt that foreigners were needed to administer the Affairs of the Pope and of Rome. It's ironic, that the Pope ruled,and was Chief of Roman politics. There was nowhere else in the history of Rome, that had been different. The population of Rome allowed The ruler's son to the throne.

He was only 16, and educated by the church, and his knowledge was limited to almost nothing. The young lad proved he also had a lust for power, when after 1 year, he appointed himself as Pope. When Octavian took the cloth for the church, he changed his name to John the 12th.

This was a tactic that all the Popes had done before him, so you might say it was a Roman tradition. The main enemy of John the 12 was the famous Berengar, who after Otto had left Italy, took over much of it. As Berengar forces began crunching on the States, the pope sent a letter to Otto, and begged for his help. In 956 Otto sent his son, Ludolf with a great force of Knights, to take care of the problem. The Knights of Ludolf engaged the Knights of Berengar, and there were small victories for Ludolf. These victories were cancelled out when he died suddenly, and John the 12th the Pope began asking for help, and so did many of the princes of Italy. Otto with dreams of the Imperial Crown, could not leave, because he was deeply involved in the Affairs of Germany. To secure the kingdom of Germany Otto had his son Otto II receive his coronation as King of Germany. Otto the Great called an assembly of all the German princes, to get their approval. The coronation of the younger Otto took place at the Great Germanic Capital of Aachen. The wheels of politics, went round and round, and I'm going to skip telling you about everybody that was appointed to every little position, because it really doesn't matter.

In 961 Otto the Great, and his German Knights had made it to the Lombard Capitol at Pavia, on the vast plain of Lombardy. There was no battle between the Knights of Otto the Great, and the Knights of Berengar. As the winter wore on. negotiations began on Otto's quest to be Emperor. Otto the great gave his word he would not take away any of the rights of the Pope, and gave his word again, that whoever he made King would show the same respect.

Otto the Great knew exactly how disloyal the factions of Rome could be, so he entered with his Knights, and he had an enormous bodyguard, of thousands. Otto the great was receiving his coronation,when he commanded the sword-bearer, while I am praying in St Peters, keep your sword close to my head. When we reach Monte Carlo again, you shall have time to pray as much as you like.

In other words he was telling a Swordsman to be on watch for an assassination attempt. Although there wasn't in fact no attempt, that does not mean they didn't plan one. Otto the great and his Knights proceeded with great caution, every step of the way in Rome, for to them it was like another world. Otto by all means did not want to stay in Rome any longer than was necessary. The coronation of Otto the Great, followed quickly after his party entered the Eternal City. Both Otto the Great and his wife were Crowned the Emperor and the Empress of the German Empire. The Imperial Crown and the powers in it, did not belong to an emperor for 37 years. In fact the title and privilege of Emperor had meant nothing for over 100 years. Otto Was now Emperor of the Roman Empire of the German Nation.

Otto the Great had sworn to uphold and defend the Pope, and from this you did not waver. The Pope showed goodwill towards past certain decrees, that made the new Emperor extremely happy. Many historians draw similarities between Charlemagne and Otto the Great, and this my friends is not right. The Empire of Charlemagne's was the whole complete Empire of the Franks, east and west. Otto the Great's Empire was only based on the Eastern Franks. In Charlemagne's empire he was ruler over all Germanic Christianity and Europe, while Otto the great ruled only a fraction of the Germanic Christian world. Charlemagne was only a link in the chain, of a long line of Kings that went back over 300 years.

Otto the great was great too, he fought Against All Odds, against powerful local traditions, and his Empire was forged in the blood of the Civil Wars of Germany. Charlemagne gained his military and political strength as the head of the Frankish masses, and they fought out of allegiance to the Frankish state.

Otto the great was head of a feudal state, and depended on the goodwill of the men he tried to control. Charlemagne's influence was the result of the institutions that have been built up for 300 years, to control Affairs by Brute Force. Charlemagne, just with a strong show of force, had been able to break down all resistance to his royal power. I know the great had to watch as local powers took on permanent form, and if they needed Direction, he always resorted to military force. When all was said and done, the West had been the privilege of Charlemagne's rule, and they had their Saxon, Otto the Great.

The last decade of the reign of Otto the Great, this man spent dealing with the power of the Church of Rome. He also spent his time Establishing the Saxon house and its Royal position.

By the time Otto the Great was done with this work, the house of Saxony would be cemented in stone. It must be remembered by the student of History, that the southeast corner of Italy, was still under the influence of the Eastern Roman Empire, or the Greek Byzantines as some called them.

The major question in the 960s was whether the Lombard princes of Italy, would put their power with the Greeks of Constantinople, or if they would place it with the Saxon conqueror. Otto the great died in Saxony in 973, and among his many credits, Otto was the founder of the Holy Roman Empire of the German nation. This name would stick to the German Empire throughout the Middle Ages, until Napoleon in 1812 abolished it.

Otto II took the Royal Crown, and his Reign lasted from 973 to 983. The policy would be with each Civil War, to gain an advantage, and then make for divisions. The main source of Otto's problems, were from the same place as fathers had been, Bavaria. The duchy Of Bavaria was in the hands of Henry of Bavaria, who also was the Next Generation.

The players had changed, but the blood line was still the same. The Magic in the blood, renewed with every generation. Henry II of Bavaria was known simply as the quarrelsome. The wheels of death and life were turning, and the plot thickens when the Duke of Swabia died.

Duke Burchard was survived by his widow, and she was the sister of Henry of Bavaria. Now the Rivalry between Bavaria and Swabia would once again be settled with swords and battle-axes. To throw salt into the wound, Emperor Otto the Great began to give power to the House of Bamberg, which was always a loyal Ally in the Eastern section of Germany. Henry of Bavaria would not take his losses lightly, and soon he would be an open Rebellion to the crown. Because Landon had been taken away from him, that would one day be the great Austria. Otto the second rode with his Saxons, they were very awesome, and after a few skulls were split wide open, Bavaria was recovered. You see the Frontier was still full of hostile Warriors, and they would not bow their heads, and accept the yoke. In the 10th century, the people of Europe were beginning to think the year 1000 would bring about a catastrophe upon the whole world. According to the church, In 1000, the world Was coming to an end, and Christ was coming to bring Heaven on Earth. The church in the 10th Century had gathered an incredible amount of will, and their power over the human mind was bordering on incredible.

The main reason for this grip on the thoughts of the population, can be explained simply as a product of no education. There was no alternative to the teachings of the church, and that's the way people became thoroughly brainwashed.

All the Christians had been brainwashed by thoughts of impending doom, and this drove many to the ways of the church, and hoped they would be saved, and not spend eternity in hell. Many offered land and money to the Christian church, and hoped that they could perhaps Secure a position, or place in the Everlasting kingdom of God. The population as a whole, were ignorant, but could not be blamed, for Education was only a wild dream, and it did not exist. In 983, the church and its Doctrine, had complete control over the minds of the people, but it would be the swords, and battle-axes, that would maintain Control over the borders.

The great work that Otto II had begun, securing the eastern border of the German Empire, was taken over by Otto the 3rd. Although the principle of Elections was beginning to be considered, the house of Saxony had complete control of the Affairs of the German lands.

In reality The House of the Saxons was overwhelming with it's hold of the politics of the Empire. Even though the young Otto was only 3, it was already decided that he would be Emperor someday. When Otto II died, Henry of Bavaria would be set free, and his first act would be to seize the young boy of 3. Henry of Bavaria declared himself Regent of the boy, and began to take the necessary steps to become King of Germany. The Princes of Saxony stood in the way of this move, and they rallied to the cause of the young Otto. it was decided by the Saxon Princes, the young Otto would be placed under the Regency of his mother. At these times of unrest in the German lands, the Slavic tribes began to make war on the border of these two peoples. The division of Otto the great was tested here, and the new Marks held off the Slavs, All those Slavic tribes.But there was Much German blood there, and the Eastern Frontier was not overrun. The Slavic Warriors must not be taken lightly, for they were ferocious, and fought like wild animals. For an entire generation, the Slavic Wars would threaten the German Nation once again. But in the end, German might would prevail.

The position of Pope grew rapidly in the eyes of the world, when the heathens of the eastern border were converted to Christianity. On Otto 111s last journey to Germany he went to Poland to the grave of his friend, Bishop Adalbert.It seems that the bishop had been killed by the Heathen tribes, and he was a martyr for Christianity. The bishop had been a missionary to the heathen Prussians, and they had executed him. As Otto the Third was received in the great lifestyle he loved most, he had the opportunity to meet with the Polish Duke Boleslaw. The Duke was perhaps the most ferocious Slav in the history of his people, and that's why he was the Duke of Poland.

No matter how treacherous The Duke of Poland was, the German Knights proved their superiority on the battlefield, and the champion the Duke became a vassal to the Empire. The Polish Slavs, as well as every conquered territory, paid tribute to the Empire.it was about the money,and all other forms of wealth.

Great Prestige went to the Roman Church when Hungary was admitted to the family of Christian Europe. Ever since the Saxons had annihilated The Hun's forces in 955, The Barbarians of this race, have been slowly transformed into a Christian state. From Wild Nomads of the steppes, the Huns had been transformed orderly people, with a government.

There were two reasons for the turnabout, one was the Christian religion, and the other was a ruling house. Just like in Germany, it took a family of vision, to place their country on the road to prosperity. In the 10th century, the rulers of Hungary had been able to look to Germany and the Dukes of Hungary had duplicated well, the lessons of the West. By the year 1,000 Hungary was ready to join the Western European States,for in reality, if you can't beat them, join them.

The Byzantine Empire send missionaries to Hungary, in the hope that they would come into their sphere of influence, but it just wasn't in the cards. The groundwork was being laid for the foundation of Hungary, and it had been sealed in blood. Henry of Bavaria married his sister to one of the Dukes of Hungary. To further the Dukes ambition, he was baptized, and even took the Christian name Stephen. Duke Stephen then made his play for the big time, and that he requested from Rome, that he be received into Roman communion, as the king of Hungary. He also asked at the Hungarian Church, that they be blessed and given the consent of the Roman Church. The pope immediately sent a Royal Crown to the Duke, and also a Replica of the Holy Lance that had pierced the side of Jesus Christ when he hung on the cross.The Holy Lance was one of the most sacred relics in history.

The same Crown and Spear are still a part of the Royal Insignia today. The New Kingdom of Hungary was allowed, with only one string attached, and that was that they stay as vassals to the Roman Church. The Magic In The Blood of the German race, had transformed the barbaric Hun's into a civilized Kingdom. What this did was open up the Valley of the Danube, to all Christians of Europe.

In the big picture, free Passage through the Danube Valley, was offered to the Christian pilgrims with access to the east. As the religion of Christianity grew, more and more pilgrims wanted to travel to the east, to spiritually cleanse themselves. A pilgrimage to the east, was the highest expression of devotion, and the doctrine of the church said, sins would be forgotten or forfeited by the journey.

In the big picture once again, the growing pilgrimages to the east, Were Meant To Shine on the holy places, in the Middle East. By shining a spotlight on the places, of the life of Jesus, and the early Christian Church, it opened the door of further Conquest in that direction. It is no coincidence, that those lands, also held the wealth of the world,and the masterplan was to get as much as they could.

Of course this part of the picture would not be coming all age until the 20th century. What this did, is give us tremendous vision, into the minds of our ancestors. Once the roads were open to the east, it was just a matter of time, that the Warriors would be on them. In reality the Crusades began 100 years later, and the holy places were captured, and the riches from them were taken back to the Empire.The empire would know,what wealth and power were all about.

The idea of the holy war, was a mighty impulse, that grew with each passing year. We have as evidence, a letter from Sylvester II, where he speaks for the Jerusalem Church, to The Universal Church of Rome. In the letter he tells the Church of Rome, to rise as a soldier of Christ, and deliver her from the infidels. This opened the door for the pope, to lead a Crusade, in the future. It staggered some Modern minds, that these men of the cloth, were also of the sword, had the intelligence to come up with this great plan of Conquest. In a few, we find genius, with vision, in the Robes of the church.

Bold, is the Disguise of the Cloth, and the modern man does not realize, the church in the Middle Ages, was a separate government, Just like the most powerful families. But there were many others in the beginning, with the culture of the past Empire or the Romans, but also the culture of the Eastern Roman Empire, which was Greek influenced, with its capital at Constantinople.

The tutor of the Young Emperor Otto, took great pains to make sure, that he would in fact, be the first truly great Emperor of the Western Empire. One of the young Emperor's first demands was a magnificent Capital, like the Roman Emperors had a long time ago. He also dreamed of living like the Greek,in luxury, just like in Constantinople. The Greeks boasted that they were the greatest in Imperial Philosophy, and greatest in their Luxury, and greatest in their power, in the Eastern Empire. His tutor kept reminding that our greatness is the Roman Empire, our might is given by Italy, fertile and fruits, by Gaul and Germany, fertile with soldiers. He was told often, that he was the Emperor of the Romans, and born of the highest Blood of the Greeks, but that he was superior to the Greeks, in power. The tutor told him often, that he ruled the Romans by right of inheritance.

The tutor was right in explaining the Learned art of Philosophy to the Young Emperor, but he forgot one thing, that no European power ever forgot. That he ruled by The Sword and the Battle Axe and the Lance, the Spear.

Otto the third desperately wanted a capital to be proud of, that would surpass all the great rulers, with more luxury than Charlemagne's capital of Aachen. Until the time of Emperor Otto the Third, even German Emperors preferred their lavish tents, surrounded by their Warriors. Usually instead of a Great Hall to sit and pass his judgments, it was most often a tent, usually in the area of unrest or War. Up until Otto the Third, the officials of the Empire, who had begun as just loyal servants, now became the heads of whole departments.

None of the things the Empire did before Emperor Otto the Third, would be allowed to carry on. It may have been good enough for his family tree, but now it was going to be different. However the young Emperor knew he wasn't endeaded to them, for giving him a solid foundation.

On a great Hill in Rome, Emperor Otto the Third built Himself a beautiful palace, and the place was called Aventine Hill. The young Emperor loved to dress himself in the long flowing robes, that the Greek Emperors of the East in Constantinople did. The Byzantine Court, was known for their displays of the Finer Things in life, and Otto the Third was going to have his.

Otto the Third called himself the Sacred Emperor,and Allowed no one to see him. It was possible to get his attention, but only after a long series of officials, had formally dealt with you. He even changed the titles of the officers in his court, and preferred that men address them, by the lavish names, The Greeks used at Constantinople. He loved to live in Rome, and did his best to recreate, the ceremony of ancient Rome.Otto the third left the administration of Rome, in the hands of two sets of his officers. One group would be with the pappel powers, and one would be at the Imperial power. This way there would be a balance and a check system. Pope Sylvester tried every Ploy he could to get the Emperor to give Superior power to his papel officers.

Otto was not about to fall into this trap, but he did give enormous grants of land to the church. The Roman population and the Pope wanted the Emperor to build a World Empire, with Rome as the capital.

The German Princes, hated their Emperor, devoting everything to Italy, and neglect in Germany. What they hated most of all, is the new Emperor neglected the German Church. Emperor Otto the Third, was so filled with religious enthusiasm, that it dipped into Madness. The Emperor traveled to Ravenna in Italy, and was influenced by the hermits. The Emperor was driven from Rome by the Roman influences that he had chosen to part with. Instead of calling his Saxons, and his Royal Warriors he spent his days fasting and praying.

He did eventually March back to Rome with an army, but he died soon after, by fever, in the year 1002. He died at the age of 22, and Pope Sylvester died, one year later. With these two deaths, died division of the resurrected Roman Empire, and the Wheels of Time kept turning, Whispering Tales of Thor. Otto tried, what future Emperors would do, and at the time of his death, he was arranging his marriage to a Byzantine princess. With the new Emperor dead the line was over. The Saxon blood would still pump in the Emperor's to follow, but the great Royal line of Otto the Great had run its course. Because of the great vision of the three Great Otto's, the German Empire was growing in size, and wealth, and in influence. All the while, Whispering Tales of Thor.

Now for the first time in many years, the Throne of Germany, and the Empire were vacant. It would be a matter, the German princes would decide. This will be the first time in German history, it would be decided by an election. The only real heir to the great Otto's was Henry of Bavaria, who was the great grandson of Otto the first. Quite naturally, everyone realized he had the blood of Otto the Great in his veins. He was cut from the same cloth of the great Saxon, and used it to his own advantage. However Henry of Bavaria could also stand, on his honor of being the head of the Bavarian stem. Herman of Swabia would claim that he was a leader of one of the most important territories.

We don't know from who, but Eckhart was murdered, as all the leaders were trying to win over the votes of the princess. In the end, when all the words were spoken, and all the promises made, Henry of Bavaria was elected.Henry of Bavaria was a master Statesman, and he promised the princes everything they wanted to hear. He really promised the princes of the German Church the most, and they flocked, and they helped sway the vote. An election was a funny thing in 1002, and it went something like this. Henry's first vote was secured, when he told the Archbishop that he wanted him to Crown him at the Coronation. Then Henry's next move was with the princes of Saxony, and told them he wanted a formal coronation at Charlemagne's capital. He didn't win, but secured the votes of Lorraine, and of Swabia. That wasn't the election, and that was the first German electoral vote. Of course to everyone they gave their vote, their Ambitions were filled. Let us set the record straight, the victor of the election was Henry .

Henry, like those before him,the main problem was the power game, between church and state, it took up the whole time That man calls the Middle Ages. All through the Middle Ages the same battle took up the time of the great Empire, and of course we're talking about the battle between Church and State. The Kings and Emperors and the Pope's wanted to rule the world, and on every issue they tried to explain why it was there problem.

Henry learned that the real centers of German political power were the great German churches. He also learned, that if he could control them, he would control the nation. If he could not control them, he knew he was sunk. The German power of the church was here to stay, and Kings and Emperors come and go. If Henry was going to rule, he had to make peace with the church, and also be there champion. First the church wanted all marriages with the priest abolished. Second the church wanted sure elections, with no bribery to win. 3rd the church wanted, the pope to be the only one over the bishop, and they wanted no other orders from anywhere.

These three demands from the German Church, would be the same demands, they would make for the next 200 years. Henry really liked the church platform, in fact he appointed Bishops every time the situation called for it. He appointed them both in Italy, and in Germany, by doing this, he showed who really was in control. Of course Henry chose loyal friends as his appointments of Bishops, just like the pope would have, if he had the choice.This endless battle between church and state was really a battle for absolute power.

When it came right down to the bottom line, the church was a luxury of the state, and the power of ruling the state, came in the form of Swords, battle axes, and spears. That's what really runs the state, always has, always will.

It must be understood that The Germanic Kings and Emperors, all knew the devious plan that Rome was playing, and they all knew what brilliant strategy the men in the cloth of the church had. The Pope's for centuries had tried to gain the upper hand, using their hold on the minds and hearts of the people. It works well with the Common Man, and great with the women, but it didn't work with their masters, the Kings and the emperor's.

They fully understood their power came from their weapons and their Warriors, and would only share it, if it was controlled by them. The world was not a place where a man of peace could get his share, and the man who seized the moment, took it all.

Henry like all who had his blood, knew the game very well, and would see that they were the winners. Henry like all German kings, had to be careful about giving real power to the Church of Rome, because it was like handing the enemy a loaded weapon. The German church had the deck stacked against them, and Rome was the dealer. However our cunning men in the cloth in Germany, would strike back at the power of Rome in 1022. The Archbishop was appointed by King Henry, but he had dreams himself. He told the Council of the German Bishops in Franconia that no person shall go to Rome, without the permission of the bishop. Also, that if any person condemned by his superiors, for a church offense, should be fired from his position for that offense.

This was the first step in the cut Of the German Church from Rome, and it was a bold move. Without the German race, there would have been no Christians in Europe, for it was German blood since Charlemagne, that had developed the church, and even carried it. No one else in the Germanic West carried the cross, and Christianity was a Germanic product. What I'm saying is, without the Germans, it would have been the Pope and his following and Rome, and that's it.

It wouldn't even have lasted either, for the Lombards would have destroyed Rome, if France had not come to their rescue. Rome had control over the German Empire, the Bible, and the teachings of the Jews, Jesus and Moses, but this was mind-control and nothing else. The Germanic control was on the field of battle, and To the victor go the spoils.

They panicked, that they were not the only players in the game, and suddenly they knew The Cunning of the German men in the cloth. These two German cannons were in reality, a declaration of independence from Rome, and they were Furious. The wheels of politics were turning faster all the time, and Whispering Tales of Thor.

Pope Benedict the 8th assembled the Bishops of Germany, and declared the National Church. The German Church men of the cloth, said that it was time that someone secured the power of the German National Church, and made sure that it was United, and now they would have a sense of their own destiny. The blinders was being removed from their eyes, and they were fast becoming mature, and wise. The Pope and the King died shortly after this hot exchange of ideas and Power, and we are left in the dark, as to what part this played in the later attitudes of Germany, and of course the popes of Rome. One thing is however clear, the wheels of politics were turning faster, and newborn Powers were being released.

Henry's part in the new plan, was to capitalize on the Revenge of the church, and take as much of their money as he could, and use it in the service of his crowd. Henry believed like those, in the Royal supremacy of the power in their blood. Only one person could rule the German Empire, and it was to be the royal power. Henry hated the great monasteries purpose, and how they danced to their own drummer. All the great places of the monks felt the hand and power of the German King. He replaced them with men of the cloth. Henry abolished the organization, and gave no pity. His name was pure. he wanted the rebellious houses, to be active centers of religious life, and if necessary he would take them back by force. This is the German Way, and this is how it was done. The monasteries were perhaps the world's first Banks, for the Vikings found many, with many Treasures, and Henry wanted his percentage.

The crown always wanted their percentage, for this is the way it was. The kingdom of Burgundy was now to have a roll, in the Affairs of the church, and of Germany. Burgundy had always been The kingdom between France and Germany, nothing more. Now the events of the empire would begin to shape the future of the kingdom of Burgundy. The Burgundian Kings had never enjoyed the power and prestige of their German and French relatives, but instead had been ruled by the power of their independent nobility. In Burgundy the nobility was powerful, and very active in the Affairs of their Kingdom. Never in their history, had there been strong and powerful Kings, and the nobility would not have allowed it.

In the year 1006 the hand of fate, and the finger of Thor, would touch their Kingdom. King Rudolph the Third who was Uncle of Henry , Proposed to Henry a plan of his liking. It seems Rudolph the third had no children, and no heir to the throne. Rudolph the third proposed that he at once, make Henry his heir, and resign his kingdom at once to him.

The swords of the nobility began to rattle, and fears dug holes in their hearts. The nobility for centuries had run their own affairs, and now a plan was being hatched, where Burgundy would become part of the German Kingdom. King Rudolph the third was pressured by all the leading families, to leave them to their own destiny, and Rudolph the third called off the plan.

A short time later Rudolph 111 Again called for Henry to take command of Burgundy, and he agreed. Henry came to Burgundy with a great show of force, and negotiations began with the noble families. Burgundy was not in the Empire at this time, and was not to be part of the German Empire, until the time of Conrad II.

In reality what this did mean, was Burgundy was no longer setting on the fence, and wasn't leaning towards Germany, or France. The possession of Burgundy, was of the utmost importance to German designs, because Burgundy was in a strategic position. Burgundy possessed the Burgundian passes, that drove straight into Italy. The holder of these valuable passes, could if need be, move straight into Italy. Also by the addition of The Burgundian passes, the German Army would not have to go over the Alps, but instead could go through the passes. The Affairs of Burgundy and Germany would never be the same, and they in time would blossom into a beautiful flower. The wheels of politics were spinning wildly, and all at the same time, Whispering Tales of Thor.

The year was now 1018, and another great man was about to enter the church and take over, and clean house. Once again Roman society was filled with Vice, corruption, and Petty ambitions. Out of this same Circle, another man, would put order and decency back into the Affairs of the Pope.This new man on the stage of world politics, was named Pope Benedict the 8th. He also used heavy reforms to enforce strong moral ideas, on the people, who by this time, we're incredibly loose and barbaric. The very fabric of Roman society had much to gain once more, and it was every man for himself. Roman society had fallen to an all-time low, and once again in history, one man would rise up, and alter the course of his time.

Pope Benedict knew without the brute force of the German Knights, there would have been no change. Henry was begged to enter Italy by a rival Pope, and once there, declared that he was there to judge the church. According to ancient constitutions this act was legal, but that mattered little to the Germanic hero. Henry decided to throw his power behind Pope Benedict. Henry was an opportunist, and also wanted to seize the moment. He agreed to enforce the power of Pope Benedict, and agreed also to be crowned Holy Roman Emperor, by the same man. For once in many years that church and state were as one, for each man promised to further, the other man's ambitions. Henry had made the Pope in Italy Supreme, so that he could counter The Growing Power of his own German Church.

Also the pope, a man with vision, could see the power of the Pope in Rome, once more work to forge the forces of church and state, and begin to work hand-in-hand, and in the same direction, as never before. The politics of Europe, make no mistake, were formed by both These great forces. In the year 1018, Pope Benedict changed the politics of the church forever. All the Lombard clergy was a symbol at the Council of Pavia in 1018, and altered the course of events for centuries. It is ironic, that the Assembly of the church men, was held in the Lombard capital, because the Lombards were the biggest abusers of the laws of the church.The Lombards for generations we're openly living with their wives, and this was forbidden. Churchman of the lower orders, as well as the highest, were openly showing their resentment to the office of the Pope in Rome.

The children of these marriages, of the men in the cloth, really made out. They had legal rights, That were unbelievable to the Modern Man. It seems the Children of the cloth, we're taking care of, and even Drew Incomes from the property of the church. This was a total disgrace, and was the custom of the cunning men in the cloth. All the children lived lavish lives, and your money like those of the Kings and Emperors went to them. The Lombards deceived the population for centuries, but then they all did. When they finally exposed all branches of the church, they swept the dirt under the rug so to speak. What the council of Pavia in 1018 had spoken by decrees, the future was going to be different.

Pope Benedict decreed that all married clergymen had to abandon their wives, or lose positions in the church. The council also decreed, the children in the cloth of the church, would from now on be deprived of all their privileges. The new law stated, the children of the churchmen, were to become Serfs, or workers of the church, and receive no money from their work. Also the children of the churchmen would no longer be able to hold property, especially property they got from the church. What a game it was then, and what a game it still is today. It is not what you know, it's who you know.

Also the act of Simony would not no longer be legal. Simony is when one gets the position, by wealth or by land. The church it is true, was more corrupt than anything in Society. Four generations of families with money and influence had bought all the positions in the church, including Bishops and Cardinals, and I would imagine even Pope's. Because in reality then and now, money talks and bullshit walks. That's probably the way it will remain till the end of time, if that ever comes. the Roman Church had always been full of scandals, and this would continue forever, only on a much smaller level, or hidden from the prying eyes of the people. these are the ways of men, and to expect different, is really pretty ignorant.

Even in later centuries and more modern times, much was swept under the rug. for a thousand years a man or woman if they had the big money, could actually purchase a pass for heaven. they actually believed it, because intelligence was at an all-time low, when there were no schools no common sense. in fact you could even pay a little bit more And reserve a spot either or Jesus left, or Jesus right, in heaven. These came at a very high price, because we're talking about eternity now, but if you had the big money it was well worth the LIE they sold you. they called this Simony too, what a coincidence.

I hope I made this action perfectly clear, because to me it is always been extremely important to know the real truth, and nothing but the truth. I am a Viking myself, in my heart, and in my mind, and I'll go with the facts,only.

 Henry II met the churchmen of Germany at the assembly in 1008. All the clergy were up in arms and Furious. However, Henry was the Emperor, and he forced the men of the German cloth to accept his demands, and did not debate the issue with anybody. Henry's decrees were even more to the point, and things were going to be different. Free born women who married a clerk of the church, where to be whipped, and exiled. and that was to take place in public. The sons of the men in the cloth, were Were to be serfs, and if an imperial judge rule different, he was to lose his office immediately. If a notary was to draw up documents, where these children of the church, could own land, he was to have his hand cut off.

For many generations the privileged men of the cloth, drained the finances of the church, and now they would have to devise new ways to play their power game. To say the churches and their Clerks we're out only for themselves, is basically the way it was.

Four generations the church had been big business, and those that hid behind the cloth of the church, where in fact excellent, businessman. The population as a whole were ignorant, and they battled daily just to feed and clothe themselves.

This my friends was the basis of the great conflict between church and state, that consumed the entire Middle Ages. I would think the average person would be totally shocked, thinking things were probably more religious back then, no they weren't. The children of the cloth, would be the most bitter, they could not live like royalty.

 It Would be strictly forbidden by the pope and the Emperor, and both great Powers worked to purify a sick Society. If anyone was ever going to totally respect the churches, and the Pope, it was necessary to clean up their act, and put on a holy front.

The Empire needed a strong church, that everyone could believe in, so that they would become more civilized. The Empire could not exist, and hope for a future, without morals, and the decency the church was supposed to provide. It would take an enormous effort, from both church and state, to accomplish this Monumental effort.

The churches of the Empire, would gather strength in every decade that followed. Unseen forces and Powers would push these churches into national powers. The idea of National Power did not come from the Kings or princes, but instead came from the National Churches, which eventually created Nations. In the champion 11th century, No One suspected the powers that were being created, but future Generations would.

Besides the great transfers of the power and the churches, and in their organization, there were also military matters that needed the desperate attention of Emperor Henry. Emperor Henry was one of the great Commanders the world has ever known. Emperor Henry led his Warriors with their German blood, to bloody battles throughout the Empire, and from one end to the other. Like A Champion chess player, Emperor Henry had to be able to read the defense, and know where they would attack. Like a master chess player Henry, had to know when to use his knights. From the days of the fall of Rome, the Empires Knights warred steadily through the centuries. Generations had spilled the blood of their enemies, and also spilled their own blood. War was the price of freedom, and in the modern world, we take it for granted. Then you took nothing for granted, for your enemies were waging Wars on every Frontier.

Emperor Henry and his German Knights answered the call to war, on many occasions, and rivers of blood were split, so the Germans could keep their women and children safe.

Thor and Odin had blessed the Germanic race, with the finest Blood in the Universe, and it was their right, and their duty to spread their blood, as far as their Conquests would take them. Every

Nation on Earth that have been blessed with the Aryan blood, has Prospered if even for a while, or until the well went dry. Europe was blessed the most, and her Heroes, prayed to the Mother Earth, that gave them birth. When the other Races attacked Europe, they were driven into the ground.

Although German blood was spilled too, in the defense of the empire, the German Knights, and German armies, killed Millions over the course of the centuries they fought. Many of Germany's enemies were hacked to death, into little pieces, and fed to the Great German Shepherds. Let's don't forget about the Dobermans, they had to eat too, and since this was a the family thing for all the Germans, the dogs ate well too. I imagine they threw up quite a bit, depending upon what they were eating, or should I say who. But let me tell you, when the Germans were totally United, with their cousins from Scandinavia fighting with them, even the Ferocious Huns were laid in the ground.It was a fact in ancient times,the Huns were like wild animals,and they ate raw flesh,of sometimes even live animals.The dogs would have the last laugh,and they would eat the Huns,sometimes alive too. So for all the romance of the old world,this is how it really was.

Thank Thor and Odin, that every time the German tribes needed a great leader, one would emerge. It must have been the Magic in the blood, of the gods and goddesses that favored them. It was a great thing for the German tribes, and basically for the whole empire, that Henry did take the throne. This was a man that cleaned up the German Church, and basically cleaned up the German Empire, and United them. For our very hostile world, One needed all the backup that they could get. Thousands of Nations have been destroyed trying to go it on their own.

Even during the time of Henry when he was Emperor, all the different races would try and break their way into Germany, but their battle-axes would keep them out. It wasn't just the weapons, it was the Warriors that held them. The great Henry would be tested many many times, and so would the empire, and every single time the German Pride grew taller, because they're enemies were buried.

The Invincible German army slashed their way through the ferocious Slavs on the Eastern borders. Many times when Henry was Emperor, Not just small battles, but enormous attacks by the German Knights ripped through the huge forces of the Slavs.At times the armies of the Slavs were hugh,and victory was in question,but still the German Knights engaged,and drove on.

The Slavs from the north we're just as vicious as the Eastern Slavs, and both needed huge forces of German Knights to stop them. This was a do-or-die situation, it seemed like every single year, but the German Knights prevailed in battle, baptized in blood.

The size of Slavic tribes was staggering, compared to the Knights that fought against them. What they did not think to consider, was the size of the German hearts beating in their chests, or the quality of the blood being pumped through them. Wave after wave of Slavic Warriors tested the German steel, and when the Eastern wars were over, plants and crops grew well on the land that had been watered by their blood. The Warriors were seasoned, but the German Knights let none through. the German Knights would also fight bloody, gruesome battles with the Vikings. They called themselves Normans from Normandy. The Normans also with the hot Scandinavian or Germanic blood in their veins, would not be denied a portion of southern Italy,and they took more than that.

Contained, but they could not be denied, for they also Whispered Tales of Thor. Henry the Emperor would also fight battles with the Greeks, and those battles were a long time coming. The Greeks All Along The Adriatic Coast, had been rebellious for centuries, and during the years of Emperor Henry, it turned into open Warfare. The German Knights each time polished their battle axes, and their swords, and each time taught the enemies a lesson in combat.The Greeks ruled in Constantinople, and always dreamed of resurrecting their empire in Italy, but they knew in their hearts, they could not beat the German Knights.

When Henry died in 1024, the German Empire lost its greatest hero, but because of Henry the Great, the Empire was left in great condition. The Empire, using Emperor Henry as an example, was now ready for the power of a strong Emperor. It had taken centuries, but now the Imperial Throne was a familiar fixture, in the political system of Europe. There can be no doubt, that Germany was by far, the leading power of Europe, and it was all due to their battle axes, swords, and great leadership.

For centuries the Duchy' s, and the kingdoms, had fought against the Imperial power, but now they welcomed it. All the nations of Europe, we're glad to have a power they could call, and receive help, if need be. From the invasions they had turned back, it was obvious, they needed to band together for military purposes. Henry was also credited for bringing Italy into the empire, and cleaning the church of its enormous sins, and unholiness.

One thing would be for sure was, When Henry died, a vacuum would be created, and there would be a major shift in power, and probably alliances. It did not take long for changes to appear, that would be bold and ruthless. There is an old saying, while the cat's away, the mice will play. The first great leader we come to is Boleslaw, the Duke of Poland. Boleslaw had been a great commanding War Chieftain for the Slavic tribes, in the wars against the German Knights. When the Slavic Wars had ended in defeats for the Slavs, Boleslaw had organized the survivors into a great Slavonic State. In the Duchy of Poland, The Chieftains power was enormous, and after the death of King Henry, The Duke took the crown of Poland as his own. You may say that the Duke seized the moment, that he had been waiting patiently for a long time.

Our great Slavic Warrior cared little about what anyone else thought, and cared even less about the consequences. The swords were rattling throughout the Borderlands, but no one moved against them. The nobility of Lombardy asked for the King of France to come to Italy, and take that Crown. Friends would say if they did not claim it, the Germans would be back. The King ordered the Duke William of Aquitaine to take the crown, if not for himself, for his son. The

Lombards had played second fiddle to the Germans for too long, and the ancient capital rose in open Rebellion against the Germans. These were all proud people, and all thirsty for power. In the Lombard capital, the Lombards destroyed the German Imperial Council. They did this because the council to the Lombards was a display of German Supremacy. On the western borders of the German Kingdom, there were always traitors to be found, but isn't this the way of men. Remember the story of Jesus Christ Turned in for 33 pieces of silver, and then put to death, because of one traitor, Judas.

The Duke of Upper Lorraine, and the Duke of Lower Lorraine, we're negotiating with the King of France, to enter into the Frankish Kingdom of the West. The neighbors treaty was ruled by the Duke of Champagne, and he was poised for a Kill. He had waited too, for the right moment to strike at Burgundy. It seems that the Duke was getting ready to lash out, at the rich lands of Burgundy, even if they were promised to the Emperor, he cared very little. the Duke of Champagne could not sit and watch these wealthy lands go to Germany. The gains the Empire had made under Emperor Henry, now seemed to be slipping away.

Emperor Henry died with no heir to his throne, and the future of the empire, was going to be left up to an election, of the German kind. For the first time in the history of Europe, each part realized the part they must all play, If The Empire was to prosper. For once everyone agreed, the transition would be better served if it was a peaceful transition, and if the winner could be judged on his merits and qualifications. They flocked from the corners of the empire, like never before in huge numbers. They would all Assemble at the historic Rhine River just outside the German Town of Worms. All five Stems made a tremendous display of unity, and raw power.

The ancient Germanic law was, every man who carried a sword, or battle axe, had a right to speak and to be heard. This right, had been the right of the Germanic Warriors for thousands of years, and even in Nazi Germany was exercised. He would be judged on their personal qualities, and also on their visions of the future for all Germans. The good old days were gone, where the top Warrior took the crown. The superiority of the Stems was not taking into consideration, and the influence of the most powerful families, was also not an issue. What was for once, in the long history of Germany, was which man would be the best ruler for all the people, and which man could do the most good for the German Empire.

The field of candidates was really narrow, down to two men, and they were both Conrad's from the Frankish house. These two German men, were cousins, and descendants of the very first Otto, so you can see, Destiny was in their veins. The two Conrad's, we are told by the Chronicles, took a bow to one another. They both realized that the unity of the empire, was the real issue, and they agreed that whoever should win, would wholeheartedly get the support of the loser. This was an important new way of thinking for the great warriors, but they realized the gravity of the situation that their country was in. United they would stand, and stand tall, but divided they would fall, and fall hard. The choice would be Conrad II, and the German king would hold to his word, to improve the lot, of every man, woman, and child. We know from the German writers, that the oldest Conrad, was a rough, and a valiant soldier in battle, with a quick mind. Conrad II did not have to face the ferocious Slavic King Boleslaw, because he died shortly after Conrad II was crowned the next King.

Conrad however would have to deal with the Slavic King's son, and that would be no simple task. The son was a chip off the old block, and he had once declared himself king of Poland. Poland was a Duchy of the Slavic tribes, but Boleslaw and his son wanted to make it clear to Germany, they would never hold and submit to them. There was just too much pride in all the Slavic Warriors, to bow heads to anybody, even if it was Germany. The new King of Poland knew he could not win a war with Germany alone, so he sought the alliance of the great Viking King Knut. Knut was the all powerful king of Denmark, and of England, and he was a tremendous power. Probably the most powerful man in the world at that time,because the Vikings were nobody's joke. the Viking king and all the rest of them were ruthless, and the greatest men in one-on-one combat in the world. This is the day before the gun and the cannon, this is where you had to show your shit. The Viking king said that he would think about it, he wasn't sure which direction he wanted to go and, he never really took the proposition seriously. If he had known world history, it Would have been different,cause every time the Vikings threw their battle-axes in, with you, you were sure to win.

Back to the alliance with the Vikings. The new Slavic King from Poland tried to make an Alliance with the Great Danes, to gang up and wipe out, Germany. Conrad II knew a witch's potion was brewing, but he had a potion of his own. Conrad II began to go see help, with the Viking king himself, and soon a deal was struck.

It must be remembered, that blood is thicker than water, and the Vikings we're cousins to the Germans. After all the land of the Great Danes was Denmark originally, and Denmark's on the very crown of Germany. The people have been mingling for thousands of years, and blood is thicker than water. Conrad II agreed to give Kent, which lay between a couple of the rivers, to Knut, for an agreement with their blood kindred. the Germans and Great Danes shared more than just the same blood, they also shared the same religion. The Danish Vikings also did ally themselves with the Great Christian King, and one day joined the family of Nations. The alliance these great warriors of the same blood made, was set in cement, and it would not be broken. This is the way of great warriors, and this is the way of Great Men, there word is truly there Bond.

The Polish Warriors would now have to go It Alone, and Conrad's First Act of diplomacy was brilliant. when these two tribes of Germans and Slavs would Clash in the future, it would now be one on one, and the Slavs could not hope to win against Thors Best. Conrad added security, and now his attention Went to the West. The great lands were at stake, just like it would always be, even up to World War II, and this land was called Lorraine. Lorraine was some of the finest lands on Earth, and it covered Much land, and all of it was good. It was some of the best agricultural land on planet Earth, and it would always be sought after by everyone that knew of it. The land was Lush, and it was held by two Dukes, and they had Ambitions of Their Own. They would bid the land to both France and Germany, and whoever would give them the best deal, that's who they would go with, it's as simple as that. This is the land of ambition and

Power, and this is how they play. King Conrad II had his Knights ready, and he rode into the Lorraine himself, and the year 1025 saw Conrad II prove his Mastery of politics.

With all the French and German Knights Armed for combat, Conrad II marched into the Lower Lorraine, and promised to the Duke, that when Fredrick died he would own half of Lorraine, and this Conrad swore to. This beautiful piece of statesmanship saved Lorraine for the Empire of the Germans. In 1033 Lorraine was united into one land, and the Duke grew richer, and more powerful just as Conrad Had promised him.

Conrad was very happy for the way he had handled the Affairs of his east and west, and now he set his sights on Rome. Conrad was not the type to wait, even for a call from the Pope, so he marched his German Knights into Italy. The Lombards as usual hated the German superiority, and the Knights of Germany battled, with the Lombard knights for over 1 year, and then it was done. When the last heroic Lombard laid down on the battlefield, the German Knights marched on Rome. The Pope in Rome at this time was John the 14th, and he was no fool.. He had no choice, Conrad II was crowned emperor on Easter Sunday 1027, and the coronation was spectacular. At the coronation of Emperor Conrad II, King knut of Denmark and England was present, and so was King Rudolph of Burgundy. Also to view at This brilliant moment, was the nobility from Germany, Burgundy, and Italy.

The Roman populations hated the foreigners, but then they hated the Romans, and this my friend is politics. But this is the way of men, and sometimes dogs have more class than men. Another major feather in the cap of Emperor Conrad II, was when he annexed Burgundy into the Empire, everyone was extremely happy. Burgundy provided mountain passes straight through the Alps into Italy, and it also provided itself a buffer between Germany and France.

 Some of the greatest of all European land. Burgundy also had a large population, that served the needs of the German Empire. The Burgundians nobility knew they would lose all the power they had held for centuries. Plus they didn't want to play second fiddle to the German government, but that's just too bad, like Mick Jagger said, You Can't Always Get What You Want. It was the Duke of champagne that would offer resistance to the rule of Emperor Conrad II. Like always it was a soap opera, and everyone trying to get as much as they could. Germany thought they would have to do battle with friends, and they were ready, but when the smoke cleared, it was the Duke of Champagne against the German Knights, and they are all Whispered Tales of Thor.

The German Knights armed themselves, and took the dust from their swords to where they were gleaming, and then cleaned their battle axes, and then they began to use them on the Knights of Champagne, but when the last man had been killed they drank champagne.

 The Germans being gods of War, also had big hearts, and the Dukes life was spared. He quickly agreed he had no right to the land, and only asked for safety in Champagne. In 1032 Burgundy was entered into the Holy Roman Empire of the German Nation.

Emperor Conrad was not a religious man, but he used religion for political purposes, like the Pope and Rome did every single day. In France the rulers ruled by inheritance, and many kings, were ruled by their more powerful vassals. They loved a weak ruler, for their nobility grew richer and more powerful, and this was France and Burgundy.

In Germany, the strongest and most powerful would rule, and this would make for a stronger Empire. In Germany instead of ruling by inheritance, It Was Always by election, and this was Germany's blessing. The strong House of the Franconians would put four generations on the throne of Germany.

In 1037 the German Knights were trying again, and the spirit of independence from the Lombards would have to be dealt with again. A conspiracy was hatched where the Knights of Champagne were to overrun Lorraine, and the Lombards were there to receive Italy and Burgundy. The Duke of champagne, and the German steel took his life like they should have years ago.

In 1039 Emperor Conrad would go to Rome, to try and bring reform to the sinful and lawlessness, of the Church Men of Rome. The pages of History tell us, the pappel office in Rome, had never been in a worse situation. The pages of History showed us what Liars, thieves, and Corruption, we're all about as far as the Pope, and his Supposed Sacred Men of the Cloth. The Tusculan family was perhaps the greatest sinners, however they cared less about the man, and more for what he could do for their power and wealth.

Corruption and lies are the very foundation of the church, but in 1039 they really outdid themselves. Pope John the 14th was a great Patsy for the Tusculum party, and when he died suddenly, holding each other in True Form, they showed their true colors, and gave us fantastic insight into the realm of the church. When Pope John the 14th died, and they had placed him in power, they replace them with another member of their house, but he was just a boy. Believe it or not, the Holy family placed him on the Throne. He was Accepted as the New Pope. If that isn't pitiful I don't know what is. But it sure made corruption a whole lot easier, getting over on a 10 year old kid was certainly no great feat. The politics of Rome and the politics of the Pope had sunk to a new level . Never in the history of the church, had there been such scandal, and this my friends was the worst.

But this is the way of Italian politics, usually those that hide behind the cloth of the church are the worst. Even in my childhood there were many scandals with child molesting. Many times, many issues of child molesting with the Roman Catholic Church, and this went all the way to the top, To the Vatican, just pitiful.

But this is the way of church politics, and The Men Who hide behind the cloth of the church. The list of scandals from the Roman Church, is too long to place in this work, but I have made sure that enough has been presented, so that the reader will know in his own mind, the truth of church power end corruption. Do not believe millions of sheep that follow the church and their power and deceit.

This my friends is life, and you must take the good with the bad, for there is no other way. Until the modern era, just speaking out against the church, would have been dealt with, with death, immediately. You would have been burned To the stake. the Catholics were so thoroughly brainwashed, they believed the pope was God's man on Earth. This is the way it was for many centuries, the population was Hoodwinked. Anyone who even argued with the doctrine of the church, was branded a servant of the devil, and then was executed, and all this did was make the church stronger.

The Pope in Rome, and his power, was the last, and only hope for the rich Roman nobility. It was through the office of Pope, that the last of the powerful Roman families survived. The Roman families never lost sight of their real power and ambitions. They all hoped their propaganda would be strong enough too, because they certainly could not beat them in war. The Pope's Throne would be the center stage, for the wealthy Roman families, and they used it for their own power, and visions, and wealth.

When the roman empire was crushed by the viking tribes over a couple
Of centuries,the richest and most powerful families,bought all the powerful positions including the Popes,For a thousand years,in this way they could continue to rule the new empire of Europe.The jews were also allowed to buy in,and this was their blueprint to power.

The power of the richest families of the Romans in truth only grew stronger,and continues to the present day.they never ever left their thrones.
Of course the German church was all powerful too,and when you fight wars you do not throw bibles at them.The killing was done with German steel,and lots of it.It was the German empire now,where might makes right.

THE BOYS ARE BACK IN TOWN

Chapter 14

What we last wrote of Britain, the Vikings were carving out their territories, against their rivals the Angles and Saxons. All of the tribes that belonged to the great Slaughter were all Scandinavian tribes, but it was a war that was unbelievable. They had to fight to see who would be Supreme, and this war had to be fought. The population of all the Scandinavian lands was exploding, and more land was desperately needed. It was a war of survival of the fittest, and the weak tribes would be fertilizer, for Mother Earth. The terrifying Angles and Saxons, and Jutes, had taken their lands by Brute Force, and it had taken centuries, to just get a percentage of the land of England. Her homegrown Warriors had fought well against Vicious Angles and Saxons from across the English Channel. Now the Danish Vikings were taking their own percentage of England, because England truly was a magnificent country, and the Great Danes had to have it.

The power of Viking Steel was creating new lands, and the warriors were brutal and bloody, and seemed to be constant. At times the carving up of new countries, covered entire centuries.

King Edmund of the Ferocious Saxons held back the Great Danes as long as he could, but in time, he too would be executed by The Vicious Men From Denmark. In 870 Half Dan and his Vikings slaughtered the Saxons, in their Heartland, West Sax.

The Brother of King Edmund, then being the King of Saxons, because of his Brilliant strategy of building castles,in four to five towns, the English gained a reprieve. The Saxons after vicious battles with the Vikings in the year 870, under Alfred, gave no more ground.

 878 saw the Army of Vikings, a whole lot bigger than the last. The Vikings began to steamroll the Saxon forces, and Alfred went into hiding. Many Saxons crossed the English Channel by the thousands, and went into the continent. Finally, all the tribes of the Saxons, Jutes, and the Angles made One Last Stand, and a heroic stand, at Devon. It was there that the great Vikings would learn a new respect for the Angles, Saxons, and the Jutes. After their great victory, Alfred

led the Saxons too many more victories, and soon peace was declared. History forever calls the treaty Wedmore. Soon the Angles, Saxons, and Jutes brought in fresh Warriors to fight shoulder-to-shoulder with the Saxons, against that men called the Great Danes. After many more Savage and bloody battles, the Angles, Saxons, and Jutes, and Danes, we're ready to slice up Germanic England.

The lands that would be set aside for the Danish Kingdom would be called the Danelaw. The Danelaw was ruled by the Danish Vikings.It was a separate country from the rest of Germanic England, and they had their own law. The Danish Vikings would not long be satisfied with their arrangement, and soon, the English soil would be sprinkled with blood again.

But to live with the Danelaw, was hard, and the Vikings tried to take West Sax, the land of the West Saxons. But here the blood stuck up in the mud, and all the time, Whispering Tales of Thor.The Saxons would not give an inch.

The Viking invasions of England and of France were overwhelming, and it was all both Powers could do to stay alive. Charles the Bald, King of the western Franks, died in 877, and his son Louis the Stammer was crowned, and died 18 months later. The drama unfolded in the world Back then, just like the drama in the world today, Non-Stop. According to Germanic law, the kingdom of Louis, was divided amongst his two sons. The kingdom of Provence went to Boso, for he was the only effective ruler in the region. The wheels of politics were spinning Wild, and would not stop here. Both sons of Louis the stammer would die by 884, and the whole Empire would go to Charles the fat. Charles the fat had proved his ineffectiveness in 882, when he let the Danish Vikings commanded by Godfried escape with The Ransom of 2800 Pounds of silver. Charles the fat also tried his hand at politics, when he made Godfried the Viking, ruler of Frisia. He did this hoping that with a Viking ruler, it would Drive Away other Viking predators. The Vikings used the rivers of France for highways and no one in France was safe.

Viking fleets kept going further and further inland, traveling all the waterways of France. The list of Viking highways were many, and all the Frenchman would see them. All the rivers were traveled from end to end, and many had twisting and turning routes. The Vikings plundered everything. Cologne was raided many times, and so were the rest of the town's. Every single town and Community along every single River of France saw the Vikings, and had no choice but to deal with them. Some just submitted, and gave whatever they had to them. Even Paris was sacked many times, and then they learned that in the future maybe they should just pay off the armed robbers, and this is the way it went.

The Vikings attacked Paris in November of 885, and it was relentless, because the Vikings had come for it all. This was no lightning raid like the Vikings were famous for, this was a full scale attack on Paris that lasted for one year. Paris had never been the capital of Charlemagne's Empire, or of Charles the balds Kingdom, and in fact had been overlooked until the Viking invasion of 885. All the forces of the western Franks were assembled here at Paris, for suddenly everyone realized the importance of this town. Paris was the key to France, and if the Franks lost Paris, they would soon lose everything else. If Paris fell, the Vikings could control all the great waterways of France. The Great Danes realizing they had the wealth of France at their fingertips, attacked the bridges to Paris, The Valiant Defenders of Paris were commanded by Count Odo, and even The Fearless Abbott Jocelyn. It was up to the Franks and Count Odo, to stop the Viking invasion of France, at the bridges of Paris, and the Franks fought with the fury of demons. The Danish Vikings offered to leave Paris, if the Franks would give them free passage out, and the Franks said hell no, it would be a fight to the Finish. The gigantic efforts of 886 by the Viking attacks, we're beating back by the Frankish longswords, and they're battle axes.

The Franks blood screamed in their Veins for victory, and their war machines, the catapults destroyed the bridges that helped the attackers.The winter floods, with the German steel, kept the Vikings from Paris. That winter, the Viking warriors plundered the countryside.

By this time the Eastern Franks had come, to add their battle axes to the fight, and the blood began to flow again. The Danish King, Siegfried, tired of the war, that took so many of his own men, told the Defenders that with 460 lb of silver he would agree to pull out. Still the Furious Viking Champions fight on and on, and they would not stop their attacks. The churchman died during the siege of Paris, however his Bible was not Missed. Count Odo rallied the Knights of the Franks on a daily basis,and he saved France.However do not forget the warriors of the Franks.

Count Odo proved The Valor of The Fearless Franks, when he and his greatest Knights fought their way through the Vikings, and went to contact Charles, and then fought their way back in. The Defenders of Paris grew Restless, but count Odo, told them, the Emperor was coming with many more German Knights, and they fought a whole lot better, knowing the boys were coming. Count Odo and his ferocious Defenders of Paris, fought on until October, and Charles negotiated a shameful peace with the Vikings. Charles Allowed them by Paris, and let them Devour the whole of Burgundy and the Western lands.

This was an act of cowardice, the brave Defenders of Paris, could not believe the shame of their ruler. To seal the deal Paris paid 7000 lb of silver, and for this Charles the fat lost his Crown. In early 888 Charles the fat was deposed, his crown was taken, but the damage was done. Deja vu, The empire was once more partitioned, and the Western Kingdom of the Franks was Odos the warrior and defender of Paris. Politics is a nasty business, but somebody has to do it. The Danish Vikings came back in 889 to claim their 700 lbs of silver, and loaded their Dragon ships with the plunder of France. But after the heroic stand of the Franks at Paris, the Viking Fleet never returned, because they had lost huge numbers of great warriors. The Pickens would be a whole lot easier somewhere else.

The Empire of the Franks would never forget the attack on Paris, or the fury of the Frankish Defenders. A new spirit of resistance to the Vikings swept the land, and in 891 the Viking forces were destroyed by Arnulf who was king of the Franks. The survivors of the Danish Fleet sailed back to England with their remaining 250 ships.

It was at this time that Hasting appeared at the mouth of the Thames, outside London with 80 shiploads of Vikings. In 886 when the battle for Paris was being fought, Alfred the Great and his Saxons took London from the Danish Vikings. After Alfred the Great's smashing victory at London, all the English people fell under his Banner and his sword, that is all the free Englishmen.

Alfred the Great, king of the West Saxons, was now Overlord of all England. In 886 Alfred the Great made a treaty, with the Great Danes, that helped the English, that were under the Yoke of the Great Danes. The Danes were using England as a base, for all their Western Raids of plunder, but the Saxons, could do nothing about it. The Danish Vikings had designs on the whole continent of Europe, but after their battles of Paris, they realized the Franks we're better organized, and their Unity was becoming extremely strong. It must be noted here, that although I use the term Danish Vikings, there were Warriors from Sweden and Norway, in all the Danish fleets.There were many Irish and Scottish with them too.
Alfred the Great and his loyal Saxons, knew that although they had a treaty with the Danish Vikings, when the fleet came back from the continent, and they were assembled in England, once more the slaughter would begin again.The Kingdom of Great Danes erupted once again in 892, and although Alfred the Great, took many hostages to ensure the peace, the Danish Army spilled over the borders again. Hasting and his Vikings wanted to enlarge the Danish kingdoms of Northumbria, and East Anglia, and these Warriors fought with him in a four-year bloody war, that spilled enormous amounts of blood on both sides. The English Army's of Saxons, Angles, and Jutes, were better trained, and ready anytime, and this the Great Danish Vikings could not believe, and they had not counted on.

The English now had a huge peasant militia, and Alfred the Saxon had divided his forces into two separate armies. That way he had the English Army ready, and staying close to home, while the others could stay active. Of course the great Saxon King, added professional Warriors to guard the all-important fortresses.In this way the English Army became more effective, and with their well-fortified fortresses were a power to reckon with. The fortresses enjoyed the military capabilities and tension was secured with them. Alfred the Great's Vision protected his people, and it also protected his kingdom.

Each piece of English land was ordered to supply a warrior, and each hide sent Warriors to the Mighty Fortresses. Alfred the Great was also responsible for the building of Warships, for the Defence of his kingdom. Alfred a man of great vision, ordered big warships like the Great Danes ships. Alfred wanted giant warships, and with these he now had the ability to take the attack straight to the Vikings. Also the Morale was greatly improved, when the ferocious Angles and Saxon warriors, could meet the Great Danes on the ocean, in battle. The war of 892 went to 896,and was a turning point in the history of both kingdoms.

The English fought a defensive War, with well-planned counter attacks, that were so effective, the Danes realized they could not win. King Alfred used his Lieutenants in his brilliantly designed attacks, the English won so many victories. The Great Danes in this bloody war, themselves Fielded two separate armies, and they lived off the countryside. Alfred the Great won a great victory at the Viking camp at Benfleet. They captured it, and it became a trophy. Among the captured possessions, were the ships of the Vikings, and also their women and children. Alfred kept them imprisoned, and showed them himself to be a human Warrior, and the Saxons collected also, the wealth of these Vikings from their raids.

It Seems As though Karma has caught up with the Vikings, and now the English were stealing from them, what they had stolen from everybody else. The wheels of karma were turning.

Alfred kept all his prisoners in jail, and knew that the Winds of Change were blowing, and always Whispering Tales of Thor. Alfred the Great as he will be remembered, truly deserved his name, and he was a great student of the Art of War. In 893 the Danish Army was bewildered when Alfred destroyed all their crops, their cattle, in the Midlands of England. With the Great at the controls the Vikings we're in trouble.

In 895 Alfred the Great had another trick up his sleeve, and this time the prize was London. Alfred blocked the course of the Lea River with two enormous forts, so that the Great Danes could not use the river. When the Saxons attacked the Viking camp, 20 miles north of London, and the great Danish survivors, escaped into the Danelaw. Alfred was the great strategist, who brought the wisdom of battle, to the Saxon Realm, and he quickly became the Toast of all of England. In 896 the Saxon Navy would be tried in battle, and Alfred the Great sent nine of his new warships, to clash with six of The Vikings. It seems the Danish Vikings had been attacking and plundering, and Alfred sent his Saxons to engage them.

The Angles and Saxon Warriors on their new British ships, could not wait to Spill the blood of their enemies into the ocean. With the warriors watching, the warships engaged over the water, and when it was done, two of the crews of the Viking ships had been annihilated. The third Viking ship sailed away with only five warriors on it. The second Clash at sea, was also an English victory, and the two Crews of these two ships were so mangled they could not even row, and ended up on the shore. The survivors were taken to the king of Winchester, where they were promptly hanged. Only a few Vikings made their way back to the Danelaw, in the one ship that remained.
When they landed in East Anglia, the word of the English Victory spread like wildfire.

Alfred the Great died 3 years after the great Saxon an Angle victory, and he died knowing that he had done well. According to the writings of the Vikings, it was because of this one brilliant man, that Scandinavia was denied, from capturing all of England. Without the brilliant leadership of Alfred the Great, there can be no doubt, England would have fallen to the fury of the great Danes battle axes. It was because of this one man, and his vision, that the Danes had been denied. The Vikings claimed that Alfred the Great was the greatest opponent, and without him, England Would have been a colony.

Alfred did not leave the English without a successor, for his brother Edward would continue the plans that Alfred had drawn up. The Vikings in England, and in Ireland, we're no longer enjoying the conquest they had once known, and were in fact being contained.In the ninth Century Scandinavian blood flowed to the West in rivers, and the northern kingdoms of the Franks had paid their dues too. The beginning of the 10th century, would find the Danish Vikings storming into northern France, and many were staying. The French could no longer take the Vikings plundering every single River of France, on a yearly basis. A plan was hatched amongst the Franks, and they prayed to the heavens, it would be successful.

Charles the simple, could no longer hold back the small Armies of the Great Danes, and their cousins the great Norwegians. Charles needed the land between the Great Rivers, so he picked one Chieftain Rolo to stop the flow. Rollo was given huge amounts of land right at the mouth of the Seine River, the river that flows into Paris. These huge tracts of land now belonged to Rollo. Rollo gave his word to the crown of France, that no Vikings would pass through his Duchy. Rolo was given a Dukedom, and he was the Duke, and he had many Viking warriors with him that wanted a better life.They would fight to the death to repel all Viking invasions.The year now was 911 and the wind kept Whispering Tales of Thor.

We do not know with absolute certainty, if Rollo was a Swede or a Norwegian. Legend has it, that rollo came from Scandinavia because he was big, so big that no horse could carry him. Legend has it that Rollo was brother to the Great Viking Ragnar. We do know that Rollo and his Viking warriors had raided Scotland for a long time, but that was before he came to Normandy.

We also know that Rollo gave his daughter a Norwegian name. We also know that the bulk of Rollo's army was Danish, although some came from Iceland, and some came from Scotland.

He Was baptized to show good faith to the French, and Many of his tribesmen said nothing, for they knew, that this was a political move, to insure an Acceptance in the establishment of Europe. Rollo was in fact , the greatest move the French could have made, for he stayed loyal, and he fought for his land, and for the French. Rolo made strict laws for the men, and the possessions of his land, and all were made to tow the line. Rollo and his Warriors strengthened the town's defenses, and the surrounding Countryside learned what real peace was all about. The vast lands that Rollo became Overlord of, Rollo cut up into pieces, and gave them to his greatest warriors. The great ones, cut their lands, and divided them into shares for the remainder of the army. This is the way it was done, and this was the story of success for France.

Now the wild man from the north, became landowners, and some had beautiful Estates. Norman Society at once was a rival power to all others, and their strength was in their character. Denmark had no system like the feudal system of Normandy. The Danish Vikings held on to their language for only one generation, and soon they were speaking French. the Vikings also intermarried with the French women, and speeded the fusion of these two peoples. Everyone began calling them Norman's, which was short for Normandy. It was not long before their Duchy became known as Normandy. The Normans would conquer all of England, and it was William the Conqueror, who was of the same blood of Rolo.

The year 911 saw Rollo transformed from a Viking Chieftain, into a Duke of his own Dukedom, or Duchy. This sent Tremors through England. In England, King Edward's cousin went on the Rampage in open Rebellion to the crown, and kidnapped a nun and went to the land of the Danes in East Anglia, and got the Danes to make war once again on English Mercia.

He also persuaded the Danes to again attack the North of West Sax. The Danes made a bad move when they made war against the Angles and the Saxons. The Angles and Saxons were at this point stronger than they ever had been, because of Their well-fortified Kingdoms. The Danes at this time had everything going for them in England, and had the English estates for thirty years. The Northman also attacked the English in 910 and hoped that their timing was everything. Danish intelligence had it, that the fleet was at Kent. The Danes attacked at full strength, and invaded English Murcia, but fate would have the last word. The Angle and Saxon armies destroyed the Danish armies.

Alfred the Great had left his country well fortified, and the Danes could do nothing. when King Edmund realized the

power the Angles and Saxons had, he seized the moment. It was at this time in Saxon history, the great King Edmund took back London, and also Oxford. To make sure London would never be captured again, King Edward had strong fortresses built, that protected the vital town. Fortresses would be built all over England to protect their vital cities, and they would hold back the Viking assaults for future Invaders. Two years later the Angles and Saxons went to war with the Danish Vikings to recapture the Midlands. The Vikings from Britney launched their massive Fleet, and they began to ransack and plunder many of the town's, but they were finally driven back into the sea. The same Fleet not to be outdone, would also stop and pillage and plunder Wales. After the huge Viking Fleet left, The English began their attacks on the Danelaw. They threw everything they had at them, and this would be a war to the Finish. By 916 the Saxons had a double line of fortresses, and now the English were secure. These double lines of fortresses not only protected the English from the Danes, they also protected them from the Irish Norse, and the Welsh, but they also acted as jumping off points for their own attacks. In 917 and 918 the English launched many attacks against the Great Danes. The army bases of that day we're confronted with a line of fortresses they could not capture, or even go near, without fear of massive attacks. When King Edward finally had the Danes in the Danelaw under control, fate would play its hand. An invasion of England came from the north, and the Invaders were the Norsemen from Ireland. This invasion was a great movement of the Norsemen from Ireland, and North West England has many place names to testify to the Irish settlers. Also the area of Southwest Scotland, came under the same fierce invasion of the Norsemen.

All over these two areas can be found sculptured stones, or monuments, the Norseman always left behind. The years of 915 to 922, the Norseman plundered Northwest England, and

Northumbria, and suddenly England had a new play again. The actual records of these times are very sketchy but we hear of the Irish Chieftains many times. The Irish after they left Ireland, tried to conquer all the lands and Wales, but they were beating off, and eventually ended up in the north of England. We also have a few facts about a ferocious Viking named Ingimund, and he too fought the same battles. We also know that he later attacked Chester, and there his raid, made himself and his Warriors quite wealthy. We know for a fact that the Norseman raids were vicious, and kingdoms felt their Terror.

In the web and spiral history of England, we see the Norwegians from Ireland fight into the Kingdoms. From Ireland came thousands of Viking warriors to conquer Northumbria, and they became part of England's History too. From 914 to 921 the pages of History tell us the warriors were like wild beasts that descended upon England. There are many Legends of Vikings that Agreed to bring their dragonships in. The Norwegians from Ireland ransacked everybody, and they reconquered Dublin Ireland. The Norseman we're cutting their section of England out, and they would be denied nothing.

The Vikings finally took York in 919, and the Viking Chieftain crowned himself the king.

This was the climax of the Furious, bloody war, between the Norwegian Vikings, and the Danish Vikings, that they have been fighting for over 50 years. During those 50 years both groups of Vikings became extremely powerful, and extremely rich, and they were forever be in the pages of the history of Great Britain. The Norseman had slain and robbed England too, as well as Scotland, and Wales, and France. They would not stop until their ships were full of gold. The Irish Norwegians we're on the move and nothing could stop their wildness in battle, and no Army could withstand them.

The Norseman, or Norwegians felt no pity for those they came in contact with. As the Irish Norwegians headed south, King Edward built several great fortresses to keep them from the Mersey river. The Vikings arrived on the scene in 920, but everywhere they Appeared King Edward had built many fortresses. The Chronicles of the Saxons tell us that King Edward was overjoyed when in that year, the king of the Scots, and the whole Scottish Nation, accepted him as their Overlord. Everyone recognize the Great Saxons King as the Overlord, and the Norwegians fell in behind them.

The Norseman Greatest Warrior died in 921, and his name was Rognvald. Of course his power was divided up amongst the other great warriors, that had gone on many raids in Scotland and England.

In 924 the great Saxon War leader King Edward died, and off to Valhalla he went. Another great warrior would try the 2 greatest forces in the world together. Of course I'm talking about the great Saxons, and the great Norse Vikings. The winds were still Whispering Tales of Thor, and everything was perfect, and there was peace, and then fate reached down and played its hand. 18 months later the great Norwegian War King Died and the Northumbrians accepted Olaf as his successor. At this time from Ireland came the king of Dublin Ireland to act as advisor to the young Olaf. He was also another powerful and fearless Norwegian Viking, who had been the king in Dublin, and had left to plunder England. England was a land of great wealth and beauty, and all the Viking Nations would definitely cut a part for themselves. Fate spins mysterious webs, and often tramples the truth. King Athelstan was now the leader of the Saxons, and he gathered all his forces and drove out of England Guthfrith and Olaf. Guthfrith Went to Scotland, and Olaf went to Ireland, and England was free of these two champions for awhile.

We know for sure that King Athelstan's armies seized Northumbria, and the Norwegians were defeated. However the Scots and the Welsh wanted the Saxons of Athelstan's nowhere near them, and tempers began to boil, and so did the blood in their veins. All of a sudden reality hit everyone in the face, and King Athelstan demanded tribute paid to him, for the northern kingdoms. This my friend was a bit much, to the fiercely independent kingdoms, and very independent Warriors, and it was only a matter of time. The Spears, bows, and arrows, and the battle axes were sharpened and Polished, and everyone waited for the call to battle.
Things became even more complicated when the Great Chieftain Guthfrith Died, and off to Valhalla he went.His son also had the power of Thor and Odin in his blood, and off to Ireland he went. The Dublin kingdom was his destination, and there he mobilized an enormous force of Thor's best warriors. The battlefield would see the armies of West Sax and Mercia fight under the Saxon King Athelstan. Also his brother Edmund would join forces, and take on the Norwegians of Ireland, commanded by Olaf.

The Furious Scott's under the command Of Constantine The Welch, would also be there, with their Knights, and they would be commanded by their war Chieftains. The battle would be furious, and The Clash of violent Warriors would be staggering, and when the last Warrior had been killed, the northern and western armies would be beaten. Thousands of Vikings, Scots, Welsh, and Saxons would lay where they were slain. Thor's eagles, and Ravens, ate the hearts, and would take care of the Corpses.

The beasts of the forest were well fed, by the slaughter of these Brave combatants. The land that men call England had never seen the violent Slaughter they saw on this Day, except long ago, when the Angles and Saxons at First Landed. Then too, The Killing was enormous, and the Angles and Saxons carved out Their Kingdoms, at the expense of so many British and Welsh lives. The Warriors of Thor and Odin, could not, and would not, be denied their Kingdom, on the Enchanted Isle.

The Norseman Fleet, with so many wounded survivors, made their way back to Dublin Ireland, and with them, the reports of the battle. Five young Kings died in the slaughter, and so did seven of Olaf's man Enforcers. The power and Glory of English arms, had never known the great victories, that they had known here. King Athelstan of the English, now took his rightful place amongst the greatest of England. The Irish Norwegians still held York, but their expansion was contained by the Saxons. King Athelstan was just about ready to call the Scandinavians into his kingdom. Many served his court, and many thought of themselves as loyal subjects.

King Athelstan was the greatest of politicians in this time. He even beat the son of Harald Fairhairs. King Athelstan had much glory in his own land, and was well-respected in northern Europe, and also in Western Europe. in 939 the King went off to Valhalla. As so often happens, when a great leader dies, a power vacuum is born, and this was no different.

After just several months, Olaf of Dublin Ireland was back at York, with his ferocious Norwegians called the Norseman. Soon afterwords, once again the countryside was raided,and a path of Destruction went through the Midlands. This time the Norwegians of Ireland came with an enormous Force big enough to do the job, and Olaf had learned a new respect for English arms.

You learn from your mistakes, and Olaf learned well. The new English king Edmond met the Norseman with the huge Army ready for battle. After viewing the enormous forces against him the New King settled for a treaty. Olaf gained tremendously, but then he had not come to be denied. Olaf and his forces we're ready for whatever came their way, and I mean whatever came their way. Olaf was now the overlord to the modern towns of Lincoln, Lincoln Derby, and several other towns. The new English king Edmond to save his own kingdom, cut the throats of the Danish and English when he gave it back to the Vikings. As soon as the English Armies had left the scene, Olaf and his Warriors butchered all the loyal English sympathizers, and began all over again, the conquest and plundering of the area called Northumbria. Both sides, the English and the Vikings, knew the future would hold Another War, but Olaf died and off to Valhalla he went. The kingdom went to the other Olaf, who was the Son Of the treacherous Viking Chieftain. The Danelaw went back to its original borders in 942.

The Viking Kingdom of York in Northumbria would not begin its transformation, when Olaf was driven out by the masses in 943. There would be a new King just like it always was, Olaf and several others went to counsel with King Edmund and received baptism. These new breeds of Vikings, played the game of politics, and submitted. The two Viking leaders began the war amongst themselves, and in 944 King Edmund expelled both of them. King Edmund of the English took the crown of Northumbria until his death in 946. The crown of the English would now go to the brother of King Edmund,Eadred. in 948 Eric Blood Axe would arrive on the scene, and change the political picture at once.

Blood Axe earned his name in Viking history, as being one of the most violent Warriors, in the history of man. His Savage exploits in battle spun Legends across the seas, and the Vikings of Northumbria were in awe of this one man.

The Vikings of Northumbria rallied to Blood Axe, and he immediately became their King. It was the magic of his name,for Heroes love Legends. This made the Vikings of England rally to him immediately. King Edmund became furious, and under tremendous pressure, Blood Axe was abandoned as the king. In 949 Olaf was back, and he too was abandoned after 1 year. This thing, of trying to create countries and Empires, was not an easy task until the pieces all fit together, new combinations would be tried. This is the only way it was ever done, and it will be the only way it will ever be done.

Blood Axe came back to the scene in 949 and this time he ruled for only 2 years. The dream that the kingdoms of York, and the kingdoms of Ireland, could be United, died because of the Norsemen's Rivalries. That makes sense, cuz too many cooks spoil the broth.

We have an abundance of coins from that era, and there would be Irish Kings on them, and they were made in Britain. But most of them we're gone soon after they were minted. Blood Axe was perhaps the most interesting of these violent Kings from Dublin, that hoped they could somehow rule all England. Like a rock and roll song says Everybody Wants to Rule the World, but nobody really does, because it's all split up into pieces, and that is the way of man.

Blood Axe was a terrifying opponent on any Battlefield, but war and politics are strange bedfellows. Blood Axe refused to give up Thor and Odin, and replace them with Christianity. Times they were changing, but Blood Axe wasn't. The court of Blood Axe was extremely Pagan, and rituals to the pagan gods were performed often. Blood Axe was driven out of York for the last time in 954, and this time it was an extremely brutal War. The Clash of arms was recorded in the pages of history by most writers, and in it it says,

Odin has always had high hopes for Blood Axe. Upon his death, the Viking Heroes Stood ready to receive him, and as he entered, they said, what Heroes attend you, from the Roar of battle. Blood axe replied, there are Five Kings, and I will make all of them known to you, and I am the 6th.

To say this was a bloody battle, will be an understatement. There were Five Kings killed, and Blood Axe was the 6th on that Bloody day.

With the death of Blood axe, The Winds of Change kept blowing, all the while, Whispering Tales of Thor. The Western Saxons of West Sax, Warred with the Vikings of Mercia, and they partitioned it. The Danish Vikings, and the Norwegian Vikings, would however not stop after brutal Wars with the English over the Treasure Island. For 30 years there would be peace, and in that brutal world, that was all you could ask for.

The 9th century for England, Ireland, Scotland, France, and Germany was like a massive hurricane, and the winds from the hurricane, gave birth to Tales of Thor.

The 10th century would feel the same forces at work, so would every century, including the 20th. To think that the Scandinavian Homeland, as small as it actually was, would go on to conquer, and slice up the Earth, is bewildering, as it is staggering. The power of these tribes, and they're fantastic Warriors, would make their presence known on all four corners of the Earth.

The Furious Warriors from the north, pretended for political purposes to become Christians, but it was their belief in Thor and Odin, that molded them into the treacherous forces that they were. All the time they attacked and plundered the Christian nations, we read of Christs' men,

Suffering . The Christian cities went up in flames, and the rulers paid the Vikings tribute, and begged like women or dogs 4 peace. The true Viking Warrior, had no need of the kind words of Christ, because he knew that only the power of Steel meant anything in this world. The power of Steel Would decide everything.

The Christian cities went up into flames, and yes the rulers paid the Vikings tribute, and they paid again, and again, whenever Thor's best arrived on the scene. The Christian nations would learn, the power of Steel, if they were to survive on this hostile planet. The Vikings to the last man believed in their own power, and deeds, and bowed to no Nation, and no Army. The Gods Thor and Odin, triumphed over all gods, and this my friends is the reality of life. In the reality of all Europe, including England, they called upon the great Scandinavian powers. It centered on the great Heathen Temple of Uppsala. As Adolf Hitler would say in the 20th century to his high command, we have not forgotten where the Images of our gods are buried, and he ordered the SS to dig them up.

Eric the bloodaxe was the best a Viking could be, and he lived by the laws and wisdom of Odin. In a later chapter we will examine the words of the most high Warlock, but for now, it is back to history. Eric the bloodaxe Died in 954, and the English seized Northumbria from him. But only Thor knew he had many more Warriors, and the war had just begun. By the end of the Teutonic migrations, or invasions, Iceland, Greenland, and North America would become part of the Vikings Realm. There would be peace in England, but there would be bloody and violent Combat too, with the Welsh in Wales.The Vikings from the Isle of Man, and also the Norseman from Dublin Ireland,would bloody their battle-axes on them. After 980 the Raids were even more intense, and much more frequent too, and the Treasures of the Norsemen grew to where they had enough to fill Fort Knox.

Between 982 and 989 at least four different invasions completely sacked the towns of Wales, and a large percentage of the population was slaughtered. The great Cathedral of St Davids, was sacked for all its riches, on at least four occasions. It must be noted, there were no banks in those days, and the biggest lumps of wealth, where to be found with the men in the cloth, or church.

Not only did the church collect the money, they spend it on their families, and of course they spent most of it on themselves, cuz this is the way of man. The pages of History, what there is of them, tell us the southern half of Wales took the full force of the Viking invasions, simply because, that's where the wealth of Wales was. The Vikings were no fools, and when they came for the wealth, they usually knew exactly where it was. Someone would always rat everybody off for a price. The Norseman were avenging the wrongs the English kings had done to their blood in the conquered territories. King Edward in 959 had treated them well, but his successors had not done the same.

974, he was succeeded by his son Edward. Edward was murdered in 978, by a twist of fate, he was made a saint. Next to the English Throne would be the brother King Ethelbert. It was during his reign, the hammer of Thor would fall. In Denmark Thor's best we're becoming Restless, not to mention the urge for adventure and wealth, when suddenly the ocean was alive with dragonships, or Viking ships. There were more Viking ships cruising the islands than ever before in the history of the world, and everyone knew they were coming. In 980 the Vikings would call the shots. The pulse of the northern Giants was beating strongly, and the magic in their blood was howling like a pack of wolves. Upon the stage of world politics was thrust A giant of a man, Olaf. There was a long line of Olaf's coming from the Vikings, because Olaf had been the baddest man in the world. In the conquest of Russia, Olaf had crushed thousands of Russians on the battlefields.

The Vikings all traveled the rivers of Russia for Generations, and Olaf would learn his lessons well. After all, he learned all he could from the Russ Vikings, he left them, and began to raid and plunder all the lands that ring the Baltic. The Baltic since the beginning of time, had been the Vikings sea.

It's because of the Vikings love, of the Baltic, that it stayed a viking playground, open to no one else. Finally Olaf launched an invasion of England, with many of the best of the Norseman. It was the battle of Maldon they gave the Norseman under Olaf, great riches. The Norsemen raided far and wide, and Olaf and his Warriors taught the English, a new respect for Thor's greatest Vikings. Olaf we are told by the Anglo-Saxons Chronicles, was a giant of a man, and his Fury in battle, only added to his legendary strength. Olaf and his Norsemen raided so much that King Ethelred made peace with the Viking Wild men. Olaf and his Norsemen came for Silver and Gold, and when they left, their hearts were full of joy. King Ethelred agreed to buy the peace, and since he could not win it, that's all he could manage.

The Vikings under Olaf were bought off, at the unbelievable price of 22,000 lb of silver and gold. The Chronicles of England always recorded the tribute paid to the Vikings, and during the same year, Olaf was back again. This time Olaf and his Warriors received 10,000 lb of silver and gold. Olaf and his Norseman left England and did not return for several years. However in 994 they landed again. The English this time fought two violent battles with Olaf and his forces. It did the English no good at all, for Olaf had plenty of great Warriors from the north, and he also had many warships. Olaf and his large ships, were Allied to the king of Denmark. The Danish fleet was enormous, but then you needed large ships, to carry 20,000 lb of silver and gold. The English won no battles, and many were ready to submit their allegiance to the king of Denmark. Many wanted to make the Vikings, Kings in England. Those that remembered the days when King Alfred was the all powerful king, cried when they thought of how things had changed. Change is the order of the universe, and England was testimony to it.

The Vikings in 994 terrorized the whole island of England, and even London experienced the Fury of the Vikings. The Vikings however were denied, a complete victory at London, and when they tried to burn the city, the Angles and Saxons rose up, and they inspired the whole city. In fact the Vikings took many casualties in their attempted conquest of London.

The Norseman or Norwegians, and the Danish Vikings would be too much Northern blood and arms, for the English, so a peace was made. Olaf and the king of Denmark would be paid 16,000 lb of silver and gold. The Norseman and the Great Danes parted here, with a job well done. Olaf left with his Norseman, but they raided and pillaged all their way to Wales, and once there, all the way to the Sea. There the Norsemen loaded aboard their dragonships, and headed for the Isle of Man, and then to Dublin Ireland.

Olaf left for Norway, where his future and his fate awaited him. The king of Denmark would never forget England, and they would have to go back, and get some more. Olaf and the King were allies in England, but they were enemies back home, for they were powerful rivals in the northern lands. However his great Viking forces Whittled down the defenses of the English, and the waves of northern Invaders would not halt. In the years 997 through 999 the king would send Danish armies to Ravish the coast of England, right at the home of the West Saxons.

The Chronicles of these years were filled with the horror and the terror of the Vikings. In 999

England would stop a massive Fleet on the Thames River, and most other rivers in England too. The armies of Kent, rushed to clash with the Vikings, and they were slaughtered. The Vikings Mounted Horses, there at the field of battle, and raped, pillaged, and plundered most of West Kent. In the year 1000, the fleet sailed away loaded with plunder, and to Normandy they would go. Normandy had always been a port for repairs, and for rest and relaxation. For many years the Danish Invaders had used Normandy, for Gathering their forces, and also as a safe harbor, on their way back to Denmark.

The Great Danes would launch another Invasion on West Sax, and the defenses they encountered, they destroyed. King Ethelred after watching the Scandinavian Mercenaries ride through his army was ready to make a deal. The Danish Vikings promised peace and were rewarded with 24,000 lb of silver and gold. The Danish Fleet and army had came for Wealth, and wealth they received, and all the time, Whispering Tales of Thor. King Ethelred within months would marry Duke Richards sister Emma, in the hope that Normans and English could land an Alliance. This Alliance could never really be, because the Normans were close relatives of the Danish Vikings, and they were in fact Blood Brothers.

When the King finally understood this, he made the biggest mistake in generations, and the English king ordered all the Danish people in England, to be killed on Bryce's day, which was November 13th 1002. The Danes of the Danelaw of course were so strong, they didn't worry, but the Danes on English soil were executed. Among the Danes that were massacred was an important Viking leader. The reaction was Furious of course, and the King launched a massive Fleet for Revenge. The best swords and battle-axes that money could buy, came from Sweden, and they also came, for revenge of the blood. The years 1003, 1004, and 1005, would see wave after wave, of vicious attacks by the Great Danes, spilling the blood of the English, in Sweet Revenge. The Vikings of course came for Revenge, however they also came for Silver and Gold. Many of the town's would fall to the Vikings quickly, and they would be plundered to the hilt. They would lose many lives, and they would lose much wealth. The English weapons and warriors could not defeat Thor and Odin. However in 1005 the Danish Vikings left England. What England still could not do, drive out the Vikings, nature could, and the Vikings left because of the famine, and the food supply would get real small.

In 1006 the Vikings were back in full force, with their lust for revenge and also for Silver and Gold. It seems the Vikings had a safe base at the island of Wright, and they had large storehouses of food. In 1007 we hear again from the Saxon Chronicle, that the Vikings were raiding far and wide throughout England, and once again, a peace was bought with silver and gold.

And the tribute was 36,000 lb of silver and gold. As an extra bonus the Vikings were given enough food and supplies to fill their ships. With all of this, plus the wealth they had already taken, the Vikings left England in their dragonships.

However the King knew the Danes would be back, and he quickly began to strengthen all the defenses. He also ordered a newer stronger Fleet to be built, that would deal the Vikings a heavy knockout blow. in 1009 the English fleet was ready and just in time, for the Viking Fleet was on the move. The English rivalries flared up again, and a great destruction came to the English Fleet, at their own making. The remaining ships were transferred to London, and right at that time, the Danes pulled in at Sandwich, and took over the facilities. The date was August 1st 1009, and by Autumn the countryside was once again filled with the mercenaries of the North.

Many of the professional soldiers were looking for Farms of Their Own, and it became obvious that many had come to stay. A new era had begun, and the Vikings could not be stopped, and they entered England at will. The Commanders of this Motley Crue, we're two brothers Destined for fame. The name say was Thorkell the Tall, and Hemming. The third power was named Eilaf, who was the brother of Ulf, a famous Jarl or warrior with very high rank. History weaves a fantastic web and Ulf was destined to marry the King's daughter, Astrid. This marriage of beauty and power would produce another, and also this would create the Royal Family Of Denmark, and they are still in power today.

One must not think of the Vikings as simply Raiders or Invaders, because the more one studies them, he begins to understand, they were a well paid professional Army. In Denmark,and West Sax there are many dug up army barracks of the Saxon Warriors, and many strong fortresses. Around the year 1000 the Danish Vikings built enormous training camps for The Mercenaries of the North. It had been estimated by many historians, that a complex so big used up over 8,000 giant trees, a small price to pay for the Millions, they received at the hands of the English, and the French. It must be clearly stated that England, France, Ireland, where to the Vikings as far as gold and silver, what Mexico and South America were to the Spanish conquistadors. It was a staggering amount, for an enormously wealthy land.

VIKING BLOOD STILL MIXING TO HELP ADD POWER TO THE NATIONS

We Must examine the tribute England paid to the Great Danes once more.16,000 pounds of silver and gold in the year 994. 24,000 lbs of silver and gold in the year 1002. 36,000 pounds of silver and gold in the year 1007. 48,000 pounds of silver and gold in 1012, and these are not all. It is ironic that England paid handsomely for her own Conquest, but by paying she secured future invasions. But then she really didn't even have a choice, the Vikings would have killed everybody and burned every town, that's why the English made the deals. They were just hoping they could gain more time to figure out how they were going to even stand up to the mighty Scandinavian Warriors. I must stress to you all modern Vikings, that these Mighty Warriors we called Danes or the Danish, we're in reality the best warriors of all the Scandinavian lands.

They were highly skilled in the art of combat, and masters of the battlefield. Sweden and Norway and Denmark came together for their conquest and their invasions, and in reality were all the same blood same race and basically the Same Homeland. All over Sweden there are Stone memorials to the Vikings that died in the wars with England. Angles and the Saxons killed many Vikings, and the land of England is sprinkled with their blood. Perhaps that is why crops grow so well, there was so much blood spilt. A historian once said that for every inch of England, there was a gallon of blood poured on it.

The Swedish Vikings kept score on the stone memorials they left behind, and told stories of who went where, and how they died. The Vikings were the first to Mark the graves of their Heroes, and of their blood, so that future Generations could know their exploits. The Vikings left these memorials all over Russia, and all the way to Constantinople.

These were proud men, who were proud of themselves, and also proud of their blood. In reality, no more ruthless than the Franks, Saxons, or the Moors, just a whole lot more heart. In Sweden there are five separate stones that tell the tale of the great warriors who received tribute in England.

The enormous wealth taken from England, France, Ireland, and Spain, went back to Sweden, Denmark, and Norway. Ever since the Scandinavians crushed the Roman Empire, the Scandinavians were becoming wealthier by the century, and they did not wait for it to come to them. You might say that many of the Vikings were born with a silver spoon in their mouth, cuz they were, unless It was a gold one.

The Viking invasions brought the most wealth back from England, and it was there, they set their sights. In 1009 the Danish mercenaries, ravaged Western and Eastern Kent, and when the last of the Warriors had lay their weapons down, the Vikings were paid 3,000, for peace. In 1009 the defense of London was once again Valiant, and the Vikings broke off the attack, for easier targets.

The Anglo-Saxon Chronicles tell us that Oxford was the next to be looted, and then put to the torch. Next the English towns that fell to the fury of the Danes were too many to even write about, I mean every single one they came in contact with, they did their thing.

The pages of History tell us that there were great battles,and the Greatest Warrior was the enormous and blood-curdling Norwegian Olaf Haraldsson. Olaf the Norwegian would become a legend to this land, and then also a legend to all other lands. For his time, he was considered, the baddest Warrior on planet Earth, and he killed tens of thousands, in man-to-man combat. The Vikings also had a great victory at Ringer Mirror, and perhaps that was their greatest victory. What it did was, drain the Manpower of the Angles and the Saxons, and opened the door for further Conquest. the Danish Vikings completely ravaged East Anglia and Cambridge and they were all stormed and looted. Oxford, and Buckingham, we're also easy prey to the Vikings, and after they were looted, they too were put to the torch.

For the next 25 years the attacks were bigger and more deadlier than ever.

Bigger than ever, The Anglo-Saxon Chronicle for the year 1010 shows there was utter confusion and Chaos throughout all the English kingdoms. In 1011 the Ferocious Viking attacks were Bigger than ever.They were launched on the wealthy land of Canterbury, but this my friends is war. It wasn't until 1012 that the Vikings were done with Canterbury. It was not until after Easter, that the full tribute was collected and paid, but when it was it was staggering, 48,000 pounds of silver. The Vikings being Men of their word left without harming another hair on their heads. I mean after all, it was about the silver and the gold. The Archbishop was captured by the Vikings, and they of course asked for another Ransom, and he shouted he would not pay, or allow others to pay. The Archbishop would be sorry for that big mouth, and in the end, a Viking crushed his skull with a battle axe .

Thorkell The Tall tried everything in his power to save the Archbishop, but Destiny had other plans. The King of the Danes had launched major attacks on England for 25 years in a row, to 1012, it just became too much.For the last 25 years, the attacks were Bigger and deadlier every single year. The Angles and Saxons still held their ground, however their leadership was nothing to write home to Mom about. All the armies were so confused with so many losses. the Danes Commanders had done well, with many victories over the English, and now it was time for the King of Denmark to enter the war. It was time for the Danish Vikings to assemble into one huge force and the King sent a message Fleet to England, of which he commanded himself.

The 25 years of war could be for the King of Denmark,so he could also wear the crown of England on his head, because he knew he deserved it. The king of Denmark was received well by the Vikings in Danish England, and all with the Viking Blood in them, submitted to the great king. The populations of Northumbria accepted the Danish King as their Overlord, but then they didn't have much of a choice. The king left some of his Warriors to guard the Danish Fleet and quickly took mounted Knights on a trip of Conquest through English Murcia. As the Danish Vikings proved to the English, they were unbeatable in combat, several towns were quickly taken. As the fury and the thrill of victory mounted, the Viking Knights stormed London itself. The Saxons of London once again Rose to the occasion, and between their Valor, and the Great Walls of the city, the Vikings were denied victory. In reality the King knew that if they took heavy losses on the walls of London, they could capture the town. Instead he chose to mount his Knights and take everything the countryside gave to him. The situation for the Angles and Saxons became very dim at best, and soon London had no choice but to sue for peace. London at that time was an island, unto itself, surrounded by hostile Vikings Whispering Tales of Thor. London realizing its strength was gone, sent hostages to the Great Danes, and promised enormous tribute.

This of course excited all the Viking warriors, because silver and gold is exactly what they came for. The king of England Knowing full well he was on a sinking ship, crossed the channel to Normandy himself.

It is amazing but true, that the king of Denmark had conquered England in 5 months, and was now the king of England, and master of all. The Viking battles had gone for many generations, and enough blood was spilled in England to fill up many of the Lakes in America, possibly even one of the Great Lakes.

They would once again have the final word, and 5 weeks after the capture of England, the great Viking king would die, and go to his place in Valhalla. On February 3rd 1014 the world would lose a great Viking, however Odin and Thor would have replacements for him.

In his lifetime of 55 years, The great Viking had seen great changes, and traveled that whole entire region of the world. The great King had sent Vikings to settle Iceland, and build bases to launch further attacks. The great King sent Vikings to settle Greenland, and he also watched when the colony in America had failed. He left his Mighty Kingdom in the hands of his son Knut, and what he might be remembered for the most, was he brought enormous wealth to his people back home, and for this he will be remembered. In the memory of the Viking Blood, the great King make sure the treasured Isle of England would get its transfusion of Viking Blood. In The End, they would be much better off for having it. We must note for the record, that although the Vikings were taking England, the Angles and Saxons were still strong and proud, and if provoked would fight with the fury of Hell's best demons. You see my friends the Angles, Saxons and Jutes, and the Great Danes, all came from the small piece of land that man called Scandinavia.

The English were down, but they were not out, and not beaten by any stretch of the imagination. When the Viking king died, the Angles and Saxons sent word to Normandy, and soon the English king was back leading the Angles and Saxons in the war again. The Angles, Saxons, and Jutes, seized the moment, and attacked the Danes and their allies. King Knut of the Royal Blood, was 18 years old. He was at a disadvantage, he had no great advisor, and his Genius of management, and opportunism was not yet developed.

The Angles and Saxons saw the death of the Danish King as a sign from their gods, and now they fought like wild beasts, and were consumed by their Fury.

Knut took his Viking Fleet to Sandwich, and there the Vikings cut the hostages in pieces. That is the ones taken from the English. War was a dirty business, and the hostages were mere Pawns in it. Not all the hostages were killed, but all of them Had been tortured, and most of them had been mutilated too. Nothing serious just eyes pulled out from the sockets. Fingers and toes cut off, but they were trying to get across a point, don't mess with us. After the hostages were put ashore, the Great Danish Fleet sailed back to Denmark, Knut took counsel with his older brother Harold who now sat on the throne. The young King would find in those around him everything he would need to execute his plans and desires on England. The great Fleet of Knut would also receive another great Viking later, Thorkell the tall. Thorkell was an opportunist like all of the blood, and he and his men added their Swords and Battle-Axes on the side of Knut.

In England, land of the Saxons, it was It was at this time with the wars on again, with the great Vikings, that King Ethelred died. The crown passed to Edmund his son, and England had a new King. You know it's funny, the Saxons said the biggest Fleet that the Great Danes had ever assembled had been pointed towards London once again, at the time the English King Ethelred died. The Danish Vikings wasted no time in their attack on London when the fleet arrived. 30 days later, all four sides of London we're under siege. The Chronicles of the Angles and Saxons tell us Edmond was successful in his war on West Sax. As soon as his victory was secured in West Sax, King Edmund attacked the Vikings, that were attacking London. The English Warriors Broke the siege on London, but in doing so, they suffered enormous casualties. The English Warriors lost so much blood, that they had to pull back from the combat. At this point, Knut and his Vikings attacked in full strength, but the Defenders of London stood firm, and would not yield.

When Knut realized he could not capture London, he disengaged his Warriors, and took his ships with all their captured livestock away. The armies of the English would Clash once again with the Vikings, and the soil of England would be soaked once again in the blood of both armies. When the last Englishmen had been cut in half by a Viking battle axe the war would be over, and this is exactly what Knut and the great warriors of the Vikings came for. And this is exactly what they got. The centuries of attacks on England, had finally paid off to the fullest extent. What had started with just small lightning raids, ended up with whole armies of Viking mercenary soldiers attacking. Edmund survived the slaughter, and went into hiding. The armed Mercenaries of Knut gave Chase to what was left of the English Army. They met up once again, and This time there would be no more fighting, and a peaceful Arrangement would be made. It was agreed by both parties the war was over, and Edmund would receive West Sax, and Knut would take the rest of the country.

In the next month, all England what have knut for their King. In 1017 Knut divided England into four parts, so that he would have a military advantage over all. Knut left his kingdom of England in good hands, and took some of the Dragonships back to Scandinavia. He returned with a fleet in the year 1020.

The reason Knut had sailed his Fleet to Denmark in 1018, was because his brother and King of Denmark, had died. To the masters of the oceans, the voyage across the North Sea was a piece of cake. King of England was also next in line to be King of Denmark, and off they sailed to settle the affairs of the Vikings. We must not think of Knut as just a conqueror, or as only a great warrior, for he was so much more. In fact he made a great king of England,and a European Monarch of the highest caliber. Knut was a patron of the church, and he guided the powers and influence of the church over the English. Knut finally brought peace to the endless Warfare in England. Knut new well the power and civilizing effect of laws, and he even established a legal code in England. We know from the Viking sagas that Knut was Fair-Haired and Green Eyed, and Valiant. The pages of History tell us that Knut as he was Brilliant,he was also extremely good-looking.Knut knew well the power and civilizing effects of the law, as well as the church. Knut helped the church to expand their power in England and he was honored from Christian Europe.

From Europe Knut Commanded the respect from the Emperor, and he received blessings from the Pope in Rome. The whole world was so happy that the fighting in England was over, and they all paid their dues. King Knut had the monasteries restored to their former Beauty, and he also had churches built. He respected the role of the church in European Affairs, and also its role in England. in the year 1026 once again, he sailed across the sea to Denmark.

A new power in the Viking world was coming of age, and he would reach all the way for the supreme power. His name was Olaf, and he had the ways of the Vikings, and he was one of their top 3 Warriors of all time. Olaf was enormous in size, and unbeatable in the Savage flurry of combat. Olaf was the royal Yngling, And the memory in his blood, told him he would be king. Olaf was The Greatest Warrior than Norwegians ever had. He was born in Norway and everyone in Norway knew he was destined to be king in his teens. Olaf had raided Sweden, Gatlin, and Denmark. No one that lived near the water would be safe from Olaf and his crew.

Olaf and his crew raided many lands and ended up fighting all the way to England. In England Olaf fought at the Battle for London, and again at Canterbury. Olaf and Thorkill also ran destruction down on France and Spain. No one was safe from the terror of the men on their dragon ships. Let it be understood, that Olaf was a mercenary, and where there were Treasures, there was Olaf's battle axe Olaf once rented his battle axe to Richard II of Normandy, and as long as he was paid, he killed his enemies. Olaf the great arrived in Norway 1014, and he had dreams of owning it.

We must remember that Norway was the smallest in population of the Great Northern Kingdoms, and Olaf took them in battle with two ships of Vikings, or 120 men. These were no ordinary men, but instead the Boldest and bravest in the world. Although Olaf and his 120 mercenaries fought several battles, Olaf's rule was only over the accessible parts of Norway. There were many areas he could not get through. Olaf was written about more than any other king in the Viking sagas periods. Olaf in the Viking age, was considered the most fierce Warrior they ever had. With King Olaf at the helm, Norway was Christian now, and this brought Norway into the family of European civilization. Olaf gave the Heathen men, in the lands called Norway, no choice,but to convert to Christianity.

Of the heathens,they were blinded, and Maimed for life. Olaf and his armed followers also entered the Heathen temples, and cast down there images. After these acts, the temples often were put to the torch. It seemed that Olaf's power grew, as much as the other Vikings. True, he had the backing of many warriors, but nothing like King Knut. In the next 25 years, it would be flexing of the muscles many times, between the Vikings of Norway, Sweden and Denmark. Much blood would be spilt, but nothing like the blood spilt in England. England Was always the jewel in the crown, but now that Knut owned it, other battles still had to be fought. The battles would go on and on, mostly posturing with armies of 3 or 4,000 Warriors. The big battles of England would never be repeated in the northern lands. for the one last great battle between Sweden and Norway and Denmark, there were just 3,600 Norwegians and 14,000 Swedes and other Vikings. Olaf had come for victory or death, and this time he received death. All the while The winds were howling, Whispering Tales of Thor.

Chapter 15

As the last chapter ended, we were watching the Viking kingdoms being forged into the blood of the Nordic race. The Viking tribes not only conquered Rome and Italy, they also conquered the entire Western Empire, but now they had conquered England and Ireland too. Never forget the Goths from Sweden had the biggest army that ever ransacked the Roman empire. They tore through Rome and conquered everything all the way to the edge of Spain.

We ended our last chapter with the Danes of the legendary Olaf of Norway. You know it's kind of Ironic that the Norwegians had destroyed the great and ferocious Olaf. He was one of their own blood, and now they received the Danish King. Under the Danes the Norwegians would be heavily taxed, and they suffered many hardships. Olaf was The Greatest Warrior that Norway had ever produced. His name would never be forgotten, in fact The Cult of Olaf grew large and Powerful for Generations after his death.

Olaf when he was alive, was a gigantic personality, and when he was dead, he was even bigger. The magic of the blood, and the magic in the blood, should not be taken lightly, and must be understood. The legends of Olaf after his death, grew to enormous proportions, and Men talked openly of the power in his blood. Vikings talked openly of the miracle properties of the blood of Olaf, where blind men were made to see, and the lame were made to walk. Many miracles did happen, and of this there is no question.

Such a fever spread through the lands of the Miracles, that the Warriors begged permission to dig up their hero, and permission was granted by Bishop Grimkell.

The same Bishop declared Olaf a true saint, and had the body of Olaf the Great transferred to St. Clement's church, which Olaf that built himself 20 years before. The Legends continued to grow at an unbelievable rate, and the Miracles became common events. Soon every village in Norway, and many other lands, openly prayed to Saint Olaf.

The Cult of Olaf, and the Miracles spread To Many Lands. They grew stronger by the year, and Saint Olaf gave the people great strength. The great Norwegian King Olav Died in battle, with his favorite Battle Axe, and Saint Olaf became Norway's Eternal King. The great Legends of Olaf lasted well past their time, that men call the Viking age, and in some parts of Norway, the cult is still alive today. Thanks to this one great man Olaf, Norway was now a Christian country, and would strengthen the Norwegians to the Pinnacle of power, and we're talking in the world. When Olaf started his long march from his base in Russia, to travel the frozen rivers, he left behind Carl. Because Olaf had his date with Destiny, and with fate, the son of Olaf was brought out to Norway after his father's death. The Vikings rallied around the blood in his veins, for he was immediately crowned King. Olaf's blood would still rule from the grave and Beyond.

On November 12th in the same year, the world saw King Knut the Great, died in England. With the death of the all powerful Knut, the empire fell apart, and once more the Battle Axes and swords would decide the borders of all Nations. To the Danish kingdoms, this was a staggering blow, however to the Norwegians, it was a gift from Odin and Thor. The ruler of Norway Died soon after words, and all the doors were open for the battle axes and swords to return. The irony of the situation was, the Anglo Scandinavian Empire, have fallen apart. But my friends, all things must come to an end.

Of all the Scandinavian kingdoms, Norway would now place their bets, and rise to fame and Power. For every action, there is an equal and opposite reaction, and Norway was coming up. Thor had his hammer, as Roland had his sword, and among the other Vikings, we have the story of Siegfried forging his famous sword. The Vikings believed these weapons were inhabited by powerful forces, and of this, there can be no doubt.

King Arthur had his sword, and so did Roland, and all were magical. The story of Siegfried the mighty Viking is carved in wood, and told in picture writing, and the memory in the blood vibrates. The first carving shows the magical sword forged, and the next carving shows the sword breaking, when it is tested by banging on the Anvil. Next Siegfried the Viking used it to kill the dragon. It shows Siegfried roasting the dragon's heart, while his brother is fast asleep. Siegfried burns his thumb as he is roasting the dragon's heart, and puts the thumb immediately in his mouth. The thumb that had been holding the dragon's heart, and the blood covering it, also went into the mouth. At once the power of magical nature is alive like never before, and the Viking at once understand the language of the birds. This story is the mystery of the cult of the blood. Make out of it what you will.

The Viking age, Like the Roman age, did not die or fall at once. In fact it happened very slowly and very deliberately. The Viking age, saw the Viking kingdoms carved out in blood, and the Scandinavian soil was soaked in the Nordic bloodbaths.

The shifts of power had been staggering, and they would continue to happen. The Norwegian farmers that had United under their Chieftains, defeated or alive, where content when he was made a Saint. The English Kingdom that had been ruled by Knut the Great, now looked to Edward, and that was both Danes and English. The Great Danes of Denmark were ruled by the son of Knut.

In 1035 The Viking North would feel a tremor, when Magnus Olaf son was proclaimed the King of Norway. Norway had always been strong, but Denmark had always held the power and the strength in the freezing North. Besides having a geographical advantage, Denmark also had a much larger population, and she was far richer to buy Mercenaries, or Vikings. The great

Canute's Son died in 1042, and Magnus Olaf's son assumed the throne. This act was unheard of, for a Norwegian to be king of all Great Danes. The smart man grinded a new Edge on his sword and his battle axe. In 1047 the Danish Vikings could no longer stand for a Norwegian to be on the throne, and the Danish rightfully crowned another King.

The Norwegians had always found it hard to gain power, in the shadow of this super powerful neighbor Denmark. No Norwegian King had ever died of old age, or one had never even died in his bed. Eric the blood axe had been driven out, and he died a very violent death. Hakkon was executed by the sons of Eric. And so the list goes on.

Most of our Motley rulers basically of Sweden and Norway where Motley rulers, and most Seized the Throne by violence, and that's exactly how they lost it too. The Norwegian history of the executions of their leaders seems very much like ancient Rome, but this is the way of men, and also the way of the cult of power. Many of the Vikings had no choice but to leave their small available lands in the Frozen North, in search of their own land for their families and their life stock. This is perhaps the biggest reason for the Vikings expansion into France, England, Ireland, Iceland, and even Greenland. Each generation of Nature's Best and strongest needed their own domain, they were real men, and they went and took it.

The reason for the change in style was simple, now these men owned land, and wanted only a peaceful development. The earlier men had only conquest and military operations on their minds, and in fact the Vikings were becoming civilized. This is not to say that all were peaceful from Norway. She would still have to fight bloody wars, for her own independence from Denmark. These ruthless Wars with Denmark would go on, and on, and on, and it was the greed of everyone that propelled these wars. All Chieftains who tried to enlarge their own power were executed in battle, and their armies were glad to dance over the soil of Norway. The king would permit only one private Army in Norway, and that was his own. In 1064 a treaty between Norway and Denmark was signed, that read that each country was now independent of the other.

As time went on, and the Bishops of Norway helped greatly to form a real civilization in Norway, and the cult of Ruthless power, was slowly turning into a civilization. The free men of Norway looked to the King now to make the laws, and also to administer Justice, for this is how men do it.

The Viking invasions of modern-day France ended when they got what they wanted, and that was the Duchy of Normandy. Slowly they began to settle and occupy the creation of Normandy, to the Vikings, it was in reality the only move possible. After the Great Viking Knut died, the ancient West Saxon Dynasty inherited England. You know life is strange and funny sometimes, and sometimes things just happen for strange reasons, but check this out. After the great king Knut had conquered England finally, many of his Vikings went back to Scandinavia.

The Scandinavians and English in the Dane law, merged together with the Angles, Saxons, and Jutes to form the greatest culture, of the greatest power on Earth, Great Britain. The

Scandinavians of England, had more in common with their English cousins who are Christians, then their Nordic brothers that were heathens. In Kiev and Russia, and France, and England, and all the other northern European countries, the masses abandoned the Viking gods, in favor of Christ. This decision weighed heavily on the minds of all the Warriors, and religion divided them into separate Nations. In Winland or America, it was Heathen, that played a major role. The heathens of America and Greenland could not be meshed together into the new mind set of the Nordics.

Scandinavian methods of Agriculture greatly improved, and great new areas were cultivated and prospered immensely. This also stopped the flow of men going to war overseas to find land, to feed their families and their people. The Winds of Thor were blowing, and Howling the name of the god of wisdom, Odin.

Attractive, successful , for their own good, they quickly found their calling, to become independent of their homelands. Iceland is a very good example, for she was a colony of Norway, and they in turn did their best to remain independent, of all the royal power. As the Vikings kept pouring into Iceland, she became her own country, remote and occupied. As early as 930 documents were drawn up it made Iceland a republic. from Iceland Expeditions were launched that ended at Modern Day Canada, and America. These are facts set in stone. Trading posts have been excavated, and the seal tools and weapons have been dug up in Canada and the United States.

The Furs were what expansion to America, and Canada was all about, for in Europe or Byzantine, the Vikings Raiders could name an enormous price for the beautiful furs from America. The same goes for the extremely valuable polar bear rugs, and the ivory tusks of the walrus. Make no mistake the Normans of Normandy were the strongest concentration of Vikings in the world, and the Duchy of Normandy was in fact the kingdom of the Vikings. The Vikings from Normandy would go on to conquer most of the Mediterranean and North Sea countries, and they would be the overlords for millions of people.

The Viking power never really disappeared, they only became stronger, and in the modern world,They call them the North Atlantic Treaty Organization, or simply Nato. The Vikings from Norway, Denmark, and Sweden learned well the language and customs, and the culture of the French, and they of course gave it a major transfusion. Normandy was a Christian Nation, and a full member of Western Europe, and they in turn, turned their backs on those they had left behind. The Normans were not runners in the pack, they became the leader, and the security of Western Europe was tied to these magnificent forgers of culture and civilization. Their Empire, like all the Germanic kingdoms of Europe, were forged in rivers of blood. But it is written, there is no other way.

History is the teacher, and the pages of history are filled with the lessons. The Normans would rewrite history, when the Vikings of Normandy conquered England And Sicily. The best defense is a good offense, and the capture of Sicily secured the southern borders of all of Europe. The Nation of Islam, and all the rest of the Arabs, for many centuries had tried to get just a foothold into Europe, at any place possible. It's like the old, if I can get my foot in the door, I can eventually Push the door open, that was their theory, and it almost worked. After the fall of the Roman Empire, all the nations came to see what they could get. Spain was completely overrun by Islam for a long time. Islamic invasions in southern France along the coast, southern Italy saw the Arabs pouring in Time After Time, and Sicily was completely overrun. This is the reason why the Sicilians are much darker than the Italians. Julius Caesar had blonde hair and blue eyes, as did many of the Emperors of Rome. The reason why, the huge land mass that surrounds Italy, had a lot of blonde hair, blue and green eyed people. If one controlled this large island, that sits at the bottom of Italy, one controlled the shipping and money making of the whole Mediterranean. It was an extremely valuable location, and just for the record, the Vikings came back to Sicily, and killed every single one of the Invaders, and changed the bloodline again. Whoever controlled this island of Sicily controlled the wealth of the West, and it had been fought over many times, and the Vikings put all that to rest. The red, blonde, and brown hair came back, thank you Thor and Odin.

The seizure of Sicily from the Arabs and the Moors, also set the stage for further Conquest and invasions, called the Crusades, or the Holy Wars. You fight them here, or you fight them there, but you will fight them.

The Vikings extended their power all the way to Constantinople of the Byzantine Empire, and of course made war on them too. For centuries the Eastern Roman Empire had counted on the Germanic Legions for their armies. The Greeks of the Eastern Empire were good poets, and philosophers, but the Germanic Warriors held down the empire for centuries. Also the Eastern Emperors of Constantinople, had enormous Bodyguards of Franks, and Saxons, and other Germanic Mercenaries. In those days it was quite different, since the days of Rome actually, a bodyguard was considered possibly 50 to 200 Warriors, not just one or two. The Vikings were always well paid bodyguards, of the Eastern Roman Empire, because of their skill in battle, nothing else.

The Vikings were so feared in the Eastern Roman Empire, that no more than 50, could enter Constantinople at any time. That's no more than 50, could be in the city at one time. The Vikings were the most treacherous group of warriors the world will ever see. As this chapter is drawing to a close, I feel I must clarify a few points on Ireland too. The Irish were always up to their necks in the Affairs of the Vikings, and Ireland would also get a Nordic transfusion of blood, and change the complete future of these beautiful people.

One must remember, that the Vikings no matter which country they came from, lived in the brutal cold and ice. For so many thousands of years, they did not even know the other world out there existed. Only along the coastlines of the big countries of Sweden and Norway, could Man live, and especially Farm, for his family and his animals. It was a hard existence In Scandinavia, but they did carve out societies for thousands of years. One of the wise men of the Vikings, said we must have the young men bring down the trees, but only cut the biggest. Then the Vikings knew they had a chance to expand their lifestyles, and do much better for themselves and their families. At first small boats went to the east, up the rivers of Russia, and the neighboring countries. Trading with whoever lined the shores, or just playing Robin Hood with those they found. This was the Viking way of life, and make no mistake it was hard, and it was brutal. Although there were no borders for thousands of years, and no names of any countries, because people didn't live like that way back then, they all came to Uppsala. From one mountain to another, Was stretched a chain, and it was a thick chain of solid gold, so that everyone could see the wealth of the Vikings, and the beauty of their gold. It was said you could see the gold glittering in the Sun for 50 Miles. It was at these meetings of all the Viking tribes, that assembled every 9 years, that first talk was made of building Viking ships, and also talk about Adventure on the high seas. When the young Vikings heard, they all wanted to go for the adventure of it all, and eventually they would go, but first they had to fight small little Wars amongst their own kind, who were happy to just go up the rivers of Russia.

It was Ragnar who would be the first to challenge the King In one-to-one combat, for the privilege of directing the Viking Nation. This is the way the Vikings did it, the King was always The Greatest Warrior of all. He had no choice but to honor the request or challenge. Ragnar killed him, and one of Ragnar's greatest friends was the boat builder, funny how fate Spins its web.

In this great work the Masterpiece, we have talked about hundreds of wars, and hundreds of places that would be called countries today. I have explained to you how they were created, and Always by Force of Arms, and rivers of blood were split, to carve out any one of the nation's I have spoken of. A great man once said, that any of the European nations, every square inch of it, had a gallon of blood spilled on it. Perhaps this is why the crops grew so well in Europe.

Ireland has been called many things, for thousands of years, but the most common is the Emerald Isle. When the Vikings found Ireland they fell in love. The red hair of many of the Irish and the Scottish women, is the most obvious trait that the Viking Blood brought to these treasured lands. And of course that is not to say, that without their red hair beauties, that the Irish would be missing something. There's been many songs written about the beautiful Irish women, and I guess that's probably one of the reasons why the Vikings stayed after all. I because they are, and will forever remain in the top three nations in the world for their women. It is unfair to say exactly who is number 1 2 or 3, and that's why I just leave It at the top 3. Of course a little red hair Flair in the little Irish Roses, just added to their beauty. It was once said by a historian that England and Ireland and the wealth the Vikings got from them, was what Mexico and South America were to the Spanish Conquistadors.

Ireland was perhaps the most important colony of the Norsemen. The Danes and the Norwegians established valuable trade trading centers at Dublin, Limerick, Waterford, Wexford, and Cork. The Vikings built all these towns, including Dublin Ireland the capital. The Vikings also built the modern docks for their shipping, to enable them to make millions of dollars. It was the southern half of the island of Ireland that was totally Conquered, and it was in the south that all the above cities I just named were built. Make no mistake the Vikings on the south of Ireland owned everything, Lock, Stock, & Barrel. But the Northern half, the Irish never let go of.

The islands off the coast of Ireland named Man, and Orkney, we're also huge bases for the Viking fleets. The Vikings needed these bases to gather together their forces, let them rest, and get them ready for more attacks. It was from the above towns I mentioned, the Vikings always gathered their forces, and they always put their fleets together. This is not to say that the Vikings never were defeated, but you could count all their losses on your two hands. And you could count all their victories, by pulling out all your hair on top of your head, each one representing one huge Viking victory. In other words there were tens of thousands of Victories by the Vikings, and their losses were real small. In Ireland the Norseman had many kingdoms, and they all Prospered greatly from the trade, and they made the Irish pay tribute to them. You know it's funny, better to let some live, and pay tribute to you, then kill everybody.

The Vikings in Ireland, just like the Vikings in Normandy France, mixed in marriage with the native women. The wars between the Vikings and the Irish were numerous, and they were all very bloody, and very brutal. In the year 902, the Irish won a stunning military victory over the Vikings, and Dublin the capital was the prize. The Vikings after recruiting many more of Thor's best, launched another Invasion in 914, and Dublin the capital was taken back. It's amazing, if you got a little gold to spend, you can hire as many mercenaries as you want, or that you might need. This is exactly what happened, when the Vikings left for a while,and the Vikings got their Mercenaries, and then they came back, and the Irish lost their Capital at Dublin once again.

The Viking warriors of 914 also recaptured Limerick, and Waterford. The Norwegians Having Ireland in check, launched their raids and war parties on Northern England once again. The raids were relentless, and for centuries they happened.

The Norsemen won great victories in Scotland, and their Treasures grew rapidly. In reality for the Irish Kings in the north of Ireland, this helped them, in their Wars with the Irish Norsemen. Now the Norwegians had to divide their forces, some going to Ireland, some going to Scotland. The Nordic Warriors however took Huge losses,in their winter battles against the Irish, and the Scots. But the law of nature says some must die, for the others to survive. Olaf of Ireland died in the north of England in 941, when it looked like Scotland was ready to submit to the armies of the Norsemen. In 951 the Norseman from Ireland, almost succeeded in capturing all of Northumbria, and their King at the time was Olaf Kvaran. By the end of his Rule in Ireland, he had given Dublin once again to the Irish. The Irish Warriors fought with such Fury, at times no one could hold them back. If their numbers would have been larger, the Vikings admit, they would have drove them back into the ocean, they came from.

It was good for the Norsemen in Ireland, that the Irish Kingdoms were not United, or the Irish Warriors would have driven them straight into the Irish sea. Make no mistake the Irish produced violent Kings, with extremely capable Warriors, however there disunity worked against them. The climax of Irish and Norsemen clashes in battle, came in April in the year 1014. The Irish had their King Brian, with all his champions, assembled a mile from the Viking Fleet, that was anchored in Dublin Bay. The Irish had assembled the most fierce Army in the history of Ireland, to meet the champions from the north. On this day it would be Champions against Champions, and the blood did fly.

With their backs to the Sea, the island of Orkney, had sent their Champion Sigurd the Stout. With him were the chosen best from his Island. The island that men call Man, sent its champion Brodir, and he brought a handful of the best in his world. From Limerick Thor sent another Champion to the field of battle, and with him came a blood-curdling crew. And of course, what battle in Ireland would be normal, without the Dublin Vikings. They showed with all their Champions. This battle saw the best of both worlds, and the Champions led the assaults on each other.

The battle itself was extremely bloody, and the fury of the champions added it to it tremendously. To add a isexual flavor to the war that day, the wife of King Brian of the Irish deserted her husband, and let it be known to the champions, that Victory would earn her hand in marriage. Dublin was going to be a Dowry, or in other words a prize. After the vicious Slaughter, Tales were told of course, including Omens and miracles. In reality, carnage was decided only by The Warriors, and their swords and battle-axes. The losses were enormous for both sides, and the bloodletting was unheard of in the battles before them. This was for all the marbles, and the right to rule, till the end of time.

King Brian of the Irish was killed, and his son and Grandson were also. Along with the complete Royal line of the Irish, there were 4,000 of Their greatest warriors killed on that day. By today's standards the 4,000 would be a day's worth, by larger armies of course. But by those days standards, they were unheard of. Many of the Viking warriors escaped the brutal carnage, and to the Vikings stronghold at Liffey they went. Those that were not so lucky, saw Sigurd fall bravely in battle, and when Brodir was killed slowly, they cut him Limb from limb. They killed this Champion slowly, and cut each arm off slowly to watch the gushing of blood. Then they cut each leg off, one at a time, to hear the Champion scream, and they did this because he dared to go against them. This is the way of men, and this is the way it was. Not only the Champions of the Norsemen were killed on the field of battle, but over 7,000 men lost their lives on this gruesome day. The battle proved two things to both sides, number one, the Irish would never submit to the Vikings or any other Army, and that the Vikings would never leave Ireland. The Vikings and all those Furious Raids on the Irishman, built and developed towns that grew into important and Wealthy trading centers. The Vikings added their powerful forces, to Ireland, and Ireland became a great nation.

Knut In England had died, and left England and Denmark his Empire with many headaches. Knut one man, one ruler, his son Hordaknut, was already firmly in place in Denmark, and he was recognized as king of the Great Danes. In normal times the son would have crossed the North Sea, to claim his title as king of England, however to leave Denmark, would have left the Danes open to attacks from the Norwegians. The times were bad with relations between Norway and Denmark. If the son would have left Denmark with his Fleet, the Norseman would have raided Denmark for sure. The English did what they were well known for, and that is they compromised once again with the Vikings.

On that day the Vikings and the Irish had 11,000 of their greatest warriors sent to Valhalla. On that day, the blood was spilled, and Combat was the reason, and the Treasure and Power were the rewards.

The new King kept the treasures of the Dead Knut at Winchester. In the land of the Scots, many Treasures were kept also. On that Dreadful day in history, Friday the 13th, when the Pope of Rome sent out the order across Europe, to arrest or execute all the Knights Templars, many escaped. It is written in the pages of History, but only for the secret societies, that all the treasures the Knights Templars had, also went to Scotland. On that Bloody day in history, when the Pope of Rome stabbed in the back the Knights Templars, many did Escape, and among the treasures that escaped with them, was the Ark of Covenant that many men seek. Also in the many years that the Knights Templar had conquered Jerusalem, they had dug for 9 years into the Earth underneath Jerusalem to find the treasures, and all the thousands of pounds of gold and diamonds, that King Solomon's Mines produced. The Knights Templars had the last laugh, and this is the way of men, Whispering Tales of Thor, done.

Made in the USA
Middletown, DE
26 December 2020